THROUGH THE EYES
OF A RAPTOR

To Sherik,
You rock!
Soar with the magic!

THROUGH THE EYES OF A RAPTOR

A Young Adult Fantasy

Julie Hahnke

Illustrations by Marcia Atkinson Christensen

iUniverse, Inc.
New York Lincoln Shanghai

Through the Eyes of a Raptor

iUniverse books may be ordered through booksellers or by contacting:

iUniverse
2021 Pine Lake Road, Suite 100
Lincoln, NE 68512
www.iuniverse.com
1-800-Authors (1-800-288-4677)

This is a work of fiction. All of the characters, names, incidents, places, organizations, and dialogue in this novel are either the products of the author's imagination or are used fictitiously.

ISBN: 978-0-595-42609-6 (pbk)
ISBN: 978-0-595-86937-4 (ebk)

Printed in the United States of America

To my grandmother, Gladys Young,
who'd have liked this story

Runes shalt thou find, and fateful signs,
That the king of singers colored,
And the mighty gods have made;
Full strong the signs, full mighty the signs
That the ruler of gods doth write.

Runatalsthattr Odins,
Odin's Rune Song from the Poetic Edda
Translated by Henry Adams Bellows

CONTENTS

Acknowledgments xi

1 To Grandmother's House 1

2 Introductions 19

3 The Diary 35

4 Library Secrets 57

5 Nosing About 83

6 The Games 107

7 Saven 127

8 Betrayal 149

9 A Faerie Grandmother 169

10 Lessons 189

11 Investigations 215

12 Gifts 241

13   The Haunted Wine Cellar   261

14   Bending Rules   287

15   Choices   311

16   Bear Baiting   333

17   The Frith   353

18   Passage   373

Lexical Matter

Appendix 1   Glossary   399

Appendix 2   The Ogham   407

Appendix 3   Fionn's Shield   409

ACKNOWLEDGMENTS

I can't imagine writing a book for kids without involving kids. I'd like to thank those who assisted me: Sara Sharp, who's been there from the beginning and who helped me understand—if one can—the inner workings of a thirteen-year-old's mind; Brianna Fogden and her then fourth-grade class, who collectively defined a character in a critical scene; David Cohen and Graham Richards for their enthusiastic support; and Ian Motha, who fancies himself my agent.

Several adults reviewed my manuscript and offered invaluable nuggets of wisdom and perspective. Louis Aszod was an early trail guide indicating hazardous pitfalls. After my final draft, further safety checks came from Lorelei and Eloise Lanum, Theresa Christensen-Kirby, and my local children's librarian Karen Nee, who has patiently listened to my prattle on the agonies and ecstasies of attempted authorship.

I would like to thank Hector MacNeil for his help with the Gaelic expressions and pronunciations used in the story. Hector is Gaelic Program Director for The Gaelic College in St. Ann's, Nova Scotia.

My deepest gratitude and love go to Marcia Christensen. Like little children we shared gleeful discoveries of myths, history, and Scottish culture, all of which shaped my story as it developed. She argued emotionally for and against story elements that I either wanted to cut, or clung to doggedly. She drummed into me the realization that a fiction writer *is* an artist, allowing me to compare the artistic process of my medium to hers. And her greatest contribution is the fine set of pen-and-ink drawings heralding each chapter. Thank you, Marcia!

1

TO GRANDMOTHER'S HOUSE

"I'd like another bag of peanuts."

The woman glanced at the name-card hanging around the young girl's neck. "You've already had quite a few, Kelly."

"Do you think I would have asked if I didn't want them?"

"I'll get them for you in a bit. We're serving coffee at the moment."

"I'd like them *now*. Please."

The flight attendant's smile faltered. She turned to the gentleman across the aisle. "Would you excuse me, sir, while I help this young lady? I'll be right back with your decaf."

At least I said, "Please."

Rudeness was a skill Kelly hadn't practiced until recently; but she found she had a knack for it.

ॐ

Her friend's parents had spoken to her about it.

"I don't know what's gotten into you," Peggy's mom said. "You're much too polite a girl to be behaving like this."

Peg's dad added, "Kelly MacBride, your mother wouldn't approve."

But that was precisely Kelly's point: her mother wasn't here, so who cared?

In the years since her father's death, her mom had only left her once before. The previous winter she'd been away for two weeks on a business trip. Every evening her mother had called to see how Kelly was doing. At first it felt like remote babysitting—as if her mom didn't trust her home alone. But when she called, she never subjected Kelly to twenty questions: did you do your homework? What did you eat for dinner? Is the house picked up? Rather, she let Kelly do all the talking; Kelly could steer the conversation wherever she chose. During these calls her mother never seemed rushed to get to her business dinners or to return clients' phone calls. Each night Kelly had all the time she wanted.

Her mom's patient listening encouraged Kelly to save up her feelings and reactions throughout the day, tucking them away for joint inspection each evening. Nothing was ever too silly or trivial to share. The nightly calls became the focal point of Kelly's days.

It was towards the end of that trip Kelly realized something—something she never let on, because at thirteen it would be severely uncool: her mom was her best friend. Not best friend as in "who you hang with"; that would unquestionably be Peggy and Jake, her pals. (Together they called themselves the Three Musketeers.) This was best friend as in best heart-to-heart friend; someone you could tell anything, and whose response meant everything.

That first time her mother was away Kelly hadn't behaved like a monster. But back then she knew her mom would return home. This time Kelly knew she wouldn't.

Kelly's decline into boorishness didn't begin until the following May. While seemingly ages ago to Kelly, it was only three short months past.

It was a warm morning and scents of daffodils and apple blossoms floated in the humidity. Kelly's barn chores were long done and she was now into serious business: breakfast. Weekdays were for school. Sundays were for church. And Saturdays were for breakfast—the kind you don't have the time to make or eat any other day of the week.

"It's to be waffles! Definitely fresh waffles." Kelly announced as she whisked the batter. "Powder them up with sugar, and then drown them in syrup—Mr. Hutchins brought us more of the dark yesterday!" By Vermont farm standards, Mr. Hutchins' maple syrup was the finest.

"The flavor's in the color," her mother agreed. "But that wasn't all he brought us …" The hint hung between them, beckoning Kelly to the refrigerator.

She opened the door to find … "Fresh eggs and smoked bacon!" How could she have missed the hickory scent? "Now I can't decide which I want."

"Then we'll just have to make both." Her mother accepted the bowl from Kelly. "You start the bacon. Meanwhile, I'm thinking of an object."

Kelly's face brightened—word games were her favorite pastime. "Is it small?"

Her mother shook her head. "Too vanilla. Use a chocolate word."

Kelly rephrased her question. "Is it infinitesimal, minuscule, or microscopic?"

"You just asked three questions, but the answer's the same to all of them—no. The object I'm thinking of is Brobdingnagian."

"Huh?" Kelly stopped licking the hickory fat from her fingers.

The batter oozed through the waffle iron while her mother attended with a know-it-all expression. "You know the rules."

Running into the den, Kelly lifted down a well-worn dictionary from the shelf. She searched the B's as her mother slowly spelled the word.

"Hey, it's not in here! No fair!"

"Serious words require a serious dictionary." Only her mom's voice could sound loving and smug at the same time.

If Kelly had to resort to the *Oxford English Dictionary* she knew she was in trouble. The OED was like the CIA of the verbal world. It didn't just give the definition of a word; it provided an entire dossier on the word's origin and use going back hundreds of years. No word could escape the OED. If it were found there and *not* in the normal dictionary, it was truly a hardened word.

Kelly hefted the first of the two volumes onto the coffee table and got out the magnifying glass. Peering at the infinitesimal, minuscule, and microscopic print, she flipped gossamer pages until she found the entry:

> *Brobdingnag: The name given by Swift in* Gulliver's Travels *to an imaginary country where everything was on a gigantic scale.*

There was of course much more, but Kelly had what she needed. She returned to the stove with a scowl. "So, your object isn't Lilliputian." She phrased her comment carefully, not wanting to burn another question on a rhetorical quip.

Her mother's laughter proved she enjoyed these games as much as her daughter did. "We haven't read *Gulliver's Travels* yet. Let's add that to our reading list."

Kelly eyes shined with flinty resolve as she considered her next question. Buildings were big. She just had to Hershify the word …

"Is it … an edifice?" Kelly flipped the bacon as she awaited the verdict. When the griddle's pops and sputters were her only answer, she looked up. "Mom?"

Her mother stood motionless beside the waffle iron for a long moment and then crumpled to the ground.

"Mom!"

The only thing notable about the hospital waiting room was how nondescript everything was: the dingy gray walls, the hard upright chairs, the over-bright lighting, and the year-old magazines. Kelly wouldn't remember any of it later. She wouldn't remember the hours of sitting—through the afternoon and evening and late into the night. She wouldn't recall exactly how Peggy's parents came to be there with her. But the doctor she'd always remember. Not the creases of fatigue etched in his face or his pained, sympathetic eyes—those she never noticed. His words were what stayed with her long afterwards, haunting both her sleep and her wakefulness. Words that at first made no sense, but whose meaning crept up and crushed her heart as she watched Peggy's parents react to them.

He'd said, "I'm sorry."

Calling anyone a liar is never polite. But screaming it in a tearful rage while pounding on a man who's just struggled for ten hours to do the very thing you wanted most—well, that's just plain rude.

It was upon the arrival of the agency woman that Kelly honed her newfound talent. Kelly hated her. She hated her squinty glasses and her bird's nest perm. She hated the stacks of papers the agency woman constantly shuffled. And she especially hated the woman's limited vocabulary.

"Aw, baby, it'll be all right. We'll find you a new home."

Baby? Only a troglodyte would use such an infantile term to a teenager. There's nothing wrong with the home I have. It's the current company I find lacking.

"It may take us time, but we'll find you some new parents. You'll have a regular family again. Everything back to normal."

One day when she appeared, the woman's smile dripped sugar. Her eyebrows twitched like caterpillars in seizure. Was she signaling news?

"I received a letter. It's from your grandmother!"

"I don't have a grandmother."

Your case file should have told you that, agency woman! My mom's mother died when she was a girl.

"But you do, sweetie—your father's mother."

Kelly tripped over the idea. Her father had died when she was so young. She never knew.

"Sweetheart, she wrote that she'd like you to come live with her, in Scotland."

෨

Kelly looked out the plane window, staring down at the ocean. Vast. Empty. Like her insides. She was going where they sent her. They said the old lady was Kelly's grandmother, but what did that mean? Family's family because you care about each other; not because you possess matching DNA.

How can she care about me if she never wrote or called—even once? Did she ever consider I might like to know I had a grandmother?

Kelly didn't have much experience with grandmothers. Back home, Peggy's grandmother visited for two weeks every July. Nana, as she was called, was a heavyset woman with ankles swollen from gout and a rolling gait, as if she'd been too long at sea. She was a fierce baker and was never out of her apron anywhere in the house. Nana had shared with Peggy and Kelly the time-honored secrets for authentic Irish soda bread. Kelly couldn't remember the recipe, but she'd never forget the dry ingredients *must* be stirred in a clock-wise direction. Nana stressed that as if it were an important safety tip, as if a chance counter-clockwise stroke might result in a fearful explosion.

When Nana wasn't baking, she'd have her feet up in the upholstered recliner, consumed with either her knitting or the daily crossword. Kelly tried knitting once. The most that can be said of her effort is she didn't poke an eye out. She'd never attempted a crossword puzzle. It seemed safer. She hoped it was a lot more exciting than it looked.

After landing, Kelly waited in her seat while the plane emptied. She was an "unaccompanied minor." The airline had to hand her over to the person meeting her. Kelly felt like a package awaiting delivery.

Eventually a flight attendant came over. "Ready to go, hon?"

"Whatever." Kelly shrugged out of her seat, leaving behind the unopened bag of peanuts.

The terminal was swarming with hastiness. Travelers were either rushing to get to their planes or to get home from them, creating a noisy sea of moving bodies. Except for one. Kelly's eyes were immediately drawn to the single immovable figure. He stood as if planted. A stout oak. His erect posture bestowed an air of strength and gravity. His steel-gray hair was close cropped, almost military, and his severe brown eyes held no laughter. In fact, a smile would have found no welcome on his face.

He was wearing a skirt—a kilt. Even though she knew it was impolite to stare, she couldn't drag her eyes away. His shoes were tied with yard-long laces that snaked up and around his ankles before ending in a bow. He wore heavy wool socks that stopped just below two hairy knees. His belt was wider than her hand and fastened with a silver buckle, mirror bright. Around the front of his kilt hung a tasseled, black leather pouch on a chain.

The man's gaze was fixed on her as intently as hers was on him. With a gulp she knew this man was waiting for her.

The flight attendant concluded the same and escorted Kelly to the dour gentleman.

"Ya'd be Kelly then," he barked in a Scottish brogue.

She nodded mutely.

"I am Allisdair, yer grandmother's *ghillie*. Her steward."

Steward? Not like a guy stewardess. Not dressed like that. Not with those knees.

He signed the flight attendant's form. "Let's go fetch yer bags," he declared as he marched off.

ॐ

A hired car was waiting, so Allisdair sat in the back with Kelly as they drove out of the airport. She was firm she wouldn't answer his questions—she'd prove how little she cared about whatever he had to say.

Unfortunately for her plan, he seemed content to ride in silence and denied her any opportunity to demonstrate her disinterest. Kelly's irritation grew with each unspoken mile, as if he were using her own plan against her.

With quick revision her plan changed to one of boisterous demands.

"So what's a steward, anyway?"

"I tend yer grandmother's manor."

Kelly's resolve was halfhearted and she abandoned her questions. Despite her irritation, she was more than a little intimidated. Maybe it was the kilt. They rode on in silence.

Gradually the countryside became wilder and less populated. Hills lifted up around them and craggy rocks and forest soon replaced maize-colored fields. Traffic thinned to nothing. They drove for another hour, the rumble of the road beneath them the only sound. Finally, the car turned onto an unmarked lane and plunged through the woods that closely wrapped the dirt road.

"We'd be here."

"Where?" Kelly's eyes tried to penetrate the leafy tunnel.

"These are yer grandmother's lands. The house is a wee bit farther."

Kelly shifted restlessly. The car would roll up. An old lady would burst through the screen door and raise her hands in delight. She'd exclaim how big Kelly had grown and then she'd throw out her arms to render a crushing hug.

How can I pretend to love someone I've never met? Someone who never demonstrated any interest in me? I feel closer to the agency woman. And she was a Grade A drip. Sappy, colorless and no flavor. But compared to my grandmother, I was tight with her.

As the car rounded a final turn, the forest abruptly halted. A huge lawn, speckled with shrubs and trees rolled away to the left of the tree-lined drive. Between the passing trunks Kelly spied a pond filled with splashing ducks and geese. They played chase around lemony water lilies. Alders stood at attention, overseeing the watery fracas, while the willows shirked their duty, drooping in a sleepy lethargy.

To the right of the drive was an assortment of working buildings. Two long, low structures were stables—she could feel their equine presence. Several smaller buildings lay beside them, one with open sides from which echoed a metallic *clang, clang, clang*. Surely a smithy. A number of large barns sat farthest from the drive, bordering the golden fields of newly cut hay.

It was only then Kelly caught sight of the house, although "house" wasn't the right word for it. "Mansion" or "castle" would have been closer. It seemed immensely old, and a stately air seeped from its beige and tan stones. At either end of the main building, long wings stretched back leading to further additions.

Kelly stared. Her head buzzed with words that tried to describe what she saw: colossal, majestic, palatial. These were rich, expressive words—chocolate words—and they all applied to the building before her. But in that buzz, one plain vanilla word was missing: *home*.

The car stopped before the manor-house steps. Allisdair got out. Kelly's heart revved like Jake's battered motor scooter. She eyed the door lock. She'd never been one for change in large doses and she simply couldn't will herself out of the car. It didn't matter that this place dashed her expectations; she was alien here. She'd abandoned any solace she could remember three thousand miles behind her. She fixed her gaze on the seatback in front of her.

Please can I have it all back? PLEASE!

She started when her door opened. She forced herself to look up, expecting some dotty variation of an aproned Nana. She was therefore quite surprised to see a woman more her mother's age.

"You must be Kelly. Welcome!" The woman's alto voice rolled through Kelly with the warming sensation of sipped hot chocolate. Her smile wasn't plastic like the flight attendant's or the agency woman's. This was a real smile. It was soft around the edges. It wasn't brittle and it wouldn't crack. And her eyes were the color of dark maple syrup—the good stuff. Eyes flavorful and rich with perception and kindness. The woman reached out an inviting hand. "I'm Jillian."

Kelly found herself climbing up out of the car.

"Ach, good. I see ya've met yer grandmother's assistant." Allisdair's voice was gritty and harsh after Jillian's. "I leave ya to her then. I have matters requirin' my attention." With a nod he turned and strode off in the direction of the stables.

Kelly searched for some snide reply, but for whatever reason she couldn't think of one. She managed a slight shrug, which appeared more nervous than aloof.

If Jillian noticed, she gave no sign. "Your grandmother sends her apologies she was unable to meet you herself. She's invited you to join her for tea at three o'clock."

Hearing the mention of food, Kelly's stomach gave a raucous growl. Her cheeks responded with a flush.

Jillian tsked. "I imagine Allisdair was all business and never thought to stop for your refreshment. His days are demanding, but that's little excuse. To us, hospitality and the comfort of a guest are ancient and sacred laws. Let's find you something to eat and when your stomach is satisfied we'll see what else you might need."

Kelly followed to the imposing double doors—doors that marked a new threshold in her life—but she failed to notice the massive snowy owl perched among the mansion's gables, silently noting her arrival.

Jillian led her through the house to an enormous kitchen overstuffed with stoves, grills, brick ovens, counters, pantries and refrigerators. The high-beamed ceiling contained openings that let the cooking heat escape and allowed considerable light, giving the kitchen a comfortable, airy feel.

The yeasty aroma of baking bread hung in the air. Kelly closed her eyes and breathed it in, allowing it to carry her back to the previous December …

It was the afternoon of Christmas Eve and preparations for the following day's dinner were under full steam. Full sweat actually, if you happened to be performing intense physical labor near the kitchen's wood-burning stove. The heels of Kelly's hands ached as she drove them down into the spongy mass. Massaging and coaxing the dough with domestic brutality, Kelly glanced at the clock. Ten minutes— no wonder her hands were complaining. It was enough. She mopped her forehead and drained her water glass. Setting the dough near the stove for its second rise, she checked on her mother's progress across the room.

The Bûche de Noël, or chocolate Yule log cake, was the sacred glory that crowned the MacBride's Christmas dinner.

The preparation of the Bûche was always her mom's responsibility, just as Kelly made the morning's Monkey Bread: balls of sweet dough fused during baking and bathed in a buttery brown-sugar goo.

Kelly observed her mother as she sculpted the whipped cream to resemble the snow covered bark of a respectable Yule log. She noted her mom's technique, fully aware that one of these years her mom would announce it was Kelly's turn to create the Bûche. The snowy log was finally complete. Kelly and her mom exchanged glances. From their expressions it was clear this was one of the finer Bûches in recent years. They both smiled.

"Mom, I know it's not Christmas yet, but there's something I'd like to give you. I think now would be the best time."

Her mother's scrutiny felt like x-ray vision. "Since I don't know what this gift is, only you can make that decision."

"Now's the time!" Kelly declared with more confidence. She thundered up the stairs to her bedroom and returned shortly with a small wrapped gift. She handed it to her mother with nervous anticipation.

Unwrapping the gift, her mother stared through the box's cellophane window. Her expression made it clear she was confused. Then she read the label: Chocolate Ants.

"Ah, there she is." Jillian's musing snapped Kelly back to the present. She guided Kelly to a woman just stepping out of one of the walk-in pantries. The woman was older and wore an apron, but that's where any similarity to Peggy's Nana ended. She wasn't heavyset; in fact, she was quite thin. Her weathered skin had the creases of well-worn leather, particularly at the corners of her eyes and mouth. Her hazel eyes had a gentleness about them, as did Nana's, but there was something more. Something not quite hidden that suggested they could flare to fierceness in a crisis. It seemed Kelly wouldn't be waiting until tea time after all.

"This young jack rabbit must surely be Kelly." The woman's brogue was nearly as thick as Allisdair's, but her voice had a singsong quality that bobbed up and down with her words. "Lassie, yer most welcome in this house and particularly in this kitchen."

Kelly believed her. The woman's voice conveyed sincerity. And kindness. It had been a long time since Kelly had felt wanted.

"Kelly, this is Maggie," Jillian introduced. "She oversees our kitchen."

"You're not my grandmother?" Kelly's surprise was so complete she blurted the question without even considering a smug reply.

"Ach, no lassie! That would be Brid. Nay, this kitchen is my domain. My kingdom. Ya needna be hungry to pop in and see me. Come visit anytime. Anytime!"

Jillian rested her hands on Kelly's shoulders. "Kelly's famished after her trip and we were hoping to find her a snack."

"Ach," Maggie cried. "Why didna ya say so! The girl's a twig, she is, an' who knows when she last ate properly."

Hmm … ten bags of peanuts probably don't count.

Maggie thought for a few moments. "Why not a slice of my bread just from the oven an' some fresh cheese?" The kitchen woman didn't wait for approval and began piling a plate. She marched off and soon returned with a glass of a dark amber liquid. "An' we're just comin' into apple season, so ya can enjoy a glass of our first cider pressin'."

Glass and plate went on a tray, but Maggie wasn't through; before they could leave, the kitchen woman deftly planted two warm oatmeal cookies on the tray.

"Thank you," Kelly murmured.

"Why don't we take this to your residence?" Jillian suggested.

They laced through a maze of hallways and corridors. Eventually they stopped before a burled oak door. Jillian led Kelly into a high-ceilinged room with a door at the far end. The mullioned windows along the left stretched from floor to ceiling, pouring in light. A warm blaze burned in the fireplace to the right. A writing desk flanked by barrister bookcases occupied the left corner; tapestries hung over any remaining wall space.

This ... is mine?

Jillian set the tray down beside two upholstered chairs that faced the fireplace.

A movement across the room caught Kelly's attention. "Look!" she gasped.

Perched in the open window, a barn owl glowed white and golden-buff in the afternoon sun. Its fathomless eyes, framed by a dark facial ring, stared at Kelly with intent.

"What should we do?" she asked.

Jillian didn't seem to share Kelly's agitation. "Don't worry about *this* owl," she reassured. "Its manners are impeccable. It comes and goes throughout the house."

The owl hopped from foot to foot and rasped a *kschhhh* of confirmation.

Jillian moved to the door. "Why don't you relax until tea? I'll come back for you before three." As Jillian was about to leave, a question slipped out of Kelly without her realizing she'd even asked it.

"What's my grandmother like?"

Jillian's eyes softened. "Brid is … well, she's Brid." As she stepped out, she answered Kelly's unspoken question. "You'll be fine here."

The barn owl *shiiiish*'ed agreement.

2

INTRODUCTIONS

At precisely three o'clock Jillian showed Kelly into Brid's solarium. A jungle of foliage bathed in the fractured sunlight that fell through the windows. Waxy orchids hung in wooden baskets from the ceiling; a red mandevilla coiled up a trellis along one wall; throughout, pots of dahlias, sedum, hibiscus, lavender, and many others Kelly couldn't name jammed every horizontal surface. An herbal scent hung in the air—not the savory tang you'd smell in a kitchen, but the more delicate whiff of tender plants busily growing.

Taking a seat, Kelly tried to swallow, but she had cottonmouth, and saliva was scarce. She sat on her hands wondering how long she'd have to wait.

"Kelly. Welcome."

Brid stood in the doorway. She had an erect bearing and she glided into the room with a perfect posture that would have overjoyed Kelly's mother; no book would ever fall from Brid's head. She had high cheekbones and refined features, and none of the loose folds of skin that Kelly associated with the elderly. Her turquoise eyes contrasted her otherwise austere appearance. They reminded Kelly of Caribbean waters—clear and deep, with ages of secrets lurking in their depths.

She floated into the chair opposite Kelly as Jillian came in and set down a tray.

"Would you care for some tea?" Brid asked in a musical voice with the timbre of a perfectly tuned orchestra.

Kelly meekly accepted a cup.

Grandmother.

She tried out the word, but it didn't fit. It was too vanilla and there was nothing vanilla about Brid. It spoke of relationship, but Kelly couldn't identify anything she might have in common—books *leapt* off her head. She wondered exactly which genes they shared.

"Tell me about Vermont," Brid bade her.

Kelly swallowed with difficulty. Sitting in the principal's office would have been more enjoyable. This was like … sitting with the Queen. What could Kelly say that the

Queen would possibly care about? Yet the Queen's polite request carried the full force of a royal command.

Vermont? It was home. I had friends there. Peggy and Jake. Right now they're probably catching frogs down at the pond—it's too late in the season for tadpoles. They'll be missing me. I had the best frog hands. We were tight. "One for all and all for one," we used to say. That was important. It meant we'd always stick together. Always, until I had to come here.

"I had friends," Kelly answered in a subdued voice.

Brid's gaze was too intense. Kelly stared down, her eyes tracing the lines of the parquet floor.

"You had a farm, didn't you?"

The farm. The meadow where we'd lie and search for comets on August nights. The oak we'd jump from, landing in a small mountain of hay. The trail by the brook where the Jack-in-the-pulpits grew. And Moonshadow. Especially Moonshadow. "Can't tell if that hawse thinks she's a paawson, or if you think yaaw a hawse," Mr. Bartles told me. He had to be the oldest living creature in Vermont, but boy could he teach riding! "Joined at the hip," he used to say. Moonshadow and me—we could practically read each other's mind. But our hips weren't joined. Our souls were.

"Yes … I had a horse."

Kelly counted thirteen separate pieces in each parquet tile.

"I recall your mother was musical. Did you also study?"

I studied. I studied the piano, but it's singing I love most. I sang in church last Easter. Mom was so proud. Nights at the piano were the best, though. We'd take turns singing and improvising harmonies. Mom's alto had the sound of warm molasses ...

Tears spilled over Kelly's cheeks. Her throat tightened until she could only nod. With an ungraceful snuffle, she wiped her nose with the back of her hand and knuckled away the tears.

Brid didn't do any of the things you might expect. She didn't cluck a "there, there." She didn't pat Kelly's hand. She didn't actually do anything. After a moment she continued as if nothing were wrong. "Do you remember Hamish?"

Kelly recalled her father had Americanized his name when her parents moved to Vermont. Hamish. James. She tried to picture him, but the only memory she had was of a photograph. "No, I was too young."

Sorry, Dad.

Brid handed Kelly a package wrapped in an amethyst-colored cloth. "I'd like you to have this."

Kelly carefully unwrapped the fabric to find a book; but when she opened it, its pages were blank.

"A diary can be a comfortable way to explore your feelings during periods of change. Your father always kept one."

"He did?"

Brid nodded. Her ocean eyes bored right through Kelly. "Is there anything else you'd like?"

To be happy ... to have my mother again ... maybe my father too. To have the normal back.

"No thank you," Kelly murmured.

"Very well. I'll see you at dinner." Brid glided out of the room balancing an entire stack of encyclopedias.

"Well, she's here." Brid looked to her guest.

"Aye, that she is."

"And?"

"Ya know my mind, *Bean-rìgh*," Allisdair replied. "It hasna changed. She's young an' unknown to us."

"She *is* my kin," Brid reminded him.

"Aye, she is. But how true is her blood? Yer hangin' on to a slim hope. An' what of the danger to us? Her presence could be a risk. Ya know my job is to protect."

"What would you do?" Brid's eyes flashed challenge.

Allisdair held her gaze. "Fer now, I'll watch her closely."

"As will I," said Brid. "As will I."

After tea, Jillian offered to show Kelly the library. The collection of books was grander than Kelly had imagined—rows of shelves towering twelve feet upward. She could smell traces of whatever polish was used to oil the wood. Few of the books were bound with cloth; most were covered in leather in an assortment of dignified colors, some even embossed and stamped with gold or silver.

Kelly exhaled a sigh. She had always loved books. She believed each one had a unique voice it was willing to share if you cared enough to explore beneath its cover. She brushed her fingers reverently across the closest spines.

"Cease that! What do you think you're doing pawing at my books? One can only imagine what you last touched. Presumptuous *girl!*"

Startled, Kelly spun around. A gaunt man stood before her. His sunken eye sockets were overly large and gave him a skeletal appearance, which wasn't helped by a complexion the color of old toenails. His voice, while not loud, pierced and grated in the back of her head.

Jillian, unfazed by the man's indignation, politely introduced Kelly to Master Roderick the librarian.

"I hardly need more miscreants underfoot. How utterly noisome!" He scowled in Kelly's direction.

Petulant. Peevish.

They looked around for several minutes more, but Kelly's joy of discovery had evaporated and she wasn't anxious to prolong her visit. As they left, Master Roderick carped after them, "See that she learns the library's rules!"

❧

It wasn't fair. Why do adults get to act like jerks, but kids have to be perfect? It wasn't her fault what she said was true. So why did *she* have to get scolded? In the hallway, after they'd left the library, she grumbled about that cadaverous crank hoarding his books. Jillian turned to her with a stern expression.

"Kelly, however you feel about an individual is your own business, but you must *never* show disrespect towards any master."

They continued back to the residence, Kelly's face burning with embarrassment.

When they reached Kelly's door, Jillian said, "I'll pick you up for dinner shortly before seven." Her tone was once again friendly and helpful, as if the earlier incident had never happened. But Kelly hadn't forgotten it, and her embarrassment had grown into resentment.

"What if I don't feel like dinner? What if I'm not hungry?" Her tone suggested her question had little to do with her appetite.

Jillian's answer brooked no argument. "It's tradition that we dine *together* each evening." Then more lightly she added, "I'll see you just before seven," and she left.

Kelly slammed the door to her residence, but Jillian was already gone. There was nothing breakable to hurl, so Kelly flounced down in a chair and glared at the fire crackling merrily before her. She punched the arm of the chair.

Rules. I hate their rules! Nobody thinks of me. How I feel. Whether or not I even want to be here. When did I agree to any rules?

Kelly was still cross when Jillian came by at dinnertime. She was mad at Master Roderick for his meanness. She was mad at Jillian for supporting him and not taking

Kelly's side. She was mad at Brid for dragging her here to live. And she was especially mad at herself for being so helpless. With little choice, she followed Jillian.

The number of people gathered in the Great Hall surprised Kelly; she hadn't expected dinner to be an event of such grand proportions. Amiable conversation filled the hall with a lively buzz. But the convivial atmosphere didn't reach Kelly; in fact, it pushed her further away. It wasn't about her and it didn't include her. It never occurred to her all she had to do was *want* to join in. Her deepening resentment was more comfortable at the moment.

Allisdair moved to the head table and the room hushed on some unspoken cue.

"Would the lower tables please assemble?"

People moved quietly to stand by their seats along the three tables that ran lengthwise down the hall. It only took moments.

"Would the high table please assemble?"

Jillian had explained the dinner protocol: in gratitude for Brid's hospitality, her guests showed their respect by arriving on time and waiting politely for their hostess. Kelly moved to the high table and stood beside the seat assigned her.

Above the mantle, a clock entwined with gold filigree chimed the hour. Each note reverberated in the silence, fading only as the next one pealed. On the sixth stroke, Brid entered the hall. By the seventh she stood at the center of the high table, erect and lordly.

As the final note died away, Allisdair turned to Brid and announced, "Yer guests are assembled."

Brid spread her arms, including all present, and called, "Welcome to my home and to my table. Leave your troubles outside these doors and relax tonight in the peace of friendship and community. Let us be thankful for the food and the company we'll share within this hall." With that she took her seat, releasing the spell that held the room silent and motionless. The hall instantly filled with the scrapes of chairs and affable banter as everyone sat and dinner was served.

Kelly took her seat at the end of the table and began eating, paying no heed to the person beside her. The mahogany tabletop was higher than she was accustomed to, and it gave her a Goldilocks feeling—like a child sitting at the adult table and someone had forgotten her booster seat. She found herself missing her kitchen table back home, of all things. While she'd never taken any special notice of it before, she could picture it now in clear detail: the rounded edge and maple grain; the napkin holder and the windmill salt-and-pepper shakers; the crystal vinegar cruet with its fluted ridges. Her mom had taught her the word. *Cruet—a small glass bottle for holding vinegar, oil, or other condiments at the table.* "It's important to know the precise name of a thing," she'd told Kelly.

"Excuse me; you must be Brid's granddaughter. Allow me to introduce myself. I'm Master David, the resident bard."

Kelly resented the interruption from the man beside her. "Hello," she said curtly, without looking up from her plate.

She tried to return to the image of her kitchen, but instead remembered an evening with Peggy's family around their dining room table. It was corned beef and cabbage night. The vinegar was on the table, and Kelly was explaining the word cruet.

"I'm a relative newcomer here myself," the bard broke in. "It can be difficult in new surroundings—hard to feel comfortable. It does come with time. And a bit of effort."

Why wouldn't he just leave her alone? She huffed a loud sigh, hoping he'd take the hint.

She looked across the hall at the lower tables. A group of kids her age clustered around the far end of the table on the right. Would they care about cruets? Or would they just think they're dumb?

"It's challenging to make new friends when you're only one in a sea of so many new faces."

Kelly started humming one of her mother's gardening songs. She knew humming at the dinner table was impolite, but she had given him fair warning and he persisted. It was his own fault.

Rather than taking offense, however, the man seemed overjoyed. "Ah, I see you know the *Skye Boat Song!*

'Speed bonnie boat, like a bird on the wing,
Onward, the sailors cry;
Carry the lad that's born to be king,
Over the sea to Skye.'

"The tune itself is based on an old sea shanty. It speaks of the boat on which Bonnie Prince Charlie escaped to the Isle of Skye, following his defeat at Culloden during the second Jacobite Rising in 1746."

At first Kelly tried to ignore his words, but his voice had an alluring quality that teased your ears, so they wanted to hear more. He made vanilla words sound sumptuous and attractive. Despite her irritation, she found it pleasant to listen to him.

"I don't even know what that is," she said dismissively, "either one: a master *or* a bard."

"Oh, how ignoble!" he cried. "What value can a life have—given to the pleasure of others—when those whom I would serve are unaware ..."

Kelly looked up. His voice conveyed distress, but his eyes said otherwise.

He explained that young people with special vocational interests come to the manor to apprentice in their craft. If an apprentice is adept and shows promise, at age sixteen, he (or she, Master David nodded to Kelly) might be accepted as a journeyman. If so, the next three years would refine and deepen those skills and then the journeyman would travel for three more years, learning how practices in his craft differ in other parts of the world. Only then would the proficient pass on to become a craftsman. "Master" designated those with a true gift and decades of experience.

"Here at this table sit the Masters Bard," he indicated himself, "Smith," he pointed down the table, "and on the far side of Brid and Allisdair sit the Masters Animal Husbandman and Ovate, ovate being an old Celtic word for librarian."

Kelly looked down and sure enough, there sat Master Roderick scowling at his plate. Beyond him, Jillian and a muscular, redheaded man were deep in conversation. Kelly learned that the redhead was Conall. As best she understood, he reported to Allisdair as *galloglas*—a sort of groundskeeper.

Master David went on to explain that a bard is skilled in music, poetry and story telling. It's an ancient profession, dating back to a time when books were a rarity and illiteracy was common. The bards preserved the history and culture of the Celtic people through their oral performances. Unlike other craftsmen who settle into a community, a bard travels, carrying news, stories, and sagas between different peoples. Just as Master Brandon, Brid's household bard was currently journeying in Wales, Master David was visiting in residence here for the next two years.

"Do you enjoy music, Kelly?"

His smile was as captivating as his voice and his question didn't irritate her this time.

"Yes," she said meekly.

"And storytelling?"

Most people associate storytelling with young children and picture books, but Kelly and her mom frequently read aloud after dinner. Many a night swelled with a soaring tale such as *Treasure Island*, *The Sword in the Stone*, or *20,000 Leagues Under the Sea*. Kelly had never considered other adults might understand.

"I did. I used to read a lot with …" She sat uncomfortably, willing her eyes to remain dry.

I'm sorry we'll never get to Gulliver's Travels.

"Be sure to tell me how you like the stories you'll hear later."

Kelly nodded mutely.

He steered the conversation to his journeys and spoke of the amazing things he'd witnessed. He told of the skalds of Norway and their poetic tradition. He described the epic sagas of Iceland and explained how they defined the heritage of the land of fire and ice. He compared the legends and beliefs of the Mi'kmaq—the native peoples of the Maritime Provinces in eastern Canada—to those of the Inuits in the farthest north (a people Kelly knew as Eskimos.)

Never having traveled, Kelly only thought of foreign countries as colored regions on a map. Master David painted her a picture where music and storytelling defined these distant cultures.

Allisdair stood up from his chair without preamble. As he did so, all conversation ceased and people rose to their feet. Kelly was unsure what to do when she felt Master David's hand on her forearm urging her up. In the quiet that would have magnified a whisper, she appreciated his silent aid and stood, joining the others.

She couldn't understand why they waited, when a low buzzing tickled her ears. A melody soon accompanied the buzz. She was hearing a bagpipe play somewhere in the distance. Its haunting notes emerged at a languid pace and she closed her eyes to better hear. When the tune ended, conversation in the hall resumed with jarring suddenness.

Retaking their seats, Master David explained. "Each evening we stand in respect as the piper salutes the setting sun, welcoming the new day."

Kelly knotted her forehead. "New day?"

"You'll find many things here different than you're accustomed to. We follow the ancient Celtic traditions, and in the Celtic calendar, each day begins at sundown."

After dinner, Kelly followed the guests to the far end of the hall in anticipation of the evening's entertainment. Portraits in gilt frames hung every ten paces down the hall's length. Their painted faces were noble, but their eyes seemed tired, as if nobility had been required far longer than they'd hoped. The room ended at a massive fireplace with a dais set in the corner.

Master David directed the musicians as they tuned their instruments. A lively dance set led off with the Master Bard on penny whistle, a woman with red hair resembling a flaming carrot on fiddle, and a slouching fellow with mouse-like ears playing a tambourine-shaped drum. For their next piece, Master David and the barbecued carrot did a slower tune with a rolling pulse reminding Kelly of the rise and fall of the sea. Musicians then traded off. The following song created a mournful longing with its sad, but beautiful, story told by harp, small pipes—a mellow, indoor version of the bagpipes—and guitar.

No two pieces sounded similar. The ever-changing combinations of musical styles and instruments produced an endless variety of effects. Storytelling was mixed into the program, but it was a high form of the art, and the storyteller's Siren voice carried Kelly into the belly of the tale.

Her knotted nerves gradually loosened into a calmer fatigue. Her day had been a long one, so she didn't stay for the end of the performance; she crept from the hall while the music played on. Heading back to her residence, she passed the main entrance and it occurred to her a night-time stroll might be pleasant before bed.

The stillness that descended as the outer doors shut was a sharp contrast to the revelry she had left behind. She let it settle over her. She ambled down the drive with no destination in mind; she simply wanted to sample the night. All of the introductions and all of the newness left her over-stuffed. She needed time to sort through her reactions to it all, so she appreciated this quiet respite.

Kelly sniffed a musky trace in the night air—to her, an unmistakable scent. The stables were just off the drive to her left. Their tug was magnetic and she was powerless to resist. Nor did she try.

They were single-story structures, long and narrow with a considerable horse-sized door mid-way down their length—now shut for the night—and a person-sized door at the north and south ends. Kelly stepped through the dewy grass and approached the nearest building. It was dark as she slipped inside so she paused to give her eyes an opportunity to adjust. She sucked in a deep breath smelling of horses, oiled leather, hay and manure. Her ears pricked at the shuffling of hooves, puffing breaths, and an occasional snort. Her face eased into a smile.

As her eyes were able to discern differences in the shadows, she edged forward down the center aisle. Curious noses poked out to greet her and she felt a swelling joy as she advanced from stall to stall, petting forelocks, patting noses, and scratching ears. A contented peace filled her. She could curl up here in the hay and sleep deeply.

Beyond the last stall, Kelly opened the south door and looked out into the lighter dark between the buildings. Soft footfalls echoed towards her and as she watched, the redheaded man, Conall, strode into view. She shied back into the shadows. She wasn't yet ready to abandon the calm she'd found.

Regardless, her calm shattered in an instant. She could only stare, opened-mouthed and numb as Conall vanished. From the spot where he'd stood a moment before, a golden eagle launched upward, propelling itself with sweeps of its wings away into the night.

3

THE DIARY

Kelly slept well into the next morning. When she did
awaken, she was reluctant to rise. There seemed little reason. In the months following her mother's death, Kelly
had been in constant transition. At first the movement
was from her old life to some new life in a new home.
Then, after learning of her grandmother, the preparations for her trip to Scotland—phone calls, tickets, visa
and passport—became the motion that filled her days.
Finally, the trip itself carried her from one continent and
way of life to another. Throughout it all, the movement
had given her purpose, albeit painful and unwelcome.

But now, having arrived at her destination, the movement suddenly halted.

Pushing aside the satin canopy, she finally climbed out of her four-poster bed. Someone had brought her breakfast while she slept, but the thoughtfulness was lost on Kelly. She only felt relief they'd left her alone.

The breakfast tray carried the ubiquitous teapot, a plate of scones and a bowl of mixed berries—blueberries and some smaller, scarlet berries that reminded her of sumac. Her mother had once warned her about the dangers of eating unidentified berries in the woods:

Many are poisonous. If you eat the wrong ones, you'll have to drink mustard-water to induce vomiting.

Kelly wasn't sure which was grosser: drinking mustard-water or vomiting. She picked out the blueberries, leaving the red ones untouched. She sniffed at a scone. It smelled lemony. That seemed safe enough, and she was hungry.

As she nibbled, she examined the fireplace set against the north wall of her bedroom. It was sizeable; the opening resembled the mouth of a bear's den, nearly shoulder-high. The stone was rose-colored, capped top and bottom by a mantle and hearth of polished black marble. Palm-sized tiles lined the arched opening, each inlayed with a pearly crossed-stick character, no two the same. Inside, the grate led to a cast iron fireback—an upright plate designed to reflect the fire's heat outward—on which a lion *passant guardant* stared back at Kelly. Unlike most heraldic lions, though, this one was neither regal nor menacing. This one was smiling.

On an impulse, Kelly ducked and stepped inside. The bricks were warm, radiating an echo of the previous night's fire. Little light penetrated behind the fireback, and Kelly inched along, feeling for the back wall with her toe. She hunched further as the ceiling pitched downward, and she stretched out a steadying hand. One pace … two … her fingers brushed a loose brick, knocking it free. It landed with a clunk.

Groping, she retrieved it from the dusty ashes, but when she found the hole and tried to place it back, it met resistance. She reached into the hollow, thinking to clear out whatever mortar had fallen loose, but found something else instead. Her fingertips swept over a soft, pebbled surface. Her thumb pushed upwards across the front of the object, feeling it yield in a familiar way. Grasping it as best she could in the cramped confines, she slid a book from its long-forgotten crypt.

Kelly returned to her bedroom, her breakfast now forgotten, to examine her chance discovery. Its leather cover was faded and caked in mortar dust. She blew a forceful puff to clear it, only to choke in the resulting cloud. She cautiously opened the book, not sure how fragile it might be. On the title page, penned in a bold but elegant cursive, she read:

The Diary of Hamish MacBride
Volume III

She stared at the lettering. She wanted to absorb every pen stroke, as if by consuming their shapes and forms she might better know her father. Finally, she dared to turn the page.

August 20

Pox Lachlan! He found it! I'm sorry I ever told him about rune codes. Now I can't keep him out of my diary. He must have cracked the code to my fireplace—that's the only way he could have gotten in.

He's probably proud of himself. Well he shouldn't be. It was obvious!

I'm tightening security. Stuart also has some ideas, but for the moment:

- I've started this diary, which will remain carefully hidden;

- New rune clues will be encoded in riddles;

- I'll make phony entries in the old diary, just to mislead Lachlan. That'll be fair payment for snooping!

HMB

As Kelly re-read the passage, the bell to her residence interrupted her thoughts. Her head snapped up. No one must know! This secret was between her father and herself. She looked about for a hiding place, and decided she couldn't take any risks. She ducked into the fireplace and replaced the book behind its brick.

Brushing ash off her sleeve, she tried to compose her expression as she crossed the sitting room to the door.

"Good morning," Jillian greeted. "Your grandmother has asked that I take you down to see Master Roy."

"Whatever." Kelly shrugged, annoyed over the interruption.

A misty drizzle shrouded the morning. The vapor wasn't distinct enough to call rain, but it clung to Kelly and coated her in a layer of damp as she and Jillian approached the barns. Kelly hadn't forgotten the previous night's incident, but despite the glances she stole, she could locate neither Conall nor the eagle.

They found Master Roy in the sheep byre, working with a younger man. The two wrestled with a black-faced ewe as they attempted to trim a section of its hoof. Master Roy scowled.

"We'll need to examine the entire lot," he instructed. "I'll not have this spreading through the flock. And quarantine this one until we're sure the rot's gone." He bent down, peering through his eyeglasses to inspect the job. "Cut away a little more from here."

The master had a wiry build and worked with a purposeful intensity that belied his years. He focused so entirely on the trimming operation that he didn't seem to notice Jillian and Kelly until he was satisfied with the results.

"Ah, yes. You'd be Kelly," he stated as he now turned his attention wholly to her.

Master Roy introduced Dougal, his journeyman. Dougal couldn't have been more opposite the master. Lanky and unkempt, he most resembled an unmade bed with dirty sheets. When he wasn't busy with a task, he fidgeted constantly—and not with any useful aim, such as straightening his hair or tucking in his shirt. His pronounced Adam's apple bobbed and quivered as he stammered something to Kelly before turning back to the ewe.

Master Roy led Kelly outside and she snugged her coat against the dewy air. They proceeded to a nearby paddock where a dozen horses milled and jostled within.

"Your grandmother says you're to have a horse. You may choose from these three-year-olds."

She stood, fixed to the ground, unable to respond. Choose a new horse? You can't just replace a soul mate. It's not that simple. Leaving Moonshadow behind in Vermont had gashed Kelly's life almost as deeply as the hole left by her mother's death. You don't just pick out a new horse and carry on where you left off. It's just not that simple.

"Enter the paddock, Kelly," the master urged.

She did as instructed, opening the gate and stepping in among the herd. It took her several minutes to reign in her grief before she took note of the horses around her. She patted hindquarters, feeling the glossy coats under a sheen of mist; sharp eyes followed her movements and ears pricked forward in curiosity. Their nickers and snorts soothed her and their presence slowly pulled Kelly up out of her sadness.

"You're to choose one," Master Roy reminded her. "Its spirit must pair to the rider. That's what you're to measure and select." He sighed. "You'll hear none of it if you're not listening."

What was he asking of her? Kelly waited for an explanation, but none was offered.

She ran a hand along the neck of a nearby roan. What was she to listen for? "Would you be mine?" she asked the beast halfheartedly.

"Not that way; with your mind!" The whisper was close. She hadn't heard the master approach. She spun around, and then stared—he was still at the fence, watching her intently. She looked at the horses and then back at Master Roy.

He stood waiting.

She'd once read that through a horse's eyes, you could sense its soul. She eyeballed a dappled mare.

Are you for me?

Nothing. This was ridiculous. She mentally questioned another. Still nothing—although she did feel hungry despite having just eaten. She queried another horse and idly thought her hair might need combing. Why was he humiliating her like this? This was hard enough. Why couldn't she just choose and be done with it? She shut her eyes as her emotions blazed.

Moonshadow, I'm sorry I broke your trust!

As quickly as her frustration and sorrow flared, it vanished, and a playfulness washed through her. She had an impulse to smile, as if she'd just remembered a funny joke. She opened her eyes and the white gelding beside her gave a soft nicker and bobbed its head. Surprised, Kelly stared at the horse.

Was that you I felt? Would you be mine?

The desire to smile returned. Kelly exhaled a long, slow breath.

A neigh from the back of the paddock interrupted her. A coal-black mare reared up in challenge. Kelly bumped and nudged her way to the back of the herd. As she reached out, the mare yanked her head away with a rebellious whinny. Kelly persisted and the black finally allowed Kelly to handle her.

Are you for me?

A stormy exhilaration coursed through Kelly, much stronger than the earlier perceptions. She felt charged with a feral electricity: less of an answer, more like a dare.

"This is my horse," she announced.

Master Roy entered the paddock with a frown. He slipped a halter onto the black and passed the lead to Kelly, signaling her to follow. "Why not the gelding?" he asked.

"He's a beauty," Kelly admitted. "But this one understands me."

"So be it."

Master Roy called over Kenna, one of Dougal's apprentices, bidding her to assist Kelly with a stall assignment, appropriate tack, and the horse's shoeing.

"I don't know where we're to find you a stall," Kenna fretted. "Master Roy has been meaning to adjust the assignments and free up some, but with all the harvest activity, who's had the time?"

Kelly had never considered herself unattractive, but Kenna was beautiful. She stood several inches taller than Kelly's five-foot-six. And compared to Kelly's athletic build, with broad shoulders and solid thighs (not that Kelly *ever* considered herself an athlete), Kenna was fine-boned and willowy. Kelly's brown hair was cut in a short, practical style, also in contrast to Kenna's long wisps of sandy blonde hair, which framed her grass-green eyes. Yet … something … seemed out of place. Her gait, in her heavy work boots, was nearly a swagger. She planted her heels with a deliberateness Kelly felt through the ground. Each step was counterbalanced by a roll of her shoulders that jangled her arms back and forth. Kenna walked like a boy.

As they reached the tack room Kenna hucked up something in her throat and spit a line drive into the corner. Kelly winced but said nothing. They entered, and the musty tang of leather and saddle soap filled Kelly's nose. She overlooked the discharge—familiar smells do wonders to cleanse unpleasantness from one's palate.

"I can't say what sort of bit you'll want for *that* one," Kenna cautioned. "She can be temperamental and you'll likely have your hands full. Be careful she doesn't throw you. You might break some bones or sprain an ankle. Maybe even hit your head." She handed Kelly a riding helmet.

Kelly sorted through the room and selected her saddle, pad, and bridle, and Kenna added a tack box with grooming tools, and a stout pair of muck boots. Then they were off to the farrier.

"Aidan's likely to be doing the shoeing," Kenna informed her. "We're the same age—fifteen, you know. He's just made journeyman, but he's an exception. It doesn't normally happen till you're sixteen. I'm not stuck as an apprentice because I'm having any kind of trouble. Sixteen is just the usual rule."

Aidan wasn't at all what Kelly expected. Unlike the hulking Master Smith, whose forearms were the size of her neck, Aidan was lean. He had a cherubic appearance: round cheekbones, pretty eyes and mouth, and a dimple on his chin. His blondish red hair, cut short, capped a high brow. The forge was responsible for his rosy cheeks, but it nevertheless added to the impression. His beatific appearance was only belied by his expression; an angel wouldn't require such determination.

He laid down his hammer and wiped his palms on his leather apron. The darker coloring along their path indicated this was a common habit. He reached out for the black's lead and ran his hand down the horse's shoulder and leg to the fetlock. With a gentle tug, the front hoof obediently sprang up. Kelly had witnessed numerous shoeings and recognized the journeyman's skill. With nips and rasp he trimmed and leveled each hoof with dispatch.

Meanwhile, Kenna perched on a nearby fence to watch. She leaned forward, held up by her hands on the rail between her legs. It was a posture Kelly's mom would have thought most unladylike. Kelly had always considered herself a tomboy—enjoying a good adventure now and again and being a Musketeer seemed proof enough. Yet in Kenna's presence, Kelly felt downright girly.

"Now be careful, Aidan," Kenna warned from atop the fence. "That black can be a wild one. Don't let her kick you."

"You worry too much," he replied.

Kenna snorted. "Oh aye, but someone has to. Growing up with five older brothers? Boys don't ever think about what they're doing—they just rush off and do it. I had to do all the worrying for them."

"Where's your home?" Kelly asked.

"Prestwick," Kenna answered. "A wee village in Ayrshire, down in the Lowlands."

Kenna didn't sound at all homesick.

"Don't you miss it?"

"I miss my brothers." Kenna seemed very specific about what she missed. "They visit when they can." She shrugged and Kelly sensed further questions might not be welcome.

"Have you named your black yet?" Aidan asked as he reached for a shoe.

Kelly hadn't. She hadn't even considered the question.

He held the shoe in the forge as it gradually brightened. When it glowed red-hot he laid it on the anvil and between hammer strikes told her, "She … is no … ordinary … mare." He shook the beads of sweat from his forehead. The air was acrid with the smell of burnt hoof as he fit the shoe. "And she'll be wanting no ordinary name."

•

Kelly had to report to Master David after lunch. Music lessons were to be a regular part of her studies. The decision hadn't been Kelly's, and she didn't welcome it. It wasn't that she minded music—she loved it, and delighted in learning more and improving her skills. It was, in fact, because she loved it so much that she was upset. Music was too personal, something precious she had shared with her mother. There was no way she was going to open herself up to a stranger—not over music.

She stepped reluctantly into the room. A piano sat beside a haphazard arrangement of folding chairs and music stands. Shelves and cabinets lined the walls, brimming with lopsided stacks of books and scores.

Master David greeted her and led her to comfortable chairs before a hopelessly messy desk.

"I'm glad you came! I'm looking forward to continuing our conversation."

Kelly sat, but said nothing.

"What did you think of last night's performance?"

She ignored the question and tried to read the titles of the books shelved across the room.

Master David overlooked her silence; he apparently didn't require answers from her.

"People's tastes differ so. We try and offer variety, hoping we can appeal to everyone." He went on to explain some of the behind-the-scenes preparations the musicians and storytellers undergo. As in the night before, she found his voice alluring. When he paused to pour them each a glass of water, she wished he would say something more.

"If you spend your days teaching and rehearsing the others, and your nights performing, when do you play for yourself?" she asked.

He flashed an easy smile. "That's always the challenge for teachers: to find time for the thing we love." He rose early, he explained, and fit in an hour of practice or composition before his day began. "And how are you finding your first day, Kelly? This must surely be so different for you. Are you managing?" His concern was audible.

It *was* different. And painful—missing Moonshadow, her mother, and her friends.

"I chose a horse this morning."

He waited for her to continue.

"But I still have to name her."

"Would you care for my assistance?" He asked gently.

She considered his offer and nodded.

"It's an ancient belief that names possess power," he explained. "That they hold some part of the individual's soul. Is your horse skittish?"

Kelly shook her head. "No. She's pure determination."

"Is she content, or is she spirited?"

"Definitely spirited."

"Does she remind you more of the day or of the night?"

"Night."

"What of her markings?"

"She's jet black, with a white blaze on her forehead … like a shooting star or a comet."

"Hmm …" The master thought for a moment. "How about *Gealach*? It means 'moon' in modern Gaelic, but its older derivation is 'bright steed of the heavens.'"

She liked the sound of it. "Gealach it is!"

A clear treble voice beyond the doorway interrupted the conversation.

> "Heaven bless thee!
> Thou hast the sweetest face I ever look'd on.
> Sir, as I have a soul, she is an angel."[1]

Master David rubbed his eyes. "Gordie, you might as well come in. We'll accomplish nothing more with you hanging about."

A boy about Kelly's age stepped into the doorway. He bowed deeply with a flourish of his arm. "Madam, might I introduce myself? I am Gordie, apprentice bard. At your service." His arm churned the air a second time and he stood upright, tousled auburn hair falling back into place. An implacable smile pushed at his freckles, and his eyes gleamed with mischief.

"Gordie, your flair for the theatrical is a bit heavy handed, don't you think?" the master chided.

"But sir, when you're a bard, all the world *is* a stage."[2]

---

1   *Henry VIII* (Act IV, scene i) by William Shakespeare

2   Based on:
"All the world's a stage,
And all the men and women merely players."
As You Like It (Act II, scene vii) by William Shakespeare

Master David snorted. "What, so now we're a bard, are we? Well my young bardling, please share with us those talents perfected by your diligent practice this week. Your audience awaits." He motioned for Kelly to remain seated.

Gordie wrinkled his brow. "How poor are they that have not patience! What wound did ever heal but by degrees? Thou know'st we work by wit, and not by witchcraft; and wit depends on dilatory time."[3]

"Ha!" snapped Master David. "You'd use Iago's words for your own dilatory ruse; and yet *your* plotting is plain to me. You'd spar away the sunlight brandishing the words of Shakespeare if it meant you didn't have to produce your instrument and reveal how little you practiced. Play for me."

As he set his instrument case down, Gordie muttered, "I pick my favorite quotations and store them in my mind as ready armor, offensive or defensive, amid the struggle of this turbulent existence."[4]

Master David leapt from his chair. "Enough!" he thundered. "Enough Burns, Shakespeare, Dr. Seuss and whomever else you fancy quoting. Now play!"

Gordie appeared to welcome any audience he could get, and Kelly was curious, so she remained for his lesson. An octopus of an instrument emerged from his case,

---

3   *Othello* (Act II, Scene iii) by William Shakespeare

4   *The Letters of Robert Burns* (To Mrs. Dunlop: 6th December, 1792) by Robert Burns

many-legged with a bulbous body. Gordie assembled his bagpipes.

Kelly had always prided herself on her musical knowledge. In addition to her piano and singing, she also understood the rudiments of the saxophone and the cello. Jake played the sax in the school band, and Kelly had pressed him into explaining the basics to her. Peggy's mother was a cellist and very willing to broaden Kelly's exposure to stringed instruments. But the bagpipes were altogether different and beyond anything in Kelly's musical experience.

As Gordie blew into the mouthpiece, the bag puffed up soundlessly. He then gave the bag a sharp spank and a ragged growl burst forth from the three long pipes that extended overhead—the drones: one taller bass drone, and two shorter tenors. He continued blowing as he snugged the fully inflated bag under his left arm. Finally the melody notes pealed with a bright tone an octave above the drones' fixed accompaniment. These notes were produced by the chanter—the recorder-like piece that Gordie fingered with both hands.

Kelly found the sound of the instrument evocative, yet the emotions she felt were as changeable as the tunes Gordie played. The martial fervor of a march made her sit up straighter and begged her to step to its beat. A lively jig frolicked and cavorted, willing her to dance gaily. And the slow air's soulful notes languished and tugged at her with a wistful longing.

"That wasn't as distressing as I feared," Master David admitted when Gordie's lesson concluded. "But it's clear you're shirking your technique. I expect a full twenty minutes every day on fingering exercises. Your embellishments should be uncluttered. At the moment they resemble neuromuscular spasms. In fact, why don't you show Kelly where the practice rooms are located, since you'll both be spending so much time there ..."

Gordie's eyebrows danced as they left the music room. "Nearly got away with it."

Kelly turned to him, quizzically.

"*Hadn't* practiced much this week. I can sometimes distract Master David into a poetic duel that eats up my entire lesson. It's a game we play; I'm not bad at it, but he's brilliant." He shrugged. Gordie stopped, as if something had just occurred to him. "If you're going to be living here now, you'd better meet the guys."

"What guys?"

"The other apprentices. Sit with us at dinner tonight."

"Okay ... I guess."

After leaving Gordie, Kelly came upon an orange tomcat meandering in the halls. She stopped to scratch his eagerly extended chin. Unsatisfied when Kelly turned to leave, however, he shadowed her back to her residence, quickly darting in when she opened her door.

"Just make yourself at home!"

The cat did precisely that. He claimed one of her chairs for his own and began to produce a series of chugging belly purrs.

"I'll call you Mack," she told him. "A respectable Scottish name."

Kelly retrieved her father's diary and sat in the unoccupied chair. Opening to where she'd left off that morning, she stroked her marmalade guest as she read:

August 22

Stuart's teaching me solar script! My words will only be visible when the sun is in the same position as the day I wrote them. That means the day after I make an entry, it will disappear until the same day next year.

Lachlan better start showing more respect if he hopes to learn any new rune codes!

HMB

Kelly turned the page. The next one was blank. In fact, the rest of the diary was blank. She stared for a long while at the empty pages. Lachlan had been her father's friend, although their relationship clearly had its ups and downs. Like the time she and Peggy clashed in the mother of all fights. Kelly had been the one to discover the abandoned cider mill. What right did Peggy have to invite Laura Lee to explore it? They didn't even like Laura Lee. Jake refused to take sides; he claimed it was an issue of girls' hormones. Yet their friendship managed to survive.

She missed Peggy and Jake. One for all and all for one is comforting in difficult circumstances. Gordie seemed friendly enough, if a bit bizarre. Kenna? She was certainly no Peggy. Peggy was bold and confident—always dreaming up new schemes for adventure. Kenna was more like a project. She was older than Kelly, but she seemed so … needy.

Kelly started mentally listing all that had happened since she'd arrived. It was a hard habit to break, even if she could no longer share it with her mom. She felt for her pendant under her shirt. A gift from her mother on Kelly's tenth birthday, it was one of the few things Kelly owned that had once belonged to her mom.

Taking out her own diary, she wrote:

August 22

Dear Mom,

I'm in my new house now. (They call it a manor.)

I've got my own room (That's called my residence.)

I've made some new friends. (They seem nice.)

I had a music lesson today. (My teacher's called a bard.)

I even got to choose a horse. I named her Gealach. (That means "bright steed of the heavens.")

It's an interesting place. But it's not the same. (I miss you.)

Love, Kelly

Kelly got up, lifted Mack from his chair, and put him out. She knew what was coming, and she hated to cry in front of anyone. Even a cat.

"Hey," Gordie cried, "pass that back! Didn't get any."

"You snooze, you lose!" the girl with the ponytail called from down the table; nevertheless, the steak pies reversed direction, the platter now a few pies lighter.

"Gimme a break," Gordie complained as he nabbed two for himself. "I was busy introducing Kelly."

Gordie could have saved himself the trouble. Kelly was horrible at remembering names. She'd already forgotten most of the names he just recited. And between her shyness and her penchant for good manners, it was an excruciating failing. She particularly hated those moments when she'd boldly introduce herself, just to be told, "Of course, Kelly, we've already met."

Beside Gordie sat Kenna, then a boy with glasses and a pronounced overbite. Ponytail sat just beyond him. Across from her, Kelly did remember Struan. He was a smith apprentice, working for Aidan. He was a stocky lad, yet his face and body lacked the clearer shaping of early adulthood, so Kelly judged he was likely twelve, the youngest age for an apprentice. A pimply boy sat further down.

Some, like Kenna and Struan, lived at the manor away from their homes; for some, the manor *was* home. Kelly was surprised to learn Gordie was also an orphan. He'd grown up here practically since birth.

Kelly was quiet through dinner, satisfied to observe the others. She didn't understand much of their conversation, and as the new kid, didn't want to annoy anyone with lots of questions.

"How's Cameron?" Gordie asked Kenna.

"He's been spending all his time with Duffy," she replied between bites. "With the games in seven weeks, he wants to be ready for the trials. Duffy's come a long way, but I don't know how he'll handle the younger sheep; they can be so willful."

Gordie was more encouraging, "Don't sweat it—Cameron's always been good with the dogs; I'm sure he'll ribbon." He turned to Struan, "Will Aidan compete in the hammer throw again this year?"

The broad youth snorted with a grimace. "That's his plan, but I couldn't tell you when he actually trains. He's *always* around the smithy to catch my screw-ups!" They all laughed, appreciating Struan's pain.

Kenna asked Gordie, "Will you be competing this year?"

Now it was Gordie's turn to grumble. "I'm trying. Having a beastly time with my reeds. Master David says it's typical at this stage of piping to go through so many, but breaking in a new reed is hard work."

"Oh, that must be discouraging," Kenna sympathized.

"If you can't handle the bagpipes, then maybe you should switch to a real instrument like the drums," sneered the pimply boy.

Gordie was quick to respond, as if this sort of challenge wasn't new. "Oh stuff it, Thomas! Everyone knows that pipers rule and drummers drool."

He shoveled in his last mouthful of pie and gulped his cider. "Come on, Kell, you'll want to see this." Kelly followed him from the hall, curious as to where they were headed.

They left the main house and cut across the court-yard. The sun was dropping quickly now, throwing off a red glow. As it reached down to brush the horizon, a fig-ure emerged from the building's shadows, striding with clipped precision. He was a piper in full, kilted attire, his tall frame made larger than life by the feathered bonnet atop his head. He marched to a gigantic rock, raised his pipes, and blew to fill them. Gordie and Kelly stood at attention, Gordie puffing his chest.

As the piper played his salute, the sun slid behind the distant hills, abed for the night. The final notes echoed in the evening air and Kelly, freed from the spell, breathed a contented sigh. The piper turned with the same precision and retreated back to whatever door had released him.

Gordie walked to where the piper had stood. "This is Winter Rock. On the eve of the winter solstice, the sun's last rays line up to fall directly on it." He smiled with pride. "I'll pipe the salute from here, one day."

The surface of the rock was covered with the same crossed-stick characters that outlined Kelly's fireplace. She ran her hands over the stony cuts, feeling their weath-ered edges. She looked at the grouped figures, imagining they spelled out, "Play bagpipes HERE."

Gordie noted her interest. "Those are runes. The pre-cise term is *Ogham* characters. They were the first alpha-bet used by the ancient Celts. They're believed to be thousands of years old. Don't know how to read them, though. Doubt anybody here does … except maybe ole' Roddy—he keeps a bunch of books on them in the library."

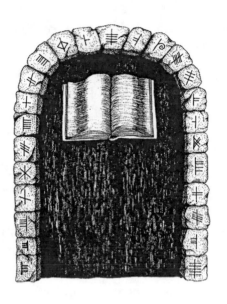

4

LIBRARY SECRETS

Kelly dreamt that night of *Ogham* characters, but not ones written on paper or carved into rock. In her dream the rune figures were stone and stood upright over six feet tall, spread over a giant chessboard. She walked among them and could feel the power radiating from the cold stone—it prickled just on the edge of perception. She knew what was needed: she must combine the runes in a specific order. But she couldn't do it. She didn't know their secrets. How could she sequence them correctly if she didn't understand their meaning?

The vestiges of Kelly's dream lingered when she awoke the next morning. What did the runes represent? She gazed at the runed tiles on her fireplace. The characters were the same as those on Winter Rock, but here each was on a separate tile—as if a primer for some ancient alphabet, and yet more than just an alphabet. She remembered the energy she sensed in her dream. Master David had said that names possess power. Could mere letters contain a natural force of their own? What mysteries did these runes hold?

Master Roderick had books, and that's what she needed. But she doubted the librarian would willingly assist her. She also didn't want to call attention to her interest in runes. The secret of her father's diary must be protected. She needed a way to get the books without anyone knowing; she required assistance, and her thoughts turned to Gordie.

After finishing her chores in the barn, Kelly found Gordie, as she expected, in one of the practice rooms. He was playing through a jig when she entered, but when he saw her, he stopped abruptly. He didn't squeeze the air from the bag to make the clean cut-offs he'd demonstrated at his lesson. Rather, the pipes expelled their air with the ragged squeal of a dying animal.

"Thanks for the flatulence," she remarked dryly.

"Huh?"

"The passing of gas."

"Oh." He giggled. "You mean a fart. Why didn't you just say so?"

Kelly clucked. "For one, because it's crude. For two, because it's so … vanilla. You really should try to use more chocolatey words."

Gordie wrinkled his nose. "Chocolatey?"

"More descriptive, expressive words. Not plain, dull … or rude."

"What if I like vanilla words better?"

"Ugh—boys!"

She slid into a chair, unsure where to begin, or how much to say.

"Gordie, I need your help. There are some books I need, but Master Roderick is so horrid: he doesn't care for girls; he's whiny and insulting; and his expression is such a … pickle-puss."

Kelly stopped when she realized what she'd said. She braced herself for another scolding and awaited Gordie's reaction.

His eyes danced. "I wouldn't repeat that to Master Roderick, but you're safe with me. Pickle-puss … I like it! And you're right; he can be a bloody bore. What kind of books are you looking for?"

Kelly hesitated. The trouble was, she couldn't see how Gordie could help her without knowing which books she needed. She answered him, but let him believe she was interested in learning more about Winter Rock.

"And I'd rather do this without anyone ... else ... knowing."

Gordie thought for a moment. "Need to run a secret mission."

"A clandestine operation," Kelly amended.

He frowned. "That's what I said."

"How would we do it?"

Grabbing a sheet of paper, he started making notes. "Every good plot deserves a plan, I always say."

"That's redundant."

"What?"

"Plot and plan mean the same thing. You might as well say, 'Every good plan deserves a plan.'"

"They are not the same. A plot is what you intend to do. *You* want to run a secret mission; that's what you're plotting." He waved the paper in his own defense. "To do that, we need to develop a plan ... of action."

She crossed her arms in stubborn refusal. "They most certainly *do* mean the same thing. My plan is to run a clandestine operation. Now we need to plot out how to do it. Plot, plan. Plan, plot. Same thing."

Gordie scowled. "And you're complaining that Pickle-puss is a nag?"

"Fine, fine. Go ahead and plan the plot."

They outlined the steps they'd need, talking through each one, often going back to add something they'd overlooked. Then they tried simplifying some of the trickier elements. Finally, they divvied up assignments. In the end, their plan for OPERATION PICKLE-SLIP read:

1. Reconnaissance—Gordie
2. Diversion—Gordie
3. Insertion—Kelly
4. Extraction—Kelly
5. Get Away—Both

They decided noon would be the ideal time to launch their operation; most people would be at lunch and the library was more likely to be empty. That gave them just over an hour to prepare. They split up with the promise to meet at precisely twelve o'clock just down the hall from the library.

At noontime Kelly was at the rendezvous, but there was no sign of Gordie. The minutes crawled as she tried to make her loitering appear to have purpose. She wondered if he'd ever show when he dashed around the corner out of breath.

"I had a spot of trouble," he wheezed. "Things took longer than expected."

He wore a baggy coat with bulging pockets that dripped onto his muck-coated shoes. First one pocket writhed and then the other.

Kelly didn't know the particulars of his planned diversion, and decided she didn't want to.

Gordie's face curled into a wicked grin. "It's been a good summer—they're *really* big!"

She shuddered, then got down to business. "You ready?" she asked in a no-nonsense tone.

"Check."

"You have the marker?"

"Check."

"A heads-up *where* you drop it would be helpful."

"Check."

"You've got to give me as much time as possible. Keep him busy for at least two or three minutes."

"Oh, don't worry about *that*," Gordie reassured her with a sly chuckle.

She shuddered again. And then it was show time. They nodded a silent "good luck" to each other and he headed in.

෪

Pickle-puss rose from his desk as Gordie entered. "Well, what is it?" he demanded. "What do you want? I'm busy and can't be bothered with foolishness."

"Master Roderick," Gordie gilded his tone with innocence. "I was here earlier and I saw Thomas shelving a book about runes in the wrong section of the library. I thought you'd want to know."

"What's that? Reshelving books incorrectly breaks Rule Five! Very serious. You children are so annoying. You shouldn't be allowed library privileges. And use the correct term: it's *Ogham* script. Runes, indeed!"

Pickle-puss marched off bleating complaints. Gordie hid a smirk as he followed behind. They stopped a third of the way down one of the middle aisles where Pickle-puss scanned the volumes along the top shelf.

"They all seem to be here …"

As the librarian inventoried his books, Gordie slipped a cookie from his pants pocket and let it fall to the ground, hiding it from view with his foot.

"So that's where they're kept: the fourth aisle in, on the top shelf," he called out in a stage voice.

"Silence, you vexing child! I know where they're kept and I'm not deaf. Rule Two is cardinal in any library; if you must speak, and personally I'd prefer if you didn't, it must be in a whisper and not a cattle drover's bellow!"

"I can show you where Thomas put it …" Gordie offered in a virtuous tone. He led the master deeper into the library, away from the door and the fourth aisle. He unbuttoned his pockets and slid his hands in.

"Oh no!" he cried, "How did *you* get out?" A large toad plopped on the tiled floor bellowing a throaty *rrrrRup, rrrrRup!* Within moments three more toads joined the first; each scuttling off in a different direction, each joining in the bassy chorus.

"What's this? What's this?" Pickle-puss shrieked, his voice an octave higher than usual. "*Bufo calamita* are not permitted in the library! It's simply unheard of. I need a rule for this. Get them out! Out!" He bent to catch one of the offending amphibians, but with an uncooperative *rrrrRup* it scooted away with a surprising burst of speed.

෯

Kelly heard the commotion from the hall and knew it signaled her turn—insertion time. She dashed in and counted four rows of bookcases. Scanning the fourth aisle, she spotted the broken cookie. (It wasn't the most durable marker, but they'd chosen it because it broke Rule Seven: no food or drink in the library.) She ran to the cookie and looked up to the top shelf. That's when she realized she had a problem.

The bookcases were tall—*very* tall—and the top shelf towered six feet above her head. There had to be a ladder about, but Kelly didn't have the time to hunt for it, nor could she risk being seen. She'd have to improvise. She tugged on a shelf. It seemed sturdy enough. With nothing else to do, she began scaling the bookcase, clinging to the shelves with taut fingertips.

Her eyes finally drew level with the books on the uppermost shelf. She read the titles: *Cuneiform Characteristics of the Ogham Script*, *Early Celtic Pre-History and Writings*, *Indo-European Alphabets and their Origins*, and other equally unlikely—and dull—titles. Then she spied just what she needed: *Understanding the Ogham Script.*

As Kelly reached for the book, a guttural *rrrrRup* from the floor startled her and she nearly lost her grip on the bookcase. Steadying her hold, she tried to hurry; her uninvited friend was likely to draw attention quickly. Then things got worse.

"Roderick, what is goin' on!"

Kelly froze. Of all the people to show up—Allisdair! Panic started to crowd her thoughts. Someone would walk past her aisle at any moment and she'd be impossible to miss, hanging in the air, clutching the shelves like a sneakered spider.

There was no time to climb down and if she jumped, she'd probably break her tibia or fibula or that other bone in her leg. That left only one option. She grabbed the book and clambered up on top of the bookcase, flattening her belly against it. She could hear Allisdair's shouts cutting through the chaos in the back of the library. She had to make her escape quickly; Allisdair in a mood was a fearful motivator and she knew the roundup would soon be over.

She slithered along the top of the bookcase, making for the corner nearest the door. She had a few precarious moments climbing back down, but she managed to not break any leg bones. Her luck held as she dashed for the doorway unnoticed, fleeing the scene with all possible dispatch.

Back in the practice room, Kelly had barely caught her breath when Gordie joined her. His pockets were once again buttoned and wriggling. As he closed the door behind him, they disintegrated into laughter, sustained by Gordie's squeaks of "Oh my!" (his rather excellent imitation of the distressed librarian.)

Gordie seemed pleased Kelly had found the book she wanted, and Kelly was relieved his scolding hadn't been more severe.

"Are you kidding?" he chortled, "To see Pickle-puss on his knees chasing natterjack toads?" Another bout of laughter consumed Gordie, through which he managed to gasp, "It was worth it!"

❧

Back in the privacy of her room, Kelly opened the *Ogham* book. She took her time reading its pages. The first chapter described how Irish monks cataloged ancient *Ogham* manuscripts in the ninth century, some of which dated back fifteen hundred years. The history didn't particularly interest Kelly so she skipped ahead to the next chapter.

The alphabet was made up of twenty-five characters: fifteen consonants, five vowels and five special characters that represented double letters (such as "TH" or "CH") and diphthongs, whatever they were.

Twenty-five characters. She walked to her fireplace and counted the figures. She was right! This was a primer of sorts; they were all here. Her hand lingered on one of the tiles for a few moments, and with a start Kelly realized that the pearly character was glowing! She yanked her hand back and after several seconds the light faded to nothing.

Her finger trembled as she tapped a different tile. Nothing. She held her hand against it and counted. By the "pi" of "two Mississippi," the inlaid character radiated the same soft light. Kelly experimented with the tiles and discovered some basics of rune behavior: casual contact wasn't sufficient—the runes needed a full two-count to light up; runes would only glow individually, never in pairs; and once a rune did its thing it needed a rest of several seconds before it would respond again.

An idea was slowly shaping about the rune codes her father had mentioned. If you touched these tiles in the right sequence, might it trigger something? Kelly grabbed her father's diary and searched its pages, hoping for clues. She gasped as she saw that his last entry had vanished— the entry made using solar script.

☙

"So have you figured it out yet?" Gordie asked between mouthfuls of lamb.

"What?" Kelly poured herself a second glass of cider. She didn't know what local variety of apple produced it, but it was tangier than the sweet cider of a McIntosh, Vermont's staple.

"What it says … Winter Rock."

"Shhh!" she hissed. "That's a classified project!" She looked about to see if anyone had overheard. It was only her cover story, but it was still "need-to-know" and the others didn't need to know.

"Relax," Gordie said, lowering his voice. "I didn't say a thing about the book or the library. And we've all wondered what the rock means. Hey guys," he called out, "Kelly wants to know what the runes on Winter Rock spell—"

He winced as Kelly delivered a sharp kick to his shin. So much for Gordie and sensitive information.

"Well it should say, 'No Loitering.' Then maybe the pipers would get the hint," Thomas carped.

"I'm sure it's some dire warning." Kenna said with resigned worry. "But, we've forgotten how to read it so it can't save us."

"*I* think Winter Rock is covered with ancient piping music," Gordie announced, still rubbing his shin. "Pipers long ago were lazy learning their tunes, so they carved them there."

Kelly rolled her eyes. "Don't you think remembering a few notes would be easier than carving a rock? Don't be such a … diphthong!"

ॐ

Rune characters represented more than just letters, Kelly learned. Each was also associated with a certain tree, and twelve of them additionally stood for months of the year. For instance, the character *beith* ⊦ signified the letter "B," a birch tree and the month of November.

The more she read, the more Kelly kept coming back to a single question. Her father had said the code to his fireplace was obvious. Assuming he spoke of a rune code, what combination of letters, trees and months would have been obvious to him? She had an idea and started looking up letters: *fearn* ⊧ for "F," *iodho* ≢ for "I," *ruis* ≸ for "R," *eadha* ≢ for "E," and that's where she halted. There was no rune for "P."

She considered her father's birthday. (She always used hers when she needed a password.) But there were no runes for numbers.

Maybe it was simply his name? But her hopes deflated when she found no character for "J." Possibly last name? She copied down: ┿╀╢╟╪╪┩╪ for MacBride. She stood in front of the fireplace, touching each tile in turn and holding it just long enough to make it glow. But when she finished, the last character faded with no result.

She sat back down and looked over at her father's diary lying on the chair beside her. That was all she had to work with, and until another entry appeared, it wasn't much. She absently opened it. There on the first page he'd written, "The Diary of Hamish MacBride."

Of course! She grabbed her pencil and started copying: *huathe* ┤ for "H," *ailim* ┿ for "A," *muin* ╈ for "M," *iodho* ╪ for "I," *saille* ╠ for "S," and *huathe* ┤ again for the final "H." She fought down her excitement as she pushed the tiles: ┤┿┝╪╠┤. Again nothing.

Now she was getting mad. He said it was obvious; he taunted Lachlan that it was so. And in taunting Lachlan he was also taunting her. He said he'd leave clues. Why didn't he start with the first entry?

Or did he? She flipped the pages and re-read his initial entry—the one he'd made before he learned solar script. Could it be that simple? She placed her hand on *huathe* ┤ and then *muin* ╈ and finally *beith* ┝. She wasn't tense this time. As the glow from *beith* was about to fade, all three runes suddenly glowed together, twice as brightly for twice as long. He hadn't signed his entry "James," "Hamish," or "MacBride." He signed "HMB."

Through the floor, she felt the rumble of stone grinding against stone. It came from within the fireplace. She stooped under the arch and squeezed behind the fireback. There was a soft light ahead—the back wall of the fireplace was no longer there! The low passage opened up into a corridor with walls of rough-hewn rock. The single layer of bricks that bordered the ceiling luminesced with a milky light, similar to the glow of the rune tiles—not bright, but enough to see by. It wasn't bad for her first secret passageway: dry, sufficiently lit, and no rats.

The floor of the passage was also of stone, with the same rough cut, so Kelly had to take care not to stumble. As she stepped down the corridor, a scraping noise behind her caused her to spin around. She was just in time to see the door slide shut with a weighty *thunk*. She pulled and tugged at it, but it refused to yield.

She peered at the door in the dimness. On this side, it wasn't camouflaged. The lintel was arched and lined from above by the very same rune tiles that encircled her fireplace. On the door itself was a carving of the smiling lion that adorned her fireback. Kelly reached up and pushed ┼╫┝ in succession. The tiles glowed as the others had, first individually and then together, and the door receded into the wall. Kelly was relieved to see the silhouette of the fireback ahead.

Assured of her exit, Kelly continued her exploration of the passageway. The corridor ran straight for a distance and then down a series of irregular steps, which she cautiously descended (there's nothing more humiliating than following up clever deduction with a careless injury.) Further on she came to an intersection. The left passage eventually terminated at a door similar to the one leading back to her bedroom. Above the doorway was the same runed arch; however, this door held a carving of an open book. She again pressed *huathe, muin,* and *beith,* but here they had no effect. She tried several other combinations at random and finally abandoned her attempts.

Down the right branch of the intersection she found another runed door with a carving of an arched doorway. She was equally unsuccessful opening that door and she finally retreated to her residence.

Back in her bedroom, she stared at her father's diary with frustration. She glanced at her own diary and then back at his. Her eyes rested there.

I don't even know my father. I admitted I couldn't remember him. And yet half of me comes from him …

Now I have a chance to learn about him when he was my age. What was important to him? What was so personal he wouldn't share it with his friends? What did he do when he felt lost—like the last thread from a blown dandelion floating helplessly on the wind?

Now he can tell me, as he might have, were he still alive. He can guide me … as a father would.

… My father …

And all I'm hoping for are rune codes.

The late-morning sunlight filtered down to the counter where Kelly perched, noshing on an oatcake. She watched as Maggie scissored a side of venison into fillets, steaks, and chops. The kitchen woman's practiced non-chalance with the butcher knife raised goose bumps on Kelly's skin. She avowed she would *never* fault Maggie's cooking.

"So lass, what brings ya to me this bonnie mornin'?" The counter trembled under Maggie's knife blows.

Kelly wasn't sure why she was there, although the mid-morning snack would have been reason enough. She barely knew Maggie. Yet she felt comfort here. Kelly's mother once told her that food has a magic that nourishes the soul. Was that it? Were these kitchen smells, sights and sounds, even the shuddering countertop, a soothing balm?

"Did you know my father?"

Maggie suspended her hacking and looked kindly on Kelly. "Aye, lass, I did. From the time he was a wee bairn."

"What was he like?"

Laying down her weapon, Maggie wiped her hands on her apron and settled on a stool beside Kelly. "Ach, now that's a muckle question."

"A what?"

"A tall question," said Maggie. "What words can capture a person? If I told ya yer da was bold an' feisty, yet at the same time thoughtful an' kind, it'd be true, but ya'd hardly have a sense of him."

"Was he ever … unsure of himself?"

"Well I'll tell ya a story about that." Maggie swept the counter clean of crumbs as she spoke. "Yer da had a confidence about him—the surety of a stone—even as a lad. He'd cook up some daft plan, but he could sell ya on its merits an' convince ya it was the only thing to be done. I only knew of one time when his belief was in doubt. He knew what he wanted right enough, but he was worried about the doin' it. He was afraid he mightna be good enough. An' that was a strange feeling for Hamish; it troubled him."

Kelly lingered over Maggie's words, trying to picture her father when he was younger. What was it that so challenged his self-assurance? Having so little of her own (those genes must have sunk to the bottom of the pool), she was certain it had to have been something dire: a fierce contest of wills or an act that would put him at grave risk.

"What was it he had to do?" she whispered.

Maggie gazed at Kelly before answering. "He decided to marry yer mother an' to raise a family. He didna know about parentin'. He was afraid he might not be a braw da—a good father."

He was afraid of me?

August 26

Dear Dad,

I know it was important to you that we be a family. I guess none of us knew how things would work out. Mom and I did okay, but it would have been nicer if you could have been with us. Still, I know it wasn't your fault.

Love, Kelly

Kelly closed her diary and got up from her chair. The barn owl had shown up while she'd been writing and it watched her from its perch in the window. She saw that it had brought her a gift. The limp body of a mouse lay next to the taloned feet. Kelly nodded thanks as she climbed into bed. Her sniffles mixed in odd accompaniment with the owl's lullaby of rasps and hisses.

ॐ

The following day a new entry appeared in her father's diary.

August 27

I'm so frustrated! Stuart's been busy, so we haven't had time to work together. I know I need to be more patient. His schedule's hectic and we have to take care we aren't discovered. Still, waiting is hard.

To busy myself, I've been studying esoteric texts. I've discovered some curious passages. This one is particularly revealing:

"The deathless singer and the flowers
He sang of live together …

How thus, they spell a chance to read
New pages old and pleasant!"

HMB

Kelly fought the disappointment rising in her. She told herself there was more to her father's life than just rune code riddles and she shouldn't expect every notation to hold some secret promise. She made herself re-read the entry—this time trying to envision her father as he wrote it. He, too, seemed to struggle with the frustration that hidden knowledge wasn't as forthcoming as he wished.

I understand, Dad. Waiting is hard. I'll try to be more patient.

The quote in the second paragraph was as esoteric as he claimed. She had no idea what it meant and wondered what in it had touched him.

It was always easy to locate Gordie—she rarely had to look beyond the practice rooms.

"Gordie, you work too hard. You need to get out more and have fun."

"This is fun."

"I mean there's more to life than just bagpiping."

"No there's not."

She let it drop. "Do you know who the deathless singer was?"

"Sure—Robert Burns."

"Burns?"

Gordie nodded "It was a description of Burns, by the poet John Greenleaf Whittier—one of the more enlightened American poets of the nineteenth century. He revered Burns." Gordie laid down his pipes, bowed to Kelly and recited:

> "The deathless singer and the flowers
> He sang of live together.
> Wild heather-bells and Robert Burns!
> The moorland flower and the peasant!
> How, at their mention, memory turns
> Her pages old and pleasant!"[5]

It took Kelly a few moments to realize something was wrong. "Could you repeat that last part again?" As Gordie did so, she shook her head. "That can't be right. It's 'How thus, they spell a chance to read new pages old and pleasant!'"

"I think not." Gordie shot her an indignant frown. "Trust me. I'm right. Besides, your version doesn't make any sense."

It didn't make sense, Kelly agreed later that evening as she copied her father's entry into her own diary. At first she assumed Gordie was mistaken. But his version was both meaningful and poetic; her dad's was neither. How could her father have been so far off?

---

5   *Burns* by John Greenleaf Whittier

"The deathless singer and the flowers
He sang of live together …"

That much was true to the original poem. And according to the next two lines, the ones her father didn't quote, Burns was the deathless singer and heather was the flower.

The trouble lay in the last two lines. Her father wrote:

"How thus, they spell a chance to read
New pages old and pleasant!"

The meter was correct, so the mistake had to have been deliberate. What was it he was trying to tell her … Could this be a rune code riddle? If so, it would have to do two things: identify the door it opened and provide the appropriate rune code.

"… a chance to read …" An image of a book carved on a stone door floated into Kelly's mind. She thought about "new pages old and pleasant." At first it seemed an oxymoron, but that's how riddles are. She turned the words over in her mind. Couldn't that describe a book you hadn't yet read? No matter how old the book, it would still be new to you.

That might mean "Burns" and "heather" were the clues that opened the door she'd discovered in the tunnel. Heather seemed familiar … Kelly recalled that some of the "trees" represented by the *Ogham* characters were in fact shrubs and brambles. She checked the book; sure enough, *úr* ≢ was the rune for heather.

Five minutes later Kelly faced the carved image of the book. She could feel the coolness radiating from the stone door. Taking a deep breath, she reached up and pushed in succession: *beith* ├ for "B," *úr* ╪ for "U," *ruis* ⧻ for "R," *nuin* ⧲ for "N," *saille* ⧲ for "S," and *úr* ╪ (this time for "heather.") Nothing. Kelly was learning that the one thing her father's riddles required even more than creative thinking was perseverance.

She sat down on the uneven floor and reconsidered the clue.

> "The deathless singer and the flowers
> He sang of live together …"

The first two lines gave her the answer—Burns and heather—while "… a chance to read new pages old and pleasant!" identified the door. That left "How thus, they spell …" They spell … *spell!*
Spell them both, dummy!

Hopping up, she began again with ├╪⧻⧲⧲, but this time rather than adding *úr* ╪ for heather, she spelled out the word: *huathe* ┤ for "H," *eadha* ╪ for "E," *ailim* ┼ for "A," *tinne* ⧦ for "T," *huathe* ┤, *eadha* ╪, and *ruis* ⧻ for "R." When she finished, the tiles glowed together brightly and rewarded her with the soft grinding of stone as the door slid into the wall.

Holding her breath, Kelly entered the warmly lit room. Her steps echoed softly on the parquet floor and she stared at the walls lined with dark mahogany bookcases. It was a library—a secret library!

Other than the single door, there wasn't an inch of wall space free of books. Floor to ceiling, on every wall—books so old they made Pickle-puss' collection seem contemporary. The air held the musky scent of leather bindings and the dry smell of old paper. On the topmost shelves rolled scrolls of parchment and vellum lay stacked like cords of wood. The center of the room was equipped for the enjoyment of reading. For serious work there was a long table with upright chairs, also of mahogany; for the more indulgent, deep plush armchairs beckoned.

With as grand a library as Pickle-puss governed, what manner of books would be housed in a secret library? Kelly moved to a bookcase and removed a volume. The cover was free of writing. She opened it and saw that it was an original manuscript, the title page penned in a spidery longhand that was difficult to read:

Shape-Shifting:
The Art and Science of Taking on Animal Form

—Translated from ancient texts
by Dingus Feorag—March, 1736

She stared stupidly at the page. It simply wasn't possible. It was easier to accept the things around her. Secret doors and passages that opened with ancient runes, talking horses and visiting owls—these she could somehow explain. Somehow. But the notion of a book that could teach you to shape-shift as easily as teach you to cook or play bridge or speak French? *That* was unbelievable. Yet, here was the book.

Kelly tucked the book under her arm and headed for the door. She pushed ├ ╪ ╪ ╞ ┤╪┼┤┤╪╪, to let herself out, but this time nothing happened. The individual runes didn't even glow. She tried the sequence again slowly. It was long; perhaps she'd flipped some of the characters. Again no response.

A bitter taste grew in the back of her throat and her heartbeat quickened.

She knew panicking wouldn't help, but telling yourself not to panic is like trying *not* to think about something. She walked over to an armchair and sank into it. She pressed her hands together and took a deep breath, as she would before singing. She exhaled slowly. She had no idea what to do. The door simply *had* to work.

The deep breathing helped calm her and she got up to try again—not because she had any clever ideas, but simply because she couldn't think of anything else to do. This time, however, as she touched *beith* ├, the rune glowed as it should have. She continued, carefully pressing each character. With the final ╪, the runes glowed together and the door opened. Kelly unloaded her fear with a heaving sigh. She stepped to the armchair and retrieved the shape-shifting book. The door had slid shut, so she again pressed ├. Amazingly, it failed to glow, as did the other tiles.

Kelly stared at the door, her mouth half open, for a long minute. She walked back, laid the book on the table and returned to the door. The rune tiles responded to her touch and the door opened; yet when she tried again while holding the book, they ignored her.

Tired and more than a little unnerved, Kelly reshelved the book, memorizing its location, and let herself out. She conceded this battle to the mysterious library. It didn't need a Pickle-puss as guard dog; it was quite capable of protecting its secrets itself.

5

NOSING ABOUT

The heightened awareness of a creature's spirit occurs at three levels: Perception, Transference, and Influence. Each is more challenging and holds greater risk than the previous; therefore, the practitioner must master each in turn before advancing to the next.

This book focuses on Shape-Shifting—one of the Transference techniques. Prerequisite is a

fluency in the School of Perception. The descrip-
tion herein is in summary form only.

—Shape-Shifting: The Art and
Science of Taking on Animal Form

Nothing's quite as alluring as forbidden knowledge. Except, perhaps, forbidden magical knowledge. The idea she might teach herself shape-shifting tantalized Kelly, but she also recognized the need to avoid suspicion. She became the perfect child by day, meticulously executing her chores, her lessons, and her practicing, never deviating from expectations. But by night, she studied in the secret library: reading, re-reading, and taking notes.

She started with the Perception techniques. As Kelly understood it, Perception is the ability to read an animal's thoughts. The three primary skills are centering, sensing, and strengthening. Centering calms your mind, making you more receptive to an animal's mental energy. Sensing is where you actually "push" your awareness outward, trying to touch the subject animal's mind. Once contact is established, strengthening reinforces the connection by focusing on its source.

Even with the shape-shifting book to assist her, Kelly was having a difficult time with the preliminaries. The book stated *what* she had to do, and often provided brief explanation, but it stopped well short of describing precisely *how* she was to do it.

Her early attempts at Perception training were noteworthy not only for their failure, but also for the chaos they wrought. On one occasion, Kelly had settled cross-legged on the floor of Gealach's stall. She focused her attention on a field mouse nudging about in the straw beside her as she tried to touch its mind.

Dougal entered the stall carrying a bucket of water. He wasn't watching his feet and he didn't see Kelly. Kelly was staring at the mouse and she didn't notice Dougal. When he tripped over her, she reared back yelling. This only further startled the journeyman who tossed the over-filled bucket with his own cry of alarm. As the water doused her, she hollered another yelp—it was cold.

"What are you doing?" His words were an angry mumble as his Adam's apple danced the tarantella.

Kelly shook the water from her head. "This is *my* horse's stall. I was just … resting."

Dougal gulped to catch his breath. "Well you shouldn't do that!"

He'd been the clumsy one. And he failed to apologize for soaking her. Nevertheless, it didn't seem prudent to argue with the journeyman, so she said nothing as he trudged off.

On her next attempt, Kelly decided a bit more privacy was in order. She scooped a field mouse into her pocket and headed back to her residence. When she entered, she didn't notice Mack napping on her bed in the next room. Nor did she realize what a light sleeper he apparently was. Taking a seat, she placed the mouse on her lap. But her effort to calm her thoughts was shattered as the cat—materializing from nowhere—flew across her lap. She cried in pain, looking down to see bloody scratches on her legs. The mouse leapt two feet into the air with a frightened shriek. When it landed, it darted behind a nearby chest. Mack pursued from above, leaping up on the chest, scattering a pair of candlesticks and knocking over a lamp. At that same instant the mouse shot out and ran behind the damask drapes.

A spirited game of blind-man's bluff ensued, in which Mack tried to skewer the mouse behind the curtains. By the time Kelly got a hold of Mack, the draperies sported a new fringe along their bottom edge.

"It's my guest," she told the squirming feline as she headed towards the door. "And it's never polite to eat a guest."

After evicting the cat, she turned to locate the mouse and start over. Instead, the barn owl greeted her, perched nonchalantly in her window. A tail hung from its beak. With a jerk of the owl's head, the last trace of Kelly's guest vanished.

☉

"Are the bagpipes hard to learn?" Kelly asked.

He didn't answer. She wasn't even sure he heard her. He folded his face in concentration as he placed his hand around the flat rock … just a certain … way. Holding his breath, he cocked his wrist and snapped his arm, timing the flick of his hand just so. He watched his stone hit the water … and then sink out of sight. He blew out a dejected sigh.

"Gordie, I asked if the pipes were hard to learn."

"Show me again," he said.

"Only if you answer me."

She chose a stone and held it casually. She reached back and flicked her own hand. The stone jumped across the surface of the pond ... once ... twice ... and a third time before it sank.

"Three ..." Gordie sighed. He shook his head. "They say, best men are moulded out of faults, and, for the most, become much more the better, for being a little bad."[6]

"Ixnay the Burns ..."

"Shakespeare," he corrected.

"... and don't even think of giving up; it's not hard once you get it. For the moment, however, pay attention."

"I was paying attention. I suppose they're hard to learn. They take more time and practice than other instruments, but if you enjoy it, it doesn't feel like work."

Drips of rain spattered around them without conviction; the rain fell with greater zeal beyond the willow's leafy canopy. Gordie hunted among the stones that edged the pond, looking for the round, flat ones she'd said made the best skippers.

"Thinking of learning?" he asked without lifting his eyes.

"No." She stared at the ripples formed as each raindrop hit the pond. "But if I wanted to, could I teach myself?"

"No way."

"Even if I had a book that explained how?"

"Not if you want to play them correctly."

---

6   *Measure for Measure* (Act V, Scene i) by William Shakespeare

Kelly turned to him, eyes alit. "Why not? Why wouldn't it work?"

"Because it's a complicated process." He abandoned his search and began ticking off on his fingers. "First you have to learn the fingering and the embellishments on the practice chanter. Then you play a tune slowly, gradually speeding up until you can play it at tempo. When your fingers can play with minimal babysitting, you can start on the full set of pipes. You have to build up mouth strength and blowing stamina, and learn how to balance your blowing and your arm pressure so that your drones remain steady. When all of that becomes second nature, you add the chanter melody and try not to squeal like an asthmatic pig.

"You can't learn it from a book, because each skill builds on the previous one. A book won't tell you when you're slightly off, and those tiny imperfections pile up until they block further progress. You never make it, and you don't know why."

As she listened, Kelly's intensity relaxed into the sparkle of wonder felt when someone explains a knotty brainteaser.

"Thanks …" she said softly. Then, with keenness, "Now show me the stones you've found …"

If the basics weren't sound, according to Gordie, you couldn't achieve the end result. Suspecting that was the problem with her failed Perception attempts, Kelly went back and focused on her centering. The difficulty was that when she tried to think of nothing, it was as if her brain laughed at her and filled itself with every conceivable and inconceivable notion.

She remembered the raindrops striking the pond. Their ripples spread outward, colliding with other ripples. They created complex patterns on the surface of the water, but they also obscured what was below. To see to the bottom, the surface had to be calm. Perfectly calm.

Kelly found that by concentrating on her breathing she was best able to quiet her mind. She would close her eyes and take full, slow breaths, thinking only of the breaths themselves. She'd imagine the air's journey: in through her nose filling her sinuses, down her throat inflating her lungs. A short pause and then the breath would travel back up the same path seeking its way out into the world. She breathed with deliberate slowness again and again. Perfectly calm.

During these moments, when Kelly was able to achieve the most profound inner stillness, it was as if her consciousness floated. It wasn't a physical sensation like dizziness. It felt more as though she could detach her mind, as though she could simply "let go" of her psyche, freeing it to drift: a sort of out-of-mind experience.

Drifting. Like a single downy feather molted from a chickadee's breast. Carried by the wind ... must she always be so helpless? Couldn't she steer? Just once? She tried a mental nudge. The drift responded along a specific course. Another nudge pushed it further, suggesting intent. The third nudge confirmed that it was moving by will and not by coincidence. With the babiest of steps, Kelly was learning to direct her extended consciousness.

The first time she actually brushed a mouse's mind, she didn't recognize it for what it was. It was as if she were suddenly preoccupied with the sounds and smells around her. After a few moments she realized the sensations weren't her own, but came from a tiny mouse that shared her perch in the haymow. When the impressions started to fade and her own senses tried to reclaim their place, she worked to bump and wiggle her focus back to the mouse. It was trial and error, and therefore neither efficient nor particularly responsive, but gradually she learned to sense and maintain contact with the mouse's mind.

Kelly taught herself the strengthening skills in much the same way, although she wouldn't have been able to describe precisely how she did it. Once she established a connection, she simply experimented with a variety of mental gymnastics, carefully noting which ones brought the sensations into sharper focus.

After several more days of practice, Kelly's confidence in her Perception skills grew and she returned to the shape-shifting book to learn the lessons of Transference. The three foundational skills of Transference are anchoring, patterning, and shifting. Kelly had trouble understanding the purpose of anchoring until she read further about patterning: in order to shape-shift, you have to be able to model your own mental processes after those of the subject animal. To become a mouse you must think like a mouse. Your sensations, thoughts, and reactions must be 100 percent pure mouse before a shift can occur. You achieve this with patterning.

The trick is, if you shift with a 100 percent mouse mind, you may never shift back—a mouse would neither understand the notion of shape-shifting nor feel any desire to return to human form. Anchoring allows you to compartmentalize a small portion of your human mind that will remain human throughout the shift; it will be the place that calls your mouse mind back when you're finished.

Kelly found that anchoring requires enormous discipline. Only the calmness achieved with the deepest centering could clarify the blur between the walled-off areas in her head and hold them separate. It was here that the book's exercises were particularly helpful. The one that Kelly practiced most frequently was to have her human consciousness direct the untying and retying of her shoelaces, while her mouse consciousness went freely sniffing after crumbs and seeds. It was with diligent repetition in this manner that Kelly readied herself for her first shift.

September 19

Important safety tips for shape-shifters:

1. Never forget who you are. Always set a firm anchor *before* you begin patterning.

2. Never shift over your head. Start with smaller, less complex animals and ensure you've

mastered Perception skills and patterning before you attempt a first shift.

    <u>3. Never become someone's lunch.</u> Don't shift into an environment where factors hazardous to the subject animal might exist.

ᚼᚴᚢᚢ

(Kelly chose to emulate her father's practice of signing with his initials, but she added her own flair by using runes. Unfortunately, there was no rune for "K"; she considered "MB Jr," but there was no "J" either; likewise, "MB 2" was out—no numbers. She finally settled on "MB II.")

⁂

It was a soggy morning in late September when Kelly finally felt prepared for the attempt. She'd given serious thought to what location might be best suited for her debut as a rodent. Privacy was paramount, but even more so was a guaranteed scarcity of cats. In the end, she chose the stable's feed storage room. The room was always securely shut. The intent was to keep vermin from the grain; that it would also keep the stable's cat population from Kelly made it ideal. After the livestock received their morning feed—routinely completed by 8 AM—no one used the room again until evening, so interruptions were unlikely.

On the stainless counter she laid the contents of both hands—a poppy-seed muffin saved from breakfast in her left, and a mouse in her right. The bare bulbs overhead threw off a harsh light, and she knew from her Perception experiments the mouse didn't care for it. She unscrewed the overhead bulbs, leaving only one burning in the corner, and broke off some muffin for her furred accomplice. Flanked by bins of grain and feed, she settled on a stool and cradled the mouse in her hands, just as it cradled a muffin fragment in its paws.

She closed her eyes and proceeded to center. Breathing deeply, she willed her mind into quietude.

Feel the breath flow in and fill me. Ride with it as it softly escapes. I'm one with my breath ... in ... out ...

With the surface clutter stilled, her mind relaxed into an awareness beyond itself. With each exhalation she slipped deeper, growing more receptive to the subtle energies surrounding her.

The tingling of another presence tickled the edges of her extended consciousness. It was unmistakably mouse. She focused her awareness, pointing it at the source of the tingling. Slowly the fuzz sharpened and the contact stabilized. She was seeing the world through the mouse's mind!

She could feel its belly drawing up the warmth from her palms. Its muffin snack, delicious, but not satisfying, stirred an insatiable craving for more. The nearby smells and sounds, all with a foreign flavor to Kelly, were perfectly ordinary to the mouse.

Kelly fixed her anchor and began to pattern her mind after the mouse's, giving herself over to the mouse's sensations and impressions. She smelled what it smelled. She heard the sounds around her as it did. She tasted the muffin, so delectable a change from the usual seeds and grains. She saw what little it saw. And she felt the tactile sensation of sitting within her own cupped hands. She gave her anchor a final test by counting the feed buckets stacked in the corner beside the salt blocks. Nine buckets and her patterning didn't waver a whisker. She was ready.

She had to push her mind even deeper for the actual shift. She had gone down to this level only twice before. She knew when she was there, because the switch wasn't evident until she was. It was as if suddenly she could see it in her mind, where there'd been no trace of it before. The book described the actual shift as "executing the jump," but Kelly thought of it more as throwing the switch.

To her, the concept of a jump suggested her mind would leap into the subject mouse's body. But that wasn't how it worked. She used the subject mouse merely for patterning. When Kelly shifted, *she* would transform into a mouse—whole and separate from the fellow in her hands. The switch was the trigger point between her human self and whatever form her patterning determined.

Breathe … in … out … there—there it is!

Mentally, the switch became as solid to her as the stool upon which she sat. She directed her thoughts to the switch and gave it a nudge. Nothing happened. Taking in a deep breath and holding it, she delivered a solid shove. No response. Perhaps "jump" wasn't so far off after all. She bunched every ounce of her psyche and hurled it at the trigger …

A wave of vertigo swamped her senses. She tried to clear her thoughts, but her brain was slow and stupid.

Her eyes focused lazily, the colors around her smeared into a blurry rainbow. Sounds jumbled together creating a wall of noise. But overshadowing it all was the assault of smell. It was as if her whole life had been spent sampling the air with cotton up her nose, cotton that was now suddenly removed. As with the sights and sounds, there was no discernable smell—neither smoky nor floral, neither musty nor rotten—there was simply the overpowering sureness of smell, a mountain of it, whatever its specifics.

As her daze slowly cleared, her senses began to measure up particulars. The smells came to her first. There was a familiar scent, like the downy aroma of a favorite blanket or pillow. Her mouse mind knew it was her own smell. There was an unfamiliar scent with a similar, yet different, musk that registered as a possible menace. Beyond that hovered something tantalizing. After a few moments she realized it was the remains of her unfinished muffin.

Her hearing cleared next, but she could make out nothing beyond the raucous chitters that accosted her ears. Their patterns were familiar, yet she couldn't quite place their meaning. She seemed to be dreadfully nearsighted and could barely detect a sizeable mass wiggling nearby, trying to right itself against the cool hardness she felt beneath her. She realized that the squirming hulk was a mouse. A massive, human-sized mouse. And then she corrected herself with a start. It was *she* who was mouse-sized. She had shifted!

Kelly rotated her ears forward as she concentrated on the other mouse's chitters. He—Kelly somehow knew he was a male; her nose was certain—didn't use words as such. What he said, together with the way he said it, conveyed impressions. And Kelly's current impression was one of agitation. He'd fallen and he was furious.

She looked down at her hands. Hands that were now tiny paws. Hands that until moments ago had supported the offended rodent.

Note to self: it will be easier to make friends if I set the subject down before shifting.

He rolled to his feet and shook himself. Then he launched into a new tirade. Her smell was wrong. She clearly wasn't related. It was *very* wrong. He didn't know her. After announcing that, his chitters grew more belligerent. He tried to bully her into leaving.

Kelly, wondering how to make herself smell friendlier, took a sniff; a prickling in her cheeks startled her—whiskers! She twitched her nose and her whiskers danced and flopped, sending pin and needle darts into her face. It wasn't so unpleasant once she got used to it. With another sniff and twitch she decided her companion's odor was nothing to brag about. Then, a more alluring scent commanded her attention: muffin!

Stand aside, rat breath! No more of my muffin until your manners improve.

She tried to shoulder past him, but a tug against her rear end brought her up short. She had a tail. She attempted to swish it back and forth, but its spastic jerks were none too fluid.

The muffin scent crowded out other thoughts, driving her to seek crumbs. Her legs instinctively scurried towards the strongest whiff. Locating a sizeable chunk, she sat erect, balancing on her tail, and greedily gnawed.

As her stomach grew sated, a restless energy filled her, coaxing her limbs as if whispering, *keep moving, keep moving!* The other mouse's whining was getting tiresome anyway, so she set out to explore. Poised on the edge of the counter, she sprang forward, executing a pinpoint belly flop onto the floor below. Surprisingly, it didn't hurt, which only affirmed the other mouse's complaints overstated his mistreatment.

Her hearing was keen and her ears told her of horses shuffling and snorting in their stalls beyond the closed door, sparrows playing amongst the roof beams, and distant voices.

She poked among the grain bins, her whiskers compensating for her poor eyesight—they scraped the floorboards and brushed the air ahead of her, alerting her to obstacles just before she could scurry into them. Her nose continually sought morsels inadvertently scattered across the floor, and it wasn't disappointed. Before long she had sampled whole oats, rolled barley, the molassesy sweet feed, and an occasional flax seed.

Kelly scampered about, gradually acquainting herself with her form, although her tail continued to vex her. (It was easy to trip over, if she swished it at the wrong moment while running.) Finally, stuffed and exhausted, it was time to shift back.

That was more difficult than she had imagined. Mice aren't known for their exceptional focus. Constantly distracted by their surroundings, they're the attention-deficit champions of the animal kingdom. She felt for the trigger, but she couldn't locate it in the disorder of her competing perceptions. She felt panic welling up. *Never forget who you are*, echoed in her brain. She remembered that her anchor was her safety line back.

With difficulty she transferred her focus to that reserved corner of her human self. Looking inward with her stilled human senses, she could see the trigger bold as day. Wasting no time, she leapt at it with all the mental force she could muster.

The transformation occurred in less than a tail swish. She was back in her body, lying face down on the floor beside the stool. She was dusty, covered with bits of grain, and the flax seeds left a funny taste in her mouth, but she had made her first shift!

⚙

He's going to do it again …

Kelly watched surreptitiously as Niall, one of the stable boys, took the last two dinner rolls before he passed the empty basket on to Robert, a fellow stable boy. Robert seemed likeable, but he appeared simple—as Kelly's mom would say. She taught Kelly that different people's brains worked at different speeds and if you needed to speak about a slower-speed brain you shouldn't use insulting words like idget, moron, or retard. "Simple" was nicer.

Robert peered into the basket. His expression flitted from expectation to disappointment to resignation. Earlier, Niall had taken the last two salmon cakes in the same manner, leaving Robert none. This was no accident. Whether Niall selfishly wanted the extra food, or simply took it to be cruel, Kelly wasn't sure.

Idget. Moron. Retard. Bully.

"Here Robert," she offered, handing over her roll, "I'm not that hungry—I'll wait till they bring more."

The younger boy's face brightened, never suspecting the meanness represented by the empty basket. Kelly returned Niall's glower with a smug smile.

"Look," Kenna exclaimed, "it's Cameron!"

A kilted lad approached in worn hill boots rimmed with mud. The weathered earth-tones of his tartan complimented his loose, wheaten curls—if he were a sheep, a shearing would be in order.

"Aye weel," he said as he slipped into the seat beside Kenna.

Kenna, less sparing of speech, gushed like a ruptured cataract—fretting over the weather in the mountains, asking after the condition of the flock, and curious how Duffy's training was progressing. Her questions and worried assumptions poured out, not waiting for answers. The whole while she gazed at the newcomer with frank adulation.

Kelly recalled the name; it belonged to an older apprentice who worked the sheep on the upper hills with his border collie, Duffy. He was scarce around the barns and stables, however, and tonight's appearance was the first Kelly had seen of him.

As Kenna finally paused for a much-needed breath, Cameron considered his words, as if he had to pay for each one and was on a limited budget.

"Aye, the braes be damp. 'Tis the season. Sheep dunna care. Warm coats."

Cameron similarly parsed through Duffy's progress with the sheep. Kelly listened to the lilt and lift in Cameron's speech, letting her hearing unfocus. Her thoughts wandered, finally settling on her experiences earlier that morning. She mulled over the more challenging aspects of tail coordination, and was trying to work out a cadence for running without tripping (such as: *step-step-swish, step-step-swish*), when she realized someone had asked her a question.

"Er ... sorry! What was that?" she blurted.

Kenna peered at her, "You're sitting there quiet as a mouse. You okay?"

"Oh ... yeah ... I'm fine," Kelly squeaked. "I was just ... eh ... wondering if you could pass the muffins."

Robert smiled at her and shook his head. "Muffins? It's dinner, silly. There are no muffins."

"Ah ... right. I ... eh ... meant the dinner rolls."

September 25

Dear Dad,

I wanted to tell you I'm learning shape-shift-ing! But I don't think folks around here should know. (I think you'd agree.) Did Stuart teach you when you were my age?

I've only ever been a mouse, but I'm getting good at it. I've learned what the book calls "unassisted shifting." That was tricky at first, but it's convenient since I can pattern without using a live mouse.

I hope you're proud of me.

Love, 十卜丰丰 (a.k.a. cheese breath)

It was bound to happen sooner or later. Perhaps Kelly should have been better prepared, but she never imagined her stretch of good luck might turn. Yet it always does.

She was working late in the secret library. The shapeshifting book and her diary were both open, as she transcribed centering exercises from one to the other. Midway through the word "discernment," her pen froze—there were voices just outside the door! She grabbed both books, and lacking any better hiding place, stuffed them under a chair cushion. Now to hide herself. It was no good—the room was too open. There was no place to hide. She was too big … too big …

There was a grind of stone as the library door recessed into the wall. Neither of the two who entered seemed to notice the gray mouse that scuttled beneath the armchair.

"Yer still plannin' a visit to the *Sidhe*?"

The voice was Allisdair's. Her myopic vision could only make out his brogues and twined laces—above the ankle all was a blur. She backed further out of sight.

"I must."

Kelly's mouse gut did a queasy flip-flop. The answering voice was Brid's. Things couldn't get worse.

Except they did.

Allisdair's feet approached and he claimed the chair above her—sitting on the books! Kelly hoped the cushion was thick enough to hide their presence. His shoes were inches from her face and she wrinkled her nose at the odor. She edged backwards.

As Brid's feet moved to a bookcase on the right, her voice continued, "After a millennium, events are finally in motion. But I'm blind to what we're heading towards. We need answers; hence, I *must* go."

Kelly's nose twitched, and it wasn't from Allisdair's feet. There was a crumb out on the floor! Her mouse instincts took over and her anchor watched helplessly as she scurried out after it. She ran through the canyon between Allisdair's shoes, praying he didn't shift his feet.

HALT! What are you doing?!!!

Her anchor screamed into her mouse mind at full volume.

Get your tail back under that chair before he smushes you!

Luckily, her person-sense prevailed. With a spin, she dashed back through his feet to safety.

Apparently unaware of the breathless eavesdropper beneath him, Allisdair responded, "*Bean-rìgh*, I've been uneasy of late. Somethin's not as it should be. Yet, I canna see from what source my caution grows."

"Is it Kelly?" Brid asked.

"I dunna know," the steward answered. "I'm watchin' her. As an unknown, she is a risk, but I canna say if she's the cause of my disquiet."

"All the more reason I should visit my people." Brid's voice moved towards the door.

The floor under Kelly shook as Allisdair stood. "An' all the more reason I shall be vigilant," he said as they left.

The mouse under the armchair was uncharacteristically still; the crumb forgotten. In fact, it was Kelly's anchor doing all the talking.

You're my grandmother. How could you not trust me? Isn't family supposed to be there for each other? That's what Mom always said. She trusted me. Not even the benefit of the doubt? I can't ask you to love me ... yet. I know that takes time. For me too. But I've tried so hard: to fit in, to please you. What have I done wrong?

Kelly didn't think mice could cry. She was wrong.

It was some time before she shifted back and packed up her work for the evening. Her actions were listless, as if the night had sucked all the determination out of her. Perhaps that's why she was receptive to the external mental energy. Whatever the reason, she heard a soft voice in her mind.

"Don't worry, no one suspects me. They think I'm one of them. I'll make my move soon ..."

Kelly stopped and struggled to understand what she was sensing. She tried to strengthen the contact, hoping to trace the source of the sending. That was a mistake. Two things happened then: the contact was immediately broken and Kelly heard a noise from around the corner just ahead. She'd been detected!

Footsteps approached and for the second time that evening she crash-shifted back into her small, furry form—once again, barely in time. The footsteps rounded the corner and a pair of muddy work boots stopped beside her. She crept close to the wall, where there was less chance of becoming a mouse pizza. Her ears picked up the person's breathing, but could tell her nothing of who stood above her.

When the boots moved on and the footfalls faded down the passageway, Kelly scurried along the wall as quickly as her half-inch legs could carry her. She would turn the corner before risking a shift back.

Suddenly the floor leapt under her. Her fur jolted straight up and her feet scampered wildly as her mouse instincts kicked into autopilot. She zigged and zagged first in one direction and then another. Every alarm in her mind was shrieking:

CAT ATTACK! CAT ATTACK! POUNCE WARNING—FULL EVASIVE MANEUVERS!

A blur of orange fur flew past, narrowly missing her.

"Nooo! Mack, no—it's me, Kelly! Cease pouncing immediately! We don't eat our friends!"

On some level she knew her mouse chitters would only further incite the cat, but she couldn't help herself. Her mouse instincts were running the show for the moment. It was just as well. Not only did Kelly lack personal experience in pounce avoidance, she was also afraid if she thought too hard about it, she'd trip over her tail with an unlucky swish.

Somehow in the melee she spotted a doorway she might just squeeze under. She faked a zig to the right and then skittered hard to the left towards the door.

Whump!

An orange mallet with five extended claws hammered down so close, she felt the breeze. That was motivation enough. Kelly shot under the doorway with such force she scraped a furless stripe down her back. She didn't notice. She didn't care.

It's quite stressful to be the object of someone's dinner plans. It was some time before she could calm herself sufficiently to shift back. During that time her anchor chanted over and over her new mantra, the third safety tip for shape-shifters: *Never become someone's lunch.*

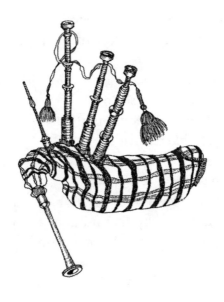

6

THE GAMES

The strong, steady beat pulsed. He took four strides forward (eight if you count both feet,) each landing precisely in time. Four more steps in place turned him to face the way he came and then he started back—feet falling to the beat. Marching a short line to and fro might have looked weird, but the stentorian tune he piped gave his movements a martial purpose, as if he were defending this particular spot of floor to the death.

Before he completed the cadence, however, he stopped and swore—the ragged cutoff of the pipes echoing the sentiment.

He sighed. "Firmness, both in sufferance and exertion, is a character I would wish to be thought to possess: and have always despised the whining yelp of complaint, and the cowardly, feeble resolve."[7]

Kelly waited.

"Burns," he added.

"Why do you push yourself so hard, Gordie? I love my music too, but forty-five minutes a day is plenty of practice for me. You work for hours and you're still not satisfied."

He shrugged. "If I know I can do a better job. I'm not satisfied until I do."

"That sounds like a lot of work."

He grunted agreement.

"When are the games?" she asked.

"Two weeks from Saturday." He reshouldered his pipes. "Two weeks to get this right …" He struck up the tune and resumed his march.

&

The next two weeks carried all the signs that summer had passed and winter wasn't far off in the Highlands. The air was cooler. The purple hillsides of heather darkened to a coffee brown and the trees melded into golds,

---

7   *The Letters of Robert Burns* (To Miss Chalmers: 14th March, 1788) by Robert Burns

reds, coppers, and bronzes. Surprisingly, the weather was drier and sunnier, although the days were noticeably shorter, with sunset piped earlier each evening. The smell of freshly cut hay was everywhere, as the last of the harvest was collected and stored for the winter.

The morning of the games dawned an overcast gray, but those with savvy weather sense knew it would burn off to a beautiful day. A festive delight energized the manor folk and most opted to walk the five miles to the Great Fields, the site of the games. The excitement was contagious and Kelly found herself keen to experience her first games.

From what she had learned, Highland games were a potpourri of Scottish culture and heritage. Centuries ago these same athletic events tested a warrior's strength and skill. The piping competitions dated back to the Falkirk Tryst in the late 1700's—Scotland's largest cattle market of the day. The Highland drovers, who carried their pipes with them, decided to see who among them blew the best tune. Gaelic *mods* began as competitions of singing, poetry, and storytelling, in an effort to preserve Gaelic as a spoken language.

Even the dancing was rich with symbols of Highland life. The Highland fling represents the movements of a rutting stag. The dancer's upraised arms symbolize the stag's antlers. The fast footwork and leaps … well, Kelly had never seen a stag rut, but she imagined it was a lively act.

The uniquely Scottish sights and sounds that met Kelly when she arrived at the fields sent a shiver of thrill coursing through her. Everyone wore a kilt—wee bairns in sandals, somber old uncles with scraggly white beards, and the women in their longer skirts and plaid sashes—each showcasing his or her family's tartan. The ever-present buzz of drones accompanied the spectacle. The sound of the pipes spilled from the fields and surrounding forest, as if the trees hid distant hives of giant bees.

Kelly made her way to a fenced swath of grass running up a hillside. It was dotted with gates, and a large pen sat within at the base of the hill. The sheepdog trials were already underway and Kelly was eager to watch Cameron and Duffy perform. She spied the young shepherd and his dog a short distance away where they awaited their turn. Cameron was speaking with Dougal, who was busy filling the dogs' watering trough.

Kenna joined Kelly along the fence and climbed atop a post for a better view.

"Oh," Kenna sighed, "I *do* hope they have a good run."

Kelly cupped her hand to her mouth and shouted, "Come onnnnn, Duffy—kick some woolly butt!"

A mob of sheep meandered about the crest of the hill as Cameron and Duffy entered the competition area. Shepherd and dog waited, poised for action. An official pointed to the pair with a nod. A stopwatch started ticking. Cameron uttered a word. And Duffy sprang up the hillside as if shot from a cannon.

"First the outrun," Kenna said wistfully.

Duffy's leaping strides covered the distance quickly and he angled around behind the milling flock.

"Now the lift."

Was Kenna's running commentary offered in explanation or was it merely to soothe her own anxiety?

Duffy slowed and assumed the low crouch of a stalking wolf. The menace registered and persuaded the flock to start down the hill. The sheep huddled close to one another trotting towards the first gate. As they passed through, one sheep balked at the gate and broke away to the left.

"Get him!" Kenna urged in a tense whisper.

Duffy dashed forward cutting off the runaway and headed it back to rejoin its mates.

Kelly sighed.

"Come on … drive them straight!" Kenna leaned forward, her eyes locked on the brown and white Border collie.

Duffy trundled his charges along with a good sense of the task at hand. Cameron only had to assist with an occasional short whistle. As the flock entered a large ring painted on the grass, Duffy finally allowed them to come to a rest.

"Okay boy," Kenna prompted, "let's see you shed."

Kelly glanced at her friend. The image of a bald dog stuck in her mind.

Cameron cued with another staccato whistle and Duffy worked the herd, trying to separate two unwilling sheep from the flock. It wasn't easy. The sheep had little desire to leave the safety of the group and tried to flow back to it like a sticky bead of mercury. Duffy was relentless, however; he darted with quick, precise turns continually cutting off any attempted reunion. The sheep were stubborn in their efforts, but Duffy proved more so and the pair finally yielded.

"Just the penning left now."

Cameron walked to the pen and swung the gate open. He spoke a clipped word and Duffy herded the sheep forward. An escapee, towards the back of the fold, attempted to flee, but Duffy would have none of it. After brief consideration, the fugitive grudgingly turned and followed the others into the pen. Cameron shut the gate.

"Ahh …" Kenna exhaled.

After leaving the competition area, Cameron headed towards the girls with Duffy trotting behind, barely winded.

Kenna beamed as the shepherd and his dog joined them.

"Aye," Cameron nodded, "'twas a braw run. Good dog." He scratched Duffy behind the ears.

They stood along the fence watching the subsequent competitors. Kenna offered a free-flowing analysis of the different pairs, which Cameron punctuated with an occasional, "Oh, aye." But to Kelly, it all looked much the same and before long she grew restless. She wasn't alone; Duffy cavorted with the other dogs near the trough, as he sought his own entertainment.

"Here, boy!" she called.

Duffy pranced to her and sat prettily. He cocked his head and stared with intelligent brown eyes.

With a laugh, Kelly sat in the grass and administered a much appreciated belly rub. There was nothing lazy or indolent about Duffy's pleasure. He wiggled and frisked under Kelly's hands with a coiled energy that begged for release.

"You want to play, don't you?"

She must have spoken the magic word—he wriggled over, mid-pat, hopping to all fours. With an eager bark, he wagged his tail so hard she feared it might fly out. A suitable stick lay nearby so Kelly gave it a side-arm flick, as if she were skipping stones. Off to the right it flew, with Duffy in pursuit a moment later. Her next throw was a flick to the left. Exit dog, stage left. This was too easy. For both of them.

"Okay, Duff, show me what you've got."

She faked to the right and tossed to the left. He fell for it.

"Sucker ..."

The next time she reversed it, faking to the left, with the intent to throw to the right. Duffy's eyes narrowed as he watched her moves. He didn't budge to the left, and sprang after the stick before it left her hand, nearly the moment she committed to the right.

Hmm ... not bad. Quick study.

She tossed a fast one at him, to see if he'd flinch. He caught it mid-air with no fuss. The next one was thrown three feet over his head—another quick toss. He sprang up like Nureyev executing a perfect entrechat, except Nureyev (to the best of Kelly's knowledge) never caught a stick in his mouth.

All right, show off ... this one's going deep ...

Duffy broke into a run the moment she released the stick. When the stick came down, he was right where he needed to be to pick it off. He'd anticipated it perfectly. As if he'd read her mind …

Could a dog be sensitive to the mental energies of a human consciousness? It was a crazy notion. It suggested that Duffy might be capable of the same Perception techniques that Kelly herself had only just learned. No way … and yet, who was she to say what was possible? Perhaps a closer examination was in order. She sat in the grass, calling Duffy to her, and began to center.

"Kelly?"

She abruptly broke off and focused on the speaker.

"Cameron and I want to go see if they've posted the results yet." Kenna stood over her, blocking the sun. "Would you keep an eye on Duffy?"

Perfect! Some privacy. Centering, she reached out for Duffy's mind. Contact was initially elusive. She sensed the dog's thoughts, but they were slippery and kept sliding from her mental grasp. Unlike a mouse's mind, which seemed motionless in comparison, Duffy's consciousness wouldn't sit still. It was also more expansive, harder to wrap her thoughts around. She had to make several attempts and hone her focus before she was finally able to establish the link.

Being inside the mind of a Border collie was akin to being in the mind of a precocious child, but with a decidedly doggie twist. Duffy was curious about everything—particularly if it moved. He was currently staring at a swallowtail skipping over the grass, searching for a game he might make out of it. He had an overpowering need for … well, play wasn't exactly the word. It was a feeling of work and play together—something he felt compelled to do, yet something he thoroughly enjoyed and couldn't get enough of.

Kelly noted the keen sense of smell and that his ears detected pitches beyond human hearing. His eyes couldn't see as far as a person's, but they were acutely sensitive to motion (the butterfly held all of Duffy's attention as it flitted along.)

Afterwards, Kelly wasn't sure if her impulsiveness was her own idea, or a suggestion from the Border collie's psyche, but she didn't stop to consider it. Duffy was having too much fun to not share it. She reached down into her mind and threw the switch. Suddenly she was eye-to-eye with Duffy, who yipped a bark of greeting.

"Hi yourself," she barked back.

Being a dog was nothing like being a mouse. For one thing, she was no longer a floor-hugger; hopefully she wouldn't get quite the nose-full of dust. Her tail was an altogether new experience as well. A mouse's tail is snaking. It swishes across the floor in a whip-like motion, bent on tripping the unwary. A Border collie's tail has two discrete movements (neither of which threatens entanglement.) One serves as a counterbalance: head up, tail up; head down, tail down. The second motion expresses the dog's mood. When content, the tail snaps back and forth with the precision of a windshield wiper. *Tic-tic-tic.*

Self-awareness was also something she hadn't experienced as a mouse. As a collie she was conscious of her own being, her desires as a dog (to play) and her insatiable need for approval.

I am a good dog, aren't I?

Tic-tic-tic.

Duffy yapped again and Kelly realized that barking wasn't so much doggie speech as it was an attention getter. She understood Duffy's intent, not by his barks, but rather by his expression and body language—and his body said, "Let's play!"

Yes, yes, yes!

Tic-tic-tic.

They ran and jumped and darted and rolled as if there were nothing more important at that moment. But there was. It was a pressure building up inside Kelly's doggie thoughts. Her mind, once it grasped the notion, held onto it like a prized bone, and she finally understood obsessive-compulsive behavior—compulsive, because she felt driven and obsessive because she could think of nothing else …

Sheep!

She and Duffy charged up the hill towards the grazing flock. While Kelly lacked Duffy's experience and finesse, her herding instinct was strong and she knew what was required. She took the left side as the flock began to move with purpose.

Move along smartly. Whoa—watch that flank! No, not in that direction. This way, you mutton-heads!

Things seemed to be under control when suddenly the flock stopped, stubbornly refusing to go on. She approached the lead sheep. It was a brute many times her size and it had a vacant expression that suggested its brain was undersized for its girth. This would be a contest of wills and she had to show this lug who was in charge.

Kelly crouched down, assuming a wolfish stance. She narrowed her eyes and held her opponent with a piercing stare. It gazed blankly and didn't budge. Her tail was low. She crept forward a foot and laid her ears back. She bared her teeth and gave a low growl. Fleece-for-brains didn't respond.

This was a game of poker. Kelly had to convince the leader that she was the predator and that it was the prey. It was all a bluff, but she couldn't let the sheep know that—it had to believe that she'd attack with the intention of ripping its throat out unless it moved where she commanded. If it called her bluff and didn't respond to her menacing gestures, it would be game over; there'd be little more she could do. So she continued to play-act as a pup in wolf's clothing.

Narrow the eyes. Don't break contact. Bunch up my hind legs. Ready to spring forward. Show a bit more teeth.

She shifted her weight back the slightest amount, as she would if she were preparing to launch at the leader's jugular. At that moment it turned with a bleat and pushed into its nearest neighbors. Mutton-chops conceded the fight—she'd won!

I'm so good. Doesn't everyone love me?

Tic-tic—

A whistle stopped her tail mid-tic.

"Duffy!"

Oh no … they'd returned! Kelly followed Duffy as he bounded down the hill towards his master. Cameron searched among the faces of the bystanders.

"And where'd be Kelly?" A frown chiseled the shepherd's tanned forehead.

Kenna sighed. "How could she leave Duffy? How horrible!"

"Aye." His soft reply was loud in the awkward silence.

Kelly's person thoughts and doggie thoughts were both churning, but in different directions, creating a schizophrenic cacophony in her head.

Guys, it's not what you think!

Those sheep were great! That was a nice move I made to the left—beautiful anticipation. I'm such a good dog, such a good dog!

Tic-tic-tic.

But what can I tell them? They can't find out about my shape-shifting.

More sheep. More sheep! They need me (because I'm so good.) I'm a good dog. Good dog!

Tic-tic-tic.

I have to think up something. What a mess!

Cameron gave Duffy a tousle. "Ya took second place, boy—a braw job ya did. Come then."

Pet me, pet me! I'm a good dog too!

Tic-tic-tic.

Kenna, Cameron and Duffy left Kelly among the other milling dogs. What should she do? They had good cause to be angry, except she *hadn't* left Duffy unattended. She hated the thought of lying to her friends; besides, she couldn't think of a plausible lie. She could say nothing, as if it never happened. But that would be worse—that would appear as though she'd forsaken Duffy and didn't see anything wrong with it.

Struggling with unattractive choices, Kelly didn't notice Master David walking past. He spotted her, however.

"Hey there pretty girl," he said, kneeling to pet her.

Oh yes. Aren't I? More pets, more pets. Don't you love me?

Tic-tic-tic.

"But where's your trainer? You shouldn't be running around loose like this."

Uh oh …

Before she could react, he had her. He led her to a post by the trough where he tied her with the other dogs.

No, no, no!

Master David ignored her protesting barks, and with a parting pet he continued on his way.

Tic-tic-tic.

Stupid tail.

What now? The trough sat along a heavily trafficked path; she didn't dare shift back here—this was too public a place. She didn't have any practical suggestions, so she gave into her collie-mind's only thought: when in doubt, bark.

Twenty minutes later, having annoyed most of the passersby, her throat was hoarse and she remained tied up, so she sat quietly awaiting inspiration. Her sharp hearing picked up the snippets of passing conversations. She knew it wasn't polite to eavesdrop, but she didn't think social etiquette applied to border collies, and besides, she had nothing else to do.

"… We're going to miss the caber toss if we don't hurry …"

"… What time will they start serving lunch? I'm starved …"

"… I understand one of the dancing judges couldn't make it. I hope that doesn't slow the schedule much …"

"… Keep a sharp eye. There's trouble afoot. I'm sure of it."

The last voice was softer. Her head shot up as she identified Allisdair as the speaker.

"What do you sense?" Conall asked in an equally subdued tone. "Thus far we've uncovered nothing."

"That itself is a concern. Whoever's behind this is coverin' his tracks well. Too well! If he's guardin' his plan this carefully, it must be big …"

They passed out of earshot (even for a dog) before Kelly could learn more.

Something big … What could Allisdair's warning mean? Another familiar voice broke through her thoughts.

"This way—quickly, before someone sees us!"

She spun her head, but couldn't locate this speaker. She didn't need to, however; only one person mumbled so indistinctly: Dougal. Was he somehow connected with Allisdair's investigation?

"Zach!"

Kelly left off her speculation as a boy called to the dog beside her. The boy apparently meant to untie Zach, but the dogs' lines were so badly tangled he untied Kelly by mistake. She realized it a moment before he did, and that was all the time she needed. With a parting bark of thanks, she bounded off into the trees.

Gordie was competing today, and Kelly wanted to hear him play. Homing on the distant buzz of drones, the piping area wasn't difficult to locate. Brightly kilted pipers with drones overhead covered the field like a species of giant showy insects. Some tuned or warmed up on familiar songs, and some performed under the watchful scrutiny of a nearby judge. Surprisingly, the overall effect wasn't raucous. The qualities of the sounds were similar and complimentary—like an orchestra tuning before the conductor steps onto the stage.

She found Gordie sitting on an outcropping of granite, his pipes resting across his lap. He said nothing as Kelly settled down beside him.

"Finished?"

He nodded.

"No medals?"

He shook his head.

"Do you want to talk about it?"

He sighed.

She knew what this meant to him, and she envied his passion—so similar to the Border collie's obsession for herding.

Great ... a dog has more in common with my best friend than I do ...

Gordie reached down and scooped a handful of leaves. He tossed them up and they danced away on the breeze.

"It's windy. My drone stopped." His voice was flat.

"It stopped ... what?"

"It stopped *playing*. Right in the middle of my march. That'll cinch a last-place every time. I practice indoors."

"Gordie, I don't underst—"

"Drone reeds are sensitive to changes in air pressure. If I suddenly give my bag a hard squeeze, I can shut the drones off. Just as a gust of wind can ..."

"... and there's no wind in the practice rooms ... so you couldn't have known." She finished his sentence.

He nodded. "The judge said if I strengthen my reeds they'll be less sensitive to the wind. He said other than that I played well."

"That's encouraging!"

"Last place is last place."

"No," she argued. "That's a loser's attitude."

"I *am* a loser."

"No! A loser doesn't bother to prepare, does poorly and then feels sorry for himself." She stuck her chin out. "You work harder than anyone. In this case your performance was hurt by something you didn't know to prepare for."

"Result's the same."

"No, it's not!" She jabbed a finger towards him. "Your playing has improved, hasn't it?"

He nodded.

"You gave it your best shot today—correct?" Another jab.

Another nod.

"The judge said you otherwise played well, didn't he?" Jab.

Nod.

"And you've just learned something that will make you better next time."

"Yeah, I should practice in a gale."

"Gordie, it's good to want to win. But you shouldn't pout when you discover it's not as easy as you'd like."

"I'm not pouting!"

"Yes you are."

He looked at her crossly.

"… But only a little. This is just the start. The next time you compete, try and improve on today's performance."

"That shouldn't be hard."

"Well, *I'm* proud of you."

Gordie sat in silence for a time and then blew out a sigh. "It stinks. When something goes wrong that's not really your fault, yet you're still responsible.

Kelly thought back on her own morning. "Yeah … it stinks like a maggot-filled rat carcass rotting in the sun."

Gordie glanced up, the sparkle returning to his eyes. "You know the next time I'll still be trying to win."

"I know," she acknowledged with a laugh.

Gordie led Kelly to the food tents where they each consumed several bridies, traditional Scottish meat pies. After stuffing themselves, they proceeded to the dance championships where the sword dance was underway.

Atop the dais, young men and woman leapt between the sharp blades of crossed swords.

As Gordie watched he commented, "All our yesterdays have lighted fools the way to dusty death. Out, out, brief candle!"[8]

"Kindly elucidate." Kelly cocked her head.

"In Shakespeare's play, King Macbeth is trapped by his ambition and actions, which ultimately bring about his own death. Resigned to his fate, he speaks of the futility of life."

"So?"

"It's the dance," he stressed, pointing to the stage. "The sword dance dates back to 1057 when Malcolm Canmore killed Macbeth and himself became King of Scotland. To celebrate his victory, Malcolm crossed his sword with Macbeth's and danced between them."

"For real?" Her eyebrows pushed up at her scalp.

Gordie nodded. "Macbeth murdered King Duncan, Malcolm's father, years before. Just as in the play, it was Macbeth's actions and his ambition that lead to his own death."

As Kelly watched the dancers' nimble footwork she considered Gordie's words. She never gave much thought to the consequences of her actions. It was sobering to think that something she did today might ultimately lead to her own death in the distant future. In Macbeth's case he'd killed a man, but couldn't innocent acts also have unforeseen effects?

---

8   *Macbeth* (Act V, Scene v) by William Shakespeare

Deliberate movement through the milling spectators caught her attention. She winced as she saw Kenna bee-lining towards her with a scowl. Kelly braced herself for her friend's displeasure.

"Where did you go? Abandoning Duffy like that! You just left him!"

I didn't. I was there. Really.

"He could have run off searching for Cameron. He might have gotten lost in the woods. What would he have done at nightfall? All alone ..." Kenna gasped at her own suggestion. "We're in the Highlands—wild things come out at night!"

"I'm sorry. I ... wasn't myself this morning."

Before Kenna could respond, Conall stepped up.

"You're needed immediately, Kenna. See Master Roy in the dog trials area." He walked off, not waiting for a reply.

Kenna glared at Kelly. She cleared her throat with a guttural huck and stalked off. Whether it was phlegm or displeasure, Kelly was unsure.

Gordie reappeared at Kelly's elbow. "Trouble?"

"She and I had a misunderstanding this morning. That's why I missed hearing you play. I ... got tied up."

"Just as well. No witnesses."

As the afternoon drew to a close and they headed home for dinner, Kelly and Gordie came upon a small gathering near the dog trials area. Kenna and Master Roy knelt by the water trough, their faces creased with worry; an unconscious dog lay before them. Dougal attended another sick pup nearby. Behind, several other Border collies panted and whimpered their discomfort, while anxious trainers tried to soothe them. Allisdair and Conall stood nearby, conferring quietly.

Struan's tall figure was easy to spot among the onlookers. "It's terrible," the smith apprentice told them. "Someone poisoned the water!"

Poison? Kelly's insides froze as she thought back to that morning. Had she drunk from the trough? She didn't recall doing so, but then a more dreadful thought occurred to her.

"Struan, is Duffy all right?"

"He seems fine, but some of the other dogs are quite sick."

A sob cut through their conversation. Master Roy stood slowly. With a shake of his head, he walked to Allisdair. But it was Kenna who'd made the sound. She remained beside the still form of the dog, weeping. Cameron, fighting back tears of his own, stepped to her and laid a comforting hand on his friend's shoulder.

7

SAVEN

Poison. It's no accident. Nor is it a bit of bad luck. It's premeditated, malevolent, and plain old not nice. That it's also deadly made the manor a dangerous place. Someone among them was not whom he or she seemed.

Kelly's secret was making her life more difficult, as well. Without divulging her shape-shifting, she couldn't explain to Kenna she hadn't let her down. Whenever their paths crossed Kenna simply looked past Kelly as if she weren't there. Kenna's shunning was especially painful because

Kelly longed to share with her that she too felt badly about the dog that had died; that the poisoning scared her too; and that Kenna wasn't alone. Yet Kelly didn't know how to move past Kenna's disapproval, and it left her feeling awkward and embarrassed. So she said nothing.

⛬

"What's been bugging you lately?" Gordie peered at Kelly's face, looking as if he might find the answer there.

"What?" She answered snappishly.

"You haven't been saying much."

Must your speech always be so pedestrian?

"Laconic," she replied.

Gordie furrowed his brow. "Milky?"

"No, that's lactic. Laconic: concise; terse; one who uses few words."

"Incoming Hershey moment," he muttered.

"How can you strive for such perfection in your piping and allow such sloppy speech habits?"

"Be laconic!"

"No, no, no! It's declarative, not imperative. If you use the word like that no one will understand you."

"If I use the word *at all*, no one will understand me. Besides, it's imperative that you shut up now."

"Don't you appreciate that I'm trying to help you?"

He glared at her. "I've got a good chocolatey word— Kelly: it means crabby and grouchy, which was exactly my point. What's eating you, anyway?"

Was she really being such a grouch? "There's nothing to do," she complained.

Gordie thought for a moment. "Saven's next week. We could carve a turnip ..."

"Saven?" she asked.

"October 31—it's our New Year's celebration."

She studied Gordie for some sign of teasing. "Why would anyone celebrate New Year's on Halloween?" She wasn't buying it.

He seemed indignant. "Because it's an ancient custom."

She almost took him seriously ... but to carve a turnip?

Kelly smirked. "So on Halloween we'll celebrate New Year's and carve some turnips. Then we can hide Easter eggs and hang our stockings."

Gordie slapped his hand down. "Is your way *always* the only way? Would it shock you to learn that while your country is barely two hundred years old, our culture and traditions are thousands of years old, and that just maybe some of your holidays are borrowed from ours? Not that you've done them any justice. Saven is a beautiful holiday, and has nothing to do with begging for candy. It's when we honor our ancestors. We particularly remember ... any ... family members ... we've recently lost." He finished in a subdued voice.

She squeezed her eyes shut, but she couldn't shake the image of sitting on the kitchen floor hugging her unconscious mother.

"Saven's my day then," she whispered. She fingered the flat disk of her pendant under her shirt. An awkward silence fell between them. Finally she asked, "Do you really carve turnips?"

He nodded, pushing his bangs out of his eyes. "Work with what you've got. Pumpkins were a New World crop; turnips are what we had."

Kelly couldn't imagine carving something as solid as a turnip. "Is it easy?"

"No!" After a moment he asked, "Would you like to try?"

Gordie led her down to the root cellar. He poked into several storerooms before announcing, "Turnips!"

Kelly looked at the heaped baskets filling the room. "These aren't turnips; they're rutabagas—and they're the biggest ones I've ever seen!"

"Oh aye, they're turnips to us. And here in Scotland they grow big and braw."

"How do you carve *this?*" She hefted one out of its basket. "It's a bowling ball. A chain saw wouldn't dent it." She heaved it into the air to demonstrate her point. It thudded to the floor and exited the room with a wobbly roll.

"That's a great idea!" Gordie ran out of the room. "I'll rack the pins …"

He soon emerged from a nearby storeroom with two handfuls of carrots that he tried to set on end. Kelly caught on and explored several other rooms. The parsnips looked promising, but they refused to stand upright. There was, however, a brown dirt-crusted root cut into segments. It stood on its smooth cuts more willingly than the carrots. Eventually ten roots stood upright in the rough shape of a triangle.

From down the hall, Kelly cocked the rutabaga back between her legs, and swung it forward, propelling it with a grunt. It wove an erratic path, nearly missing the roots, but at the last moment it wobbled to the right, nicking the corner one. It didn't take much; the roots were eager to fall and Gordie and Kelly cheered the lucky strike.

The appeal of the game was short lived, though, given the effort to rack the pins. Snooping through the store-rooms, Kelly pulled a potato out of a basket.

"How about 'baga bocce?"

"How do you play?" Gordie asked.

"First you roll the little ball." She tossed the potato down the hall. "That becomes the target. We then take turns trying to roll our balls closest to it."

Gordie nodded. "It sounds like curling."

"Curling?"

"It's a Scottish game that's played on ice. But we don't roll balls; we slide stones—big ones."

"This big?" Kelly held up her rutabaga.

"That's a runt. We're talking forty-pound stones."

Kelly cradled her rutabaga protectively. "Well, 'baga bocce sounds better than 'baga curling."

"Excuse me, Miss 'Precise Meaning,' it's *turnip* curling."

Kelly's jaw tightened. "At the moment we seem to be out of forty-pound rutabagas. Furthermore, you said curling requires ice. Do you see any ice? No ice, no sliding. No sliding, no curling."

Gordie thought for a moment. "We could make ice! Maggie stores jars of olive oil in one of these rooms."

"That would be *simulating* ice, not making it." Kelly imagined pools of olive oil up and down the hallway. "Er ... why don't we skip the ice? But we can call it turnip curling, if you insist.

Gordie seemed disappointed there'd be no ice.

Kelly assembled her four rutabagas behind a starting line of carrots. Gordie searched for balls of his own and soon emerged from a room laden with four enormous cabbages.

Taking the first turn, Kelly launched her rutabaga down the hallway. It lumbered to a stop well short of the potato. Her next roll would need more *oomph*.

Gordie addressed his cabbage pile. "To roll, or not to roll: that is the question. Whether 'tis nobler for the head to suffer the flings and taros of playful fortune, or to steam in a pot of bubbles and by composing dinner, oneself condemn?"[9]

Kelly groaned. "That was more *ham* than Hamlet."

---

9 Based on:
  "To be, or not to be: that is the question:
  Whether 'tis nobler in the mind to suffer
  The slings and arrows of outrageous fortune,
  Or to take arms against a sea of troubles,
  And by opposing end them?"
  Hamlet (Act III, Scene i) by William Shakespeare

"Please," Gordie entreated, "the cabbage is a gentle vegetable with tender sensibilities. One must treat it delicately."

"Oh, horse hockey! Take your turn."

Gordie bowed to the cabbages. "You who are about to roll, we salute you!"

"TAKE YOUR TURN!"

Gordie raised his cabbage with deliberate care. He wound up, swung his arm forward and released—the cabbage hit the ground with a *thwock* and lumped down the hall. As it rolled, it dropped its leaves, strewing the playing field with a carpet of vegan debris. It first threatened to overshoot the potato, but the shedding slowed it sufficiently that it shuddered to a halt just beyond the target tater.

"You're going to have to clean that mess up before I can take my turn."

Gordie shook his head firmly. "No way—you don't remove any ball from the field until you've played them all."

"Don't remove your cabbage, just its droppings."

"Those droppings *are* my cabbage—most of it, in fact."

Kelly was about to protest, when a door opened atop the nearby stairway.

"Quick," Gordie hissed, "someone's coming!"

They darted into a storeroom and made for the farthest corner. Behind the stacked bins and baskets they discovered a pile of empty burlap sacks. They slithered under, ensuring any telltale limbs were safely out of view.

Footsteps descended the stairs ... a pause ... and then ...

"Look at this mess! Who's responsible for this?"

Kelly recognized the voice. It belonged to Rhona, a kitchen woman who worked for Maggie. Kelly didn't care for Rhona. It wasn't Rhona's unwashed hair with a shine more from grease than lustrous beauty; nor was it her grating voice always raised in complaint; rather, it was how she bossed and ordered the other kitchen crew around, as if their work had no value.

Steps approached their storeroom with pauses every few seconds.

"Shhh ..." Kelly whispered.

The footsteps stopped just inside the doorway. Kelly tried to lie still, but the burlap was scratchy and her itches demanded attention. After what seemed like an eternity, the steps moved on and Kelly allowed herself to shift to a more comfortable position.

"I don't have time for this ... he won't wait ... always nervous about getting caught ..." Kelly could only catch snippets of Rhona's complaints.

"What was in this sack?" Gordie whispered. "It stinks."

"Onions," she whispered back. It did stink.

The air under the sack grew stifling and drops of sweat ran into Kelly's eyes before she finally heard Rhona's footsteps retreat back up the stairway. When she and Gordie finally crawled out, a sheen of sweat covered them and bits of onion skin dotted their hair and clothes.

Gordie wiped his face on his sleeve. "We didn't carve a turnip, but we did invent several new vegetarian sports, and we managed to *not* clean up after ourselves. I'd say our afternoon was a success!"

"Come on," Kelly said, "I'm hungry and it's nearly dinner time."

Gordie wrinkled his nose. "I hope they're not serving onions."

"Or turnips," she added.

෪

As one of the four great fire festivals in the ancient Celtic calendar, Saven commenced with the lighting of the First Fire at sunset on October 31. The bonfire glade—the site of the ceremony—crowned the bald peak of Ben Abba, the wooded mountain that rose up behind the manor house.

By late afternoon on the thirty-first, the day's earlier rain had ended. The skies still brooded, but an occasional glimpse of blue offered some hope for a clear evening. Jillian joined Kelly for the walk to the mountain-top glade. They climbed the path, a slick carpet of wet leaves, in silence for a time. The growing chill of the approaching night affirmed that this was indeed the eve of winter. Golden birch leaves, the last to fall, danced above the trail as if waving good-bye to the passing year.

Jillian laid a hand on Kelly's shoulder. "How are you?"

Kelly didn't have a ready answer. She'd been here several months now. She considered her lessons and activities. She thought of the people she'd met—some she liked and some she could do without, but she suspected that was the case wherever you were. What did it mean to be happy? Was the absence of *un*happiness the measure?

She answered honestly. "I don't know … I'm okay I guess."

Generations of past bonfires left their blackened scars on the natural limestone that paved the clearing atop the mountain. In the center, a mound of logs and branches towered fifteen feet in the air. Brid stood closest to the pyre, flanked on one side by Allisdair holding an unlit torch, and on the other by a kilted bagpiper. Brid's tall and lordly figure brought to mind Kelly's recent attempts to balance books on her head. Her bruised toes summed up her lack of success.

A sizeable crowd had already assembled, and as the sun eased downward, the glade quickly filled with people. As the sun approached the horizon, the onlookers quieted in anticipation. Allisdair handed the ready torch to Brid. At the very moment the sun brushed the earth, Brid thrust the torch skyward and called a clear voice:

"We stand in a moment outside of time.
We light this First Fire in the interval between
    yesterday and tomorrow.
We light it on the day between the passing of the
    old year and the start of the new.
We celebrate life while remembering and hon-
    oring those before us, in this space and in
    this time between death and rebirth."

All eyes followed the sun as it slid behind the distant hills. As the last glimpse slipped from sight, a blinding flash returned Kelly's attention to the raised torch, which now flared brightly. Brid touched the torch to the base of the pyre and the fire eagerly caught. The hisses and pops of the hungry flames accompanied the soulful air the piper played in salute to the passing day and year.

As the final notes faded, Brid spread her arms and called out, "All other fires have been extinguished. The First Fire burns alone, representing our unity. From it, let us re-light our candles and hearths, remembering that our souls and the souls of our ancestors likewise came from a single, divine spark. May we nurture and aid one another honoring this oneness throughout the coming year."

When Brid finished, a small group approached and lit torches from the bonfire. They then passed through the crowd, lighting the candles that onlookers held forward. As each new candle sputtered to life, it in turn served as source to kindle the next. In this way, the glow of the clearing steadily waxed into a bright nimbus.

"Hello, Kelly!"

Kelly looked up to see Master David's features dancing behind the flickering light of his candle.

"Good Saven to you," he said, holding out his taper.

She lit her candle from his. "Good Sa—ah!" She gasped, for in the darkness beyond the master, a glowing skull floated and bobbed in the air!

He turned. Seeing the cause of her dismay, he gently took her hand and urged her towards the apparition. As they approached, a young child emerged from the darkness; he held a basket that glowed from within.

"Have you never seen a carved turnip?" Master David asked.

"They're real? I thought Gordie was making all that up!"

"He can be a tease, but in this he was telling the truth."

Borrowing the turnip from the child, Master David held it up for Kelly's inspection. The top had been cut off and the inside hollowed out. A candle burned within and a string served as handle. The turnip's purple upper half gave the carved-out eyes a sunken appearance. The bottom portion glowed an ivory-yellow, the sallow complexion of a real skull. In the spooky category, a carved pumpkin couldn't hold a candle to a turnip.

Kelly struggled to reconcile the familiar customs of Halloween with the origins and intent of this ancient holiday. "If Saven is about remembering our ancestors, are we supposed to carve their faces on the turnips?"

The bard returned the turnip to its young owner. In the reflected candlelight, Kelly could see the amusement in his eyes. "No—carving *any* face on a turnip is work enough. Portraits aren't required."

He went on to explain the unique nature of the holiday: Saven falls into a crack in the Celtic calendar. It begins the day after the old year has ended, but one day before the new year begins. Technically, it belongs to neither year, which was what Brid meant when she said, "We stand in a moment outside of time." The early Celts believed this made Saven magical. They believed that on Saven the veil that separates our world from the Otherworld is at its thinnest and that it's possible to pass between.

"We set out candles," Master David pointed to the carved turnip, "to guide ancestors who might choose to visit us tonight. We'll set extra places at the table to show them they're welcome in our homes."

They joined the crowd as it headed in small groups back down towards the manor, lured by the night's promised feasting and festivities. Behind them the bonfire crackled blithely. It would be well past dawn before it would collapse, its fuel consumed, into a bed of red-hot coals.

"I don't know anything about my ancestors," Kelly admitted as they descended the mountain path. She had to step carefully in the meager candlelight. "Six months ago I didn't even know I had a grandmother."

Master David gazed up at the stars glittering in the now clear sky. "That's what makes Saven such a special holiday. By telling their stories we remember their lives. We honor them, yes, but we also keep a part of them alive—as something more than faceless names."

They walked the rest of the way in an easy silence, Kelly grateful for the Master Bard's company.

Kelly wasn't surprised those around the dinner table shared reminiscences of family now gone and stories of earlier generations. Kenna talked about her youngest brother, who died from pneumonia when he was six. She described his whippoorwill laugh and she named all his favorite songs. The boy beside Gordie told stories of a long-dead great uncle, once a clan lord and a bold warrior. The boy's eyes glistened with clan fervor as he spoke. That his stories suggested his great uncle was a kleptomaniac cattle thief seemed not to bother him at all.

Aidan joined them for the feast, and he remembered his grandfather, a coastal fisherman who, one winter, saved his village when food supplies were dwindling. He sailed into a North Atlantic gale to catch enough fish to feed the villagers through the winter's remainder.

Then it was Kelly's turn. She didn't know what to say. That it would be about her mother was certain—she'd been thinking about her all day. But what? There were no brave or courageous moments she could think of, and any funny anecdotes escaped her at the moment.

What do I miss most?

That was easy—it was her mother's smile. Kelly imagined that smile, and as she did her mother's laughter cascaded through her mind. A memory suddenly flashed from an evening of playful challenge. Whether or not it was Kelly's happiest moment hardly mattered—it represented all of those happy times in its warmth, unabashed delight, and free-flowing love.

"In the winter my mom and I would spend our after-dinners in the family room with a fire burning. Sometimes we'd read aloud, but sometimes we'd play … word games!

"My favorite game is simple in theory. It requires an unabridged dictionary. On your turn, you choose an unusual word from the dictionary that your opponent won't recognize. Then you either copy its real definition or you make one up for it. You write it all down and your opponent has to decide whether it's the actual definition or not." Kelly beamed with the brilliance of the game's simplicity. "It's fun to think up elaborate definitions that are bogus—those were my specialty. I used to prepare days ahead trying to outfox my mother. And that was hard to do; she had a prodigious vocabulary."

I didn't always win, but I lived for her surprised smile and short little laugh when I presented her with a particularly fine word.

Gordie nodded. "Can you recall an example?"

Kelly closed her eyes for a moment. "No ... not off the top of my head ..."

... Zeugma. That was my tour de force. When Mom realized it was a real word her laugh was half snort, half bark.

Zeugma: 1. A grammatical construction where one part of a sentence governs two or more other parts of the same sentence. 2. An ancient city on the Euphrates noted for its pistachio nuts.

I miss your laugh, too.

After dinner their personal stories gave way to the more formal tales and songs planned for the evening's entertainment. The music and verse wove a fabric of melody and harmony, plot and dénouement. Each saga, ballad, and tune plaited the threads of so many lives long since removed, knitting a tapestry of remembrance.

Kelly allowed herself to fall into the fabric, to wrap herself in it and feel all the textures and hues with her whole being. She could taste the salt spray and hear the sailors call during the sea shanties. Her ears rang with the clank and crash of swords on shields when a beloved lord led his men into combat. Her nose caught the smoke of peat and the sweetness of the heathery braes in a song about a traveler on the moors. The grief of an untimely death moved her to tears in a lament for a hero. She could practically see their faces and sense their features.

They are alive. Here. In this room with us.

Exhilarated, but also exhausted, Kelly left the hall close to midnight with the entertainment still in full sway. The last chorus filled her head with the image of a warrior poet standing against a craggy peak, as she paced sleepily back to her residence. The light was dim as she entered her sitting room. That's when she heard the voices.

Kelly crept to the bedroom door—they came from within.

"Hamish, that's a big decision. Are you sure you're willing to give all this up?"

Kelly instantly recognized the voice, although it was one she thought she'd never hear again. She stepped into the bedroom. "Mom?"

There she was, unbelievably. Standing by the bed, talking to … it was her father—the eyes and shape of his nose were unmistakable. Neither noticed her.

Kelly's dad clasped her mother's hand. "Gwen, it'll be the best for all three of us," he said, laying his other hand on her swollen belly. "By the time the baby is born, we'll have established a new life in the United States. That's where we'll raise our family. It will be our home."

"Mom, Dad … hey!" Kelly tried to interrupt, but she couldn't. Her parents were unaware of her presence. "Hello?"

"Could you be happy there, Hamish?" her mother asked.

"Guys? Can't you see me? Please talk to me …" Kelly's brief elation faded as she realized she was to be an observer and not a participant in this conversation.

"Darling, I could be happy anywhere, as long as you and our daughter are with me."

The kiss drove Kelly from the room. If it had been a proper peck, no problem. But it wasn't. It was one of those sloppy ones of the most unhygienic kind.

Confused, Kelly stepped into the brighter hallway. Distant singing still echoed from the Great Hall. But returning to her sitting room, the light again dimmed. There were still voices coming from her bedroom, but something was different. She edged towards the doorway.

Her parents were gone. In their place stood a man addressing a boy. She stared at the boy sitting on the edge of the bed. She was sure she didn't know him, and yet … there was something familiar.

"I know this is difficult for you," the man said. "It is for me also. I too miss her."

They also took no notice of her presence. To prove the point, she jumped up, waving her arms and shouting, "Ha, ha! You can't see me!" Neither responded.

"But it's Saven and we need to remember your mother," the man continued. "You want to let her know that you still love her and won't ever forget her."

"Ninety-nine bottles of beer on the wall," Kelly bellowed. It wasn't terribly musical. It was also unnoticed.

The boy looked up. Kelly could see tears glistening in the corners of his eyes. "But father, sometimes I can't remember her face. Sometimes I try to think about her and I can't see what she looked like." His voice broke as he said, "I can't remember her ..."

Kelly was staring cross-eyed at the pair, with her tongue thrust out. But the boy's pain touched her. She gave up the face, feeling sorry for him.

The man knelt by the bed and placed his hands on the boy's knees. "Son, it's all right. Remembering her is about cherishing the things she taught us and loving the ways she touched our lives. The image of her face and the sound of her voice will fade. Let them go. Remember instead what her face and her voice gave us: smiles and laughter."

The man stood and held out a hand. "Please, Hamish—please, come with me to dinner?"

Hamish?

Kelly's mind raced as the boy slowly stood and followed his father out of the room. Of course—that's why he looked so familiar—it was her father as a boy!

Wait! Don't go!

Kelly hurried to catch up. She stood blinking in the hallway's brighter light. The pair was nowhere to be seen. Singing could still be heard in the distance.

Tired and perplexed, Kelly returned to her residence. The light again dimmed. This time, there was no conversation from her bedroom. Peering in, she found a woman lying on the bed. A man sat in the chair, watching the sleeping figure. His eyes were red and swollen, and a frown ridged his forehead. The woman was comely—beautiful, in fact. Her blonde hair had a luster that shimmered in the diffuse light. Her aquiline nose and high brow balanced the other noble features of her face. She lay very still, and Kelly suddenly wondered if she were merely asleep.

"Aye, ya were right," the man spoke. The textures in his voice were chewy and resonant, but they carried an overwhelming grief. "Alas, I was right too; the risk was too great. Yer sacrifice will buy us peace for a time, but at what cost? Fiona, we canna afford to lose ya." He stepped to the bed, looking down at her and choked, "*I* canna bear losin' ya." He stood, his gaze never leaving her form.

"Ya kenned the ancient lore aright. But at yer peril …" he wiped his tired eyes, shaking his head. "There's danger in that knowledge. Perhaps it's best hidden. In lesser hands it's deadly. In the wrong hands disastrous … an' yet, I sense we may need it before all is done."

If his eyes could have willed the woman back to life, she surely would have obliged him, if only to lessen his sorrow. He bent down and took her hand. He brushed his lips over it and gently removed a ring from her finger. "I'll need this fer a time." He then removed a silver pendant from around his neck and clasped both in his hand. "Together these will form the key."

He glanced to the foot of the bed where an oversized book with a stout binding lay. "I shall lock an' hide yer diary, an' the secret of its key. As I shall also hide my line. Thus my children's children will lie beyond reach—in safety, until the appointed time approaches." He looked up, focusing on something beyond the walls of the room. Clearing the husky grief from his voice, he pronounced, "Ages hence, an heir of our blood, with power eclipsin' even our own, shall discover what is hidden, trip what is locked, an' wield a magic long believed lost. With that one lies the hope of our people."

He again held the lifeless hand. "An' I promise that yer courage an' sacrifice shall be remembered in song. Our people will never forget ya, or the lore's promise for our future." He then fell to both knees and wept quietly, pressing Fiona's hand to his cheek.

Feeling like an unwanted observer, Kelly crept from the room, leaving the man to grieve in private. Standing in the bright hallway, she tried to understand what was happening.

This time when she entered her residence, the lights didn't dim. She slipped hesitantly into her bedroom. It seemed free of visitors, but she checked under the bed to be sure.

She lay in bed a short time later, her head crowded with the scenes she'd witnessed. The grieving man and the woman Fiona were unknown to her. His words meant little, but his speech and attire suggested the distant past.

She thought of her father as a boy. She could appreci-ate his fear of forgetting his mother. She often shared that worry. There was comfort in knowing he'd understand.

But Kelly was most drawn to the scene with her par-ents. It was from a time before she'd even seen their faces through infant eyes. Yet the solace she felt wasn't of remembrance. It was of wholeness. There they were, all three of them, together. Her family.

Something tugged at her subconscious. A stubborn half thought demanding attention pulled her back. Back to the scene of her father as a boy. What was it? What neglected observation itched so? Her father had been young, perhaps a year or two older than she was now. The older man was his father, a grandfather she never knew. The unasked question rose to the surface with a dread urgency: if, in that scene from long ago, her father's mother had recently died …

… *then who is Brid?*

8

BETRAYAL

Brid lied to me ... I have no grandmother ... I have no one ...

Kelly's mind stumbled from one awful idea to the next as she lay in bed. Despite her exhaustion, sleep eluded her. The betrayal was too fresh, too pointed. In one excruciating blow, it had wrenched any bits of recovered meaning from her life.

By the time dawn lightened the windows, Kelly still lacked answers and the questions themselves had become a jumbled knot in her head.

She opened her father's diary hoping she might find an entry that would fix the horrible truth; that would offer some unlikely, but acceptable, explanation. The pages, however, remained blank.

She dropped into an armchair and closed her eyes, her hand clasped around her mother's pendant.

Mom—can I be with you? Please!

Sleep finally overcame her; she dozed for a time until the presence of another in the room woke her. She was groggy and slow to grasp what she saw. She stared at her guest for a long, confused moment.

"Mom? Is that really you?"

Wordlessly her mother crossed to her and wrapped her daughter in an embrace. Kelly burst into a torrent of tears that tried to wash away the last six months as she clung to her mother.

"I don't know what to do," she whimpered. "If Brid's not my grandmother, then who is she? I can't face these people. I don't know who they are …"

Kelly's mother finally spoke, but it was as though her voice came from a great distance. "Don't be afraid to trust the people you love. You may sometimes get hurt, but life's about risking trust and love. Good Saven, sweetheart." Her mother kissed Kelly's forehead. "Now sleep …"

Some time later Kelly woke in the chair. The room was empty. She rose and gazed out the window at the teeming rain. The angry sky reflected Kelly's mood.

Why would Brid lie to her? That question haunted Kelly more than any other. Why build this elaborate ruse around Kelly's ancestry? Why had they lured her here? Child slavery? It seemed unlikely. Besides, most slaves don't get their own horse.

What did she have that they wanted? Nothing; she was just a thirteen-year-old gi—

Kelly had read about Turkish pirates kidnapping young maidens and selling them into harems, but that was centuries ago. And it was in Turkey. She'd never heard of a Scottish harem.

Could they mean to sell her off as a child bride? There were laws against that in the United States, but Kelly didn't know much about the Scottish legal system. The hopeful groom must have paid a lot of money for Brid to go to all this trouble. That could be how she supports the manor. Kelly might simply be the latest victim. It's always the fat, ugly ones who want the young girls. They can't attract a wife on their own, so they pay to have one stolen for them.

The thought of some yellow-toothed sot, reeking of cigars and stale scotch, pinning her in his clasp and then trying to kiss her … ugh! She shuddered with revulsion. Maybe it was child slavery after all.

Her unanswered questions stacked up like a proper Vermont woodpile. If she were strong she might have gone to Brid and demanded an explanation. But she wasn't. Instead she nursed a victim's resentment mixed with a solid dose of guilt over her own weakness.

It was her stomach that finally drove Kelly from her room—breakfast was long past. She trudged down the hall feeling none of the airy pleasure she usually did on a trip to the kitchen. That was because she realized the head kitchen-woman must also be a part of this deception.

Kelly saw more of her mother in Maggie than she did in Brid: the easy laugh and ready smile; the application of food as a balm for minor irritants; the fierce defense of pot or bowl, should a filching hand stray near. Maggie's kitchen was a safe zone where Kelly could go and breathe the familiar scents of a loving hearth ... until now.

The kitchen was always busy mid-day, but with the Saven feast later that afternoon, Kelly was met by culinary bedlam. The room seethed with an army of peelers, choppers, mincers, and stirrers, all pressed into service for the day. The job of managing this chaos required the planning skills of a master architect crossed with the steel of a drill sergeant, and it belonged to Maggie: whether it was the scaling and gutting of the fish, the scrubbing and peeling of the vegetables, or the seasoning and turning of the meat spits, little escaped her notice. At the moment, she was supervising the decoration of pastries that would grace the feast's dessert. A call from across the kitchen interrupted that operation to confirm the baking time of the steak pies.

Did you intend to lie to me? Or did Brid force you to ... even though you knew it was wrong ... that it would hurt me?

Maggie noticed Kelly's presence and flashed a cheerful smile. After imparting instructions to a young girl tasked with chopping leeks, Maggie walked over.

"Ah, lass, a good Saven to ya."

I know. There's no need to keep pretending.

Maggie's face folded in what could have been concern, except Kelly knew better. Still, it was a good act.

"Lassie, what is it that's troublin' ya?"

... unless ...

"Are ya all right, dearie?"

Is it possible you were deceived too?

There was care in Maggie's eyes that stirred Kelly's heart. From somewhere nearby the smell of bacon carried Kelly's thoughts to her kitchen back home. Her mother's words echoed in her head.

"Don't be afraid to trust the people you love."

Images of her mother overlaid Maggie's face. Kelly could only blink, confused.

Mom?

"Kelly?" A hint of worry was audible in Maggie's voice.

"Do you ... need help?" Kelly asked hesitantly. "Cooking ... can I help cook?"

Maggie nodded thoughtfully. "Aye. Perhaps a wee bit of cookin' will set ya right. Danu knows we could use more hands the now."

Maggie guided Kelly through the throng of workers to a table set back along the far wall near the cavernous brick ovens. Pale mounds of dough lay in orderly rows. They soaked the air with their yeasty fragrance as they basked in the heat thrown off by the ovens. Kelly closed her eyes and breathed deeply.

"Ach, there ya'd be," Maggie said as a young boy stepped around the corner. His skin glistened and beads of sweat fringed his eyebrows. Maggie took the long-handled bread peel from him and reached into the nearest oven. "Hmm …" she mused, "they'd be nearin' doneness, but I'd give them another few minutes." She set the peel down. "Now young Will, Kelly here is goin' to help with the cooking. Get her whatever she needs. An' mind ya, keep an eye on this bread—I'll nay be serving burnt loaves this Saven feast."

The boy appeared to be several years younger than Kelly. He had yet to say a word; he simply stared at his feet. His slumped shoulders and tucked chin suggested an effort to achieve smallness. He buried his hands in his pockets.

"I'm Kelly." She stuck out her hand.

No response.

"Your name is Will?"

He looked up with doe-like eyes. "Willie." He practically whispered.

Her hand didn't budge. She left it hanging there in the space between them.

Give a shake. We can be friends.

Ever so timidly, Willie dragged his hand out of hiding and reached out with it. Before he could change his mind, Kelly grasped it and gave a solid shake. "Hi, Willie." Her smile sealed the bond.

"What do you need?" Willie spoke in a diffident voice.

Kelly hadn't considered what she'd actually make. She looked at the peel and then at the ranks of dough balls.

"How about pizza?"

"Pizza?" he asked.

"You've *never* had pizza before?" She couldn't fathom such a staple in her diet—pizza was its own food group—might be completely absent from another kid's. Growing up without pizza. It was serious. Bordering on child abuse. They'd have to correct the problem. There was still time to save him.

Willie stuffed his hands deeper into his pockets and stared at the floor, shifting his feet. Realizing how her question must have sounded, she felt badly. Willie seemed earnest in what he did, acting as though he should take the world at face value. Kelly feared it might leave him vulnerable to those who did not.

"I think you'll like it," she promised. "I'll show you how to make it."

They began with the dough. She taught Willie how to use his closed fists to spread the dough into a flat disk. Willie learned the two hazards of spreading pizza dough. The first occurred quickly and with little warning. His eyes widened in alarm as a hole tore across his disk where the dough stretched thinnest. Kelly reassured him and stretched and pinched some of the thicker areas to patch the tear. The second near-catastrophe followed soon after the first. The dough behaved like an under-filled water balloon and one side rolled away from his fists and oozed down to the floor. Willie gasped. Kelly managed to catch it just before it hit. With more massaging they eventually had a heavily repaired disk of dough, ready for the next step.

"Now we add the sauce," Kelly explained. "Any tomato sauce?"

He shook his head. "We have other sauces."

"All right, we'll improvise." Kelly sent him with a bowl to find something suitable. When he returned she looked doubtfully at the bowl's contents. "What is this stuff?"

"It's the gravy for the roast. It's made with potatoes and bacon and celery and port wine."

Not trusting herself to respond, Kelly simply smiled and showed him how to spread the reddish-brown goo on the dough.

"Next we need cheese. Is there any mozzarella?"

He shook his head.

"Ok … what *do* we have?"

Willie led Kelly to a bench stacked with wheels of fresh goat cheese. Fingers were the best way to crumble the soft cheese, and soon sticky white gobs coated their hands. Kelly gave a trial lick. It had a tangy, sharp flavor; she hoped it went well with bacon and port wine.

"Last come the toppings. Pepperoni?"

He shook his head no.

"Then I'll rely on you to choose. Pick a few things that you think will go well together."

Willie nodded solemnly, accepting the assignment.

A raspy hiss overhead caused Kelly to glance up. Perched in the rafters above her, the barn owl reviewed the scene.

"I'm sorry, but you cannot choose the toppings—there'll be no mice on this pizza!"

The owl ruffled its feathers and hissed a *shiiish*.

Willie was soon back, juggling three bowls in his arms. The first contained walnut halves. The second, raisins—Kelly had to get this boy some real pizza—and the third bowl held pieces of a dark meat.

"It's venison!" Willie seemed pleased with his selections.

Kelly did her best to look encouraging.

We're making a Bambi pizza. Maybe I shouldn't have been so hasty about the mice.

Willie spread the toppings with the care of an artist, as if one misplaced raisin might ruin the whole creation. Finally he exhaled a long breath and looked expectantly to Kelly.

She nodded encouragement. "We'll hold the baking until just before the feast. Congratulations—you've made your first pizza!"

Sort of …

The kitchen boy glowed with pride.

"Willie!" a voice shrilled.

Marching over to them, Rhona paused to examine herself in the high polish of the stainless counter top, smoothing her hair back to her apparent satisfaction. She didn't even bother to look at Willie when she addressed him. "We've no time for your foolery on a feast day. Go down to the wine cellar and fetch some bottles of claret." She straightened her apron as if it were precious silk and not threadbare cotton soaked in dishwater. "And then finish your chores *without* distraction," she ordered before she paraded off.

Dismissive and self-absorbed. Over what—Raggedy Anne hair?

"Why can't she go get them herself?" Kelly muttered.

"She's afraid."

"Huh?"

"The wine cellar is haunted." His expression was sincere as always.

"No kidding ... aren't you afraid to go down there?"

Willie shrugged, "I don't have trouble, but when she goes it upsets the ghost."

Smart ghost.

"Willie!" Rhona's voice carried across the kitchen to them.

"You go ahead," Kelly waved him on. "I'll watch the bread."

&

The crusts gradually deepened to a dark golden-amber. Maggie appeared as Kelly was about to slide the peel in for inspection.

"Aye, I thought they'd be nearly done."

Kelly's defenses snapped back into place. Had Maggie been a part of the deception? If so, her pretense now was cruel. Yet Kelly couldn't fully accept it. Not Maggie.

She silently helped Maggie extract the baked loaves and replace them with four of the risen dough mounds awaiting their turn. Kelly set the floury peel down and rested her hand on the countertop as she struggled for something to say into the uncomfortable silence. Maggie gently laid her own hand atop. Kelly wanted to yank her hand away, but for whatever reason, she couldn't bring herself to do it.

"I saw yer smiles earlier, lass. Yer's an' young Will's. They were sunshine, they were."

That was private. Between Willie and me. It doesn't make what you've done all right.

Maggie's palm was warm from handling the just-baked loaves.

Tell me you didn't do it. Tell me you didn't know …

"If ya dunna wish to talk now, ya dunna have to."

Tell me she made you do it …

"But know yer always welcome here!"

After Maggie left, Kelly's hand remained on the counter, now strangely missing the contact.

Kelly busied herself, helping around the kitchen for the remainder of the afternoon. The activity was sufficiently distracting for a time, but as the hour of the feast approached, the acid in her stomach churned with the vigor of a washing machine. The thought of confronting Brid terrified her: coyote scared. Like a coyote caught in a trap, she'd chew off her own leg if it meant she could escape. She longed for the anonymity of the lower tables, but tonight was a high feast and she was to sit at the high table. Beside Brid. A seat of honor. A coyote-scared-chicken seat.

Allisdair assembled the guests and Brid glided into the hall on cue. Brid's bearing, so dignified and erect, reminded Kelly of her failed attempts at balancing books. She felt foolish and embarrassed—not because her posture stank, but because of her own gullibility. To have been sucked in so easily. She'd allowed herself to believe because it was attractive to do so. They must have been counting on that. The thought made Kelly even angrier.

As the dinner guests took their seats, Brid placed a hand on Kelly's arm and bid her a good Saven. The touch scalded, but Kelly somehow managed to choke out, "Good Saven" in reply.

It wasn't long into the dinner when things went from horrible to truly ghastly. Brid announced to the table, "Kelly has a surprise for us this evening."

Kelly's eyes bulged, as if shocked with a mega-amp jolt.

"She's made us pizza," Brid told them.

No! I meant that for the lower tables! They'll eat anything.

The oxygen seemed to suck out of the room as the pizza was brought to the head table. The masters murmured with curiosity and Brid asked if Kelly would do the honor of serving them. Kelly stood on jelly legs as she served up the pie. Nobody moved as she retook her seat; they were all watching her. What now?

Brid leaned over and softly asked, "Would you like to take the first bite, Kelly?"

Kelly bit into her slice, but her mouth refused to work. Lockjaw set in and her tongue flailed about helplessly.

She somehow managed to swallow the bite whole, not even noticing how it tasted.

To survive dinner, Kelly imagined herself sitting at a bus stop surrounded by courteous strangers. Whenever asked a question, she'd answer politely with remote detachment. She shoved her roiling emotions and unanswered questions behind a door in her mind that she locked tightly. They didn't go away. They just festered, bunched and ready to burst out upon their release.

Kelly flinched at another touch to her arm. "Is everything all right? You're very quiet." The bus-stop woman had spoken.

"I'm just tired. I didn't sleep well last night," Kelly answered.

"Why don't you retire then? I hope you feel better in the morning. Good Saven, Kelly."

Back in her residence, sleep was impossible. She was too tired, too hurt, and too angry. The mullioned windows became bars, her room a cage. They let the cub out during the day to get exercise and fresh air, returning her to her cage at night. Except tonight the cub couldn't rest. She paced behind the bars. Trapped and betrayed, Kelly didn't want to play the zookeeper's game any longer.

She escaped to the liberty of the hall, unsure what she wanted. She wandered heedless of where she headed and grew accustomed to the echo of her footsteps, so was quite surprised when she nearly ran into Master David.

"Kelly, what are you doing up at this hour?"

"I … couldn't sleep."

The bard's expression was inscrutable. "Really? Your grandmother said you were exhausted and retired early. Or so I thought."

"I was … I mean, I am … but I couldn't!" Fatigue and frustration clamped down on Kelly's brain, paralyzing rational thought. She turned away from the master, wishing he'd just leave her alone.

"Kelly … Kelly?" He gently, but insistently turned her shoulders back towards him. "I wouldn't be much of a bard if I weren't adept at reading an audience. It's obvious you're struggling with something. Come," he bid, guiding her down the hall. "Sit with me while I enjoy some of this wine Rhona was good enough to leave out for me." He raised the flagon in his left hand.

Back in the music room, he filled two glasses, setting them on the table between them.

"Take a sip. It will help calm you."

Kelly dutifully drank a small mouthful. It tingled as she swallowed, with a warm sensation that began in her mouth and slid down into her gut.

"Ah," the bard breathed, following a healthy swallow, "she rewards me with fine vintages on feast nights in appreciation of my labors." His face flushed with the contentment of a cat as he savored the wine.

They sat in silence. Each afforded the other privacy for thought—Master David because he was in no hurry, and Kelly because she wasn't yet ready to unlock the door in her mind. It was a patient silence. Kelly didn't feel pressure to speak just to fill the quiet spaces. After a time, Master David picked up a pennywhistle and played a slow air. The sound was of wind blowing through cattails beside a pond. When the tune ended, he played another and then another, swelling the silence that wanted no words more aptly with music.

A particularly mournful air caught Kelly's attention. "What was that song?"

Mom used to hum that when she was out cutting flowers for the kitchen table. I thought it was just something she'd made up.

"It's called *Morgan's Lament*. Morgan lived a thousand years ago, the greatest bard since Cairbre in the days of myth." Master David's baritone had the sonority of a cello, beautifully complimenting the high pipe of the penny-whistle. "He grieves for Fiona, the woman he loved. She discovered an ancient power, but in trying to wield it, it killed her. In his song, Morgan tells that he hid her secret. But he vows that a descendant of his and Fiona's will one day rediscover that secret. That's the riddle he leaves us, for they never had a child together. It's a mournful tune, but did you hear the modulation to a major key in the final phrase?" Master David replayed it. "It ends with a glint of hope."

"I never knew it had words," she confessed; her mother had only ever hummed it.

Master David laid the pennywhistle on the table. "You're hurting."

Kelly stared at the glass in her hands, intent on the trembling surface of the liquid. She wasn't ready to unlock the door yet, but perhaps she could talk *about* what it held back.

"Someone I trusted lied to me. A terrible lie."

"Have you spoken to this person?"

"No," she answered softly, "I'm not sure how to."

"So, you've bottled all this up inside you, and now the pain won't even let you sleep."

Kelly could only nod at his shrewd guesses.

"Have another sip. It'll relax you." He pointed to her glass and waited while she obeyed. "Have you considered that there may be some other explanation—that perhaps your trust wasn't betrayed and this person didn't lie to you?"

Kelly shook her head. "In this case it's obvious."

"Hmm … I've found life to be subtle and rarely obvious. There's typically an 'obvious' answer to any question, yet it's amazing how often an overlooked, improbable case ends up being the true explanation. I've come to learn that I should doubt those things I feel most sure of.

"Kelly, there's comfort in seeing the world as black and white. It's easier to understand the things around us if they're either one or the other. But despite how we'd like to have it, the world exists in countless shades of gray. Some are darker and some are lighter, but seldom is there pure black or pure white. Right and wrong, good and evil—these aren't conditions where you cross a threshold and you suddenly switch from one to the other. They're merely the extreme end-points of a continuous line—a line on which our lives exist in the middle. Not black. Not white. Just shades of gray."

Master David leaned forward and wrapped his hands around Kelly's as she held her glass. "Kelly, you've got to speak with the person you believe wronged you. You can't assume a lie until you've heard both sides of the story." He let her hands go with a gentle squeeze and instructed her to finish her wine. "Do you think you can sleep?"

"I don't know," she answered truthfully.

"Well, if not, a bit of fresh air might help—just don't venture far at this hour!"

The idea of slipping out was appealing. Leaving the manor house, Kelly stepped out into a wild autumn night. The chill wind was bracing; its gusts scattered the fallen leaves up into the air and then in turn collected them in the crannies and corners of the buildings, where they waited to be scattered again. The moon was nearly full and it painted the world in the shades of gray Master David had described.

Kelly found herself walking to the stables out of habit. As she entered, Gealach's nicker surprised her.

"Hey, girl, can't you sleep either?" She reached to pet the white blaze on her horse's forehead.

In answer, Gealach pranced about her stall with a rebellious snort.

"What's gotten into you? You act like we're going riding."

Gealach kicked up, neighing in affirmation.

And that's when Kelly decided. It normally wouldn't have occurred to her. Riding at night in the Highlands of Scotland isn't safe; the rocky, uneven mountain trails can be treacherous in the dark, and the deep, untamed forests that bordered the manor are home to any number of nocturnal creatures—harmless enough by day, but an entirely different matter at night. There was probably even a rule against it, but Kelly had never bothered to find out, because she had more sense than to try. Until tonight. If Brid wasn't her grandmother, then Kelly didn't belong here, and in her mind that placed her above the laws of the household.

Whether it was the feral wind that goaded Kelly, or Gealach's conspiratorial encouragement, once Kelly had the idea she never stopped to consider if it was wise. She saddled up her horse and mounted. With a mighty spring, Gealach plunged out into the world of shadows, leaving the safety of the stables quickly behind.

They raced across open fields and meadows, eventually crossing under the dark cover of the forest. Kelly rode recklessly. Defiant. Urging Gealach to run faster. As they settled into the rhythm of the gallop, she found Gealach anticipating her commands. Her legs could feel the hardened horse sinews flexing and driving beneath her. In the stillness of the forest, she could hear Gealach breathing to the beat of hooves striking the trail.

She listened to the rhythmic breaths, her mind slipping further and further into the sound until it enveloped her. She felt an insistence to run—to escape the civilized world, to race ahead of the wind. Kelly's consciousness slid deeper, drawn down by a great weight. She saw the forest through Gealach's eyes; she could feel the ground as each hoof landed. Gealach's breathing was an irresistible pulse beating through it all. In, out; in, out. Down—further down she slid.

Then she sensed an echo of hoof beats. She was aware of Gealach running beside her. Her equine senses vaguely registered that she was now a horse running abreast of her own. She didn't care, though. Horses aren't concerned with shape-shifting and her mind had slipped so far, there was no conscious part of Kelly left. Running was everything—the thundering drumbeat of her hooves, the bunch and spring of her powerful legs, the stretch and counterbalance of her neck.

On they ran. Branches and brambles whipped out at her, bouncing painlessly off her tough hide. She could feel a sheen of sweat form, but she wasn't tired. Blasts of wind swirled the leaves around her hooves and still they ran.

An animal scream slashed through the tempo of their cadence and Kelly reeled under a tremendous blow. Her strides faltered. Her shoulder and back burned with white-hot pain. She reared up and neighed defiance. Turning, she spied her assailant, just as the large mountain lion jumped back at her with a snarl. The cat locked claws and teeth on Kelly's neck. She again reared, striking out with her hooves, trying to shake her attacker free. Again and again the cat sprang and Kelly defended. It was getting harder. Time seemed to run in slow motion. The world around her became muffled and distant. She could hear Gealach's neighs, but they sounded far off. Her nostrils flared as her horse senses recognized the metallic smell around her—blood. And then darkness.

9

A Faerie Grandmother

A grizzled wolf bounded up the trail, the dark overhang of the trees camouflaging its shadowy form. It halted when it came upon the gory tableau: one horse stomping and rearing, a distressed sentry guarding a second—a still form awash in a sea of blood, legs tangled with those of a mountain lion, also lying motionless.

The wolf settled back on its haunches. Raising its muzzle, it trumpeted a howl that reverberated off the nearby pines. Allisdair suddenly stood where the wolf had been. He moved to the mountain lion, laying his palms on its side. After a long minute he turned to the injured horse. Cradling its bloody head in his arms, he closed his eyes and drew a deep, steadying breath.

The percussive beat of wings shuddered the night air. An eagle descended through the pine boughs and alighted beside Allisdair. A moment later, Conall stood there.

He took in the scene. "What's happened?"

"Danu knows how she shifted," Allisdair answered. "It's Kelly."

"Is all of this blood hers?"

"Aye," Allisdair shook his head. "It's bad. Her physical wounds are mortal; psychically she's extremely deep without an anchor; an' that cat was no ordinary beast—I sense a strong evil at work. We've got to shift Kelly back *now*; if she slips any further she'll pass beyond any of our skill."

Stripping off his gloves, Conall knelt on the bloody ground. He placed his hands on the horse's neck, trying to avoid the hemorrhaging rents and gashes. "You lead," he told Allisdair. "I'll anchor you. Draw upon my strength as you need."

The only measure of time's passage, as they concentrated on the shattered body before them, was the dying horse's breaths, each weaker than the last. Finally, a shudder rocked their bodies and beneath their hands lay Kelly's wracked and bloody form.

Conall stood, wiping sweat from his brow despite the chill night.

"Go! Let her know we're comin'," Allisdair commanded. "An' then scour the forest. I want answers."

The *galloglas* nodded. A moment later the golden eagle launched skyward and flew off.

Gealach's ears laid back flat and her eyes swirled white with distress. Allisdair fixed those eyes with his own. "As ya love yer mistress's life, ya must carry us both with the speed of the wind if we're to save her."

Gealach quieted as Allisdair mounted with Kelly in his arms. "Go then!" he cried and Gealach sped into the night, as fast as any horse could run.

A silent and grim-faced gathering met Allisdair in the manor courtyard. Jillian and Conall carefully lifted down Kelly's body and laid her on a waiting stretcher. Brid assessed her condition, and then waved for them to take her in.

She turned to Allisdair, her expression grave. "It's too soon to know."

His face was inscrutable.

"We each have much to do. We'll speak later," Brid said before she turned and strode into the house.

The lights shone brightly in the infirmary throughout the night, as Brid fought to keep Kelly on this side of the Otherworld. Under those lights, Kelly's eggshell pallor suggested she'd already left this life, but her irregular breaths belied her appearance—breaths so feeble a whisper could snuff them. Under those lights, a bluish tinge developed around her lips, hands, and feet. Not a good sign—it represented cyanosis: through internal injuries and loss of blood, Kelly's body was starving for oxygen. As the night wore on, red-soaked rags piled up in harsh contrast to the room's antiseptic whiteness.

Brid worked on, mending torn organs, shredded muscles and severed blood vessels. A quiet woman, petite in stature, assisted with practiced hands. Ina, a journeyman herbalist and healer, had trained under Brid herself. Now, with silent determination, she applied all of her skill to help Brid save her granddaughter.

Hours passed. At some point after a disregarded sunrise, Brid stepped back and shook her head. "We're losing this battle. Might there be something else at work here?" She thought for a long moment. "Conall reported a powerful force had twisted that cat's being. There may have been a psychic attack as well ..."

Brushing aside their fatigue, Brid and Ina redoubled their efforts, this time focusing their healing on Kelly's mind. The hours crawled by. Exhaustion creased Ina's face, causing her seventeen years to appear several times that. Brid's features were unchanging. If she tired from her labor, she showed no sign.

Gradually, ever so gradually, Kelly's erratic breathing evened. The blue that fringed her extremities faded and her complexion seemed less cadaverous. The vertical rays at the windows suggested a noonday sun before Brid and

Ina finally pulled back from Kelly's mind. They took seats beside the bed, noting the subtle yet important changes in Kelly's appearance.

"It was well we checked," Brid said. "At least now she has a chance."

"She's young." Ina massaged her temples. "And I sensed a strong resilience under the dampening evil." Her eyes were a hazel wash of sympathy and admiration for her mentor. "Would you like me to sit with her?"

"Nay," Brid waved aside the offer. "You go rest. I'll stay with her. I have much to think on."

Ina bowed her head. "As you wish."

☙

Sometime later the infirmary door opened, interrupting Brid's vigil. Allisdair took a seat beside her and waited for her to speak first. She was a long time gazing at Kelly's unconscious form, and when she did address him, it was without turning away from her granddaughter.

"What have you learned?"

"Little, as yet. Conall's men are combin' the forest, but it appears there was just the one cat …" Allisdair trailed off. "I'm sorry, *Bean-rìgh*." The remorse in his whisper was plain.

"No—I'll not have you apologizing, Allisdair. You've been cautioning of a lurking threat. You're ever insistent that we remain watchful. You have served me well. This shall *not* lie on your head."

They sat in silence for several minutes until Brid turned to him with eyes of blue-diamond hardness. "You've spoken of what you're certain. Now tell me what you suspect."

He nodded. "A mountain lion attacked her. Not a Scottish native, it's proof this was deliberate an' well planned. The ... derangement of the animal's mind was complex an' skillful. An' equally merciless. There's no question an agent of Bres arranged the attack. There's also no question the individual responsible is among us."

"I guessed as much," Brid mused. "Nor is the timing coincidence." She gave an indignant *humph*. "How like Bres to stage an attack on Saven and try to force his own ending to the prophecy."

Allisdair grunted. "We havena yet spoken of the *Sidhe*. Did yer visit offer any answers?"

"Yes," she sighed. "But not in the manner expected." Kelly's weedy breaths could be heard behind Brid's pause. "Ages ago, in a time when the hills were still young, Cairbre spoke to me of my path.

"He said,

> *'Victory in your struggle shall not belong to you.*
> *Another will one day come for whom that path is true.*
> *You first must become lost for life's road to be discovered.*
> *Only in your wandering, will your purpose be uncovered.*

Bereft of guide you'll be; blind of sight and deaf to kin,
And from within that darkness will your life's true task begin.'

"Following Fiona's death, on the eve Morgan left us, Riagall came to me in my garden. I waited for some message, some sign, but he simply blinked his eyes and flew off. I didn't know it at the time, but that was the last I was to see him."

"Bereft of guide?" Allisdair surmised.

"Thus, I believe. Then, just after Hamish and Gwendolyn moved to America, my second sight left me. The loss of my future-vision has been a heavy one—particularly now when we most need answers.

Allisdair held her gaze. "An' 'deaf to kin'?"

"It's been many seasons since I last visited the *Sidhe*, but the undying race changes little. Until now. When I went to my people on Saven Eve, they knew me and greeted me—their eyes told as much—but when they spoke, it was as if a great wind sucked the air from their throats before any sound could escape.

"Cairbre's words from an age long forgotten have thus been fulfilled. Presumably, I shall hence learn my true contribution to life's wheel."

Allisdair stared down at his brogues, weighing Brid's news. "I canna see the prophecies in this time an' this place. To me, they belong to an age now remote."

Brid's eyes unfocused as though gazing inward some great distance. "Perhaps they do belong to an earlier time, when Gods walked freely among men, when a blessing could treble a harvest or a curse maim a body. And yet these prophecies come down to us out of that past. Their power is dormant but not diminished."

Allisdair rose from his seat and paced to the window. "If the prophecies direct our lives, why should any of us act?"

"Our actions *do* have effect, Allisdair. They can alter futures and color inevitabilities. A prophecy is not a promise that something *will* happen. It's more of an offer that something *could* happen."

After a thoughtful silence, Brid turned to her granddaughter's bed. "Do you have any idea how Kelly managed to shift?"

Allisdair threw up his hands. "By the sword of Lugh, I canna answer that—either how she learned or from where she drew the power. Roy was as stunned as I when I told him. The only journeyman adept enough to teach her would be Dougal."

Brid's face grew stern. "He hasn't been long with us. Does Roy think Dougal might have broken his oath?"

"Accordin' to Roy, there have been incidents with some of the apprentices, but not of sufficient substance to accuse him of somethin' so serious. Roy doesna believe Dougal's the answer. I have to agree. But I'm without any other explanation."

"We shouldn't discount the possibility that Kelly shifted on her own," Brid mused.

Allisdair shook his head. "Ach, that's impossible. She's too young. Seeds of latent power, perhaps. But as complex a shift as a horse? Absolutely not. Most of our journeymen dunna have the psychic strength to accomplish it."

"I understand your skepticism, but we have no other explanation. Until we do, we have to consider it a possibility—however unlikely."

"This takes us back to a fifteen-year-old question: who was Gwendolyn?"

"Unless Kelly herself holds the key to her mother's lineage, we will not learn more than we already know." Brid's eyes rested on her granddaughter, whose skin now showed the first hint of color. "Last night's events carried Kelly into the center of our struggle, whether or not it was our intention to involve her. If she recovers, Danu willing, I sense she'll play a part in whatever's coming. We must prepare her."

As Allisdair drew breath to respond, Brid raised a hand.

"I know well the risks of training one so young, but hasn't Kelly demonstrated the risk of no training? I don't want to lose her, Allisdair. I *will* protect her."

"Could it be that ya love this one?" he asked softly.

Brid dismissed his question with a wave of her hand. "I loved all my children."

"Aye, as a mother would. But a mother can also have a special one—a child who's touched an unplayed string in her heart."

They stood in silence gazing at Kelly. Allisdair, apparently reaching some decision, dropped to one knee and pledged, "We will train her. *We* will protect her."

⚭

She was underwater. She thought herself a jellyfish. Undulating. Buoyant in the bathtub-warm waters. She felt safe, which seemed important. The little light there was came from high above and was fractured and distorted by all the sea in between. Sounds were muffled and distant. The sensation of floating suffused her, as if that were the only possible state of being.

Her mind was lazing and not interested in sharp thought. Still, she thought it curious she wasn't out of breath. The notion that she might need to breathe nudged her upward. Pulsing through the currents, riding the rhythm of the ocean. Up. Unhurried upward.

The surface was slow to draw near. She must have been deeper than she realized. But no rush. No urgency. It was a leisurely undulation and that seemed fine. Gradually, the lights brightened and sounds were discernable. Dancing sparkles told her she was close. With one final thrust she pushed up to break the surface.

Kelly vaguely realized that she hadn't been in the water at all. Her thoughts were slow and heavy as if every idea weighed a thousand pounds. Even simple thoughts were laborious and tired her. Her eyelids were crusted shut and refused to open.

"Kelly, how are you feeling?"

She knew the voice was a familiar one, but it was too much work to identify its owner.

"Kelly?"

"I'm okay," she tried to say, but the words croaked out like coarse sandpaper scratching her throat.

"Are you in pain?"

Pain? Was she in pain? Whatever the answer was, it weighed too much; it was too heavy for Kelly's brain to consider.

"I'm okay," she rasped.

Someone held her hand and gave it a gentle squeeze.

That's nice. Like mom used to do.

"Sleep, dear one," the voice urged.

And she did.

෴

"Kelly?"

That voice again.

"Brid."

Kelly pried her eyes open, letting the room's light spill into her head. She blinked and squinted until her vision slowly adjusted. But when she finally could see, the room wasn't familiar.

"You're in the infirmary. Are you in any pain?"

What Kelly felt was sensory overload. But pain? When she gave a test squirm she gasped. She drew a deep breath in through her teeth and concentrated on lying very still. "I'm all right if I don't move," she admitted groggily. As the pain's sharpness faded to an ache, a parching thirst replaced it. "May I have a glass of water?"

Brid held a cup to her lips, letting her sip it at her own pace. "You'll be thirsty. You lost a lot of blood and will have to build your fluids back up."

What was Brid talking about?

"Tell me what you remember." Brid pulled her chair closer. Her voice was soft and encouraging. It brought back Kelly's earlier sensation of floating. Of safety.

"I … I'm not sure. It was dark … and windy … Gealach—I went riding …" Kelly tried to recall. "It's fuzzy after that."

"You went for a ride at night. Think about the ride. Do you remember setting out?"

Kelly nodded.

"You left the stables. Then what happened?" Brid's voice had a soothing quality that urged Kelly to answer.

"We were galloping … running. Running was everything. Yes … I remember Gealach galloped … beside me." Her voice was distant as she relived the scene. "We were in the forest … on the trail … we were going to run all … Nooooo!" Kelly's body arched as her anguished cry held in the air.

"It's all right Kelly—you're safe now. It's only a memory. There's no danger here—you're safe!" There was a note of command in Brid's voice that could not be ignored.

Kelly trembled in her bed, still caught in her recollection of the attack. "It kept leaping at me. Biting. Clawing." Tears ran down her face. "I tried to fight it, but it just kept coming …" she sobbed.

"Hush now!" Brid gently ordered. "It's all past. You're safe." She held tightly to Kelly's hand. The physical contact slowly brought Kelly back to the present. "Take deep breaths; they'll help calm you."

Kelly did as she was told. Gradually the tightness in her chest eased and her body ceased shaking.

"That's better." Brid still held Kelly's hand. It was an anchor of reassurance. "We can continue later, if you wish."

The concern and caring in Brid's voice were like a drug that smoothed the sharp edges of Kelly's distress. She didn't want Brid to leave her, to release her hand, to stop speaking to her. She didn't want to continue later. She'd do it now if only to keep Brid beside her.

"I'm all right," she whispered. The meager strength she had was fast waning.

Just stay with me.

Brid's voice was comforting. Safe. "Kelly, who helped you shift that night?" she asked with perfect calm.

... Who helped me? That's a funny question. Well, I suppose ...

"... Gealach did." Kelly's words had a distant, dreamy edge. Sleep was claiming her.

"Gealach?"

Kelly's eyes fluttered shut. "I was listening to her breathing ... and then I slipped into her mind ... I didn't mean to shift," she answered lazily.

"Have you shifted before?" Brid's eyes sparked with a bright intensity that belied the gentle lull of her voice.

"Oh sure. Just never by accident ..." And with that Kelly was fast asleep.

☙

Soft activity in the room woke Kelly, but Brid was no longer present. She didn't recognize the young woman who placed clean linens in one of the many cupboards lining the wall. She watched her for a time, but the journeyman healer's skills were attuned to her patient; it wasn't long before she turned, aware that Kelly no longer slept.

"That was a good rest," she said by way of greeting. "You'll find you'll tire easily for several days." She continued tucking linens into their assigned cubbies. "Don't fight it; give in to the desire to sleep. Your body knows best what it needs." Her tone was professional, but not perfunctory. Her words carried concern, as did her expression.

"I'm Ina—I'm helping care for you. I hope you're comfortable; it's difficult to be so in a strange bed." Ina gestured to the south window. Clustered pots covered its sill, displaying sprays of flowers in vibrant hues. "Scotland's an unlikely place to raise orchids, but I can't help myself—I love them so much. I thought you might enjoy them while you recuperate." The orchids gave off a delicate fragrance that lingered in the air. If you sniffed too hard, you'd breathe right past it.

Ina's kindness did lift Kelly's heart, but it also embarrassed her: that someone she didn't know should worry so much about her.

"Th … thank you."

"Oh, no worries!" And as if Ina's words had power, Kelly's unease evaporated.

"Your grandmother should be back soon. Since your accident, she's barely left you. She never steps out for long."

My grandmother …

Kelly smiled to herself, remembering the comfort Brid's presence had been … of her holding Kelly's hand …

… my grandmother …

It was at that moment all the memories of Saven Eve and Saven Day came flooding back. Despite her pain and fatigue, she was fully alert when Brid stepped into the room a short time later. Kelly watched stiffly, without comment, as Ina took her leave and Brid settled in the chair beside the bed.

"It's good to see you stronger," Brid began.

"Who are you?" Kelly's demand dripped with accusation.

"Whatever do you mean?"

"I know you're not my grandmother. So why do you pretend to be?"

"What makes you say this?" Brid appeared baffled.

"I know my father's mother died when he was young." Her smugness slapped at Brid.

The older woman's eyes widened. She nodded slightly. "And thus fate drives our choices," she murmured. "Kelly,

I'm going to answer you with a story—a story that begins in Ireland."

Brid's voice took on a rich, musical quality not unlike Master David's when he regaled the Great Hall with a tale. The sound was pleasant and made Kelly want to hear more. It also made her want to believe, and her suspicions ebbed as Brid wove her words.

"In the days back beyond the memory of men, there lived a race of tall, comely people. They possessed deep knowledge of the earth, the elements, and nature. They reveled in music and cherished wisdom and learning. They were called the *Tuatha de Danann*, the children of Danu. Among them, the bards safeguarded the music and history of the people, protecting the knowledge of the race and passing it down to future generations.

"When their kingdom was overrun by the mortal Sons of Mil, the *Tuatha de Danann* departed, leaving Ireland to the humans. Some chose to go to *Tir na Nog*—the land of youth—a far off isle in the west. Some chose to reside in *Tir fo Thuinn*—the land under the waves. Most went to live in the *Sidhe*—the hollow hills. Calling upon the secrets of the earth and the energies of nature, what men would call magic in later times, they created these hidden places beyond the realm of human perception.

"A very few of the *Tuatha de Danann* chose to remain among men, helping to protect and defend humans against an ancient evil that still existed in their world." Brid paused, a curious gleam in her eyes.

Kelly wondered what musty legends had to do with her.

"I am *Tuatha de Danann*, Kelly. One of the first. I am the last of my people living in this world. You are descended from me in direct lineage, so I *am* your grandmother, albeit hundreds of generations lie between us. Have you never considered your surname? Mac, *mhic* in Gaelic, means 'the child of.' Hence, MacBride means 'child of Brid.'"

They sat in silence while Kelly slowly absorbed Brid's news. "You look good for your age," she finally said.

"The *Tuatha de Danann* are unfading. While we can be killed—and Danu knows many kith and kin died in our early wars—we do not grow old. In the *Sidhe*, all are strong and beautiful. I've chosen this appearance, because it raises fewer questions."

Kelly asked, "Am I … tu … tu-a …"

"*Tuatha de Danann*," Brid spoke the name slowly. "You have some Tuathan blood, as your shape-shifting ability proves. However, intermarriage with humans over the centuries has thinned the bloodline. Its strength and power are now greatly diminished. Only once in a very great age will it run nearly true, and that hasn't happened in a millennium. Morgan, the bard prophet, descended from the great Cairbre, had nearly pure Tuathan blood, as did Fiona, of my line.

"Enough family history." Brid stood. "You've much healing left to do." She gave Kelly's hand a squeeze. "I bid you sleep now."

Kelly stared at the door long after Brid had left.

I'm glad you're really my grandmother …

"*Bean-rìgh*, may I speak with ya …"
Bean-rìgh. He always calls her that. Like a nickname. But he doesn't say it like you would a nickname. He's never casual and friendly when he says it. Always respectful and very serious. Bean-rìgh …
"… is very sick. Aye, Ina helped to heal …"
"… what were the symptoms …"
"… dry mouth … sensitivity to light … very seriously ill."
In her dream, Allisdair and Brid were discussing her. But dreams can be funny—they can trundle along just fine, when they'll suddenly go all weird.
"… has had no voice these last two days."
Huh? My voice is fine.
"Are you sure? Do you know what this means?"
Laryngitis?
"Aye, which is why I came right to ya after Ina told me."
"Allisdair, it can only be deadly nightshade. Belladonna. Someone's poisoned David."
That roused Kelly awake as she realized this conversation wasn't the fuzzy creation of her dreaming sub-conscious. Kelly lay there feigning sleep as she continued to eavesdrop.
"Do we know how it happened?"

"He's convinced it was in the wine he drank two nights ago, after his performance on Saven night. He was most distraught when he heard it was poison; he had shared that wine with Kelly when she had trouble sleepin'."

"Belladonna! That would explain why we struggled so to keep her alive. Allisdair, I must ensure David is out of danger. Take me to him at once!"

⚬

Bella. It means beautiful. Kelly knew a smattering of Italian. Louisa Scardina, a music teacher who'd worked with Kelly's mom in the school back home, had taught her. Whenever Louisa stopped by their house to visit, she set to work on Kelly's linguistic tutelage.

"Where is my bella bambina?" she'd demand, until Kelly was seated before her—usually with a glass of sparkling water for each of them.

The trick to proper Italian (or English, with a proper Italian accent) is to identify the special syllable. In each word, one syllable stands above the others and gets all the emphasis. Take "bella." To say it correctly you have to hang on "bel" until you're practically out of breath. Then in that final gasp before you pass out, you squeak "la." Now take "bambina." (It really means very young child. At age thirteen, Kelly might have been offended being called a bambina, except that one, it was Louisa doing the calling, and two, she'd been doing it since Kelly had been a bambina.) In "bambina," the second syllable is the special one. Bam-biiiii-na. Belllll-la bam-biiiii-na. It means beauuuuu-ti-ful chiiiii-ld.

Poison.
Belladonna.
Bella.
Beautiful.

A beautiful murder.
Beautifully dead.
Lights out.
Buonanotte.

10

LESSONS

"Listen carefully. What do you hear?"

"I ... I'm not sure ..." Kelly answered. "It's *very* different."

"That's why I've chosen a sparrow for this lesson," Master Roy explained. "You've experienced mammalian shifts, but the avian mind is a foreign one to us. Birds are nothing like their furred cousins and provide an excellent opportunity for strengthening perception skills."

Kelly was having difficulty extending deeper into the bird's consciousness. "It's … so … noisy," she murmured.

"That's right. While some birds act individually—like the jay or the hawk—sparrows live in close community with one another. They think and act together; their mutual protection relies on it. What you're hearing are the voices of other sparrows nearby."

"Can they read each other's thoughts?"

"Ach, goodness no! They don't need to. Your feathery companion has spent its entire life minding the chirps and flutters of its fellow sparrows. If it were a human, it could sit in a crowded café and tell you at any moment what every person had just said and what each was currently doing.

"That's the challenge of this exercise, Kelly. I want you to sort out *this* sparrow's consciousness from the other voices in its head. At the same time, you need to maintain your anchor, and not let the avian sensations overwhelm you."

Kelly tried to search for the strongest presence. It was difficult, though. The impressions were all *so* alien they seemed alike. It was as if Master Roy had asked her to detect the regional dialects within a Swahili-speaking group. Kelly concentrated on what she thought to be this sparrow's perceptions and tried to ignore the rest of the chirpy babble.

"No, no!" Master Roy corrected. "Don't shut out the other voices. That's the human thing to do, but it's not the sparrow thing to do. Learn to hear them and listen to what they're saying. You'll need to heed those voices when you shift—they'll keep you safe. Just don't let them interfere with your focus in the subject's mind. Learn to think like a sparrow ..."

Shape-shifting lessons were a new addition to Kelly's routine since her recovery. Although typically reserved for those of the rank of journeyman, Brid had thought it best for Kelly to receive proper instruction, given her demonstrated aptitude. Brid had stipulated ground rules, however. Kelly wouldn't take the Journeyman's Oath, but secrecy would bind her studies. She wasn't to speak of shape-shifting or her lessons to anyone other than Master Roy, Allisdair, or Brid. That was easy enough, as she never discussed her shifting in the past.

The second rule prohibited extracurricular shifting. There was to be no shifting beyond her lessons or assigned homework. For Kelly, this rule was more problematic, but she reluctantly agreed to it since it was the only way she'd get the training—and she *did* want to learn everything she could about the subject.

It was late morning when Kelly finished with Master Roy. She instinctively headed to Gealach's stall, as she had for the last several days. She hadn't realized how much she'd missed her horse's companionship until her first morning out of the infirmary. When she'd shown up in the stable, still shaky on her feet after her long convalescence, Gealach's neighs and whinnies could be heard across half the estate. Since that happy reunion, Kelly had taken every opportunity to stop by and reassure her horse that all was well.

Little had changed around the stables in the weeks Kelly was abed. Niall still bullied Robert, and Robert still accepted Niall's bullishness as part of a normal day. Several stalls away, Kelly could hear Niall's current plan as he presented it to the younger stable boy: Robert was to muck out each stall and Niall would then spread the fresh straw. Hardly fair. Mucking—cleaning up and hauling out the messy straw—was all of the work. Kelly smoldered as she heard Robert accept the plan; they each had a task, so to him it seemed equitable.

You should be shoveling the poop, you poop!

Later, with Gealach curried and brushed, Kelly stopped by the tack room to see whether her saddle needed a polish. She found Kenna and Cameron in deep discussion perched atop milk cans. They jumped up as she entered, their eyes glinting suspicion.

Cameron moved stiffly to the door. He nodded to Kelly. "Aye, heard ya recovered. Good on ya." His words were polite enough, but his tone held all the warmth of an ice cube. He slipped out the door.

Kelly was unsure what to say.

"I tried to come see you. They wouldn't let me. They wouldn't say what was wrong with you. You were in the infirmary for so long." Kenna spoke in a strident tone, as if she blamed Kelly for being ill. "There must have been complications. But I didn't know what you'd complicated, because they wouldn't tell me anything. 'She's doing better, but it will take time,' was all they'd say. I did try to see you."

Was she mad at Kelly for causing her concern? Not likely. The only thing Kenna didn't worry about was that she worried about everything. She kept glancing at the door as she spoke, despite the fact that they were alone.

Kelly peered at her. "Are you okay?"

Kenna straightened and her eyes widened. "Me? Of course. I'm fine!" She left the room, banging the door behind her.

ॐ

Her reunion with Gordie had been nearly as disastrous. He had pressed her for all sorts of particulars about her illness, which she could only answer with vague half-truths. (Allisdair had forbidden her to speak of the attack or the poisonings to anyone. He feared the culprit would go into hiding if he learned they were on to him.) That was fine in theory, but it didn't accommodate a kid's inquisitiveness. Gordie must have felt she was putting him off. When he asked how much time she'd been spending with Ina lately, it was clear he thought she'd dumped him as her best friend.

The only encounter that hadn't been a train wreck was with Master David. He'd been overjoyed to see her.

"I was terribly concerned. I'm so glad you're well!" His smile was genuine and glowed with feeling.

He always seemed to know the right thing to say. Kelly felt as though she could start a thought and he would know how to finish it perfectly. As if their spirits were somehow attuned to one another. He also seemed to know what not to say. Or to ask. She wanted to talk to him about the poisoning—she'd worried for him and figured since they both knew about it anyway, it wouldn't really be violating Allisdair's dictum. But before she could frame a question, he shook his head and held a finger to his lips.

"Shh … it's too monstrous to speak of. We're both well. That's enough."

That noon, the situation with Gordie worsened. Kelly had saved a seat for him, as they customarily did for each other at meals. When he arrived, however, he made quite a show of moving farther down the table and sitting with another boy. It wasn't long into the meal when Gordie announced his views on his most recent Shakespearean study.

"It's *Julius Caesar*," he said in an overloud voice. "One of Shakespeare's earliest plays. The hero, Brutus—"

"Protagonist," Kelly uttered.

"*Excuse* me?" Gordie's drawl silenced all conversation at the table. Kids have an innate sense for impending combat, and the wagons were clearly circling.

"The leading character in a story is called the protagonist."

Gordie flashed a patronizing smile. "That's fine, Kelly. In your stories you can be the protagonist. I'm sure you'll be extremely protagonizing. Me? I'd rather be a hero."

Sniggers erupted around the table and Kelly's face burned.

"As I was saying," Gordie continued with starchy melodrama, "Brutus is the hero of the play, but is undone and later killed for his tragic flaw—he betrays Caesar, his close friend, when he supports the conspirators who would kill the emperor. It's tragic because Brutus believed he acted in the republic's best interest. Yet betrayal is betrayal:

> *'For Brutus, as you know, was Caesar's angel:*
> *Judge, O you gods, how dearly Caesar loved him!*
> *This was the most unkindest cut of all;*
> *For when the noble Caesar saw him stab,*
> *Ingratitude, more strong than traitors' arms,*
> *Quite vanquish'd him: then burst his mighty heart;'*[10]

Kelly lost her appetite, but she refused to leave the table and admit defeat, so she pushed the food around her plate until the meal was over.

As they rose to leave, Gordie was beside her and said sotto voce, "Et tu, Kel-ly?"[11]

She spun around to him and hissed through clenched teeth, "You—you stay right there!" She waited until the

---

10 *Julius Caesar* (Act III, Scene ii) by William Shakespeare

11 Based on: "Et tu, Brute?"
    Julius Caesar (Act III, Scene i) by William Shakespeare

room had emptied before she continued. "I've done nothing to you, so you can knock off the aggrieved act. I was sick. And I nearly died. Ina helped save my life. If I spend some time with her out of gratitude, how dare you complain!" Kelly's outburst was as brief as it was intense. She faltered, searching for something more to say, but she'd spent her steam and could only stare at Gordie.

Gordie, for his part, could only stare back at Kelly. "Wow," he said in a soft, stunned voice, "I didn't know you were that sick. Are you okay now?"

"Yeah."

"No one told us anything. I had no idea it was so bad." He scuffed his foot back and forth across the floor.

"Brid didn't want the other kids to worry, so she asked me not to talk about it." Kelly's lie wasn't precisely true, but she wanted Gordie to know that she hadn't willingly held out on him.

"Sure you're okay?"

"Yeah."

After an awkward pause Kelly asked, "Did I miss anything exciting?" just as Gordie said, "Maybe you could help me with a project." Their faces relaxed into smiles, recognizing the return to peaceful relations.

Kelly nodded. "What do you need?"

"A lookout," he replied. "The details are need-to-know. And you'd rather not." In a whisper he added, "Meet me at the old barn—the one that edges the pasture—in an hour. Stay out of sight!"

※

One hour later, Kelly was at the designated rendezvous. This was the oldest farm structure on the estate and it didn't appear as though it received visitors with any frequency. She worked the door open, the long-neglected hinges offering squeaky resistance, shutting it behind her as she slipped inside.

While livestock hadn't been sheltered here for many years, the air still held the musky traces of cows and sheep. Since that time, the sidewall planking had dried and shrunk, as old wood will, leaving vertical slits between some of the boards. These intermittent chinks passed slivers of afternoon sunlight into the shadowy gloom, but they did little to light the barn's interior.

Long-disused farm equipment filled the dark belly of the barn, some of the larger pieces brandishing sharp edges and pointed blades. Kelly hung back near the safety of the door. She thought she was alone, so she started when a voice spoke out of the shadows.

"Did anyone see you?"

"Of course not."

"Good." Gordie spoke in a hoarse whisper. "I need to climb up into the rafters. You stay here as lookout."

"What's up there?" she whispered.

"Need-to-know," he reminded.

"Well I do."

"What?"

"Need to know more." She crossed her arms stubbornly.

"I need to collect some ... ah ... samples for a ... science experiment." In the darkness she could just make out the covered pail he held up.

"I don't know ... I think I've stopped needing."

"If anyone comes, hoot like an owl and then duck out of sight."

Out of sight? Ducking wasn't required.

"Let's hear it."

"Hear what?" she whispered.

"Your owl hoot."

Kelly pursed her lips and gave a hoot.

"I see." He sounded unimpressed. He moved past her, softly singing:

> *"O hoot, an' I'll come to you, my lassie;*
> *O hoot, an' I'll come to you, my lassie;*
> *Though father and mither should baith gae mad,*
> *O hoot, an' I'll come to you, my lassie."*[12]

Just as the darkness seemed to absorb him, she thought she could see his feet moving upwards. Curious, she crept along to discover a ladder affixed to the wall. She climbed up through a hole in the floor above and found herself in the haymow. The air here was thick with particles that

---

12　Based on:
　　"O Whistle, an' I'll come to you, my lad;
　　O whistle, an' I'll come to you, my lad;
　　Though father and mither should baith gae mad,
　　O whistle, an' I'll come to you, my lad."
　　Whistle An' I'll Come to You, My Lad, by Robert Burns

tickled her nose and made her eyes itch. She tried to muffle a sneeze, but the dusty stillness magnified the sound.

"Go back down—now!" Gordie ordered from somewhere across the loft.

There was even less light up here. Kelly couldn't see the floor in front of her, let alone the opposite wall. His voice was above her; he was probably climbing another ladder, or the hay bales themselves.

He spoke with urgency. "It's dangerous up here—there's a huge hole they lift the hay through. You'll never see it in the dark. Climb back down and get back to your post!"

Kelly reluctantly did as she was bidden, feeling unneeded. Why did Gordie require a lookout anyway? In this murk no one would ever know they were here. They could be sharing the barn with a felon in the act, and they'd still not be aware of each other's presence. Kelly would only learn of her danger as she stumbled over the victim's still-warm body ...

She jumped at a sudden fluttering overhead. The high-pitched *eeks* surely belonged to bats. A missing roof plank allowed a narrow patch of light to penetrate the dark upper reaches of the barn. It fell upon a section of the wide beam running just below the roof ridge. Kelly gazed upwards, trying to imagine a murderer's shadowy crimes. She realized with a start that a foot dangled from the beam high above her. A corpse!

It wiggled.

Not quite dead yet ... She made out an elbow and realized Gordie was her corpse, inching along the beam on his belly. She followed his progress until he was once again swallowed by the darkness. What was he doing up there?

Maybe the murderer took a swing at him with a rusty sickle, and Gordie narrowly escaped evisceration (and tetanus) by crawling across the roof beam. Even now the villain, neither nimble nor agile enough to follow, would be down here with her, looking for a way to climb up and meet him at the other end. She'd better watch her step— he'd likely be cranky after missing Gordie. How typical: Gordie has all the excitement and leaves Kelly to deal with the disconcerted killer.

She continued to explore, squeezing between a plow and an aged tractor, careful not to bang her shin on the tractor's hitch. She halted mid-step feeling the hairs prickle on the back of her neck. Something was wrong. Wholly dependent on her hearing, she tried to identify the source of her unease.

The occasional slithering noises and bat squeaks above her weren't a threat; she discounted those. No … there was something else. Far across the barn there was a soft buzzing, barely audible. It hadn't been there when she first arrived.

Perhaps she was hearing the cold-blooded fiend sharpening his blade on a leather strop, preparing for his next attempt. She must investigate!

She hugged the outer wall, working towards the distant sound. She edged past a corncrib, above which hung the plow horses' hefty yokes. Just beyond a feeding trough she spied an assortment of pitchforks. Weaponry! She armed herself with one.

As she drew closer, the buzz resolved into subdued voices—Kelly was hearing a hushed conversation. She crept along the wall hoping to catch what was said. (A lookout has broad license and eavesdropping isn't merely permissible, it's strongly encouraged.) The speakers were outside, separated from her by the scant wallboards. She drew adjacent to the voices with silent, catlike steps.

The deeper tones of the closer voice were definitely a man's. Kelly could just make out his words.

"… Don't worry about her. I've sent her up with the tups. That'll get her out of the way."

The second voice spoke, but it was both softer and more distant. Kelly couldn't distinguish any words.

"I know, but we still have to be careful. With Allisdair on the prowl, the chances of getting caught are greater," the first voice answered. "Look, just because we didn't succeed last time doesn't mean we won't eventually. If I can manage to get rid of her for good this time, we should be able to pull the whole thing off with no one the wiser."

The second voice responded. Then the first.

"Leave that to me—she's thwarted our plans enough already! Don't forget the timetable. We'll meet in the usual place."

They were about to leave and Kelly *had* to find out who they were! She looked wildly for a window or a chink in the wall. She spied a knothole, low to the ground. She dropped to the floor and stuffed her eye up against it. Her sharp intake of breath wasn't intended, but she couldn't help herself—right there, a foot from her face, was a pair of muddy work boots! She tried to see past the confines of the knothole, but it was no good. As she watched, the boots walked away, carrying their owner's identity with them.

A soft yelp overhead, accompanied by shuffling and muted curses, reminded Kelly of Gordie's yet-to-be completed science experiment. She made her way back to her lookout post.

When Gordie rejoined her there, he was a mess. Dust and cobwebs clung to him and small sticks of straw poked out of his hair. Kelly squinted in the meager light. A large pink lump swelled below his left cheek.

"Gordie! Your face—what happened?"

He pushed his shoulders back. "It was a hazardous mission. I knew the risks going in. It's a mere flesh wound."

"But what happened?"

"Need to know?" he asked.

She nodded.

He held up his pail. It emitted a low drone. "Some of the samples resisted collection," he admitted wryly.

"Are those bees?"

"Wasps," he corrected.

"No, no!" she exclaimed as he reached for the lid. "No need to show!"

The wickedness in his smile made her queasy. "Thomas left his drum in the practice room last night."

"Need-to-know—and I don't!" she blurted.

Ignoring her, he continued on. "Not that difficult to remove and replace a drum head. These little fellows ought to enjoy a nice, cozy winter … provided they're not disturbed by any loud banging …"

Kelly shuddered. "I need to go. You're on your own for that part of the operation."

"Okay, but you'll be missing the best part," he said as they stepped out into the late afternoon, leaving behind the barn and its secrets.

The morning dawned clear with a light northwesterly breeze (four to five knots steady, Kelly estimated). She gobbled her breakfast and hurried through her chores before seeking out Master Roy.

He looked at her bright eyes and her body coiled with anticipation, knowing the question she needn't ask. "All right then," he answered, "we'll do it today. But you had better calm yourself if you hope to center sufficiently to manage a shift."

"Yes, Master Roy!" she promised, grinning. Today she was going to learn to fly!

She had hoped to, three days ago, but a storm had grounded all air operations. During that time, Master Roy had forced Kelly to sit through dull classes on topics that seemingly had nothing to do with flying.

For instance, she learned that sparrows have monocular vision. With eyes on either side of its head, a sparrow can see in all directions at once. (Master Roy explained this is a useful safety feature for those living at the bottom of the food chain.) On the other hand, hawks and other raptors—who have few natural predators—have binocular vision with their eyes set in the front of their heads. He said this provides better depth perception, which raptors need for gauging their swoops and dives.

As boring as that had been, rods and cones were even worse. Master Roy taught her that rods and cones are the two types of cells in the eye that help us see. Rods detect very low levels of light, while cones differentiate between colors. Sparrow eyes are made up predominantly of cones, while the eyes of nocturnal birds, like owls, are densely packed with rods. After three days of such tedium, Kelly had nearly given up on the prospect of flying, but today's fair skies afforded her the opportunity at last.

Master Roy selected a grassy patch behind the stables for Kelly's initial flight practice. He wanted to minimize distractions, he explained, so they'd start in an area devoid of birds. Kelly was giddy and had to quell her excitement in order to center adequately. After establishing her anchor to Master Roy's satisfaction, she patterned the image of a sparrow's mind and let herself sense its being. Holding these impressions, she willed her mind to push the switch.

The first few moments as a new creature are most bewildering. Animals are so varied in how they perceive the world around them that it takes time to acclimate to a new mind and body. Kelly didn't rush the process. She simply waited while her sparrow brain sorted out its new inputs.

I find the best way to accustom to a new form is to inventory your senses, one at a time, Master Roy thought into her head.

She started with her vision: out of her right eye she saw an old riding plow resting behind the stables; out of her left she saw Master Roy, himself a sparrow (flight training always observes the buddy system.) She concentrated on his coloration—it was … different. His feathers displayed complex shading and more color gradations than she remembered of sparrows.

You forget your lessons, Kelly. You can see more colors now—sparrows have a much higher concentration of cone cells in their eyes than humans do.

Rods and cones. Right.

Kelly took a couple test hops, chirping out a metallic, "*Chik!*"

"Let's begin with some straight line flying." That's what Kelly understood Master Roy to say. What he really said was, "*Chik-chik, chip!*"

Kelly knew takeoff required a springing hop followed by sure, steady down-strokes of her wings. However, on attempting it she only lifted a foot in the air before tumbling back into the grass.

"*Chik, chit-tchup,*" chirped Master Roy.

Yeah … forgot that. Tail up to fly up.

Kelly tried again, this time holding her tail up. As she launched airborne, her wings lifted her off the ground and she rose up, if a bit erratically. She was flying!

"*Tek, tek,*" he commanded.

She lowered her tail and headed in for a landing, as requested. Well, crash and roll would have been a more accurate description of what actually happened.

Master Roy landed neatly beside her. "*Tiwi-twit-iwit*," he twittered.

He was right—she needed to lower her secondaries more for takeoffs and landings. Her secondary feathers on the inner back edges of her wings acted like the flaps on an airplane. Her primaries (on the outer back edges) were her ailerons—used for mid-air turns.

With practice, her takeoffs and landings improved. Master Roy then had her try some touch-and-go landings, where she'd barely touch down before hopping back into the air again. That seemed a useful trick for hot landing zones, when things turned out to be not as safe as first assumed. Turning in-flight took some getting used to, but once she got the hang of it, she enjoyed some aerial hot-dogging, showing off her banks and veers. Master Roy chirped she should take her lessons more seriously, but she didn't think he really minded.

This isn't to say all of her flying skills came easily. The first time she landed on a branch, she came in much too fast—the branch was closer than she realized. Her feet locked with a vice-like grip (which luckily held), but her momentum was such that she spun around the branch three times before her wings could brake her. Yet again, Master Roy alighted with pinpoint precision and chittered the explanation and solution.

Kelly repeated the lesson he cited.

Birds with monocular vision suffer from reduced depth perception ...

Kelly thrilled over her lightness and buoyancy in the air, and was wholly consumed with her flying. When Master Roy would have called a halt to the day's lesson, she cajoled him into continuing in the afternoon.

When they resumed after lunch, Master Roy announced that Kelly was ready to join the rest of birddom. He led her to the near paddock. The bordering shrubs were alive with sparrows darting to the ground, stealing morsels of overlooked grain, and then flitting back to the cover of the bushes.

Master Roy instructed, "You've got a solid grasp of the fundamentals of flying. Now we'll add your earlier work on filtering voices and maintaining a steady anchor."

This time when she shifted, Kelly's head was filled with a twittering cacophony. The voices of so many made it hard for her to concentrate on the mechanics of flying, so she hopped up into a bush to observe for a while.

She watched as a sparrow flitted out to the clearing to search for grain. Then sparrows two and three joined it. Then fourfivesix. And then suddenly the bush was empty of birds—as if they all decided to go and no one wanted to be last. Just as suddenly, they flew back en masse, as though they'd never really meant to leave. Kelly found a schizophrenic rhythm to their behavior: the lure of the grain, the safety of the bush. Wherever they were, the other was better.

"*Chik, chip,*" Master Roy reminded her. Don't forget to listen.

Much of the birdie jabber was little more than nervous twittering, as if the overwrought creatures were sighing, "Oh my!" again and again. An earnest *tchup* was often heard. Watching and listening, Kelly noted it immediately preceded the frenzied exodus back to the bush. It must have been the call of alarm.

"*Twit-itwit.*" He was pleased she picked that up.

Most of the balance of the chirping was observational:

"Grain here."

"Missed some seeds—plenty left."

"Brown cap with white wing bars coming in."

"There's some grain under that horse poop."

"Wind's freshening."

"Puddle here for a drink or a splash."

And so forth. It wouldn't have been such an effort to sort the voices if they took polite turns speaking, worthy of a well-preened tea party. But they didn't. They constantly interrupted with chirps and chirrups tripping over one another in no discernable order. It's no wonder there've been no great philosophers or famous authors who were sparrows—they couldn't hold a single thought long enough.

Kelly found it funny how amidst all the avian chatter, nothing said was ever personal. Constantly fluttering and bumping one another, you never heard, "Sorry." There were no hellos or goodbyes. No one ever chirped, "How are you?" or twittered, "Thanks for the grain." They spoke so much and said so little. Master Roy had said sparrows live in close community, yet to Kelly, close community suggested you cared for and about one another. Sparrows didn't seem to do either.

Her lesson ended as the afternoon shadows drew long. She was exhausted from her extended class, but the mixed exhilaration of shifting and of flight filled her with a euphoria that masked her fatigue. Nevertheless, Master Roy gave her the next day off, promising she'd be more tired than she expected and she'd need the rest.

Rather than head in, Kelly wanted to savor the echoes of her day before rejoining the company of others. So, hugging her memories close, she sought Gealach's companionship, knowing her horse wouldn't mind an impromptu grooming.

An hour later, her excitement comfortably settled, she stood outside the stables and inhaled the crisp autumn air. Darkness came early to the Highlands in late November, and while the winter snows hadn't yet arrived, the night chilled quickly after the sun set. As she gazed up at the diamond-bright stars, a noise from the byre caught her attention. It was late. Who'd be working at this hour? She went to investigate.

She found Kenna topping up the hay for the young calves.

"Why working so late?"

Kenna's head popped up from behind her armload of hay. "What do *you* want?" she groaned with a pinched face. "Why can't you just leave me alone? Haven't you already done enough?"

Eyebrows arched in question, Kelly could only stare back.

"And to think how I fretted while you were sick," Kenna plunged on. "Did you come to gloat? Sure—it's easy to be magnanimous when you have everything, and I have … nothing." The last word came out half gulp and half sob.

Kelly shook her head as though that might rattle some comprehension loose. "I have no idea what you're talking about."

"Oh, don't play the innocent. I saw it with my own eyes!" (Eyes that now glistened.) "He was with you the entire day. The entire day! You think you can keep it a secret? You must take me for an idiot."

She saw me with Master Roy. She must have seen me shift …

"It wasn't the first time either. You started as soon as you got out." Kenna stuck her chin out defiantly. "You planned it in the infirmary, didn't you?"

"It was Brid's idea," Kelly admitted with reluctance.

That news hit Kenna like a slap. All the color drained from her face and the tears rolled freely down her cheeks. "Brid? It was her decision?" Kenna deflated with the news. Her lower lip trembled perilously. "Does anyone else know?" There was no anger left in her voice, only pain and humiliation.

"Allisdair," Kelly answered softly.

The last was too much for Kenna. She broke down with gushing tears and bawling yelps.

"I'm sorry," Kelly offered. "They asked me not to talk about it."

Kelly didn't think one could cry any harder or louder, but she was wrong. It was difficult to make out words in the animal wails Kenna produced, but Kelly caught an "I can't go home!" occasionally mixed in.

Kelly was baffled by Kenna's reaction, but carrying on a conversation with someone seriously invested in a good cry is about as successful as trying to teach a dog to speak. (Speak as in talking with words, not as in barking—the latter's what you settle for after failing at the former.)

Eventually the torrent of tears subsided. "He's never satisfied," Kenna gulped between sniffles. "He finds fault with everything, even when there's nothing wrong. As punishment, I have to do extra chores—work that *he's* supposed to be doing." Kenna paused to wipe her nose on her sleeve.

"*Who?*"

"Dougal." Kenna moaned. "He's complained about me to Master Roy and today announced that I'll be sent home if I don't shape up in a hurry." Kenna's chin started to quiver and Kelly was afraid she might start crying again. "I *can't* go home! Animal husbandry is all I've ever wanted to do." Kenna cleared her throat and spewed the results into the hay at her feet. "My stepmother's never liked it—'it's not proper,' she says. If I'm sent home she'll pack me off to finishing school. She wants me to be a *lady.*"

"But why are you upset with me?" Kelly asked.

"I thought they were going to give me a chance. I thought if I really dug in, I could prove to Master Roy that Dougal is wrong and I do belong here. But they're not even waiting. If Master Roy's training you to replace me, his mind must be made up. And if Brid and Allisdair have already decided, then there's nothing I can do."

"Kenna, I'm not being trained to replace you. And I don't think Brid or Allisdair know anything about your trouble with Dougal. When I was sick, Brid was concerned that I wasn't learning enough about … the family business. She and Allisdair asked Master Roy if he'd work with me personally. They did ask me not to speak about it, but I can assure you it has nothing to with your apprenticeship."

Kenna heaved a sigh and rubbed her puffy, red eyes.

"That doesn't help you with Dougal, however. Could you talk directly to Master Roy about it?"

Kenna shook her head. "After what Dougal's told him, it would just look like I was trying to shift the blame."

"So that's why you're here working so late."

Kenna nodded. "Dougal's got me up in the high fields with the tups all day, which should be his job. When I finally get back, I still have to do all of my own work."

"Tups?"

"The rams," Kenna explained. "It's breeding season, so we take the tups up into the hills where the ewes winter …"

"… and they have wild, woolly sex together," Kelly finished. She was rewarded with Kenna's sheepish giggle.

"It's real shepherding, which I love, but walking and climbing all day is tiring. And it isn't fair to have to come back to all of this work afterwards. Besides, he'll just find fault with it anyway."

"Well, with two of us at it," Kelly offered, "it won't take any time. Just tell me what you need me to do."

"Really?" She could hear the relief and gratitude in Kenna's voice.

Kelly winked. "If I don't want your job, we'd better make sure you keep it!"

It wasn't until later that night Kelly suddenly realized where she'd heard the word "tup" before. The day she'd been lookout in the old barn, Mr. Muddy Boots had said, "I've sent her up with the tups. That'll get her out of the way for a while." If that had been Dougal's job and he reassigned it to Kenna, then he had to be Muddy Boots! That meant the extra work he was loading on his apprentice wasn't as punishment … he was trying to keep her away from something. There was nothing wrong with Kenna's performance. Dougal was simply using her.

The thought that Dougal falsely maligned her friend to Master Roy enraged Kelly. And now Kenna, heaped with double works shifts, was in real danger of being sent home in disgrace. What was *he* up to? Why, Dougal might be slinking around at that very moment. A bit of late-night aerial reconnaissance ought to ascertain whether all was well. Centering easily, she patterned her mind on a sparrow—all memory of her promise to Brid forgotten as she made the shift. She hopped up to the windowsill, spread her wings, and took off into the night.

With steady wing beats, she flew straight in the direction of the barns. Despite the clear skies, it was very dark and visibility was poor. She strained to see the barn's outline against the sky.

Slam!

She flew beak-first into a tree. Her bird brain was so concussed, she was lucky to maintain her anchor as she fell, limp, down the length of the trunk to the ground. Lying in a crumpled heap, she managed the weak command to shift back.

Kelly sat up slowly and leaned her back against the felonious tree (growing in this particular spot seemed crime enough). Gradually, her head stopped spinning so violently. She got up, unsteady on her feet, and wobbled back to the house, nursing a cauliflower nose that was bleeding profusely and two eyes that were sure to bloom with color by morning. At least she'd have the day off.

As she walked, some rebellious part of her brain recalled a flight school lesson: *Rods enable night vision. Sparrow eyes are densely packed with cone cells and contain very few rods.*

11

INVESTIGATIONS

December 8

I'm learning mind-bending! I finally persuaded
Stuart to teach me, but his paranoia is starting
to make me edgy. He'll only work with me well
away from the manor where there's no chance
of getting caught. I can only wonder where he
learned it.

Today we used a tit to carry messages between
us. It wasn't very reliable; it tended to substi-
tute words it didn't understand. Stuart sent: "If

Allisdair catches us he'll flay us." I received: "If a man sees us he'll feed us worms."

HMB

Kelly reread the entry several times. Mind-bending. What was it? An inquiring mind was bent on finding out! But she could hardly raise the subject with Master Roy; what she needed was a book. And if the knowledge was as closely guarded as her father suggested, such a book would surely be kept in the secret library.

Only later that evening did Kelly learn how difficult her search would be. Before, she had selected the shape-shifting book at random. This time she was looking for a specific topic. For that she needed a library catalog or at least some knowledge of the filing system, and she had neither. The floor-to-ceiling shelves held thousands of books. A book-by-book search could take years.

She sat in an armchair staring at the books, trying to formulate a plan. If her shape-shifting book was in the "how to" section, perhaps a mind-bending book might be nearby. She gathered four or five books to either side of the shape-shifting book and sat to examine them.

She made slow progress. Some of the books didn't have titles. Many lacked a table of contents, which might have suggested what they were about. Several were original manuscripts written in longhand and difficult to read, and two were written in Gaelic.

With persistence, Kelly managed to identify: a book on the breeding of Highland sheep; a retrospective of early bardic poetry; an anthology of Celtic myths and legends; and a collection of bawdy drinking songs (while Kelly wasn't familiar with all of the terms, their context suggested great color). The breadth of subjects confirmed an even more Byzantine filing system than she'd feared.

The night crept on. The only sound was the intermittent turning of pages. Kelly's eyelids slumped from staring at the fine text and cramped cursive. Slowly—imperceptibly at first—the room began to change around her. The armchairs grew plusher, almost shaggy. Their brass feet lost their luster, taking on earth tones and the sheen of horn, strangely resembling hooves. The shelves of books faded, transparent with a swirling whiteness behind. The lighting dimmed and the room grew cold, bitterly cold. Kelly was barely aware of the room's transformation—it was measured and subtle, and her mind was sluggish with sleep.

When it was complete, she was no longer in the library. She wasn't even indoors. She stood on a hillside, in the dead of night, caught out in a late winter storm. A merciless wind threw snow horizontally, piling it into chest-high drifts, which threatened the sheep huddled close for warmth.

Nor was the library the only thing to transform. Tall and muscular, Kelly was now a grown man. She could feel the man's emotions, but she couldn't read the thoughts behind them. He fought a sorrow that was couched in frustration. Something terrible had happened, which he'd been powerless to prevent. Yet this wasn't a weak or impotent man. Kelly sensed reservoirs of strength: physical, emotional, and moral. He was torn by recent happenings, however, and the choices he faced. He sought a deeper answer to a problem, and while he was certain a solution existed, he was unconvinced where it might lie.

Through the blur of swirling snow and sleet, another figure emerged from the storm. Kelly couldn't discern his features, for the newcomer was as tightly swaddled in his woolen cloak as was the person she inhabited.

"I didna ken ya were up here, Bearach," the newcomer yelled into the flying snow. "I've bin searchin' these few hours fer ya. Yer needed down at the manor. Now."

"The storm weel bury the sheep," Kelly's host explained in a deep voice blown hoarse by the wind. "They dunna ha' the sense Danu gave a rock in weather such as this. Weel lose the lambs."

"Thar be others who can sit wi' the ewes. The laird is dead. Go down to yer grandmother." The newcomer's order stuck no better than the sleet bouncing off his cloak.

"Aye," Bearach replied. "I felt him pass—an' I could feel his shock o' the betrayal. An' I ask mi'self how takin' his place will end the blood. The hatred."

"Fer the love of Lugh, man—yer the tanist and Bres killed yer da! And yet ya sit here ruminatin' with the bloody sheep. Yer da was strong, an' he didna fear the job he ha' to doo. What manner of son are ya?"

Kelly felt Bearach's fury as he grabbed the other's arm, snarling, "Ya go too faar, steward!" Then regaining control, he released his bear-like grip. "Tha' I struggle wi' questions no one else stoops to ask, makes me more of a man, nay less. Mi da taught me tha' much."

Bearach turned and stepped further up the ice-crusted hillside. He called back over his shoulder, "I weel go ta Brid when I'm ready …"

The scene suddenly shifted.

The sun was brighter than Kelly ever remembered; the grass was a vibrant green; even the sky was a picture-book blue that seemed out of a story. Kelly knew she was someone else now. Bearach's earlier sorrow and uncertainty were replaced with an exultant joy that wanted to burst her rib cage. The howl of the winter wind was replaced with an equally loud roar, but this rose from the throats of the men around her. Her eyes sparkled with sunlight mirrored off shining armor, as a gilded army ran at an easy lope towards battle.

A soldier, three men over, shouted, "Long may the bards remember the Battle of Moytura!" He spoke in an ancient tongue that Kelly couldn't place, but she somehow understood.

The soldier next to her rallied, "Aye, and may Balor and Bres not soon forget our vengeance!" In response, the men around her—all beautiful in their youth and glorious in their battle raiment—sang out a war cry with a single, pure voice.

Kelly was a soldier in some primeval battle, fighting for a cause she knew with unshakeable certitude to be just.

An officer ahead called back, "Forward, with Lugh! Into battle for Danu and for Tara!"

"For Danu and Tara!" the soldiers sang back in unison, and they surged ahead to defend their homeland from the evil that threatened their families, their land, and all that made them a people.

And then with no warning, she was back in the library, easing cramped muscles up from the pile of books over which she'd been sleeping. Reshelving the books—her mind-bending quest laid aside for the moment—she made her way back to her bed where she slept soundly, and dreamlessly, for what remained of the night.

Kelly braced herself outside the door. She didn't want to enter and she was stalling, looking for some excuse to walk away.

"Kelly, can I help you with something?"

Kelly looked up into the face of Master David. She hadn't heard him come down the hall.

"I … need a book on an ancient battle. But facing Master Roderick is worse than fighting one of my own."

Master David's smile was supportive and understanding. "Perhaps I can spare you needless wounds. Old battles are a bard's specialty. Would you care to tap my knowledge, before braving Roderick's domain?"

Kelly heaved a sigh. "Thank you!"

They returned to the music room, where they each settled into a chair.

"Now of which battle would you like to hear?"

"The Battle of Moytura." Kelly hoped he knew of it.

"The first or the second?"

"I didn't realize there was more than one."

"In the First Battle of Moytura, Nuada, king of the *Tuatha de Danann*, fought the Formorians for possession of Ireland." The pitch and timber of Master David's voice carefully balanced his precise pacing; this was the lyric voice he reserved for storytelling.

He recounted how the *Tuatha de Danann* had beaten the Formorians, but that Nuada, the Tuathan king, had lost his arm in the battle, forcing him to abdicate the throne. Bres, son of a Formorian father and a Tuathan mother, took his place, in the hope he would bring peace between the two races. Over time, however, as Bres proved to be a poor ruler, he was driven out and Nuada was reinstated as king.

In the Second Battle of Moytura, the mighty warrior Lugh led the Tuathan armies against the Formorians, who were in turn led by Balor and supported by Bres. When Lugh killed Balor, he ended the reign of terror against the Tuathans and peace returned to the land.

"What happened to Bres?" Kelly asked.

"He was defeated, but allowed to live."

"Why? Didn't he side with the Formorians in the end?"

"Yes, but remember, Kelly, that he was half Tuathan and had once been their king. He made a bad decision, but the Tuathans forgave him for it.

☙

"Is this a bud?" It was hard for Kelly to keep the excitement out of her voice.

Ina stepped over and peered closely at the plant. "I believe it is," she confirmed, "but I wouldn't have spotted that for several more days. You must have telescopic vision."

Not telescopic … binocular.

"How long before it will bloom?" Kelly asked expectantly.

Ina smiled. "Orchids may yet teach you patience. That flower spike will develop for two or three months before it blossoms."

Kelly drooped with the news.

Ina added, "It's exciting to discover them, though. And after watching the spike grow and the buds swell, the resulting flowers will be all the more beautiful."

Patience was a trait that Ina had in abundance and which Kelly lacked. The young healer possessed a quality of stillness Kelly could only marvel at, because it was so foreign to her. It wasn't the patience of a cat that, stalking its prey, could hold motionless for ages waiting for the right moment to pounce. That's patience as a means to an end. Ina's was stillness as the end itself. It was a cessation of activity, yet it was as apt as an iguana basking in the sun, or a lily floating on a pond's surface.

One day while recovering in the infirmary, when Kelly was particularly restless, Ina had explained how there's healing in a pause. Patience was necessary so the body could be afforded that pause when it most needed it.

She'd told how, as a healer, she practiced quietude so that she might help bring some to those under her care.

Kelly's reaction at the time had been, *A patient patient? Hardly me.*

Yet Ina's efforts weren't wholly lost on Kelly. The two met frequently in the greenhouses—Ina instructing on orchid care and Kelly learning and sharing her friend's passion. They'd often work in silent stretches, relaxing into the moment without trying to fill it up with chit-chat. Kelly had come to love the quiet work as much as she did the excitement of a newly discovered flower spike. It wasn't dissimilar to her centering before a shape shift: the ability to calm her mind so she could extend her awareness and tap energies beyond herself. She wondered if this was how Ina healed.

Kelly had been practicing her own exercise in patience that afternoon. The night before, she discovered a new entry in her father's diary:

> December 19
>
> Stuart was late for our MB lesson today and when I asked where he'd been, he became eva-sive. I have a suspicion … I'll be watching him closely before our next lesson.
>
> Allheal's parents will lead you to worship.
>
> HMB

The last line of his message had "rune riddle" stamped all over it, and Kelly thought she might know the door it would open. About a month before, she'd found a new passage down one of the more distant tunnels. The passage dead-ended at a door with a Celtic cross sculpted into its stone. Unfortunately, "allheal's parents" meant nothing to her, but she hoped it might to Ina.

Her quiet work this afternoon had been pleasurable—she always enjoyed her time with Ina and the orchids—but she was sitting on a rune riddle and enough was enough.

"Does 'allheal' mean anything to you?"

Ina paused in her watering. "Yes—it's a common name for mistletoe."

"Mistletoe?"

Ina nodded. "It's an ancient folk medicine."

Ina didn't miss Kelly's surprise.

"Nature can harm us, Kelly. And for some who've had that experience, it becomes their view of the world …"

An image of a mountain lion filled Kelly's mind, quickly replaced with the dark berries and plum-colored flowers of the belladonna plant.

"… but it also heals us, as mistletoe, and whatever skill I possess, demonstrate." She placed a hand on Kelly's shoulder. "Don't miss the one, because of your experience with the other. They're two sides of the same coin. We couldn't have the healing and the good without the risk of the hurtful.

"Mistletoe has a broad spectrum of healing properties," Ina went on, "and has long been revered by the Celtic people. We'll be cutting it in a few days as part of our Yule tradition."

"What are its parent plants?" Kelly asked.

Ina seemed confused.

Kelly pulled the tag from the orchid before her. "'*Mystic Jewel x Dragon Flag.*' Doesn't that mean that *Mystic Jewel* was one of this orchid's parents and *Dragon Flag* was the other?"

She thought those were cool names for parents. She would've liked to call her mother Mystic Jewel. And what dad wouldn't want to be Dragon Flag?

Ina nodded. "Orchids are often crossed like that, applying the pollen from one species to a different species in order to create a new hybrid. But mistletoe is a pure species—it doesn't have parent plants in the same sense that hybrid orchids do."

The explanation did not, unfortunately, make the rune riddle any clearer.

"If you're interested in mistletoe," Ina offered, "I have some folios on medicinal herbs you can borrow."

Kelly accepted the offer and spent that evening learning everything she could about mistletoe. Known by many names (bird lime, devil's fuge, golden bough, herb de la croix, mistal, and viscum), mistletoe is a small bush that grows in the branches of a host tree. It's considered a parasite because its roots tap into the tree's bark and it steals nourishment from its host. The name comes from old English: "mistle" meaning dung and "tan" meaning twig. When birds eat the mistletoe berries, the berry seeds get passed along in the bird droppings, spreading the seeds to the branches of new trees.

"Poop branch." Gordie would love it …

When Kelly read that oak and apple trees are mistletoe's most common hosts she had an idea: might "allheal's parents" mean allheal's hosts? Continued reading uncovered that mistletoe occasionally grows in other types of trees, but the book neglected to mention which ones. That tidbit fired off an intensive bout of study and cross-referencing, as she worked to identify all the possible "parents." It was late (or early, depending on whether you considered the old day or the new) before she was satisfied her list was complete. She had: *quert* ᚊ for apple, *duir* ᚇ for oak, *eadha* ᚓ for poplar, *huathe* ᚆ for hawthorn, and *ailim* ᚐ for fir. Elm was also on the list, but there was no *Ogham* character for elm.

According to Ina's sources, some of these trees were rather unlikely hosts. Kelly wasn't sure which ones her father intended, but with a short list of five, she was confident she could solve the riddle.

Despite the hour, Kelly opened her fireplace and made her way to the door with the cross. (If allheal's parents were to lead one to worship, then a cross was practically an "X" marking the spot.) She looked over her list. Mistletoe grew on apple and oak trees with such a greater frequency that Kelly was willing to bet both *quert* ᚊ and *duir* ᚇ were part of the answer, perhaps even the entire answer. She touched ᚊ and then ᚇ, reversing their order when nothing happened. She then added *eadha* ᚓ and tested all of those combinations (ᚊᚇᚓ, ᚊᚓᚇ, ᚇᚊᚓ, ᚇᚓᚊ, ᚓᚊᚇ, ᚓᚇᚊ.) Still nothing. She threw *huathe* ᚆ into the mix and when that didn't work *eadha* ᚓ was removed.

Lastly, *ailim* ✝ was added and *eadha* ≢ and *huathe* ⊣ were removed sequentially and then together.

Kelly knew that persistence was a trait common to all great explorers, but as she tried the final runic permutations her palms were clammy. What if this wasn't the answer? It was on her next-to-last combination that she was finally rewarded with the sweet sound of stone scraping against stone. In the end, the correct sequence was *duir, quert, eadha* and *ailim* (⊣≣≢✝); elm was ignored and hawthorn wasn't used (hawthorn being a rare host for mistletoe at best).

The tunnel that lay beyond headed off with direct purpose, lacking twists, turns, or intersecting passages. Ten minutes later, Kelly pushed open a stone door at the tunnel's terminus and stepped into the chancel of the small abbey that sat on the far side of Ben Abba: a woodland chapel nestled in a quiet birch grove. This was Brid's abbey and was used for special services and holidays (as it would be on Christmas Eve). The overland path to it wound around the broad foot of the mountain, so this tunnel represented a more direct route.

Kelly had been here before, but it was always with the distracted restlessness reserved for dull church services. Tonight, however, the abbey was a magical find led to by a secret tunnel opened by rune codes. She lit an altar candle to inspect her discovery.

The tall side windows were set with stained glass shaded in greens and browns. Without sunlight behind them, their color was uniformly dark, but their images were clear from the shapes of the cut glass and leading.

Each depicted a different woodland creature: a white stag, a boar, a broad-shouldered bear, a golden eagle, a wolf, and a gigantic snowy owl.

The surrounding walls were a copper-brown stone, their shadowy color just visible in the light of her candle. These walls were unadorned, but the wall behind the altar displayed elaborate carvings. The mural on the left depicted a fleet of ships landing on a sandy beach. Basalt cliffs towered in the background—either shielding or warning those about to disembark. The relief to the right was of a strikingly handsome man playing his harp in a sylvan glade. His audience caught Kelly's attention; before him, some with eyes closed in obvious delight, the animals of the forest stood, sat, or lay listening. Kelly ran her fingers over the stony ridges of a fox, a badger, a raven, a mouse and a bear. She wondered what song the bard played; what song did they all enjoy so much—bear, mouse, and bird alike?

Carved verses crammed the margins of the wall, some in a language that might be Gaelic, some in *Ogham* characters. Centered between the murals was a chiseled disk. The center held what could have been a starburst or a compass. Arranged around the center were a dozen or so panels, like pie slices, each with the carving of a plant and its name.

In the candle's flickering, shadows danced across the carvings. The wall hinted of a purpose beyond worship. There was a magic here. But for this night, at least, it remained hidden. Satisfied with her discoveries, Kelly extinguished the candle and returned through the tunnel to her bed.

The following day was December 21; that evening would mark the winter solstice and the start of Yule. At the manor, the Christmas season was referred to using its ancient name, Yule (derived from the Scandinavian word *jul*, meaning "wheel"). The Yule holiday actually combined the observation of the winter solstice—the shortest day of the year—with that of Christmas, so it began on the eve of the twenty-first and ran through the twenty-fifth.

Making wholesale changes to traditions rooted in one's earliest childhood memories can be disconcerting. But for Kelly the opposite was true. Had she been in Vermont trying to celebrate Christmas, her mother's absence would have painfully amplified Kelly's loss. Here, however, the differences in her grandmother's holiday traditions actually afforded Kelly some relief. (And who wouldn't love stretching Christmas over three additional days?)

Christmas couldn't seem more different from the holiday Kelly knew. The Yule log wasn't a chocolate cake. It was a mighty stump that was lit on Christmas Eve and burned through the night and all through Christmas Day. Here, there were no Christmas trees or brightly colored lights hanging inside and out. Rather, mistletoe was cut and set over doorways to bring peace and prosperity to those within, while candles glowed warmly in the windows that looked out on the long Scottish nights. This year Kelly wouldn't be watching *The Nutcracker* on television; she'd be Wassailing on Christmas Day with the other youths of the manor. Gifts were still exchanged, but they weren't bought; they were handmade.

Yule began at sundown—barely past mid-afternoon this time of the year—when people joined to see the final rays of the setting sun line up through a narrow gap in the trees and fall directly upon Winter Rock. These were the last glimmers of light from the shortening days, and were sped on their journey with the bagpipe's soulful farewell. At sunrise the next morning, the first light from the now-lengthening days would be greeted with the continuous pealing of the abbey bells.

Following sunset, everyone retired to the Great Hall for the First Feast of Yule. Before they sat, Brid lit the single white candle centered in a large, evergreen wreath. The wreath represented the wheel of life—Yule—and tonight the candle-lighting celebrated the renewal of light; on Christmas Eve the taper would again burn, symbolizing the renewal of life.

There was no head table this evening. It was tradition at the First Feast for the servants to join the celebration and for the masters to serve the meal. Maggie, Willie, Rhona, and the rest of Brid's staff were seated about the hall, and in their unlikely role, the masters walked among the tables pouring pitchers of cider and wine, carrying platters of meat and winter vegetables, and clearing away the emptied dishes. Even Allisdair and Brid participated. While Kelly expected expressions of resignation and forbearance on the servers' faces, she was surprised that they dispatched their duties cheerfully, genuinely concerned that those they served left the table satisfied. (Mostly. While he wasn't actually rude to anyone, Master Roderick scowled throughout the evening.)

The next morning Ina persuaded Kelly to join her for the cutting of the mistletoe. A thin layer of snow crunched underfoot as the two girls negotiated their way through the ancient oak grove to a massive tree a full twelve feet across.

A group had gathered there and Kelly followed their upward gazes, spying a man in white, swinging in a harness through the upper branches. He brandished a long-poled sickle with a blade that sparkled golden when it caught the sun's rays. He was moving towards a clump of green nestled in the bare branches that could only be mistletoe.

"We've harvested the Yule mistletoe in this manner since the first days," Ina explained. "The privilege falls to the highest ranking male on the estate, who by custom dresses in white wool." She paused and looked at Kelly. "I understand your father held the honor for years."

A smiled curled at Kelly's lips. She was pleased she had a connection to this seemingly important ceremony. She tried to picture the man above as her father.

The highest ranking male ... there was something familiar ...

Allisdair? That's Allisdair up there? Allisdair who's never out of a kilt?

She was suddenly grateful for the white wool trousers.

As he reached his pole towards the mistletoe, Jillian and several others positioned themselves directly beneath, holding a sheet to prevent the sacred herb from touching the ground. As Jillian called ready, Allisdair gave a swift pull and a sprig wafted down, landing squarely on the sheet.

Kelly watched Allisdair's relaxed movements and heard the easy tone of his voice. It wasn't his typical gruff. There was more Ebenezer and less Scrooge. This was the second time in less than a day his manner had surprised her.

Because precise sickle placement was awkward from the end of a pole, the pruning operation wasn't a quick one. After a time, Kelly grew bored; as she looked around, a furtive movement caught her attention.

A figure darted behind a nearby tree; then, after a brief pause, ran behind the next tree further back. His shirt tail dangled carelessly and his hair stuck up on one side as if he'd slept on it: Dougal was easy to identify, even at a distance. What was he up to, sneaking away from the group one tree at a time?

Now it was Kelly's turn to slip behind a tree. Closing her eyes, she slowly exhaled; as she found her center, she made the shift and a chestnut-red squirrel (with rather handsome ear tufts) clung to the trunk.

Squirrel shifts had been her most recent subject of study and she was eager to test out her latest form under field conditions (or in this case, forest conditions). Kelly's promise against extracurricular shifting hadn't been wholly forgotten. But once you bend a rule, it's easier the next time. Besides, this reconnaissance was in everyone's best interests.

The fissured and furrowed bark of the oak provided her needle claws an excellent gripping surface. She scampered up a hundred feet to take a sighting. Kelly located Dougal slinking through the grove back in the direction of the manor. Surveillance was better suited to the lower branches, so she ran back down and then out along a bough. As the branches shrank to twigs, she pumped her tail twice to prime herself for the leap to the next tree.

Master Roy had chosen the squirrel to teach the balancing of consciousnesses. The importance of anchoring is stressed in early shape-shifting training, because it's an important safety skill. However, finesse shifting requires a degree of trust in the subject animal's instincts; for this to happen, the anchor must release some control. If there's not enough anchor, you'll think entirely like a squirrel and never have the sense to return to your human form. But if there's too much anchor, you'll run around acting like a person in a squirrel's body and miss the whole point of being a squirrel.

The trick is knowing when to let each mind assert itself. A squirrel teaches this because leaping through the air at distant tree branches is not something the human consciousness readily agrees to. To a squirrel, on the other hand, it's business as usual, *and* quicker transportation is a handy thing when your legs are only three inches long. So without relinquishing her anchor, Kelly had to ease its control enough to allow her squirrel consciousness to take over for leaps.

Soaring through the air fifty feet up caused her anchor some mental shrieking initially. But she had practiced with Master Roy, jumping between trees in the apple orchard, and her training did kick in.

Red squirrels, unlike their larger gray cousins, are more nimble and move more quickly through the treetops than they do on the ground, so it didn't take long for Kelly to catch up with Dougal. This gave her some time to concentrate on her jumping technique and work to fine-tune her control. For a squirrel to perform a properly executed leap, it must extend all four feet spread-eagle in order to maximize glide while in the air. Kelly repeated a mantra of "pump, leap, glide, grab" as she approached the end of each branch, but after the first dozen trees it became second nature. She discovered subtle changes in leg position enabled her to drift right, left, and even downward, should the target branch be slightly out of line. Where she at first clutched wildly for *any* branch to grab onto, relying on the holding power of her prickly claws, she gradually grew more confident and started choosing her target branches, landing with far less fuss.

As Dougal left the grove, pines and birches replaced the oaks. The chunks of reddish-orange pine bark required a slightly different hold, but Kelly adjusted easily. With birches she had to be more careful; the papery bark would sometimes peel away when she grabbed onto it.

Running slightly ahead of Dougal, she stopped for a short rest when she spotted a crossbill twisting open the scales of a ripe pine cone. Lunch time!

She muscled him aside. "*Tjuk-tjuk-tjuk*—outta here, bird-brain, this baby's mine!"

She was halfway through her appropriated snack when something bowled into her from behind. She spun around to face her assailant and was astonished to see another red squirrel chattering excitedly at her.

"*Cheeek, cheeek!*" she scolded. "What do you think you're doing? And stop calling me 'baby!' No, I do *not* want to be your girlfriend! Get off me, what are you doing? I said no. I meant no. 'No' doesn't mean, 'sure thing.' Where'd you get that idea? Would you stop climbing on me! I'm not playing hard to get—I'm not interested. Ugh—you've got *fleas*!"

Ignoring her, the squirrel persisted in his attempts to woo her—although as courtship went, his was rather paltry. Kelly, a furry half-pound of indignation, decided to reinforce her message. She swung her neck around and dug her incisors into his foreleg.

That's for the fleas!

Shoving her anchor into the back seat, she took off at a breakneck pace. Charging down branches and then hurling through space, she was the Evel Knievel of squirreldom trying to outdistance her amorous shadow. After a series of fur-raising leaps (even for a squirrel), he finally abandoned his pursuit. Once safe, she halted to catch her breath and to scratch away one of the small gifts he'd given her.

By now, Dougal was again far enough ahead that Kelly had to scramble to catch up. The forest was thinning as they neared the manor grounds and Kelly found herself having to leap farther and glide longer to reach each successive tree. But her skills had improved with the practice and she was quite pleased with herself, soaring effortlessly while her anchor silently attended each maneuver.

It was on her very next jump that things went downhill. Literally. As her glide ended she reached for the approaching branches, but before her paws could grasp them, she felt the tug of gravity. She stretched her forelegs, scrabbling in desperation—but they only met air. The branch was just beyond reach.

It's funny how fluid time can be. In some instances a minute can seem like an hour; at other times, hours can run by in moments. During a crisis, time somehow slows so that more thoughts and observations fit into the briefest instant. At her current height, Kelly was 1.76 seconds above the earth. In 1.76 seconds she'd run into the ground at 38.52 miles per hour. While 38.52 doesn't sound like a large number—and as speeds go, 38.52 miles per hour isn't impressively fast—if you're a petite, fine-boned rodent, 38.52 might as well be a hundred or a thousand. A splat is a splat.

While her squirrel instincts continued to reach for the branches (squirrels are eternal optimists), her anchor took charge. Unfortunately, panic thinking—and who wouldn't be panicked—isn't always well considered or productive in an emergency.

How could I be so dumb?

Tick …

I'm a squirrel, after all.

Tock …

I should have remembered that. What made me think I could fly?

Tick …

And that's when she hit upon a desperate idea.

Once the whisper of the notion floated past her consciousness, her mind grabbed it and forced it into action without waiting for orderly thought. Afterwards, she wasn't even sure how she'd known what to do. But wanting to become a bird at that moment was so powerful an image in her minds (both person and squirrel) that it somehow wrenched her from her red, furry form into the lithe, feathered body of a tree sparrow. Passing control to her bird senses, she brought her tail up hard. She pulled out of her dive precisely 1.75 seconds after she began her fall, and as she did, she felt the grass tickle her breast feathers.

What she had just done was known as direct transference—shifting from one animal form directly to another without shifting to a person in between. It was an advanced technique and was covered in one of the later chapters. Kelly hadn't read that far yet, so was surprised she'd managed to pull it off. That must be what "on-the-job training" meant.

Dougal was heading for a door on the east wing of the manor house. There was an open window beside it, but Kelly's disguise was a problem. Birds flitting through the windows were a common enough occurrence, but tree sparrows tended to be shy around people and buildings; as one, she might draw attention. She landed on a nearby branch and tried to repeat what she had just executed in sheer panic. It took a couple of attempts, but she finally managed a direct transference from a tree sparrow to its slightly larger and less timid cousin, the house sparrow.

By now Dougal was inside. Kelly hopped from her branch and easily glided towards the building, chittering away the whole time. She decided that house sparrows were the blabbermouths of the bird world. She much preferred the tree sparrow, who only chirped when it had something useful to say. In fact, she was so busy chirruping about how the humidity was frizzing her feathers, the deplorable state of nests these days, and how the jays were ruining the neighborhood, she hardly noticed Dougal moving down the hallway. It wasn't until he was passing through the far door that she realized what was about to happen. Her anchor issued the order to shut her beak and she aimed at the fast-closing door as speedily as her wings would carry her. She covered the distance quickly, but the door shut just before she got to it. She was trapped on this side.

A mouse makes a rather lacking spy because of its poor vision. However, when the task at hand is to squeeze through tight spaces, a mouse is perfect for the job. Kelly landed on the stone floor and centered her anchor on the image of a mouse. The direct transference was getting easier and she was soon twitching her whiskers and swishing her tail. She smushed her belly against the cool stone and pressed herself flat as she squeezed under the door.

On the other side she popped back into shape and tried to get her bearings. Her rather excellent hearing picked out Dougal's mumble. She was trying to make out what he was saying when there came a sudden shriek.

"Eeeeee! You let a mouse in with you!" Rhona could pierce even a mouse's ears.

Her cover blown, Kelly pancaked herself and started to squeeze back under the door when the floor shook with a violent *thump!*

She was lucky to have started back under when she did—the broom only caught her tail. Still, it was an agonizing blow. When Rhona opened the door looking for the suspect mouse, she didn't notice the sparrow with crumpled tail feathers flying a ragged line for the far window. Kelly's butt would be sore for days.

12

GIFTS

Kelly arose early. She was excited, but not with expectation; it was simply because it was Christmas morning.

The sky was the gray of a dull nickel. A gentle flurry drifted down, unpressed by wind. Kelly built up the fire in her sitting room and warmed her back to it, as she gazed at the snow floating against the silvery light of the pre-dawn.

There was time enough before her day would begin. The chapel service had been the afternoon before, marking the start of Christmas at sunset. Breakfast with Brid wouldn't be until 9 AM. Lulled by the unhurried solitude of the snow, Kelly watched as the flakes lazily accumulated on her windowsill. She removed her pendant and gripped it in her left hand. The snow had piled several inches deep when she reached for her diary.

December 25

Dear Mom,

It's Christmas. This will be our first one apart. That made me sad, but then I realized Dad had to get used to it. I suppose we will too.

Here at the manor we don't buy gifts for each other. We make them. It's much harder, because you have to think about people and decide what might have special meaning for them.

It's snowing this morning. Christmas snow. It's so peaceful. Like a soft, white blanket wrapped around me. Warm and safe. And it covers the sadness.

I'd like to give you the snow for Christmas, Mom. Merry Christmas!

Love, Kelly

The Christmas breakfast table, set for two in Brid's residence, sparkled like a shiny ornament. It was a good-china day and the crystal and sterling glittered merrily. Kelly shared with her grandmother the traditional holiday fare of mince pies and fresh-baked oatmeal bread, and other delicacies covered the table in generous abundance: pheasant sausage, smoked salmon terrine, leek and mushroom quiche and a citrus salad. It was only afterwards Kelly guiltily wondered how early Maggie's own Christmas morning must have begun.

Following breakfast they retired to the sitting room, where Brid presented Kelly with a princely set of tack, dyed a deep forest green. The bridle and reins were braided with a supple yet strong leather, and tooled hillsides of wild horses galloped across the saddle. She also received an ermine-lined wool cape of the same color, with gloves and cap to match.

Then it was Kelly's turn. She carefully set a bulky parcel on the coffee table before her grandmother. Brid teased the tissue paper apart to reveal a potted bonsai grove. Kelly's breath caught in her throat as Brid examined the miniature trees. Ina had instructed and guided Kelly in the creation of this gift, but the hours spent over anxious decisions of which branches to prune and which to preserve had been Kelly's. Even the selection and placement of the trees forming the grove had presented choices requiring thoughtful consideration. She gulped a swallow as she awaited Brid's reaction.

"*Beith*," Brid reflected. "Birch. The first of trees to seed and establish a new forest. *Beith* signals healing and rebirth—the release of those whose time has come to completion. The first month of the Celtic calendar. It's the lady of the woods, yet within its slender form lie vast reserves of strength."

She turned the pot to better see one of the trees near the back. "And what's this among the birches?" Her eyebrows arched in surprise. "*Nuin*. An ash. Of *Yggdrasil* and the World Tree. It's the symbol of change, the battling of fate. It's the giver of wisdom, the bringer of visionary dreams. It grows tall with a broad crown and its branches reach heavenward as its roots delve deep within the earth. It stands as the gateway between worlds."

The blue of Brid's eyes drilled into Kelly with intensity. "Why a single ash among the birches?"

Kelly's gaze flicked down to the diminutive trees as she tried to structure words around the gut feelings that prompted her choice. She'd intended a birch grove. The ash was only added at the last minute on an impulse. Yet having done so, the whole felt so incredibly right she never second guessed it.

"The sameness of the birches felt like … a melody sung in unison. The ash added … harmony to the song …" She trailed off, hoping her explanation didn't sound ridiculous to her grandmother.

Brid slowly passed her outstretched palms around the form of the bonsai grove. "Yet not all notes combine to create harmony," she said more to herself. "This is a most unlikely of pairings … yet its resonance is profound." Her eyes narrowed, locked on the single ash. "*Beith* is my tree." Her words were hardly more than a whisper. "Who then does *Nuin* represent?"

After a thoughtful silence she looked up with a softer expression. "Kelly, the newness of your stay here has passed. This is your home now, regardless of where your future may lead you. We are your kith and kin. Is there anything you desire?"

What do I want? People have been asking me that for eight months. At first the question made me angry. As if the person asking had the power to give me what I wanted most, but chose not to. I don't know where the anger's gone anymore. And the person asking doesn't have to give you back, Mom, because it feels like a part of you is still with me. As though you refused to be sent away. At first I just wanted things to be the way they had been. Normal again. None of it's the same now. None of it. Yet, oddly, it feels normal enough. Who have I become?

Her eyes followed the black veining that highlighted the white birch trunks. Bonsai was the art of growing dwarf trees in a way that made them appear far older than their actual age. The trees Kelly had planted to make this grove were close to her own age, yet they appeared ancient— many generations older, as if they'd lived through the ages to reach their current state of veneration. As if they carried the collected wisdom of the past in their bark and leaves.

"I'd like …" She hesitated. "I'd like to learn more about … my heritage."

Kelly left her grandmother with a promise to join her later for a private dinner, and she made her way to the kitchen where the revelers were to assemble for the Wassail.

She arrived to find Willie tying strips of red ribbon bedecked with tiny gold bells on the handles of a large wooden cauldron. A battery of spices stood in line beside bowls of waiting ingredients: orange slices, roasted apples, brown sugar and lemon peel. Maggie was busily pouring gallon jugs of cider into a massive stock pot atop a nearby stove.

A voice could be heard approaching the kitchen:

> "*Some say that ever 'gainst that season comes,*
> *Wherein our Savior's birth is celebrated,*
> *The bird of dawning singeth all night long;*
> *And then, they say, no spirit*
> *dare stir abroad.*"

Gordie strode into the room with his left hand clutching his chest and his right arm spread theatrically.

> "*The nights are wholesome;*
> *then no planets strike,*
> *No fairy takes, nor witch hath*
> *power to charm,*
> *So hallow'd and so gracious is that time.*"[13]

---

13   *Hamlet* (Act I, Scene i) by William Shakespeare

He made directly for the bowls of ingredients, but Maggie got there first, turning his shoulders and propelling him in the direction of the cauldron.

"I'll nay have young Will doin' all the work while ya eat yer way through my pantry. Why dunna ya lend him a hand there?" She firmly suggested.

Gordie threw up his hands with a look of unwarranted persecution, but nevertheless assisted Willie with the ribbons.

As others started to arrive, Kelly stepped to the stove and admitted in a soft voice, "I've never done this before."

Maggie looked up. "Ah lassie, is this yer first Wassail then?"

Kelly nodded.

"No worries—everything must begin sometime." As Maggie lobbed orange slices and lemon peel into the pot, she explained the Wassail is a hot, spiced apple punch The group of carolers would carry it around the manor house in the bowl the boys were decorating, offering a cup to any who'd like one. They were to finish in the West Room where they'd exchange gifts.

Maggie's warm features suddenly hardened and she placed a firm hand on Kelly's wrist. She dropped her voice, but Kelly had no difficulty hearing words that sliced into her with knife-like precision. "Dunna leave that cauldron alone with anyone. Anyone! I'll nay be havin' Christmas Day tragedies this holiday." Maggie's hazel eyes were as steel-hard as they'd been jovial moments before.

Kelly gulped agreement, wondering how the savvy kitchen woman knew of the Saven poisonings.

"Ach, then," Maggie chuckled, erasing all tension, "We'll be havin' a fine Christmas fer sure!"

Wassailing proved to be Christmas caroling with portable refreshments. They took turns in pairs carrying the jingling Wassail bowl as they moved from room to room throughout the manor. Assorted Christmas cookies stuffed several baskets that also accompanied them and were passed out with the cups of steaming holiday punch. It wasn't long before Kelly decided they'd consumed more than they'd given away.

Kelly knew some of the carols they sang and some bore resemblance to ones she recognized. She tried to improvise harmonies to the ones she'd never heard before, but was only partially successful. Still, none minded as they merrily trooped through the manor singing and proffering cookies and cups of Wassail to all they met.

Gordie had a roguish grin as they stopped outside one door. "Watch this!" he whispered.

His knock was met with churlish cries from within.

"Go away you miserable children! I know what you're about and I'll have nothing to do with this foolishness. Be off! Stop bothering me!"

Kelly winced at Master Roderick's voice. Gordie's smile was so infectious, however, her wince melted into laughter. Doing as they were bidden, they proceeded down the hall, singing gaily.

The cookies ran out before they'd finished, and Kelly offered to return to the kitchen and refill the baskets. When Gordie announced he'd come along, she wondered how many cookies would survive the return trip.

When they got back, they were surprised to find only Aidan. He leaned against the wall, the cauldron at his feet. Alone with the Wassail bowl.

Kelly's eyes narrowed. "Where are the others?"

"We finished up," he answered. "They went on ahead to the West Room. I waited so you'd know where to find us."

It was odd the others hadn't taken the Wassail bowl with them. She chose to say nothing, however. She merely looked from Aidan to the bowl and then back to Aidan. Gordie, suspecting nothing, gave Aidan a hand with the cauldron as they went to rejoin the group. Kelly followed with the cookies.

Over the last month, Kelly had learned how much harder it was to make Christmas gifts than it was to buy them. She always tried to choose a gift that would be special for the recipient, but this Christmas her choices were limited to things she could make herself. Nevertheless, after some weeks of imaginative thought and hard work, Kelly was pleased with her results.

Gordie was a sponge for new tunes, particularly ones he could play on his bagpipes—although he was a fine singer, as well. For him, Kelly had written out the sheet music for a dozen traditional American folk songs she was sure would be new to him. She bound the individual sheets into a sheaf tied with a ribbon on which she'd carefully drawn notes and other musical markings.

Kelly gave Ina a bottle of herb-infused oil, made from the herbs she helped tend in the garden. Ina could use the oil for the healing properties of the herbs, but it would also make a tasty addition to many dishes.

With all of the time Kenna was spending in the icy, high pastures tending the ewes and tups, Kelly thought warm gear might be appreciated. She sewed Kenna a pair of sheepskin mittens figuring if the fleecy hide could keep a sheep warm, it should do likewise for Kenna.

Gordie presented Kelly with a *bodhran*—the handheld Celtic drum she'd seen many nights during the after-dinner entertainment. He'd learned to make it as part of his bard apprenticeship, but he admitted he could never let Thomas catch *him* playing a percussion instrument. It was roughly the shape of a tambourine, but more than a foot across; the goatskin head stretched tight over a birch frame. Gordie showed her how to strike it using a double-headed drumstick, known as the beater, with a rocking hand motion. She'd need help learning to play it, but she was looking forward to the challenge.

From Ina she received a book of tree and plant lore. After seeing how voraciously Kelly studied the reference books in the herbarium, Ina decided to compile some of the more obscure texts into a single volume for Kelly's personal research. Kelly looked at the pages painstakingly copied by hand. This must have taken Ina weeks to assemble. It was a trove of information Kelly was anxious to explore.

Kenna also gave Kelly a musical instrument—a carved wooden flute. "My brothers taught me to whittle," Kenna explained. "It gives me something to do in the upper pastures. I made myself one, but I stink at playing it … although the sheep don't complain. I thought you'd do it more justice."

Kelly blew into the mouthpiece and was delighted with the breezy note that floated from the flute. She grinned her thanks.

Aidan surprised Kelly when he stepped up and handed her a package. She never spent time with him and hadn't considered exchanging gifts. Unsure of what to say, she unwrapped the box. Inside she found a squat pewter bowl with flat handles—lugs—on either side. Flattened hammer-marks dimpled the bowl and attested to the physical effort that had gone into the gift.

"It's a *quaich*, Kelly. It's the Highland cup of friendship." He gently took it from her by one of the lugs. "The two lugs represent the sharing expected of Celtic hospitality." He reached the *quaich* down into the Wassail bowl and drew up a cup of punch. He held one lug as he offered her the cup.

She accepted the *quaich* in silence, grasping the free lug as he passed it to her. She could smell the apples and spices coming off the still-warm liquid. She stared at the surface of the punch as if her eyes could see *everything* that had been added to it. Then, with uncharacteristic clumsiness, she bobbled the *quaich* and the Wassail poured down the front of her.

"Darn! Now I'll need to change." She turned to run from the room and knocked into the Wassail bowl, splashing its contents across the floor. "Oh! It's all wasted!" she exclaimed as she hurried out.

When Jillian led Kelly into Brid's salon that evening, Kelly was surprised to find no table set. Had Brid changed her mind about dinner? Or had she simply forgotten? Either was unheard of. Kelly settled into a chair to await her grandmother. She hadn't sat for long when the ghostly figure of the barn owl glided into the room, alighting on the chair beside her.

"Merry Christmas, Master Owl!" Kelly bade.

The owl spread its wings, snapping its beak as one might tsk a tongue.

Had she missed something?

"You'll need to be more observant if you wish to correctly sex an owl."

Kelly jumped at her grandmother's voice. Brid sat calmly beside her, the owl gone. Kelly stared stupidly, no words ready, as her mind struggled to connect the dots. Those bedtime appearances soon after her arrival, when the owl would rasp her to a teary sleep; the daytime vigils it sat in the infirmary during her long convalescence; the overhead oversight from the kitchen's ceiling beams on her visits to Maggie—it had all been Brid. It had simply never occurred to Kelly that Brid, lord of her people and of pure Tuathan blood, could do something Kelly had figured out on her own: she could shape-shift.

Brid's ever-serious features held a fleeting hint of bemusement.

"Your heritage, Kelly, is a long and tightly woven tale. To learn it all would take a lifetime. Perhaps longer. But the story surely encompasses your gifts. And that's where we'll begin this evening.

"What birds have you become in your studies with the Master Husbandman?"

She had been a tree sparrow and a house sparrow, but the house sparrow was unauthorized. She hadn't really broken her promise—in the bird world, tree sparrows and house sparrows are practically related. Brid might understand … but Kelly didn't want to risk it. She didn't want to let her grandmother down. Her churning thoughts raised a flush to her cheeks.

"Sparrows," she answered obliquely.

"Not well-suited for night flight," Brid mused.

Kelly's blush flared. Luckily, her grandmother didn't seem to notice.

"Would you like to try something more vigorous?" Brid offered.

Kelly once again started when the owl suddenly replaced her grandmother. The mahogany eyes seemed to swallow Kelly like pools of molasses. They blinked with deliberateness, and just that quickly Brid was back in her seat.

"I feel like dining out this evening," she informed her granddaughter. "Would you care to join me?"

Kelly's puzzlement must have shown on her face.

"Would you care to become an owl?"

Her eyes widened as Kelly realized Brid's meaning. She nodded slowly.

"In your past shifts you've imprinted the pattern of the animal's mind by perceiving it directly. Tonight I'm going to give you the imprinted pattern. Steady your centering."

Suddenly, Kelly's mind filled with an owl's sensations, as if they'd been cut and pasted into her brain. Kelly studied the image of the owl's mind and filed it in her own memory.

"Do you feel you can shift with that image?"

Kelly nodded to Brid's question.

"You may shift when you're ready."

Kelly expected the first moments of disorientation that accompanied any shift, but she was unprepared for the searing pain behind her eyes.

"Kschhhhh!" The shriek that escaped her was as instinctive as the defensive posture of her hunched body and raised wings.

Shift back. Brid's calm voice spoke in her mind, addressing her anchor.

Despite the clouding pain, Kelly managed to do as directed. The pain vanished. She sat breathing heavily and looked to her grandmother for explanation.

"A barn owl's eyes are very sensitive to light—much more so than a human's. This provides exceptional night vision, but can also make a well-lit room painful to bear."

"But you often fly about during the day."

"I found it bothersome, at first, but after a millennium or so, I got used to it." Her grandmother stepped around the room turning the lights down.

In near-total darkness, Kelly again made the shift. After a few moments of orientation she rasped a short, "*Shiiish!*" Better this time. She cocked her right wing and absently straightened some misaligned feathers with her beak. When she looked back up, she was perched beside a second white and tawny barn owl.

Brid hissed a sustained wheeze that could only be described as a snore, indicating they should head to dinner. With a sweep of her wings, she led Kelly out the window into the nighttime blackness.

Kelly was surprised at how different an owl was from a sparrow, although both were birds. Sparrows are small and vulnerable—ever alert to potential danger. A barn owl, on the other hand, lives atop its food chain with few natural predators. The sparrow's nervous paranoia was absent. Instead, a calm self-assurance was hard-wired into her genes: Kelly knew she was the biggest, baddest bird on the block.

Her wings allowed a different kind of flight, as well. Their sweep was so great, relative to her body size, that with rapid downbeats she could practically hover. She used this technique to slow her forward speed as she stretched her talons forward to land on a branch beside

Brid. Kelly continued her earlier preening while Brid hissed and rasped owl fundamentals.

"You've probably noticed that your night vision and depth perception are excellent; your hearing, however, is your most important sense."

Kelly objected with a series of guttural screeches, explaining that she couldn't, in fact, hear anything. As a sparrow, she'd gotten used to the sound of her own flight—the sound of the air displaced by her wings—just as one becomes accustomed to the sound of air rushing by an open car window. As an owl, there was no sound in flight, as if someone had turned the volume off. Might she be deaf?

Brid snapped her bill in reply, explaining that Kelly's hearing was fine. Owls are silent in flight due to their wing design. The wing feathers have a velvety pile that muffles sound and there's a comb-like fringe on the leading edge of the wings that minimizes air turbulence.

Kelly's beak poked at her wing, confirming what Brid had snapped.

I'm designed with stealth technology! Very cool!

Brid continued to explain that while silent flight makes an owl undetectable, it more importantly allows the owl to locate its prey by sound. Owl ears are extremely sensitive and are positioned on the front of the face so that the facial bones funnel and amplify sound.

"Come, let's try it."

They flew out over a field. Kelly focused on her hearing and became aware of the soft scrabbling of an entire host of nocturnal critters under the snow. Listening carefully, she could differentiate each by its direction and distance. Her owl mind could instinctively tell the difference between a vole six feet ahead to the right and a rat scurrying directly beneath her. Having identified these contacts, her whole body tugged at her consciousness.

"*Kschhh!*" Brid called, "Go ahead—give in to your instincts."

Kelly released her anchor's control and she instantly dove on the rat, feet forward, talons spread wide. Her ears directed her to it as surely as sight. Before she'd fully reengaged her anchor, her expandable mouth tossed down the rat body in four gulps.

Note to self: rodent shifts shall be discontinued immediately!

Brid demonstrated an alternative hunting technique Kelly referred to as "perch and pounce." From a fence post or tree branch, she would merely wait until something scampered by on the ground below, and then pounce. It made for a more casual dining experience, allowing one to eat at a more leisurely pace.

Experimenting with both methods, Kelly consumed one rat, four short-tailed voles, two wood mice, one shrew, and one bat (the last tasting somewhat like chicken). She was sated and didn't believe she could eat another thing. She was about to say as much when she burped up a pellet of compressed bones and fur.

Owl puke. Ew …

⚘

Back in Brid's salon Kelly was giddy with the excitement of her experience. "That was wonderful! I could do that *every* night."

Brid nodded sympathetically. "Now you can see why it's my preferred animal form. But try not to skip dinner in the hall *too* often—we'd miss your company."

"You mean … I can …"

"Yes, Kelly. It's a safe form. You may shift to an owl on your own, outside of lessons. Just don't stay out too late."

Her day had been a full one and Kelly was exhausted. Yet even fatigue couldn't rob her of the warm glow she felt. Nor did it stem her routine. Before she climbed into bed, Kelly extracted her father's diary from behind the loose brick in her fireplace. As if her final gift of the day, an entry awaited her.

December 25

I was right! I followed Stuart after breakfast. He's been sneaking looks from a book on MB before each of our lessons!

How he ever learned the vault combination, I'll never know. Being a decent spy myself, I now possess it too! Now I understand his paranoia about being caught.

Fionn's shield guards the hidden wisdom. Only the freshly cut golden bough can penetrate his shield.

Merry Christmas and thank you, Stuart!!

HMB

A book *did* exist! And Kelly now knew where. While she didn't exactly know where the vault was located, she'd somehow find out. Her father had also supplied her with the rune code riddle necessary to open the vault. Not a bad Christmas present. Not bad at all.

Merry Christmas and thank you, Dad!!

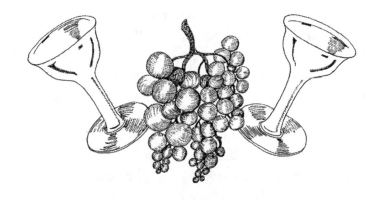

13

THE HAUNTED
WINE CELLAR

"Two more ewes missing—because of your carelessness! At first light I want you in the upper pastures searching every drift and snow bank large enough to bury a sheep. Think on *that* while you clean this place—I don't care if it takes all night!"

Dougal's rebukes were becoming common occurrences. Barely a day would pass before he'd find some new fault with Kenna's work. The outcome was equally predictable: he'd punish her with overloaded chores—typically jobs that should have been his.

Kelly witnessed this evening's encounter from outside, through the sheep byre's far window. Aside from her concern for her friend, she snooped hoping to learn Dougal's purpose. Why did he want Kenna out of the way? More importantly, what was *he* up to while Kenna was busily performing all of his work?

Kelly withdrew from the window, stepping silently on the crusted ice underfoot. Instead of sliding into the darkness beyond the window's light, however, she backed into someone directly behind her. She spun with a start.

"Niall! What are you doing here?"

"It would be more interesting to know what *you're* doing," the stable boy sneered. "Eavesdropping on a journeyman. I wonder what Master Roy would say."

Kelly had no desire to tip Dougal she'd been spying on him. On the other hand, she really didn't think Niall would go to Master Roy. That wasn't his style. He was more likely to blackmail her with the *threat* of telling. And once done successfully, he wouldn't quit. It would provide him a constant series of petty victories over her. She wouldn't allow this pustule the satisfaction. She decided the best way to defeat a blackmailer was to out blackmail him.

"If you insist on going to Master Roy, then by all means." Her silky tone dared him to tell the master. "Eavesdropping isn't polite—you're right—and I'm sure Master Roy would ask me to be more careful. Of course, I'd need to mention how you move logs from your pile to Robert's. He'd likely be more interested in that …"

This was a shrewd guess. As part of their chores, the stable boys each had a pile of wood to chop every morning. Kelly couldn't help but notice how Niall's pile was always smaller than the younger boy's. Her surmise seemed to have hit the mark.

"You little witch! You're spying on *me*? You just keep your trap shut or I'll make you really sorry!" Niall darted off into the darkness before Kelly could say anything more.

She turned back to the byre, alarmed to see that Dougal had already left. Another opportunity to tail him lost!

Her hoped-for surveillance had thus far yielded little. When her schedule did allow her to observe his activities, she simply couldn't get close enough to trail him undetected. Dougal's duties ranged across the manor, from the barns and stables to the hillside pastures; it was simply too vast a territory to stake out effectively.

Yet … Dougal wasn't in this alone. If Rhona were his accomplice, perhaps she might lead Kelly to some answers. At the very least, Kelly knew where to find her. One merely needed to spend time in the kitchen …

It was uncharacteristically quiet when she arrived. The solitary figure present was standing on a crate, hunched over a deep sink, scrubbing a massive stockpot. Steam rose from the hot water as the fog might rise from a mountain *loch*. Sudsy peaks floated on the surface. Kelly cleared her throat so as to not startle him.

Willie turned. He nodded a shy hello and scratched his nose, wiping away a glob of suds.

"Are you here alone?" Kelly was surprised that Maggie would leave Willie here by himself if there was work to finish.

He nodded. "Maggie's nephew is fiddling after dinner. She wanted to hear him."

"What about Rhona?" It wouldn't surprise Kelly at all that Rhona would abandon Willie.

"She's working late down in the wine cellar."

"Wine cellar? I thought it scared her."

"Oh aye. But she's been going down more these last few days."

Kelly found it unlikely Rhona had discovered reserves of courage. Unless … the wine cellar's reputation was a hoax … and Rhona knew it!

"If Rhona's spending so much time down there," she suggested in what she hoped was an innocent tone, "it can't be too scary. Would you take me down sometime?" She backed away several steps; Willie was rinsing the pot and more water was spraying around the sink than into it.

"I can't. She has the only key."

How convenient: a base of operations, to which Rhona had sole access, possessing a creepy enough reputation to discourage visitors.

Haunted, my foot! I bet she's the one who started the rumor.

Kelly helped Willie finish up—it went much faster when your arms could reach the bottom of the sink—

and walked out with him. But no sooner had they parted than she doubled back to the darkened kitchen and the door that led to the wine cellar. She slipped in and started down the stairs. The stone steps were narrow and steep, and she needed both hands on the walls for balance as she descended. The stairway spiraled down in a tight corkscrew. Kelly was careful to place each foot along the outer edge of the treads—they were widest there with less risk of a misstep.

She tried to listen over her own breathing for any sounds coming up from below, but she heard nothing beyond the hesitant scrapes of her own feet. The stairway ended at a stone door with barely enough room to stand between it and the last step. Kelly tried the door, but it was locked. Locked from this side. Rhona was *not* in the wine cellar.

No sooner had she released the handle, than a sound rose up from behind the door. It filled the cramped passage, echoing off the close walls. It was a thin, scratchy wail that climbed high in pitch like a siren. After a brief pause, another cry followed—one that began to rise and then fell off like a moaning sigh. It was no human sound. Nor was it any animal call Kelly had ever heard. Overcome with terror, she turned and fled up the stairs, not caring where on the steps she placed her feet.

꙰

"But master—"

"No, Gordie, we're finished."

"But sir, I was hoping to go over my strathspey and reel one more time."

"No, Gordie. We're done. It's time for Kelly's lesson."

Kelly's arrival seemed to interrupt some disagreement between Gordie and the Master Bard. Both appeared vexed.

"Sir, there are only two weeks left until the Indoor Games! I know I could medal—possibly even win Piper-of-the-Day—if I can just get my tunes in shape. Considering what's at stake, I'm sure Kelly wouldn't mind if I took her lesson time this week. Would you, Kelly?" He turned to her earnestly.

Master David shook his head with a sigh. "If I thought it would impart even an iota of Fionn's wisdom, I'd cook a fish for you myself. Gordie, you're confusing success with excellence. Strive for the latter and you will, at times, achieve the former. Your goal should be to play well. *How* you get there is more important than *if* you get there. Now, your lesson is over. It's not Kelly's decision. It's mine."

Kelly could see the dejection in Gordie's eyes as he packed his bagpipes and left.

"Sir, what's wrong with wanting to win? Gordie's so passionate about his music. That can't be bad."

Master David assumed a more patient expression. "His ardor is admirable. But it's my job to ensure he aims it in the best direction. The desire to achieve is important, as is the discipline to work towards that goal, but the act of winning shouldn't overshadow the importance of playing well. If Gordie plays poorly and still manages to win a contest, is that more noteworthy than if he plays the best performance of his career, yet doesn't win?"

"It's not whether you win or lose, but how you play the … instrument?"

The Master Bard nodded.

"Sir, one more question before we begin?"

He peered at her. "If I suspect you're using Gordie's stalling tactics because you haven't been practicing … Very well. One more question."

"What did you mean about Fionn and a fish?"

Master David had no issue spending lesson time reviewing Celtic mythology, which was the basis for his reference to Fionn MacCumhaill and the Salmon of Wisdom. He told how the warrior-poet in his youth was tasked to cook the Salmon of Wisdom for his master, the bard Finnegas. Finnegas warned Fionn not to taste the fish—that was for the master, because the first taste would impart all the wisdom of the ages. While the fish cooked, however, its skin blistered up. Fionn tried to pop the blister with his finger, burning himself as he did so. He instinctively sucked on the burn and the fish juices on his fingertip were sufficient to carry the knowledge of the ages to the boy. When Fionn explained to his master what had happened, Finnegas realized that Fionn was the one destined to receive the Salmon's knowledge.

Master David walked to one of the shelves along the wall and thumbed through an oversized book until he came to the page he sought. "This is known as 'Fionn's Wheel.'" He showed Kelly a drawing that contained five concentric circles. At the cardinal points on each circle were hash marks—five at each point on the innermost circle, decreasing to a single hash, north, west, east and south, on the outermost circle. The effect was like a compass rose. "This is an early depiction of the *Ogham* alphabet, which in the days of Fionn symbolized the height of bardic knowledge."

He went on to explain how years later, the Tuathan god, Manannan Mac Lir, inscribed Fionn's Wheel onto a hazel shield he crafted for the warrior, thus creating Fionn's Shield. Fionn went on to found the Fianna, a group of lords many believed to be the basis for Arthurian legend and the famous Knights of the Round Table.

Kelly silently absorbed his words, but something nagged at her. She couldn't shake the feeling she'd seen Fionn's Wheel someplace before …

A few days later the weather finally broke, and Kelly took a frisky Gealach for an afternoon ride under the pale winter sun. Over two feet of snow had fallen during the last several weeks, but there was rarely that amount in any one place; some spots had blown clean to bare earth, and in others the wind had piled drifts many feet tall. The snow was fresh, and Gealach enjoyed kicking up the sparkling powder like a child might shake a snow globe. The drifts in the lee of the stables muffled Gealach's hoof falls; that was why Kelly could hear the voices before their owners came into view.

"I want you to do it tonight!" The slurred consonants were Dougal's.

"*How* I handle it is not your concern!" The second voice was Aidan's.

She turned the corner between the smithy and the stables. Spotting her, the two journeymen fell silent, acknowledging her with sullen nods.

Back in the stall, as she rubbed Gealach down, Kelly wondered about the conversation she'd interrupted. What was it that was to occur tonight? That Dougal wanted it to happen meant that Kelly didn't. Might someone be in danger? There were simply too many loose ends for Kelly to see any overall pattern. But how to learn more? By the time she had Gealach cooled and dried, and her own tack cleaned, Kelly had determined an evening patrol was in order—an owl patrol!

☙

Kelly had logged considerable time as a barn owl of late, and with the practice she'd developed an easy balance between her anchor and her owl self—in fact, so much so, her anchor could have some fun.

"Command and Control, this is Owl Patrol One: Ready for take off." Kelly hopped from foot to foot and gave her wings a shake before she answered herself.

"Proceed, Owl Patrol One," she replied. "You are cleared for takeoff."

With sweeping, silent wing beats, she took to the air. The first part of her mission would be to secure the perimeter; she would fly a wide circuit around the manor buildings. She'd then methodically patrol within that perimeter, hoping to sight any suspicious activity.

She was delightfully buoyant in the air—barely a pound in weight carried by wings with a four-foot span. She could glide for long periods without the incessant *flap-flap-flap* other birds required.

Coasting silently over the ground, her ghostly white form slid through the night, camouflaged against the snow. A fierceness coursed through her—she, the supreme hunter, stalking not just suspects, but also her dinner. The small creatures of the field had no defense against her; they could run, but they couldn't hide. She marveled at her ability: she could transition from glide, to dive, to veer and turn with pinpoint precision, guided by her highly sensitive vision and hearing. Armed with her owlish gifts, she *knew* she owned the night.

"Owl Patrol One, this is Command and Control: Proceed to terrain-hugging mode," she ordered herself.

"Roger, C&C." She dropped down until she was gliding a mere foot off the ground. On down beats, her wing tips brushed the snow as she flew inches above the earth—this was true nap-of-the-earth flight.

As she flew out over the duck pond, she dropped her feet down from their tucked position and dangled her talons, dragging them through the icy water.

"C&C, OP1: We are feet wet," she announced to the night.

A talon snagged some slimy pond plant that stubbornly held on as she flew back over land. It took several forceful leg shakes to kick it free.

"We are feet dry." She turned in the direction of the barns.

A sound ahead and to the left commanded Kelly's attention.

"Target acquired."

"OP1, C&C: You are cleared to engage."

A moment later Kelly was standing in a snow-covered field with a chittering vole squirming in her beak. She knew it was customary to interrogate prisoners before execution, but she had missed her dinner; she was bingo fuel and starving. Under her rules of engagement she was authorized to use proportional force—that is, in proportion to her hunger—so she decided to eat first and ask questions later.

She made several other tasty interdictions as she completed the perimeter sweep. Most were soft targets she could swallow in a single gulp; one brown rat was particularly large, however, and took several good swallows to get down.

"C&C, OP1: The perimeter is secure. No sign of suspects."

"Roger, OP1: Proceed with Phase II of the mission."

Phase II was the barn-to-barn search. Most of the barn buildings had small owl doors high up near the rafters to encourage owls to roost in them, helping to control the rodent population. For an owl, a barn was a target-rich environment.

Kelly started with the cow byre. She flew into the dark hayloft and perched on a roof beam that gave a view of both the loft and the floor below. With vision one hundred times more sensitive than a human's, she could easily distinguish the gray shapes that filled the barn's dark interior. It was her ears, however, that provided the most valuable data.

"C&C, we have multiple contacts! The first has a bearing of 245 degrees, range 14.375 feet."

"OP1, you may proceed at will. Remember to maintain radio silence."

Dive, dive, dive!

She jumped from the roof beam and was down to the floor like a bolt, razor-sharp talons extended before her. One mouse later, she was back up at her perch choosing her next contact. After about ten minutes of air-to-ground attacks and no sign of illicit activity, she decided to move on and search the next building.

The second building she flew into was the disused barn where Gordie had collected his wasps. Here she perched on the ladder leading up to the haymow. She worked the outer area of the floor, which was relatively clear of derelict farm equipment.

She was trying to decide if a bank vole, despite its saltiness, was more savory than a ground vole, when she heard something unexpected. She concentrated on her hearing and only slowly realized that the sound wasn't a sound at all. It wasn't coming through her owl senses, but through her anchor. It was a faint signal. A psychic sending. And if she was able to "hear" it, the sender must be close by.

Kelly pushed her center deeper, trying to strengthen the signal.

"… an eagle removes … bothersome nest … killing … or the mother before she's fledged her brood …"

She was on the verge of a titanic discovery—this could break her investigation wide open, possibly revealing not just the perpetrator, but also uncovering his plot! The gaps in the message could undo her, though; she was losing critical information. Her frustration at being so close pushed Kelly beyond common sense and she extended her awareness in an effort to boost the weak signal. It worked … sort of …

"… I agree. Wait—someone's here! Sendings aren't safe; use birds in the future!"

With that the message abruptly concluded. The sending didn't exactly end, however. Kelly could feel the presence of another mind surging outward, searching for … her!

OP1, C&C: ABORT, ABORT, ABORT! EXIT HOSTILE TERRITORY IMMEDIATELY!

She made for the owl door at top velocity, blessing the barn's darkness and her silent flight. Shooting straight back to her bedroom window, she willingly relinquished any ownership of *this* night.

January 9

Lachlan found the cellar's back door, but he doesn't know its secret—he'll never work the code.

Before he can enjoy the fruits of Bacchus, he must first satisfy the doorkeeper, who has different tastes.

HMB

Once again Kelly sat in Lachlan's shoes. She'd found the door several weeks earlier. A plump bunch of grapes with a wine glass to either side marked what was most certainly the alternate entrance to the wine cellar. Yet, like Lachlan, she didn't know its secrets.

January 13

- Bacchus = God of Wine
- Wine = Fruit of the vine
- *Muin* ✝ is the *Ogham* character for vine.

I still don't get the second part of the riddle.

╬├╪╪

Kelly didn't think *muin* alone would open the door, but for the moment that was all she had to work with, and in the interests of being thorough she thought she should at least rule it out. The thought of confronting the door, however, made her skin prickle.

After dinner that evening she made her way down the passage in question. She stood looking at the carved grapes for several minutes before she reached up and pressed *muin* ╋. The runes ignored her.

The ghost, however, did not. A noise arose from within that nearly peeled back Kelly's skin. It was an eerie wail, high-pitched and rasping. It had the quality of fingernails dragging across a blackboard, but brought on the feeling of claws dragging through your gut. As the tone slid up and down, the sound changed. It was as if the voice, escaping from a strangled throat, was trying to say something, but couldn't manage to form the words.

Terror piled up inside Kelly. At first she was frozen to the spot, but then all at once she couldn't run away fast enough—back to the company of the living. She had the door, but to gain entry she would have to somehow satisfy the ghost within. *Not* a task she relished.

"Hey Kelly, pass the neeps?" Gordie slurped down some fish stew before he reached out to accept the bowl. He continued his point as he slapped a mound of mashed turnips on his plate. "You're not alone, Kenna; bardic lore is filled with tales of the oppressed and unjustly accused."

Kelly looked at him puzzled. "How does that help Kenna?"

Gordie continued, ignoring the question. "Take the song, *MacPherson's Farewell* ... "

Kelly helped herself to a second portion of tatties—one could never have enough mashed potatoes. She elected to pass on the neeps.

"... Jamie MacPherson was the Scottish equivalent of Robin Hood, born of a gypsy mother. His archenemy, Duff of Braco, despised him for his gypsy blood and hunted him down, eventually imprisoning him. MacPherson was tried by the Sheriff of Banff, who himself had been bought off by Duff ... "

Kenna listened with a rapt expression. "What happened? How did MacPherson escape?"

"Oh, he didn't," Gordie informed her. "They hanged him."

Kenna pulled back as if slapped.

Gordie leaned forward and dropped his voice. "The treacherous part was that a reprieve from the Lord of Grant was on its way. Duff knew this and set the village clock ahead fifteen minutes so that the reprieve would arrive after MacPherson was already dead."

"He died?" Kelly demanded. "Gordie, why are you telling this story? What does this possibly have to do with Kenna?"

"I thought it might help her to know she's not alone. At the end he played under the gallows tree and afterwards asked the crowd who would take his fiddle. None would claim it, so he smashed the fiddle over his knee and cried, 'There's nay a han' shall play on thee when I am dead and gone.'"

Kenna's eyes looked watery and she wiped her nose on her sleeve.

Kelly delivered a sharp kick to Gordie's shin. "Robin Hood? That's just a romantic name for a highwayman. He ripped off people! That's why they hanged him. This has *nothing* to do with Kenna's situation. Can't you see you're upsetting her? Next time you feel the urge to help someone, DON'T!" Kelly rose and stomped off, leaving her tatties unfinished.

More snow the following morning again thwarted Kelly's plans for a ride. She swung by the kitchen, filling her pockets with apples—Gealach would require a peace offering if she weren't going out today. Kelly grabbed a bunch of green grapes for herself and bit into their cool, wet sweetness. As she walked, munching on the grapes, she wondered if Gealach might like to try some. Probably not—particularly once she smelled the apples. She'd much prefer those to grapes. Kelly paused mid-stride, a grape lolling in her mouth. Her mind grasped for something just beyond reach. Why was it important that Gealach would prefer the taste of apples to grapes …? Of course!

She turned and dashed back to her residence, first flipping through her diary and then the rune book. "Before he can enjoy the fruits of Bacchus, he must first satisfy the doorkeeper, who has different tastes." You weren't likely to find bushels of apples in a wine cellar, but Kelly would bet all the grapes from last fall's harvest there was cider down there.

The rune for apple tree was *quert* ▤. Abandoning her trip to the stables, Kelly hurried through her fireplace and down to the wine cellar's back door. At the moment there were no noises coming from behind it. She stood facing the door, hesitant to disturb it. Slowly she brought her hand up and held it for a long moment over *quert* ▤. She tensed, not sure what might happen when she touched the cold stone. Sucking in her breath, she pressed the rune. The silence continued. She then pressed *muin* ✝, and the door slid open.

Kelly stood motionless, paused at the threshold. Her curiosity eventually overcame her fear, however, and she ventured in. She moved with a wary caution, placing her feet gingerly, as if each step might trigger some violent response.

The cellar was dimly lit and it was difficult to see any distance. The occasional stone pillars that ran up to the vaulted ceiling were set with luminescent bricks, but their feeble light fell off quickly, leaving most of the cavernous vault in dusky shadows.

The room was a maze with tall racks of bottles forming narrow alleys. Casks and barrels of all volumes were piled everywhere, from the smaller kegs of ale and cider to the larger casks: hogsheads holding over sixty gallons of wine and spirits, and the giant tuns at four times that size.

Kelly crept deeper into the cellar. She wanted to believe the eerie silence meant the ghost wasn't home. She knew better, though. And that was the trouble. The silence was more sinister. Not only was she certain the ghost *was* here; she was equally sure it was watching her … and waiting.

The long rows of wine bottles, stacked one above the next, stretched off into the darkness. Kelly couldn't fathom how this much wine could ever be consumed in a lifetime—either human or Tuathan. How long had these bottles lain here … hundreds of years? … longer? She reached out to inspect one, curious what its label might reveal. But as she touched it, bottles overhead started to rattle. It began at the far end of the rack behind her and spread down the row, as if a strong wind blew through disturbing the wine's repose.

Kelly snatched her hand back. "I was just looking! I'm not going to steal any of your wine," she called to the shadows. "I'm an explorer!" Her attempt at bravado did little to embolden her.

Almost at once a whispering sprang up around her. It was a soft, sibilant buzz, lacking discernable words. And then, just as suddenly as it had begun, it ceased—silence again reverberating off the cold stone.

Kelly edged on, careful not to touch anything. She came upon a stone arch that opened into a smaller side chamber. The air was cooler here. And damp. Moss carpeted the far wall, a lush green running up to the ceiling. As Kelly looked, it glistened in the dim light—water from some unseen source trickled down through the green and vanished into a crack in the floor. This room was also filled with casks and racks of wine. In the far corner, Kelly could make out a pile of glass shards and the fractured remains of bottles. She moved to investigate, but the moment she stepped into the room a deafening shriek froze her bowels, halting her mid-stride. She hastily backed into the main cellar.

"All right, all right! I won't go in!" she cried back.

Once again the whispering started. Kelly tried to stand still, but she felt tiny tremors throughout her body. She strained to understand the wordless message if, in fact, it had any other meaning than, "Go away!" And again it stopped.

She suddenly had the oddest feeling she wasn't alone. She knew in that moment she had the full attention of the spirit that haunted this place. What she didn't know was whether its intentions were malevolent. She realized that coming here may not have been the wisest idea, and all at once wished she could click her heels three times and send herself back to her room.

Maybe she could ... She'd certainly shifted out of tricky situations in the past. (She ignored the fact she'd also shifted *into* quite a few.) Forming the barn owl image, she began to center. No sooner had she started, however, when a second bone-jolting shriek rocked the cellar. The horror in that cry tore her mind from its task. It seemed the ghost would not permit her to shift and escape.

The feeling of another presence overwhelmed Kelly. Her desire to identify the source battled her fear of what she might actually find. She slowly craned her neck, trying to avoid any sudden movements that might alarm her excitable host. She scanned the surrounding racks looking for ...

It was high up, atop the wine rack behind her. In the dim recesses of the ceiling a pair of obsidian eyes stared down at her. She could see nothing else—just the eyes. Their purpose was impossible to read; they just stared. Focused entirely on Kelly.

Suddenly they were gone. In the rack across from her, the bottles began to rattle—the disturbance rippling down the row. Then silence. Kelly looked up. The eyes were back. This time looking down from the rack before her.

She wondered what the ghost's intentions were, and it occurred to her the eyes might be wondering the same thing of her. Kelly returned their gaze, preferring to keep her opponent in view. She wasn't sure how long she stood there, riveted in time, pinned down by those eyes. At some point she realized her foot was asleep. She edged backwards until she bumped into something. Without dropping her gaze, she reached a hand behind her and identified a cask. She slowly climbed up on it maintaining eye contact, now from a seated position.

Her stomach gave a protesting growl. She watched, but the ghost didn't react. She dug in her pocket for one of Gealach's apples, but as she took a bite, the eyes blinked. She chewed nervously, but not quite sufficiently and swallowed her chunky mouthful. She took another bite. The eyes pressed closer.

Maybe eating just now wasn't the smartest move. If the ghost was hungry, she hardly wanted to suggest she stay for lunch. *As* lunch. She set the apple down on the cask beside her.

Something flickered across the icy gaze. The eyes pressed even closer. They were nearly out of the shadows. In the scant light, Kelly struggled to distinguish any features that might give name to her adversary. And then another flicker. Whiskers!

Remembering the doorkeeper had specific tastes, she held out her half-eaten apple. "Would you like this?"

The whiskers jerked a strong twitch and the eyes crept forward to the edge of the rack. A pink nose and the pink insides of two large ears were evident. The creature's face was covered with a silver-gray fur, except for two black rings that circled its eyes—giving the eyes a much larger appearance.

"It's all right; I won't hurt you … see?" She placed the apple on the cask and backed away. "You can have it. I won't get close."

The pink nose began twitching convulsively and the creature scampered along the wine bottles, rattling them in its wake. With a squeaky grunt it launched itself across the aisle and landed on the cask with a splat. It grasped the apple without hesitation and gnawed away with vigor.

Kelly had no idea what type of animal it was. It was squirrel-like, but shorter and plumper with a bushier tail. Its head and face were mouse-like, but larger and broader than a mouse's. Its paws—pink and furless with five digits each—were nothing short of human-like.

Her curiosity overcame, and quickly erased, her earlier fright. She couldn't help wonder how this creature viewed the world around it. And what it thought of her.

She centered and pushed her consciousness outward, feeling for the creature's psychic force.

It sprang up on its hind legs chattering. "Now dunna ya try yer tricks on me, lassie! I'll have none of tha'."

Kelly nearly fell over as she realized the creature was speaking to her in English ... well, English with a thick Highland brogue.

"You can talk!"

Its pink-fingered paw groomed its whiskers as if it were considering her words. In a thin, scratchy voice, more than half squeak, it answered. "Aye, I'm surprised too." It paused and took another nibble of the apple. It chewed thoroughly and swallowed before it continued. "It's been so long. I had to think fer a moment before I could find the words."

"What are you?" The question blurted out before Kelly considered it might be rude. She hoped she hadn't insulted the creature.

"Ach, now what kind of education have they been givin' ya tha' ya dunna know a dormouse when ya see one?"

The Highland accent and inflection would have been challenging enough, but spoken in a hoarse screech, it took Kelly several moments to interpret the dormouse's words.

"I'm from America," she explained. "We don't have dormice there ... I don't think."

"Ah, the colonies."

"It's ... a country now."

"I havna looked in several years." The creature paused, as if coming to some decision. Nodding to itself it continued, "I'd be Dingus, an' I'm right pleased to make yer acquaintance … particularly seein' as ya were kind enough to remember me a snack." The dormouse stretched his left paw in front of him and dipped his head for a long moment. Kelly wasn't up on dormouse etiquette, but she believed he had just bowed to her.

"I'm Kelly MacBride. It's a pleasure to meet you."

"Ah … one of Brid's … and who would yer parents be, lass?"

"My father was James … Hamish. Hamish MacBride."

"Hamish … Hamish … ah yes. When he was a wee bairn, he used to bring me apples too."

That explained how her father knew Dingus' predilection for apples. She wondered how many of her other ancestors had journeyed down here bearing treats for the resident ghost.

"Have you always lived down here?"

"Ach, no lassie," he wheezed. "I was one of Brid's masters. Do ya know how some grow a wee bit batty as they age?" He stretched forward as if leaning in to share some juicy gossip.

Kelly nodded.

"… Well, I grew more … mousy. Round about my second century, I became less interested in the affairs of the manor." Dingus took another bite of apple, chewed and swallowed. "I found I was spendin' more time as a dormouse an' less as a man. So I decided to retire in this form."

He dropped the apple and cocked his head. "Tell me, is young Roderick still hidin' himself in *my* library?"

"Excuse me?"

"Ach aye, he couldna wait fer me to step down. He never was much with people—always preferrin' the company of books. He wasna always like tha'. As a youth he had promise. Loved his studies. An' tha' fair wife of his. But after she died he turned bitter. He hid behind the books. They became a shield to keep out the world. He cared less fer safeguardin' their knowledge. It's no wonder when I retired Brid didna give him care of the abbey vault or the private library. Those things didna matter to him. Just the books."

"Yes," Kelly answered thoughtfully. "He's still there."

"So tell me, lass, who was yer da?"

Their conversation went on like that; Dingus would often repeat his questions, forgetting they'd been asked and answered, and he seemed to thrive on old gossip (particularly about Pickle-puss and the library). He told Kelly stories about people she didn't know—not the high tales of great deeds or famous legends, but the everyday goings on from his youth. She wasn't particularly interested, especially after the fifth retelling, but she never let on. He was a loveable old dormouse and she enjoyed his company. (Out of respect for his dignity, though, she did restrain from petting him.)

Dingus gave Kelly a tour of the wine cellar, pointing out his mossy nest in the small side chamber. The broken bottles piled in the corner had once held cider; when Dingus felt like an occasional drink, he'd simply help himself. His diet was primarily of spiders and insects, but

Willie would often leave a handful of nuts or fruit on his trips down to the cellar.

Dingus barked a thin, screechy cackle that Kelly assumed was a laugh. "The lad doesna know what manner of ghost resides here, but he's clever enough to know tha' it appreciates a snack!"

Kelly sensed that Dingus held affection for Willie, although he admitted he did rattle the bottles from time to time, "to keep the lad on his toes." Dingus seemed to enjoy torturing Rhona on the occasions she ventured down, which pleased Kelly immensely.

She discovered that the source of the once-terrifying wail that she'd heard from within these walls was, in fact, the sound of a dormouse singing—Dingus loved music. When she learned this, she offered to teach Dingus some new songs from the colonies. He was so thrilled he broke open a bottle of cider, which they shared in celebration of their new friendship. A girl and a dormouse make for an odd duo, but neither noticed as they sat in the mossy chamber singing away the afternoon.

14

Bending Rules

It was Dingus who provided the clue she required—the missing piece to the puzzle. And like all tricky puzzles, once you see the solution, lots of seemingly incongruous elements suddenly fit together with an elegant beauty. The mind-bending book's elusive hiding place, the strange familiarity of Fionn's Shield—Dingus' words supplied the answer: "the abbey vault."

Candles once again flickered on the altar as Kelly faced the back wall of the darkened abbey. Between the two chiseled murals, she inspected the carved disk that she'd found so intriguing on her previous visit. Sure enough, the familiar starburst of Fionn's Shield sat centered on the disk. But unlike Master David's drawing, twelve pie-slice panels wrapped around the shield, each containing the carved image of a plant and the name of an *Ogham* character. There were: *beith, luis, fearn, saille, nuin, huathe, duir, tinne, coll, muin, gort* and *ngetal.* Oddly, the twelve panels didn't quite join up. There was a slight gap at the twelve o'clock position between *beith* and *ngetal,* the first and last of the panels.

Kelly laid her books atop the altar: her diary, the book on *Ogham* characters, and Ina's book of tree lore. She flipped through her diary until she found her father's vault reference.

> *Fionn's shield guards the hidden wisdom. Only the freshly cut golden bough can penetrate his shield.*

If this were the vault, the second sentence should provide its combination. Unlike the other doors that runes had opened, however, Kelly had an abbreviated set of characters to work with. Why were only twelve out of the twenty-five runes here?

"Golden bough" had a familiar ring, and Kelly thought back trying to remember where she'd heard the term. She reached for Ina's book, but she had a feeling it wasn't the source. Whatever reference she'd seen predated Ina's gift. Yet, the only other texts that came to mind were the plant folios Kelly had borrowed … during Yule … when they were cutting …

"Mistletoe!"

She opened the book to the chapter on mistletoe. Sure enough, "golden bough" was one of its less common names.

Kelly reached for the *Ogham* book, certain this riddle was all but solved. She scanned the pages quickly, but missed the entry on mistletoe, so she went back and read through with more care. Something was wrong—there was no *Ogham* character for mistletoe! There had to be a mistake. The text was difficult to read in the unsteady candle light; she'd simply missed it. Beginning again, she turned the pages deliberately. Her stomach twisted tighter with each chapter she scrutinized. No mistletoe.

What wasn't she seeing? She was sure this was the vault. Mistletoe was certainly part of the riddle's solution, but apparently it wasn't the entire solution. It wasn't even an *Ogham* character. What relationship did it have with these twelve trees? And why twelve? She traced the cut stone leaf engraved on the first pie slice with her finger— *beith*. Birch. Like the bonsai grove she'd given Brid.

What had Brid said? … *The first tree to establish itself in a new forest … rebirth … the lady of the woods …*

Kelly straightened as she remembered: … *The first month of the calendar.*

She pointed to *beith*. November. She counted each of the panels clockwise in turn, naming the months, ending with *ngetal* for October. She then pointed to the blank sliver. "Saven," she whispered. A day belonging to neither the old year nor the new; a day outside of time. Fionn's Shield was ringed by an ancient Celtic calendar.

Freshly cut mistletoe must refer to Yuletide. Kelly pressed *luis*, the rune for December, but nothing happened.

Come on Fionn—share some of that wisdom!

She'd never had a single character rune code before. Solutions were always two or more runes. Two ...

She grabbed the book of tree lore and reread the section on mistletoe. The book said it was harvested at the solstice. But there are *two* solstices—winter and summer. She wasn't sure if anyone cut mistletoe in June, but she didn't know that they didn't.

She counted out the months again. *Tinne* was June. She pushed *luis* and then *tinne*. When nothing happened, she reversed the order and smiled when, with a soft snick, Fionn's Shield swung open.

The vault wasn't large—eighteen inches tall and wide, and two feet deep. Kelly held a candle up to the opening. The meager light jumped and skipped over the stone walls, her hand was shaking so.

Safecracker. Interloper. Trespasser.

A dozen or so scrolls were stacked farthest back, behind several boxes covered in leather. A shallow wooden bowl with handles—similar to her *quaich*—rested on a small wooden chest, and lying beside it was a book.

Kelly reached for the book, but then yanked her hand back in surprise. She reached in again, slowly this time. First her fingertips tingled; then as she reached further, the tingling spread to her hand and wrist, as if thousands of pins pricked her. She grasped the book and her hand trembled even more violently as she lifted it out and placed it on the altar. The binding was worn and lacked any title or other identifying marks. She opened the cover and peered at the first page: *The Advanced Brodgar Techniques: Influence.*

She didn't disturb anything else in the vault. She swung the door shut and blew out the candles. Collecting her books, she crept back down the passageway towards her residence.

Thief.

ॐ

Mind-bending. It was a slang expression. Whereas shape-shifting was one of the Transference techniques, mind-bending was an Influence skill. It was the ability to ask animals psychically to do things. The mind-bending book proved to be much more challenging than Kelly expected, however.

The first problem was language. The book used an archaic Scots dialect. Kelly would read unknown words aloud and try to identify them phonetically, but she often had to surmise meaning from context. *Anither* was "another." *Maist* meant "most," and *atween*, "between." But the conventions weren't consistent. *Gae* meant "gave" and *hae* meant "have," but *sae* was "so" and *frae* was "from." Still, with some linguistic gymnastics, it was possible to understand that *Mind, an one restit or daur na attend, you maun try anither scheme*, meant, "Remember, if one refuses or doesn't do as asked, you must try another approach."

Kelly could tolerate the vocabulary issues, but the author thoroughly annoyed her with his tendency to interrupt useful explanations and digress into a philosophical discourse on the moral correctness of "control," and the degree of "persuasion" that was just. Still, with persistence and copious note taking, Kelly began to see a picture emerge.

The Perception preliminaries applied to mind-bending as they did to shape-shifting. First one had to center, then sense the target mind, and finally strengthen the contact. It was here, however, that Transference and Influence differed. The Transference skills of anchoring, patterning and shifting weren't used. The foundational skills in Influence were voicing, specifying, and motivating.

Kelly was fuzzy on the specifics, but she believed voicing was *how* you spoke in an animal's mind, and specifying was telling the creature *what* you were asking it to do. Motivation must be how you ensured it did what you asked.

Kelly gave a lot of thought to the practice subject she should use. She knew she should start small. But it would be helpful if whatever animal she chose could assist with her investigative work; after all, that was what mind bending was about—getting animals to help you. Convinced that the barn buildings were the scene of a fair portion of the illicit activities afoot, Kelly decided on a plan that would provide night-time stake-out coverage in each of the barns—she would practice on bats!

Colonies of teeny pipistrelle bats roosted in the barn rafters. Most hung in the lethargy of hibernation, but there were a few restless individuals actively hunting insects within the warmer confines of the barns. If Kelly could enlist the support of one pipistrelle in each of the buildings, she could create her own spy force to monitor for anything unusual.

The first step would be to train her spies. Kelly set up spook camp in a comfortable hayloft in one of the closer barns. As her first training exercise, she would teach a bat to report back what it observed. Kelly picked one of the more active bats from among those roosting and held it in her palm. The pipistrelle's ten-inch wingspan belied its miniscule form. With its wings folded, its head and body were a mere inch-and-a-half long.

Hello, Gulliver—welcome to Brobdingnag!

Aside from the leathery black of its face, ears, fore-limbs, and legs, reddish-brown fur covered its body. Its folded wings reached past its head like a pair of stilts, each ending in a single, hooked claw.

Kelly nestled in the hay and watched the bat respond to the warmth of her hand, its hind claws and forelimb claw pricked her skin as it inched about. It made a soft shucking noise that resembled rapid-fire lip smacking.

Eager to flex her mind-bending knowledge, Kelly centered and extended her consciousness, reaching out for the pipistrelle's mind. She listened for some time, but she wasn't sure what she was perceiving. The bat's sensations were alien to her. Mind-bending wasn't patterning, however, and subject familiarity shouldn't be an issue. She decided to start with something simple.

WOULD YOU PLEASE FLY AROUND THE BARN?

She hadn't intended to shout into the tiny bat's mind, but that was the effect she had. Kelly had no difficulty sensing the bat's instant terror. It was overwhelmed with raw fear and could only tremble as it repeatedly furled and unfurled its wings, unsure of the direction of the threat.

She promptly withdrew her mind. Her forefinger stroked the bat's shuddering body.

"I'm sorry, I'm sorry, I'm sorry!" she whispered.

Her voicing needed some work.

⚬

The next afternoon, Kelly spied Kenna working in the cow byre.

"I thought you were spending your days up pasture."

Kenna looked up from her inspection of a heifer's udder. "Not anymore." Kenna's words sagged with audible depression.

"What happened?" Kelly grabbed a milk can for a stool as she awaited the bad news.

"Master Roy called me in this morning. Based on Dougal's reports over the last two months, he questioned whether I had a future in animal husbandry. He suggested that perhaps I might be better suited for other training."

"Is he … sending you home?"

Kenna nodded, swallowing hard. Her jaw clenched several times. She looked up at Kelly with defeat in her eyes. "He said I have two weeks. A probationary review."

Kelly squeezed Kenna's hand. "My mother always told me there's something good waiting just around the next corner. Even if you can't see it, you've got to believe it's there." Kelly hoped she sounded more encouraging than she felt. Comforting words were one thing. Pulling off the miracle that would save her friend in time was quite another.

౸

Kelly understood the principles of positive reinforcement in obedience training; she'd often seen Cameron reward Duffy for good behavior. Next to Kelly sat a capped jar. Moths, collected from her bedroom window barely an hour before, fluttered against the jar's sides searching for escape. For a pipistrelle they were as good as a doggie treat.

Kelly touched the mind of the bat she cradled in her hands. It was still a jumble of foreign impressions, but she hoped the proverbial carrot on a stick would be universally understood. She pushed forward gently, so as to not shout.

If you fly around the barn, I'll give you a juicy moth! she whispered within the pipistrelle's head.

The tiny bat screamed a high-pitched squeak and shook violently. Kelly did what little she could to soothe the troubled creature, but ached for her own consolation. Kenna was running out of time.

౸

"What do you know about animal training?"

"What do you want to know?" Kenna stood at the counter in the feed storage room mixing a supplemental meal for the pregnant heifers and cows.

"How do you handle it when an animal won't do what you ask?" Kelly tried to keep the frustration out of her voice, hoping her question sounded academic.

As Kenna scooped cottonseed into her feed bucket she explained how you must first understand what the animal's thinking. The basic motivators are fear, aggression, learned behavior, and instinct. If the animal is acting out of fear and you respond with anger, that will only increase its fear and make the problem worse. But if it's aggressive behavior, you may need to demonstrate anger to establish your social dominance. Only then will the animal submit.

"We had some orphaned pigs a couple of seasons ago that were always acting up. Master Roy showed me how to press on the back of their necks, right where a dominant adult would bite them. It was amazing—they turned into little angels after that."

Kelly considered Kenna's words. "You mentioned … what was it … learned behavior? If an animal won't do what you ask and it ignores your treat, then what?"

Kenna scratched her armpit before grabbing a spoon and ladling molasses into the bucket. "Assuming the animal understands what you're asking, if it doesn't respond to your reward, it's because there's something else it wants more.

"Cameron learned that early on with Duffy. After finishing with the sheep, he'd whistle for Duffy to come. But Duffy didn't want to quit—he was having too much fun. So he started ignoring the whistle."

"What did Cameron do?"

"The trouble was, Cameron only whistled for Duffy at the end of the session. Duffy learned that the whistle meant 'game over.' Master Roy had Cameron start whistling for him all the time. And every time he obeyed, he was rewarded with treats and affection. Most of the time Duffy could go back to his work with the sheep, but occasionally they'd be through for the day. Duffy learned to not fear Cameron's whistle and he started to come regularly."

Kelly nodded.

"Don't rule out instinct, though," Kenna added. "If you ask a dog to run off a cliff, no reward in the world will persuade the dog to do it. You can't ask an animal to act against its instincts."

She squirted a healthy dropper of minerals into the bucket and gave it a stir. She and Kelly left, turning out the light as they went. While Kenna hadn't answered the specific reason the bats responded in terror, she did identify an overarching problem: Kelly needed to understand how pipistrelles thought, and Kelly, quite honestly, didn't know squat about bats.

❦

Kelly wasn't much of a dancer. It wasn't that she was a klutz. It was that dancing was so … public. Reluctant to make a fool of herself, she was simply too chicken to try. Scottish dancing was particularly mysterious to her. Reels, jigs, hornpipes and strathspeys—she could never tell them apart. The tunes were all lively, but to her unpracticed ear they were indistinguishable. She wasn't sure what she was listening to at the moment, but it bounced along gaily. The notes were crisp, the rhythm steady; his playing was improving. Sucking in a deep breath, she steeled herself with a grunt and opened the practice room door.

When Gordie saw her, he held the current note for a long moment and then suddenly released the pressure on the bag. Had a dancer been following him, she would have hung in the air, mid-leap, for two or three seconds, and then crashed onto the stage.

"What?"

She smiled encouragement. "That sounded good."

He didn't return the smile. "I'm sure you came here just to tell me that."

"Gordie, I was hoping we could make up."

"Whatever."

"I'd rather be friends than enemies."

He said nothing.

"Besides, I could use your help."

He pursed his lips, nodding. "I believe you were the one who suggested the next time I felt the urge to help someone, I shouldn't." He shrugged. "Sorry. Simply following orders." He reshouldered his pipes and started blowing into the bag.

"Oh, come on! Don't sulk over that. You were upsetting Kenna. I was trying to salvage the situation."

"Ex-*cuse* me—*I* was trying to be supportive. Who died and made you laird? I suppose it's not possible *you* could ever be wrong."

"Let's not argue over it. Hey, I hear Maggie's baking blueberry scones this Saturday." They were Gordie's absolute favorite. Practically a currency for him; he would barter whatever he could to get more. "If you lend me a hand I'll promise you my scones."

His face was expressionless.

"It's not much. I just need some library books. Anything you can find on bats, particularly pipistrelles."

"No deal."

No deal? To blueberry scones? She couldn't even motivate her best friend to help her. Kelly thought back to Kenna's words: *"If the animal doesn't respond to your reward, it's because there's something else it wants more."* What had she said the basic motivators were? Fear, social dominance … social dominance—he wanted an apology!

… I suppose he was just trying to help … even if he did bungle it.

"I was trying to protect Kenna's feelings and didn't realize I was hurting yours. Sorry!"

"You were rude. Admit it."

Rude? I wasn't rude. Unabashed, perhaps. But hardly rude.

Kelly drew breath to protest and then stopped. She stood with lips clenched for a long moment. "Yes. I was rude. I'm sorry."

They stood facing each other, neither speaking.

Finally he broke the silence. "Bats, you say?"

She nodded.

"I'll still be expecting your scones."

⚛

Kelly poured through the books Gordie later delivered, and she had to admit how scant her knowledge of bats was. They were winged mammals, but their wing structure bore no resemblance to a bird's. Short "arm" bones led to long, downward-angled "finger" bones, over which stretched the gossamer wing-membrane. Flight was more a matter of waggling your fingers than flapping your arms.

Ultrasonic echolocation was the technical term for how a bat perceived the world around it. As it flew, a bat chirped out high-pitched (ultrasonic) sound pulses. When a pulse hit an object, it would bounce off the object and echo back to the bat's hypersensitive ears. The direction and strength of the returning echo told the bat the object's exact position.

That bats possessed such sophisticated navigational instrumentation impressed Kelly, until she read about the amazing tricks and evasive tactics insects had developed for escaping echolocation. If pulsed with a bat's ultrasound, a lacewing would fold its wings and crash into a dive. When the bat arrived at the spot indicated by the returning pulse, the hoped-for snack would be long gone. Some moths jammed the bat's radar with their own ultrasonic pulses; some had stealth scales on their wings that absorbed the pulses, rendering the moth invisible to the bat. Tiger moths left a particularly dreadful taste in the bat's mouth. When a tiger moth was pulsed, it sent back its own pulse, as if to say, "Remember me? I taste gross!" Kelly was awed by the escalating arms race taking place between bats and bugs in the dark rafters of the barns.

She was correct that pipistrelles fed on insects, but she also learned other bat species ate pollen and fruit; several larger ones ate fish and small frogs, and a few species actually did drink blood! *How* a pipistrelle ate was also an education. She assumed they caught their dinner with their mouths, but not so. A pipistrelle scooped an insect up in its wing, mid-flight, and then would flip the bug into its mouth as it continued searching for its next snack.

The strangeness of bats convinced Kelly that she needed more first-hand knowledge. That night, back in the haymow, her first order of business was to block the owl door. She had a lingering owl memory of the delectable taste of bats. She wished her dining experience this evening to be as the eater and not the eaten.

Kelly selected a semi-awake pipistrelle and settled into the hay as she centered and reached out to the bat's mind. Her anchoring had developed sufficiently that the schizophrenic sensations of patterning no longer distracted her, as they once had; they were now second nature. Through her own ears she could hear the pipistrelle's soft, lip-smacking grunts. Through the bat's ears she heard its high-pitched squeaks—squeaks beyond the range of her own hearing, and therefore ultrasonic. These weren't the loud blasts used for echolocation, however; these were squeaks of communication. The pipistrelle was reporting the ambient temperature back to the roosting colony.

Kelly could see little in the inky blackness of the hay-mow; however, through the bat's pin-point but sensitive eyes she could make out the dim shadows of the rafters and loft walls. Through the bat's mind, she could feel the warmth of her palm radiate up through its belly fur, the heat stimulating physical activity. Kelly realized that warmth energized the bat, whereas cold brought on torpor and the long winter sleep of hibernation. As the pipistrelle warmed in her hand, a vague sensation began to grow and sharpen. As it fully awoke, the sensation turned urgent: it was hungry.

The pipistrelle bunched its throat muscles and trumpeted a shout. Almost immediately its ears detected soft pings in rapid succession. It repeated the sequence over and over: shout and listen, shout and listen. This must be echolocation. The returning echoes painted a black-and-white picture of the barn's interior—walls, beams, and solid objects were light against a black background; the closer an object, the brighter it appeared.

The pipistrelle dragged itself to the edge of the loft and launched into the air, its growing distance from Kelly quickly breaking her contact. But she had what she needed. She understood enough to pattern the creature's mind.

Kelly made the shift, but things didn't go so well. She tried to crawl across the hay, but her legs were useless; they weren't strong enough to propel her forward. How had the other bat moved about so effortlessly? Its motion had been that of a mountaineer climbing with an ice pick in each hand. She tried that—pushing each forelimb ahead of her, hooking her claw, and then pulling her body forward. Her forelimbs, which were simply her folded wings, were as muscular and strong as her legs had been weak. She spent some time getting used to the sensation of walking. As she dragged herself about, she produced the lip-smacking noise the other bat had made. It meant little more than, "Here I go, here I go."

When she attempted to flex her wings, they barely opened. As she pushed out with her arms, she felt like a convertible top halted mid-way. It finally occurred to her that her wings were more hand than arm. She tried again, this time flaring her fingers, and her wings stretched outward in a pose that would've made Batman proud. She tried several flaps, but she was too used to a bird's wings. Bat wings required a completely different technique. She discovered that it worked best if her arms remained relatively still. Her fingers, however, twitched, danced, and twirled in nearly continuous motion.

She was ready to take to the air. With strong wing flaps, she leapt up … or at least tried to. She barely lifted off the hay. Kelly tried again, gathering herself for a mightier spring. It was little better than her first attempt. Her legs were simply too scrawny. Perhaps she could lift herself with wing power alone. She thrashed wildly, but remained earth-bound.

She thought back to her sparrow flight lessons. Wings create lift via their forward movement through the air. Perhaps her forward movement was insufficient. As a bird, a good hop sufficed. But she wasn't a bird. She thought of ducks taking off from a pond. They only got airborne after first dashing across the pond's surface. Wings extended, she tried flapping in combination with a sprint. It was pitiful. Frankenstein lumbered with more speed and grace. Her legs simply weren't designed for track events. Yet the other pipistrelle had taken off effortlessly …

Of course! It had launched from the edge of the hayloft. The downward speed would generate lift, if the bat angled its wings correctly.

She dragged herself to the edge. Peering into the blackness, she took a deep breath and stepped off with an explosion of flapping. The sudden drop was frightening, but she was expecting it, so she didn't let it distract her as she quickly found the wing angle that most effectively counteracted gravity. With spastic wing beats, she slowly rose through the air, away from the barn floor, jubilant that she was—

Smack!

She never saw the beam she flew into. Lying in a heap on the barn floor, she wondered how long it took a pilot to crash when he forgot to turn on his radar. As the pain subsided, she sat up and mimicked the shouting reflex she'd witnessed. Her bat brain knew how to process the returning echoes her ears detected. She shot off several more ultrasonic pulses and formed a clear picture of the darkened barn's interior.

Climbing back up to the loft, she tried again, this time remembering to pulse while she flew. She slowly accustomed to bat flight, pulsing every second or two. She gradually added aerial turns, takeoffs, and landings to her maneuvers and grew confident in her basic flight skills. It was during one such practice flight a bright spot suddenly appeared on her mental radar map. It hadn't been there a moment before. *And it was moving!*

From *"Eep … eep … eep …"* she instinctively switched to *"Eep, eep, eep, eep,"* her throat spewing out pulses as quickly as it could. Chow time! She swooped and spun, zeroing in on what her mind told her was a moth with a 1.765-inch wingspan. As she closed the distance to her target, the returning echoes came back faster. Their machine-gun pinging whipped her bat senses into a frenzy.

And … gotcha!

Her right wing scooped up the hapless moth with the motion of a fielder's glove.

Whoa!

Her wing, wrapped tightly around the struggling moth, had all the aerodynamic effectiveness of a wadded-up dishrag. She pitched in a hard downward tumble to the right.

Thwunk!

She'd be sore tomorrow, she thought from the floor as she stuffed the moth into her mouth, but she wouldn't be hungry.

Kelly worked for another hour, trying to catch her dinner with more finesse. She tried grabbing moths directly with her mouth, but it was too much work chasing down each one. The wing-scoop method was more efficient, because precise aim wasn't necessary, but she simply didn't have the flying skills to perform it without crashing.

She finally settled on a variation of the technique. The same membrane that covered her wings also connected her legs and tail. By wiggling her legs—at *this* they excelled—she could control the shape of her tail flap. She found with practice she could snatch a moth in her tail flap, and just reach her head down to eat it, with far less disruption to her flying.

Her body ached from bruises and exhaustion when she finally climbed into bed, but sleep didn't come quickly. Her mind sifted through what she'd learned, how it felt, and what she still didn't understand. With only eleven days left, a single question overshadowed all: *How will this help my mind-bending?*

"It's missing, and it's your fault."

"I hardly need you reminding me of my responsibilities. Shouldn't you be minding your own assignments a bit more closely?"

Kelly was heading back to her residence following lunch, but the voices in the hallway brought her up short. The muttered accusation had been Dougal's and the response was Aidan's. They were quarreling again, and Kelly was curious to know what it was about. She listened from just inside the doorway.

"If you don't locate it quickly, I *will* have to report it." Dougal's words dripped with threat.

"That's brave from someone too scared to do it himself. I'll find it. I'm riding out at first light. It'll be back by noon tomorrow."

What had Aidan lost? And what was it that scared Dougal? Suddenly, Kelly's lunch did an uneasy flip-flop in her stomach. Could they have discovered the mind-bending book was missing?

Mack, unconcerned over Kelly's current troubles, purred in his sleep nestled on her bed, while she considered her next steps: how to trail Aidan; whether she should return the mind-bending book tonight; and most importantly, how to make mind bending work.

Why couldn't she coax pipistrelles to fly? Even for a moth bribe? They didn't seem to be holding out for something better; they'd been terrified right down to their toe claws. What had spooked them so badly?

Kenna had said not to rule out instinct. But how could that be the issue? Kelly wasn't asking the bats to drive a stick shift. What could be more natural than asking a bat

to fly? What could be more natural than … asking it …
She sat very still, urging the wisps of the thought to gel.
What could be *less* natural than an alien voice inside your
head asking you to do anything? That had to be it. But
that presented a dilemma. How in bat blazes was mind-
bending supposed to work if you couldn't tell the creature what you wanted it to do?

Kelly spent the rest of the day reviewing everything the
book had to say on voicing and specifying. That seemed
to be where her problems lay.

She wanted a bat to do a natural thing—fly. But she
couldn't ask it mentally, because that's unnatural. So she
needed to "voice" her request so it didn't sound like her
asking. How was she supposed to ask a bat to fly, without
its knowing that she'd asked it?

She remembered the pipistrelle's growing hunger as
it woke, and how that drove the bat to fly off in search
of dinner. Perhaps voicing wasn't about asking at all.
Perhaps it was more about cause and effect. Could she
mentally suggest to a bat that it felt hungry, without it
realizing she was doing the suggesting?

Kelly jumped up and grabbed her coat.

Ten minutes later she was once again in the haymow
with a bat warming in her hand. She recalled the sensation of empty-belly hunger she'd sensed in the previous
pipistrelle, and studied it. She tried to nudge that feeling into this bat's mind. The pipistrelle grew nervous and

edgy, but it did decide it must eat. It lunged from the edge of the loft and flew into the darkness.

After waiting several minutes, Kelly concluded the bat wasn't coming back anytime soon. Perhaps she made it feel *too* hungry. She selected another pipistrelle. This time she suggested the feeling that a light snack might be nice. This bat also fidgeted. As it considered the suggestion, she could sense subtle differences in its mental patterns; its "voice" wasn't exactly the same as the previous bat's. She tried to shape the impressions she sent so they better matched this bat's mental energies. The bat calmed down, but it still accepted the craving for a wee bit of moth. The pipistrelle leaned from foot to foot. She hinted at a bright spot moving against the bat's radar. With an *Eep!* the pipistrelle launched into the darkness, pinging away for targets. Less than a minute later it returned, landing smartly beside her.

Kelly worked with several other bats that evening, trying to better appreciate the subtle differences in voices. She had no idea how she'd get bats to spy for her, but that was a problem for another day. She needed to wrap up and get to bed; she wanted to get an early start in the morning. She had no clue what Aidan's mission would be, but it was her mission to find out.

15

CHOICES

It was still dark when Kelly headed to the stables. She set about her chores briskly with little wasted motion. Not long after, activity at the far end of the stalls signaled Aidan's arrival, but Kelly was in no rush; an inch of fresh snow had fallen during the night and that suited her plans perfectly.

Aidan had been gone perhaps a quarter hour before Kelly finished cleaning and tidying the stall, and she followed in pursuit astride Gealach. A set of fresh tracks, plain to see in the unbroken blanket of white, headed across the grounds and into the forest. A trail of bread-crumbs wouldn't have been easier.

Under the eaves of the wood, the forest lay in stillness, shrouded in the softening light of dawn. Kelly's breath swirled about her in puffy billows and she tugged her cap lower over her ears. Little snow had penetrated the pine boughs and the tracks were indefinite in places, but Kelly was certain they continued straight on. They were headed towards the abbey, and the knot in her stomach tightened.

She had considered returning the mind-bending book the previous evening, but she'd decided against it. Even if Aidan and Dougal knew the book was missing, there was nothing to suggest she was the one who had it. Alerted now that someone had taken it, they might well be watch-ing the abbey. It seemed too risky to go near the vault at the moment.

She rode into the clearing as the abbey came into view, but the tracks didn't turn off. They continued on without interruption. What is he up to? Gealach echoed Kelly's tension with a soft nicker.

"It's okay, girl." She patted her horse's neck. "We'll find him."

Twenty minutes later, she spotted him. He was in a rocky clearing hemmed by dense forest. She dismounted, loop-ing Gealach's reins to a branch, and stole forward to the edge of the woods—a perfect observation point hidden behind the cover of the trees. Aidan moved slowly across the clearing, scanning the sky. Something feathered and bloody hung from the end of a rope he swung high into the air; he punctuated the swings with short whistles.

She didn't know how long she huddled behind the screen of the trees, watching as Aidan paced back and forth, but the sun was now well up, and her shivering threatened her resolve to stay any longer. Suddenly Aidan stopped and tensed—still looking skyward. He whistled a sustained note. And then, with the speed of lightning coming to ground, a blurry streak flashed down from the sky and struck the bundle at the rope's end. Aidan released his grip as the raptor caught the lure. The light, speckled underbelly and sharply pointed wings were unmistakable—it was a falcon. The jesses around its ankles indicated it was a trained bird: an escapee, who'd obviously flown off during some previous flight.

That was all Kelly needed to see. She was frozen and had the answer she sought, although it was hardly the exposé of sinister activity she'd supposed. She mounted Gealach and headed home.

As she led Gealach into the stables, Master Roy was there to meet her.

"I know the weather hasn't been good," he began. Kelly didn't understand his stern expression and the edge in his voice. "And you've been anxious to get out on the less inclement days, but I must insist that you complete your chores *before* you indulge in a ride."

Kelly gaped, at a loss for words. "I ... I thought I had."

"Hardly. I expect better of you, Kelly. Please go see to it now." He walked off shaking his head.

Kelly's face burned. What had she forgotten? When she got to Gealach's stall, she was even more baffled. She had left it with fresh straw and a neat pile of hay in the corner. She returned to a foul mess that looked as though it hadn't been mucked in a week. Five horses with overactive colons would have struggled to produce this much manure.

Kelly first saw to Gealach's needs before she tackled the filth. After administering a thorough rubdown and curry, she began clearing the soiled straw. From two stalls away she heard snickers.

"I expect better of you," a whiny voice mimicked, followed by more snickers.

Why, that snot-crusted cockroach—Niall set me up!

When Niall showed up that morning and found Gealach's stall neat and in order and Kelly undoubtedly off enjoying herself, he must have dumped the dirty straw from every other stall into Gealach's.

She could hear his self-satisfied chuckles and she fought the urge to run him through with her pitchfork. Afterwards, she couldn't quite say how the idea occurred to her. But it was wicked. In fact, it was so wicked it was perfect.

Bent on revenge, Kelly quelled her rage and focused her mind. She extended her consciousness, attempting to touch the mind of Thunder, the large chestnut mare, two stalls down. Mental contact over any distance is difficult and unreliable. It took several tries before she brushed

Thunder's equine presence. She centered further, to strengthen the connection and steady the wavering contact. She eased deeper into Thunder's consciousness.

Kelly sifted through Thunder's perceptions and confirmed that Niall was working in the back of the stall. Excellent!

Kelly didn't fumble for an impression to suggest. She knew exactly what she wanted. She insinuated a feeling of pressure and discomfort into Thunder's psyche—not an alarming feeling, but a familiar one that was persistent and increasingly called for relief. Kelly held the sensation constant, in no rush to force it more firmly. It would happen—it was one of an animal's most basic instincts—so she was patient.

Through Thunder's senses, she felt the horse widen her rear stance. Thunder raised her tail. The mare stretched forward, arching her neck.

At that point several things happened at once: Thunder gave into the suggestion; Kelly backed out of the horse's mind; and a shout of disgust rang out from the back of Thunder's stall.

Kelly smiled. Mind-bending definitely had its uses.

When Kelly joined her friends at lunch the next day, Gordie's look of concern tipped her all wasn't well. Kenna's shoulders sagged; her movements were listless, and she could only stare at her plate.

"Kenna's giving up," Gordie explained.

"No way," Kelly objected as she took a seat. She leaned forward locking her eyes onto Kenna's. "You've got to fight back!"

Shrugging in a helpless gesture, Kenna answered, "Why bother? Dougal's going to see that I'm sent home no matter what I do. So why kill myself to complete all the extra chores he's assigning?" She pushed her vegetables around without taking a bite.

"Because if you quit, he wins," Kelly insisted.

"He wins when he sends me home."

Kelly shook her head. "No! If you give up it'll say to Master Roy that Dougal was right all along. Besides, what about the animals in your care? I know how much they matter to you. Your responsibility is to them right now, no matter what happens next week."

Gordie chimed in. "Kelly's right. How *you* feel about your work is more important than whatever Dougal and Master Roy think. If you know you never gave up, you can hold your head up, regardless of what happens." His face brightened. "Hey, I know what'll cheer you up!"

Kelly glared at Gordie; she was prepared to kick.

He ignored her. "I've written a short verse:

Thunder, the proud, was noble among mares,
And to her, Niall the young was glad to give care.
Late one morning hard at his travail,
Niall, eager to please, was a-work near her tail.
But Thunder had urges she couldn't resist,
And when she was finished, young Niall was quite pissed."

Kelly laughed so hard she had to wipe the tears from her eyes. Kenna enjoyed the poem equally. It was heartening to see her laugh. Kelly nodded a "well done" to Gordie.

They moved the conversation to less painful topics and Kelly enquired about Gordie's upcoming competition.

"Are you ready for tomorrow?"

"If I can play my tunes well, I might have a shot for the overall Piper-of-the-Day prize."

Kenna gave him a wry look. "How *you* feel about your playing is more important than what the judges decide," she parroted back with a smile.

Gordie rolled his eyes. "Oh great," he muttered.

෴

That night another three inches of snow fell, and the next morning the sullen sky held the promise of more to come later in the day.

Following breakfast, Kenna walked with Kelly down the shoveled path to the barns and stables. "I've decided you're right," she told Kelly. "Not that it's going to make any difference, but I can't stand giving Dougal the satisfaction of seeing me quit." She stopped on the path. Her eyes were pleading as she wrung her hands. "I hate it! I feel so powerless." Kenna kicked the snow into a powdery swirl.

"Doing the right thing gives you power," Kelly assured her.

Neither knew what more to say, so they walked along in silence. With a halfhearted wave, Kenna turned into the cow byre as Kelly continued to the stables, but at Kenna's cry Kelly doubled back.

Bovine bedlam greeted the girls. Somehow, the cows had escaped their stalls, clearly some time since. The floor was a mine zone. There's a reason horse manure is referred to as "horse apples" and cow manure as "cow pies." As poop goes, a cow's is among the most unpleasant. Wet pies had been tracked across the entire floor. In their freedom, the cows found the hay bales stored in the crib against the far wall. Half a dozen were pulled into the room and ravaged by the greedy ruminants. Nor had the cows missed the large bag of feed; the wide tear running down its side had spilled feed across the width of the room. Even worse, the older calves had gotten into the milk cans, with predictable results. The calves milled through the toppled cans, the clatter and clanging of those they kicked rising above their raucous lowing.

"How could this have happened?" Kenna cried over the noise. "They were secure in their stalls when I left last night."

Kelly had a pretty good idea what had occurred, but she said nothing. A quiet fury began smoldering in her gut.

"This will take me a week to clean up!" Kenna stepped aside as a cow nudged past her. "And Master Roy will be by this evening to check on my work."

"I'll give you a hand, Kenna. I have to go muck Gealach's stall, but I'll come back after. Don't worry—we'll get things in order before Master Roy stops by."

Kelly marched to the stables glowering. That Niall would target Kenna for one of his vicious pranks, right now with the rest of her troubles, was unconscionable. Kelly would help Kenna through this, but *then* she'd take care of Niall ...

Stopping by the tack room, she grabbed her muck boots and kicked off her shoes. As she plunged her right foot into the rubber boot, her toes met a viscous goo. She pulled her foot out and a brown substance with a cloying smell oozed off her sock—molasses! Choking with rage, she pulled off the goopy sock and stuffed her foot back into her shoe. Where was that piece of rat excrement? Payback wasn't going to wait, after all.

She hunted through the stables, finally spotting Niall behind the building, where he was dumping his wheelbarrow into the manure wagon. Kelly fought an overwhelming urge to shove Niall face first into the poop.

Why fight it?

Anger wasn't just clouding Kelly's judgment; it was overwriting good judgment with bad and rationalizing it.

It's his own fault. His pranks have forced me to this.

She centered and pushed her consciousness outward, just as she'd done with Thunder. The distance was again a factor. She brushed against fleeting impressions from several horses, but focused her mind forward. Kelly flowed with her breaths, full and relaxed, channeling her mental energy into a laser beam that reached out towards Niall.

Just as she was beginning to think it wasn't going to work, she sensed the whispered tendril of a thought. It wasn't a horse's—it was different from anything in an animal's mind: more complex and bound with purpose. She eased her psyche towards it, eventually grasping on and firming the contact.

Kelly wasn't prepared for the experience of being in another person's head. She thought it would be familiar, but it wasn't. Niall's mind was a swirl of activity, and it was some time before Kelly could detect patterns in the swirl, if you could call them patterns. It was as if she was watching snow fall, where the closest snow blew to the right, the snow behind it blew to the left, and the snow farthest back fell straight down.

The nearest activity was Niall's physical sensations. As Kelly focused on these, she could hear the scrape of his shovel, as Niall heard it. She felt the exertion of his breathing, and sensed the heat coming off his body under his scarf and coat.

She pushed farther, edging into the next layer. These impressions lacked a steady rhythm—some flitted past while others persisted. She felt a presence of meanness most strongly. Echoes of past pain and fear were also detectable. These were Niall's emotions.

The part of his mind farthest from her buzzed with quick and deliberate activity. She suspected these were his conscious thoughts. She didn't want to touch these, even if she could, certain of their pollution. The closest layer was all she needed.

She studied his stance at the wagon. If she could just get him to lean a bit more to the left, he'd overbalance in that direction. She softly suggested that the wagon tipped to the right. Niall shifted more weight to his left foot and inclined his body. She hinted that the wagon tipped further. Niall shifted left. Now he just had to turn his ankle inward, and his foot would slip on the soiled straw …

DESIST! IMMEDIATELY!!!

Blinding pain erupted behind Kelly's eyes. A psychic flash exploded in her mind, knocking her out of Niall's and leaving her senseless. As the shock, but not the pain, faded, Kelly found herself doubled over in the snow clutching her temples. A figure towered over her, seething anger that she felt more clearly than the wet slush beneath her.

"Come with me!" was all Allisdair said, and he turned and marched toward the manor house.

Kelly struggled to keep up, her head pounding with waves of pain. He led her straight to Brid's residence.

"Wait here." He entered, abandoning her in the foyer. The massive oak door shut behind him with the finality of a sarcophagus lid dropping down over a tomb.

I can't believe he caught me! I should play dumb. "… I don't know what you're talking about. I was just going to ask Niall a question."

Allisdair knows. He spoke in my mind. Besides … I can't lie to Brid.

No one ever told me not *to mind-bend.*

It's not as though the book and Dad's diary didn't warn me. Trying it on a person wasn't very smart.

It's not my fault; I was just trying to help Kenna.

Yeah—right. Revenge had nothing to do with it?

Deep in her gut Kelly knew she was wrong. Deep in her gut, another feeling lurked as well, but Kelly wasn't yet ready to face it.

☙

"Had anyone else brought me this, I'd have insisted the person was mistaken." Brid shook her head. "Influence? And on another person!" She looked to Allisdair for explanation.

"I couldna believe it myself. I scanned the area several times. There was no one else. Aye, it was her. Across thirty feet! She only exerted motor control, thank Danu, an' her technique was crude, but the lad was unaware. *Beanrìgh*, how is this possible? The spontaneous emergence of influence skills ... at *her* age!" It was Allisdair's turn to shake his head, the disbelief plain on his face. "I thought her shiftin' extraordinary, but this is ... unheard of."

"Her father's powers developed early, as they did with most of my line."

"But never before their sixteenth year, an' not to this degree," he countered. "She's a full two years younger."

"Fiona wasn't quite fifteen ..." Brid mused. "But this ... so young ..."

"Could we have her age wrong?"

"No." Brid spoke with certainty. "I remember the date well. It was just after Hamish and Gwendolyn moved to America. When my second sight failed me. Hmm … I'd always assumed that piece of Cairbre's prophecy was triggered by Hamish's departure. What if it was, rather, Kelly's birth?"

Silence settled around them. Allisdair waited for Brid to continue, which she eventually did. "She'll have to take the oath."

"*Bean-rìgh*, no! She's too young. She lacks the maturity an' resolve; horseplay an' mischief overrule duty an' responsibility—today was an example. If she did make the commitment, how could we expect her to uphold it? She's a child. An' the danger if she foreswore her word would be calamitous. She'd be just the pawn Bres has sought through all these ages."

"Your case is precisely why we wait until a youth is sixteen. But the power she's already demonstrated is a perilous risk in the hands of the ignorant. We simply can't delay for two more years."

"*That's* why we have rules," Allisdair argued.

"Peace, faithful one. There are always rules. Who can claim to honor them all? Without understanding the risks, who's at fault when a rule is violated? The one who broke it, or the one who withheld knowledge of the consequences? If she remains unaware of the risk of her choices, then *we* bear the blame for that risk."

Allisdair faced Brid with grim resignation chiseled into his features. "An' when she learns the nature of what we battle, where will she find the peace to sleep at night?"

Brid returned his gaze. "She'll find it where we all do—in her faith." Neither spoke for several long minutes, their thoughts searching unknown paths.

"I would speak with my granddaughter now."

Kelly's internal debate had long since quieted. She sat for what seemed like hours, nursing a sour stomach, unsure of what she'd say to Brid. She finally heard steps approach the far side of the door, and the soft catch as the latch released. She clenched her jaw. Allisdair stepped out and Kelly braced herself.

Without turning to her, he said as he marched past, "She'll see ya now."

Kelly entered with guarded steps. She'd never seen Brid angry; it had to be fearsome. She found her grandmother seated in the parlor. The crackling fire might have signaled a relaxed winter afternoon, but Kelly drew neither warmth nor comfort from it. She lowered herself into a seat facing her grandmother.

"Tell me what you did." Brid's voice was level and without emotion. That made Kelly even more tense. She wasn't sure what she expected, but anger, surprise, or even disappointment would have been easier to bear. Calm steadiness was unnerving. She described what happened behind the barn in halting sentences.

Then Brid asked the simplest and most damning of questions. "Why did you do it?"

Niall's a bully; I was angry; he deserved it!

Her head swam with retorts. Yet, as she thought each, it turned hollow and lost substance. Why had she done it? The truth crept unbidden into her mind.

Because I could. I was showing off.

A whipping from Allisdair would have been easier to bear. She had let Brid down and she knew it. The unfaced emotion stirring in her gut rose up with the force of ocean surf breaking on the beach. A wave of shame engulfed Kelly and washed away any excuses or prevarications that lingered. She was left with the certainty that Brid had expected better of her, and she'd blown it. Her jaw gave the briefest of quivers; and then Kelly began to sob.

Brid didn't react as Kelly's emotions ran their course. She sat quietly as Kelly blubbered on. After a time, she stood and surprised Kelly again—she opened her arms. In all of Kelly's time at the manor, Brid had never hugged her. It simply wasn't Brid.

Kelly stepped into her grandmother's embrace. Huddled in the safety of that moment, Kelly realized her grandmother's love wouldn't be meted out for good behavior, just as it wouldn't be withheld to punish mistakes. It was always there for her. This, of course, made Kelly cry all the harder.

After Kelly exhausted her tears, Brid offered her a cup of hot liquid with a musky scent of earth. She urged her to drink it.

"It's valerian tea; it will calm you."

Kelly sipped the smoky tea and could feel it melt her body's tension. Her breathing evened and slowed, and her chafed emotions settled into a tranquil stillness.

"Kelly, your powers are a gift of our people—one that for thousands of years has shaped our lives, our traditions, and our beliefs. With this gift comes a responsibility, however. The *Tuatha de Danann* have always employed their powers solely for good. The influence techniques you used today fall into a dark area. When you mentally influence the actions of another, you're committing psychic enslavement. As a people, we've never tolerated that. We believe all creatures have the right to act for themselves. This is why we so carefully guard this knowledge and restrict its use."

Brid's eyes grew hard. "There are ... others ... who don't believe as we do. Who think Influence is their right."

"Others?"

"The Formorians. Just as the *Tuatha de Danann* possess abilities beyond humans, so do the Formorians. *They* don't hesitate to use their powers to enslave and exploit. From the beginning we've fought to defend humans from them and have sought his final defeat."

"Whose?" Kelly asked.

"Bres."

"But didn't he live thousands of years ago?"

A half-smile played at Brid's lips. "Kelly, I am Brighde of the *Tuatha de Danann*. *I* lived thousands of years ago." Her smile vanished. "Bres leads the Formorians and has long been our sworn enemy. The threat is real. He'll try again to kill you. As Lugh is witness, I can promise Bres isn't finished with you."

"*Me?* What did I do?" Kelly gulped. "… and what do you mean, *again*?"

"The attack on Saven Eve and the poisonings were certainly his work. He has, shall we say, some *history* with our family."

"History?"

Brid sighed with what might have been weary sorrow. "Prophecy foretells that an heir of my line will finally defeat Bres. For eons he's tried to force the prophecy to his own ends by assassinating my heirs. And now, you're the last. You're too alluring a target for him to pass up. He'll certainly make another attempt."

Kelly felt small, exposed, and not at all brave. How could she defend against a threat like this? Was anyplace safe? Then a horrible possibility occurred to her. It hurt her just to think about it—hurt her in a sacred place she thought to be protected from evil.

"Did …" she stumbled over the words, "… did Bres … kill … my father?"

There was sympathy in Brid's eyes, but her answer was less than reassuring. "I've suspected thus, these many years, but could never prove it. We do know he killed Duncan, Hamish's father."

Brid barely gave Kelly time to absorb this latest news before she pressed on. "There is a danger that's even graver than the risk to your life. Your powers will continue to develop over the next several years and they'll be with you throughout your lifetime. Bres may try to subvert you to his cause. Particularly if your power is strong. He would hope to use you to destroy me."

Kelly gasped at the thought.

"What you've achieved, Kelly, falls beyond our rules' ability to safeguard. We normally wait until apprentices are older before they're given the opportunity to swear to our cause. And then we must convince ourselves of their resolve before we'll awaken their latent gifts and teach them how to use them.

"Your power is already waxing. Yet you cannot exist outside of our laws. You must commit your life to our cause, pledging to honor the code of the *Tuatha de Danann* and restricting your powers to protecting the innocent and fighting evil. If you were *ever* to break your oath, if you even once cease to respect the freedom and rights of the creatures of nature, then you would fall prey to Bres and become an agent of his evil."

Brid laid a hand on Kelly's forearm. There was regret in her voice, but Kelly sensed the same surety of love that she'd felt earlier. "If I could spare you this decision for a time, I would. But reversing the course of events is not an ability we've ever possessed—Danu, if only it were. Think carefully. Once you pledge your life you *cannot* change your mind. In the meantime, I must insist that you not use *any* of your powers until this question is settled. Is that absolutely clear?"

Kelly's mind whirled as she left her grandmother. The threat of Bres and the question of her commitment to the Tuathan cause were simply too huge for her to absorb.

She focused on less lofty matters—ones she could wrap her thoughts around: the promise she just made to Brid. If she couldn't use her powers, then mind-bending was out ... which quashed her plans with the pipistrelles ... which were her only means for helping Kenna ... Kenna ... *Kenna!*

Kelly sped from the house and raced to the barn. It was already growing dark. She wondered when Master Roy would be stopping by.

When she entered the byre, she wasn't greeted by the raucous moos of earlier that day, but by moos of bored contentment. The cows were back in their stalls busily munching on hay and feed. Kelly couldn't believe the clean, orderly interior. Somehow Kenna had managed to transform this morning's battle zone into the tidy byre Master Roy would be expecting to see.

A sound from the far end of the barn made her turn. She expected Kenna, but was surprised to find Gordie. He was kilted, with shirt-sleeves rolled up and muck boots nearly hiding his hose and flashes.

Seeing he now had an audience, he paused in his sweeping and held his broom before him, as if to address it.

> *"What a piece of work is cow!*
> *How bovine in reason! How infinite in lactation!*
> *In chewing and digestion, how thorough and complete!*
> *In action how like a quadruped. In apprehension, how like a bull!*

The dairy of the world! The paragon of
ruminants!
And yet, to me, what is this quintessence of cud?
Beef delights not me; no, nor veal neither,
though by your lowing you seem to say so."[14]

"Gordie, I thought your competition was today. What are you doing here?"

"I was on my way out this morning and saw Allisdair march you up to the house. He looked like he chewed on a hornet's nest, so I came to ask Kenna what was up. She was desperate for help, so I stayed to give her a hand." He shrugged and gave the broom a final sweep. "What happened?"

"I sort of stepped in it," she admitted. "But what about Piper-of the-Day?"

Gordie set the broom aside and changed out of the boots and back into his ghillie brogues. As he wove their long laces up and around his ankles, he answered in a lower voice, "Imagine I got a medal, maybe even Piper-of-the-Day; and in the meantime, Kenna got sent home.

---

14   Based on:
"What a piece of work is man!
How noble in reason! how infinite in faculties!
in form and moving, how express and admirable!
in action how like an angel! in apprehension, how like a god!
the beauty of the world! the paragon of animals!
And yet, to me, what is this quintessence of dust?
Man delights not me; no, nor woman neither,
though by your smiling you seem to say so."
Hamlet (Act II, Scene ii) by William Shakespeare

Just how much would that trophy mean, knowing that I could have helped her and I didn't?"

Just then Kenna, with bits of straw stuck to her sweaty skin, walked in from the back.

"You look pooped!" Gordie told her. "*I'm* udderly exhausted; I'm going to plop into bed tonight." He headed to the door. "Come on, let's get some dinner."

As they walked up to the house, Kelly put a hand on her friend's shoulder. "Gordie, you dung good."

16

BEAR BAITING

Kelly stared at the sheet of music without seeing it. The notes held no interest for her this morning. The muffled tones from the surrounding practice rooms attested that others were having more productive sessions.

Aside from some halfhearted moral support, Kelly hadn't done a thing to help Kenna, and her friend's time was up. On top of that, Brid awaited Kelly's answer on her commitment. Kelly was at a loss. The choices she regularly made influenced the activity of an afternoon, perhaps a day—never an entire life. Where did one begin?

Over the last eight months, Kelly had been defined by the things that happened *to* her—events that she was powerless to affect, and she'd chafed that she possessed so little control over her life. Now, she had the control, but was overwhelmed by the enormity of the decisions facing her. To finally have the ability to direct her own future, and not know what to do, was more depressing than her previous helplessness.

"Kelly? I asked which note in the phrase signals the key modulation. Did you even hear me?" Master David peered at her.

She stared at the base of the music stand, searching for clear order to her thoughts.

"What's troubling you?" His voice echoed concern.

"I … have to decide my life, and I'm in the middle of things I don't understand."

"Thirty-five hundred years is a lot of family history. Your confusion is justifiable."

The music stand was of cherry wood. Carved Celtic knot-work ran up each of the three legs; meeting at the base, the braids interwove seamlessly before wrapping upward towards the desk. Leave it to Master David to insist on such artistic expression in something as utilitarian as a music stand.

The master's words broke the silence. "Perhaps you aren't ready for answers yet. Perhaps the questions themselves could bear more scrutiny."

Together they examined Kelly's predicament, sifting through her uncertainty, carefully exposing her fears, and identifying those areas requiring more information. The soothing baritone of his voice and his easy, disarming words didn't speak to her as a teacher might, but as a confidant and friend. Her anxiety gradually eased. She still didn't know what she'd do, but she trusted that, together, they'd sort it out.

They deliberated on Brid's cause, Kelly's commitment, and her need for protection, and they kept returning to a common theme: Bres. Kelly knew so little about him.

Master David rose and set aside the cherry stand; Kelly's lesson had moved beyond music. "This is your decision, not mine ... but I'd be reluctant to judge *anyone* based on events that occurred over three thousand years ago. Things change over time." He took one of the more comfortable chairs beside his desk. "People change."

"But he keeps killing off my family. And he's already attacked me—and you!"

"A war started this." There was sadness in Master David's voice. "A savage, bloody war. For both sides. Sacred magical gifts, debased in their use as weapons. One side strikes; the other counters. Again and again. Even long after the cause ceases to exist, both keep attacking, because by now, that's all they know to do."

The Battle of Moytura filled her mind: Tuathan soldiers erect with righteousness. Then she flashed back into Bearach's mind, remembering his uncertainty. *He believed there could be a different course …*

"Who was Bearach?"

"An ancestor of yours." Master David told how Bearach had ruled the ancient Gaelic kingdom of Dal Riada. By the sixth century, the primeval war over the ownership of Ireland was moot—the land had belonged to the humans for over two millennia and Brid's people were now in Scotland. "Bearach sought a truce with Bres."

"Then why are we still fighting?"

"Bearach was killed before sufficient trust could grow between both peoples."

So much killing … over what?

Neither spoke for a time.

"Your grandmother thought Bearach betrayed her cause. Kelly, it was never clear that it was Bres who killed Bearach." He flashed her a penetrating look. "Understand the alternatives of the decision you must make."

☙

That evening Kelly sat in her room staring at the empty pages of her father's diary.

You took the oath, Dad. What did it mean to you? Were you eager, or did you act from a sense of duty? Did you ever regret it?

She watched those pages late into the night, but nothing materialized, so she reluctantly went to bed.

☙

Although winter persisted later in the Highlands than in the more southerly climes, by the beginning of February the signs of its passing were finally visible. Snowdrops struggled to push up through the snowy blanket that receded with the more frequent rains. Soon the lighter greens of soft new grass would color the white fields. Ravens set to building their nests; the fox vixens were in cub; and the cows and ewes began lactating, producing milk for their imminent birthings.

The ancient Celtic holiday of Imbolc marked the approach of spring, celebrating the abundance of fresh dairy products and also honoring Brid—lord and provider of her people.

Imbolc morning, everyone pitched in to produce the fresh butter and cheese that would highlight the feast later that day. Kelly donned a worn apron, eager to participate. Having always considered butter and cheese to be supermarket merchandise, she was curious to learn the process from cow to table.

The butter-making was a scene of prolonged domestic violence. The long-handled plungers of the dash churns drove down into narrow wooden tubs, repeatedly pummeling the cream within until it surrendered its buttermilk; fresh butter was the result. Kelly took a turn, but she wasn't long at the task before her arms grew heavy and tired. She investigated the cheese-making, and a woman directed her to a vat filled with curdled milk. Rather than reeking of something long-forgotten in the recesses of the refrigerator, the milk had a tangy fresh scent—almost sweet. Her job was to push a large-meshed sieve through the semi-solid curds as they coagulated. The sieve diced the curds, allowing the liquid whey to run off. Recalling the old nursery rhyme, Kelly glanced about to ensure no visiting arachnids wanted to share the experience.

The atmosphere was a striking contrast to that of the butter-making. Here it was one of sacred ritual. The women around her scooped curds into round, wooden molds called chissets. They worked with a satisfied patience, their hands reverently pressing and kneading the curds into place, as though making cheese were an honor. They salted each wheel and enshrouded it in cheesecloth before fitting the chissets into the cheese press, which would slowly squeeze out the excess moisture. These wheels would then age for several months before they'd be ready to eat. The curds Kelly stirred would become the fresh farm cheese—akin to cottage cheese—that they'd serve at tonight's feast.

Kelly worked at her vat for several hours, allowing the sanctity of the other women's motions to seep into her, filling her with a calm, contented purpose. As lunchtime neared, she stretched, inhaling a deep breath of fresh cheese as she ran her hands down the front of her apron. Her left hand ended in the apron's pocket and happened upon a note. She unfolded and read it.

R,

    Meet me during the blessing ceremony. Everyone will attend—we won't be missed.

                          —D

This had to be Rhona's apron … and she was to rendezvous with Dougal! This might be Kelly's chance to catch them and finally learn what they were up to.

⁂

The Blessing of the Cows was to take place after lunch. The first calf of the season had been born in the early hours of the morning, and the coincidence of that occurring on Imbolc was considered auspicious. Everyone would be at the ceremony. That is, *almost* everyone.

As Brid placed her hands on the first dappled brow, pronouncing the blessing for good health, strong calves, and abundant milk, Kelly slipped out of the byre. The barn buildings were still her best guess for Dougal and Rhona's meeting place. She'd search the stables first. She moved quietly, straining to detect any tell-tale voices. She checked the stalls, the tack room and the feed storage room, but the place was deserted. She stood in the south doorway considering where next to look. That was when she noticed the aviary door was ajar.

She crept up to the building and paused. She heard soft shuffling noises within. With a solid thrust she flung the door open.

The man, whose back was to her, jumped and spun around. But it wasn't Dougal. It was Master David.

"Oh!" was all she could think to utter in her surprise.

"Kelly, you startled me!"

An untethered merlin perched on a roost beside the Master Bard.

"I came looking for Conall," he explained, "just as this fellow flew in. It seems to be carrying a message." He fished into the capsule secured to the merlin's leg, drawing out the note within. Unrolling the narrow slip, he read it with a sharp intake of breath. "Where's Brid? We must get this to her immediately!" He handed Kelly the curled paper:

> *tonight*
> *I will strike*
> *the bard*

An attack tonight! And another one directed at the master. Kelly hurried after Master David as he hastened to the byre. The blessing ceremony had ended and Brid was among a small group admiring the newborn calf.

Seeing the bard's expression, Brid was instantly alert. "What is it, David?"

He handed her the note. "A merlin flew in, carrying this."

Brid passed the note to Allisdair. He read it with a frown. "Is this threat directed at David, or our own Bard, Brandon?"

Brid nodded, "Yes ... Brandon may also be at risk. We'll take no chances. Allisdair, you can get to him quickly. Take Conall and go at once. Guard him well!" She turned to Master David. "And *you* will stay beside *me* throughout this day and night. Pressing an attack on Imbolc, under my very roof—the impudence! I'll keep you safe, David."

Master David bowed his head. "Thank you, Brid."

Kelly longed to stay with Master David, as if her presence might safeguard him. But what protection could a thirteen-year-old offer a gifted bard in the face of such a threat? Was he scared? Kelly certainly was for him.

But there was still the question of Dougal and Rhona. Kelly tore herself from the byre, determined that she would assist this investigation in whatever way she could. She spent the next two hours combing through the barns and out-buildings without success. If they had been there earlier, they were now long gone.

The afternoon was getting on as Kelly headed back to the house. She'd have to hurry so as not to be late for the Service of Thanksgiving at sundown. Brid had invited her to assist in the chapel service, and then to lead the candlelight procession from the abbey back to the manor and the awaiting feast.

Yet Kelly couldn't get the note out of her thoughts. Who had sent the merlin? And for whom was the message intended? Rhona would be conspicuous loitering around the aviary. But Dougal had routine duties there and was often in and out. And what was Aidan's connection? If the intended recipient didn't know they'd intercepted the message, he might await its arrival even now …

It wouldn't take long to check. And she could always make up time using the secret passage to the abbey. She raced back to the aviary in the lengthening shadows. This time she opened the door cautiously, bracing herself for whatever she might discover within.

Floating dust sparkled in the rays of sunlight entering through the open door. No one was inside. Kelly moved past the roosts of the larger hawks—the goshawks and harriers—looking for their diminutive cousins, the falcons. A peregrine greeted her with a plaintive *we-chew* as she stepped by, and she located the smaller merlins roosting just beyond. The one she sought was easily identified by the message capsule still banded to its leg. She slid her left hand into a stiff, buckskin gauntlet and untied the merlin's jesses. It readily stepped onto her fist and she carried it to a small worktable where she sat. She slipped off its hood and returned the piercing gaze from its black marble eyes.

"Can you tell me where you've been?" Kelly stroked the merlin's blue-gray back feathers with her right forefinger. It protested with a *ki-ki-ki-ki-ki,* but seemed to enjoy the handling.

She exhaled and centered, sliding into the merlin's mind without difficulty. She slowly adjusted to a view of the world through its fathomless eyes.

Restless. Impatient. I want to fly—no ... to dart, to plunge and turn, to free myself from gravity, climbing heavenward; and then to embrace the gravity and outrace it, rushing back down to earth. Will this one fly me? Release me, untethered, free to launch into the sky? Or will she tie me back again, this just a tease, as the last one did? Edgy. Eager. Let me feel the air whistle through my feathers. Loose me into my element. Restive. Longing.

Kelly retreated with the merlin's imagery vivid in her mind. It hadn't flown recently—certainly not earlier today. Of that she was sure.

⚛

"I have no idea where Kelly is. She was to assist me with the service. I don't see her here."

"No," the bard replied, looking about the crowded abbey. "She hasn't arrived."

"Well, we can't delay any longer," Brid stated. "Would you mind assuming her role?"

"It would be my privilege to assist."

Brid nodded, "Fine, then let's get started."

⚛

The merlin hadn't flown. It had been in the aviary all along. But she had watched Master David remove the note from the capsule. Could ... *he* have placed it there? Might he have been dispatching the message *out* by merlin, when Kelly interrupted him? She suddenly remembered part of the mental sending she'd overheard in the old barn several weeks previously: *Sendings aren't safe; use birds in the future!*

Tonight I will strike the bard.

Perhaps "the bard" wasn't the target of the attack at all, but the attacker's own signature.

Tonight I will strike.—The bard

Master David ... you?

Kelly stumbled out of the aviary, staggered by the implications. As she passed the stables, Aidan and Ina emerged leading two saddled horses.

Ina called to Kelly, "You're going to miss the service; we're late already."

"I …" Kelly wasn't sure how to voice her suspicions. She threw Aidan a guarded look.

Ina placed a reassuring hand on Kelly's arm. "It's all right. Tell us what's wrong."

"I … think Master David … may not be all he seems." She had their attention now. She surged on and explained her fears.

"Aye," Aidan said thoughtfully, "the merlin is ours and it didn't fly today." He shook his head with a frown. "But your accusation is a grave one—particularly against a Master and a bard. You'll need more proof than just the merlin."

"But if Kelly's right and an attack is to take place tonight, we have little time!" Ina countered. "We should search the music room."

"No …" Kelly stared at the growing shadows on the snow, thinking quickly. "… It's too public. He wouldn't keep anything incriminating there. Students are in and out all the time."

"His private study!" Aidan exclaimed. He hitched the horses to a nearby post and started for the manor house at a jog.

A few minutes later they stood outside the bard's study. Kelly tried the door, but it was locked. A dejected sigh escaped her.

Aidan dug through his pocket and produced two small files, which he slid into the lock's tumbler. "Having made a few locks ..." he stared at the keyhole, sliding his hands back and forth in small, precise movements "... it's not that difficult ... to learn to open them." He straightened with a satisfied expression.

Kelly gave the handle a turn and pushed the door inward. They paused on the doorstep, aware of the enormity of their violation. Kelly stepped in cautiously. It was a small room, stuffed with bookcases. Musical instruments, parts of instruments, tools, manuscripts, books and scrolls crowded the shelves. The room was dominated by a large desk with stacks of sheet music around its edges. A half-empty bottle of milk sat beside a mortar and pestle in the desk's center. Ina sniffed the mortar and gasped, nearly dropping it.

"It's belladonna root—deadly nightshade!"

Kelly didn't understand. "But ... Master David was poisoned that night also ..."

"True ... but he didn't consume very much—he was sick, but his life was never at risk." Ina recalled.

Aidan spoke up. "That's a neat way to divert suspicion ... ingest a small amount of the poison yourself ..."

Kelly looked behind the desk and it was her turn to gasp. In the corner of the room, just beyond the back bookcase, was a pair of muddy work boots!

It is *Master David. But what's he up to? Am I his target?*

☙

Master David poured milk from the crystal ewer into the chalice Brid held. She raised the cup, displaying it to those assembled.

"Let us give thanks for our livestock and the generous bounty with which they provide us," she intoned. She drank deeply from the chalice.

What was the rest of the sending she'd heard in the old barn?

… an eagle removes … bothersome nest … killing … or the mother before she's fledged her brood …

Eagles … she knew they were fiercely territorial. She and her mom had spotted a bald eagle while on a hike two summers before. The white-headed and tailed silhouette soaring overhead was magnificent. It had piqued Kelly's bird-watching interest, but her mother had chuckled and told her not get her hopes up; she wasn't likely to spot anything else. Eagles don't tolerate other birds in their territory—they either drive them off or kill them …

Kelly stared at the mortar and pestle and then at the milk … milk …

"Come on!" she shouted as she ran from the study. "We've got to get to the abbey!"

Brid leaned to Master David and whispered, "After we light our candles, I'll lead out. Follow directly behind me. The rest will fall in after we've exited the abbey."

"Very good," the bard nodded.

☙

They ran from the house—Aidan and Ina making for their horses. Kelly had fallen back, unable to match their pace. She was too slow … too slow …

She held up and forced herself to center, despite her heaving chest. Moments later, a tawny-white barn owl arrowed off in the direction of the abbey.

☙

Night had settled. In the gathering dark, Brid's candle threw a pale nimbus around her face. Her breath coalesced about her like curling smoke as she waited for the others to recess from the abbey.

"Oh, Brid …" Master David said from behind.

☙

When Kelly arrived at the abbey, a scene of bloody carnage met her. A massive tiger commanded the clearing in front of the stone convent, its white fur camouflaging its movements against the snow. Its ponderous paws struck with rapier speed and the strength to fell an oak. With each snarl, its pink mouth revealed fangs that dared its prey to feel their bite.

The tiger faced a grizzly bear, a full six feet at its shoulder hump. The body of a wolf lay beside the bear, blood pouring from numerous gashes. The grizzly wasn't faring much better. Its movements were labored and sluggish. It fought its own torpor, as well as the striped adversary before it. Several deep wounds testified to the bear's flagging defense.

The tiger suffered from no such debility, and was carving up its opponent with a deadly grace.

Shrieking defiance, Kelly dove, aiming her outstretched talons at the tiger's eyes. She darted in, enraging the beast, and her feathers filled the air as it reared up, jaws snapping at her. For good or bad, her idea had worked—she'd captured the tiger's attention. With lethal four-inch claws, it sliced the air about its head, trying to quell this aerial annoyance.

The commotion grew as a snowy owl suddenly joined the fray with a stentorian *krow-ow!* Like Kelly, it also aimed for the tiger's vulnerable eyes. The two quickly found a rhythm to their counterattack that afforded each the greatest protection. While one dove, the other would beat up out of range and prepare for the next swoop. This kept the tiger constantly ducking the incoming attacks, and denied it the opportunity to strike the defenseless, retreating owl.

That's not to say that the owls weren't at risk, however. One unlucky slash of the tiger's paw caught Kelly inbound; her right wing burned with pain. Nevertheless, the owls kept up their barrage, denying the tiger any opportunity to return to the battered grizzly.

Kelly lost all sense of time. As the minutes ticked on, both birds suffered. In addition to their wounds, they were tiring. They'd eventually miscalculate in their fatigue, which would prove fatal. Yet if they retreated, the tiger would finish off the grizzly and their diversion would have gained nothing.

Suddenly the tiger howled with a renewed savagery and failed to avoid Kelly's talons as they gouged deeply into one eye. She scanned the clearing to see what had drawn its attention. On the edge of the woods Aidan and Ina sat atop two steaming horses, Aidan firing off arrows with deadly accuracy—one already stuck out from the tiger's side. Kelly turned back for another descent, and the next arrow lodged in the beast's throat, turning its snarl into a gurgling yelp. The creature went mad with fury and Kelly, in mid-descent, was the closest thing it could strike at. It sprang up on its powerful hind legs and reached overhead to crush her between two clapping forepaws.

Committed to her descent, Kelly's death was certain, but as the tiger reared, Aidan loosed an arrow that plunged deep into the cat's exposed chest, piercing its heart. With a yowl that echoed through the birch grove, the beast fell over backwards, the fight and the life pouring from it.

If time had slowed during the attack, with each action observed in excruciating detail, then it now sped forward, leaving Kelly numb to the ensuing commotion. Her attention was fixed entirely on Master David.

No longer the predacious feline, his body lay limp, pierced with arrows. He carried no menace as he struggled to breathe past the gurgling throat wound. Kelly didn't see a traitorous assassin lying there; she could only see a man, long thought to be a friend, in the throes of death.

"Easy, Kelly." Aidan stood behind her, a notched arrow pointed at the bard. "No closer."

Master David's gouged and bloody eyes opened, although it was unclear if he could even see. "Kel-ly ..." he drawled in a hoarse whisper.

Her fractured emotions crowded out all thoughts. She couldn't respond—no words were there. Master David coughed up a crimson mouthful of frothy blood. Finally, her confusion and hurt took form.

"I loved you!"

"And you ... were like ... a daughter to me," he rasped. A shudder wracked his body and he shut his eyes for a long moment.

"How then ... h-how ... could you do this? You tried to *kill* me!" Tears ran down her face.

A faint smile played about his mouth. "You were amazingly resilient." His breaths turned to ragged gasps. "As an orange cat, I nearly caught a curious mouse, and you failed to drink from the poisoned trough ..." A violent spasm cut short his confession.

"But why?" she pleaded.

His closed eyes seeped blood; his words a hoarse wheeze. "I loved you ... but my principles. My cause ... required me to do this. How could I not be loyal ... to my beliefs? This ... brought ... no pleasure. Kelly, I'm sorry ..." The bard's voice trailed off as he moved away from that place. With a final breath his body stilled, lying in a red stain of snow.

17

THE FRITH

In the days following Imbolc, sadness blanketed the manor, quieting the daily bustle and dulling spirits. It was the sum of numerous griefs and hurt, and it overshadowed any sense of victory or relief in the battle's aftermath.

Brid's drugged lethargy during the attack had left her defenseless, and her injuries had been grave. Taking the form of a grizzly had afforded some protection, but it had been barely enough. Even with all of her healing skill, she was only just returning to health several weeks later. Jillian hadn't been as fortunate. Rushing, as a wolf, to Brid's side during the first moments after Master David's ambush, she had died defending Brid. The shock of the sudden violence was only overshadowed by the shock of the betrayal. That a bard—a sacred role reserved for those held to the highest standards—and one living among them as a trusted friend could commit such a foul crime was the unkindest cut of all.

Still, over time, morale about the manor slowly recovered. As the weeks went by, shock and grief were slowly replaced with acceptance and a grim appreciation that things had not fared worse. And that's not to say there hadn't been happy news along the way, either.

The reversal of Kenna's fortune put a renewed swagger in her step. It came to light that Dougal's accusations against her were as groundless as Kelly had suspected. Dougal, it turned out, had been secretly seeing Rhona for some time. While their illicit relationship was no great crime, *how* Dougal had arranged his free time was an entirely different matter. Upon investigation, Master Roy learned about Dougal's abuse of Kenna—both how he foisted his own chores onto her, and how he falsely maligned her performance, hoping to send her home.

Dougal had also pressured Aidan to register complaint against Kenna, but the journeyman smith had refused. He didn't share Dougal's low opinion of Kenna's work and he resented the attempted coercion.

Journeymen have a solemn duty to mentor and train the apprentices under their direction. To exploit an apprentice for one's advantage is inexcusable and simply not tolerated. It was Dougal who'd be leaving in disgrace.

Kenna straddled the paddock fence eagerly recounting the story to Kelly. Master Roy wanted Kenna to continue managing some of Dougal's former responsibilities. "He said it would be excellent preparation for my passage to journeyman next year!"

There was an uncharacteristic confidence and pride in Kenna's enthusiasm.

"He said it was the support he saw from my friends that led him to question Dougal's complaints. He said a slacker wouldn't have earned that kind of loyalty." Kenna thumped her friend's back in gratitude.

Kelly smiled. Despite her failed attempts to uncover Dougal's misdeeds, it was the least of her actions—her small gestures of encouragement for Kenna—that had made all the difference in the end. Kelly pointed to a nearby holly. "Whoever spits closest to that bush wins!" she challenged, knowing she'd lose.

Brid passed Allisdair a steaming cup of tea.

"Is she prepared?" he asked.

Brid sipped at her cup while breathing in the aromatic vapor. "She understands the elements of the rite, but when is anyone ever prepared for a *frith*? Particularly one's first." Brid paused in thought. "Some of my descendents reported little during their first *friths*—nothing more than an evening spent in quiet meditation. Some experienced visions, occasionally of portents beyond their understanding." She blew absently across the surface of the liquid. "Only a few, those with nearly true blood, caught glimpses of their *fetches*."

"What was Fiona's experience, *Bean-rìgh*?"

"Her *fetch,* a white stag, went so far as to reveal the hidden path to the *Sidhe*. I know not what to predict of Kelly," Brid admitted. "I would think she'd be too young to expect much … and yet she ever seems to surprise me."

"She's been subdued these last few weeks," Allisdair observed. "Unusually so fer that one."

"I've noted it too," Brid nodded.

Allisdair stroked his chin. "What forms will she observe tonight?"

"I don't know. She wanted to plan it herself."

"Ach, why doesna *that* surprise me," he growled.

☙

A *frith,* Kelly had learned, is the Celtic equivalent of the Native American vision quest. The *fritheir*—that was her—seeks to answer a question, typically about her future. According to Kelly's sources, the answer can come in one of two ways: either the *fritheir* uses the second sight to see into the future, or she interprets portents—signs of everyday life that have special meaning during a *frith*.

Kelly's experience reading tea leaves was limited to "Lipton" on the teabag—she didn't consider the second sight one of her talents, so she studied up on portents. The books she'd read cataloged the most critical portents to watch for, but each book itemized a different list. This left Kelly with a bewildering array of possibilities. She tried to record them in her diary, but she abandoned the attempt before she'd progressed very far.

March 1

Frith portents and their meaning:

- It's a good sign if someone is walking towards you, but a woman walking away is a bad sign.
- A red-haired woman is unlucky, but a black-haired woman is lucky.
- If a trip is planned, it's good luck to see a duck, but it's bad luck to see a goat.
- A pig facing away means misfortune unless you're a Campbell.

十卜≢≢

She began to doubt anything would happen during her *frith*, but she maintained a positive attitude. She *did* have a question she had to answer, and a night of quiet introspection couldn't hurt.

�

The pinewood, in these first days of spring, had a magic all its own. Kelly walked over a carpet of needles, bracken, and woodmoss, dodging the occasional patch of stubborn snow. She kept an eye out for the tell-tale foliage of creeping lady's tresses—one of the few orchids native to the Highlands. Ina had described the rosettes of roundish leaves and the creeping stems that formed green mats along the forest floor. It would be a thrill to take the news of a discovery back to Ina. They'd both surely return to witness the tall spikes of white flowers in late summer.

Atop one of the taller pines, a crested tit proclaimed its territory with a macho *seeh-burrurrlt, seeh-burrur-rlt!* Gregarious chaffinches frolicked in the branches of nearby trees showing off their coloratura song, which ended with a *choo-ee-o* flourish. Kelly could hear the muffled scampering of a small mammal—most likely a dog fox or red squirrel—but it was careful not to show itself. The woodland creatures knew spring was upon them, and they reveled in that knowledge.

Kelly halted with a sudden realization she was being watched. To her left, half-hidden among the trunks, she spied a herd of red deer. They'd likely been grazing on the evergreen twinflower that grew at their hooves, but they were grazing no longer. Four dozen coffee-brown eyes fixed on her. Their branching antlers and grayish-brown bodies held perfectly still, melding into the shadows beneath the trees. At some unseen signal, they turned as one, springing and leaping away. Their departure was silent, but the earth reverberated under their hooves.

It's lucky they weren't pigs ... because I'm no Campbell.

A realization had crept up on Kelly over the previous few weeks. She couldn't pinpoint exactly when it had begun or where it had come from. It hadn't started with bright, well-defined edges, but rather as a fuzzy nebula of a notion, barely perceptible. As it grew, however, it gathered strength and was now a surety of adamantine hardness. Kelly wanted to commit her life to Brid's cause and to take the Journeyman's Oath.

The process seemed straightforward enough. Tomorrow, following her *frith*, Kelly would sit for the Questioning. She would appear before the Council of Masters and answer the questions they posed. If she could satisfy the Council, they would hold her Ceremony of Passage that evening, where she'd take the Oath.

The Questioning wasn't so much a test of knowledge or ability, as Kelly understood it. It was more a test of intent. Kelly had always performed well with verbal exams; linguistic precision allowed her to articulate subtleties clearly, and that always makes a good impression. The trouble was, no matter how precisely you expressed yourself, you couldn't articulate what you didn't understand. *Why?* That was certainly going to be one of their questions. Why did Kelly want to do this? Why was she so certain? And there lay the problem. She had no clue why.

Kelly's research into *friths* had stressed the importance of "in-between" times and places. Calling upon the *Sidhe* for guidance needed to be done in a time and place where they could most readily respond. As on Saven Eve, that would be where doorways between our world and the Otherworld were likely. These doorways existed at "in-between" moments and locations.

The most in-between time of day was nighttime, especially just before dawn. And the period when the moon's phase begins to wax, as it would tonight, is potently in-between. In-between places contain boundaries, such as land and water, forest and clearing, field and alpine rock. In-betweenness filled Kelly's thoughts as she hiked along.

She liked that this ritual stressed in-between. It made it more personal. More hers. Life for her didn't exist at an extreme, as it seemed to for so many others: Gordie in his piping and Kenna in her husbandry of farm animals. Kelly's life was always in the middle. Moderate. In-between. A famous poet once asked if anyone could make poetry out of the middle way.[15] Kelly never forgot that question, because to her it asked, "Can my life be poetic?" During *this* in-between night, at the in-between spot of

---

15   Former poet laureate Robert Pinsky shares his thoughts about the world after September 11, *Jim Lehrer News Hour*, November 6, 2001:

"In these times, we're encouraged to be cautious, but not frightened; to be courageous, but not foolhardy; to be steadfast, but not stubborn. In other words, the wisdom seems to be, take the prudent middle ground in our actions and in how we deal with our emotions. Can anyone make poetry out of the middle way? Can anyone be lyrical about moderation? ..."

her choosing, her *frith* offered her both meaning and poetry.

Kelly chose to conduct her *frith* in a dell she'd discovered the previous autumn. She and Gealach had been riding; they were miles from the manor and not just off the beaten path—they were far from *any* path. From the moment she'd ridden into the clearing, she knew the place was special.

The dell snuggled into a broad cleft in the surrounding hillside, sheltered from the ever-present mountaintop winds. Birch and brightly-berried rowans fringed the clearing with white and red, contrasting the greens of the grass and lichen-covered rocks. Across the downhill face of the dell, just within the birches' cover, a lively stream (a *burn* to Gordie) cavorted. The closeness of open space besides dense forest, grassy lawn interrupted with rocky outcroppings, all bordered by running water, shouted to Kelly of in-betweenness.

She hadn't been to the glade since the previous fall, and she was unprepared for the changes of spring. It was still too early for the yellow-green tinges of emerging leaves, and the rowans' berries were long past. But the earth pushed up its own palette of delicate colors. Mixed among the greening grass were the lavender and purple bells of spring heather. Pink spikes of bergenia and the white-starred flowers of wood anemone dotted the clearing. Bright yellow marsh marigolds edged the stream bank, while young ferns growing along the edges of the woods framed the scene with a ruffle of emerald lace.

Kelly was well down the eastern face of the hill and the sun was already past the mountain's peak. Night would come on quickly. She set down the armload of fallen branches she'd collected and kindled a fire in a rocky depression. Hunting about, she added more wood to her pile, until she was satisfied she had enough to last through the night. As the trees' shadows marched across the dell, a strident *kya!* pierced the stillness from far aloft. The last light of the day lingered on a golden eagle soaring high overhead. Its wings blazed until the sun slipped further down and extinguished their fiery glow.

Unpacking her knapsack, Kelly laid out a thick wool blanket where she could sit beside the fire, with her back against a granite outcropping. She set out a plate with bread and cheese, and filled a pewter goblet with cider. But the food wasn't for her—she had to fast for her *frith* and hadn't eaten all day. The food symbolized her welcome to the *Sidhe*. She then took off her socks and shoes, and found she wasn't too uncomfortable if she stretched her feet right to the edge of fire pit. Bare feet demonstrated a supplicant's humility.

The moon was the thinnest sliver of a crescent and threw scant light. The night thickened around her, quickly swallowing the glade. In the background, Kelly could hear the musical tumbling of the stream. It was out in the darkness, as if it were the song of a disembodied voice. The fire's pops and crackles existed here in the light, and that made them more real. Kelly let the dancing tongues of flame lull her mind into a quietude not unlike centering.

Why do I want to do this? What makes it so important to me? Thirteen years of dreams and priorities pushed aside by something I didn't even understand a few months ago. How do I know it won't happen again? After it's too late to change my mind?

She thought of Peggy and Jake, but the memories seemed flat and lifeless. She then thought of Kenna assisting a new-born calf to stand; she saw Gordie's purple, puffed face blowing into his bagpipes. These images were more colored and textured.

Something rustled in the trees beyond the fire's light. Kelly sat up, fully alert. It made too much noise to be a small animal. The sound came again. She could hear the crunching of twigs—closer this time. Whatever it was, it didn't appear to be shy about approaching her fire. She grabbed a stout branch and stood, edging closer to the fire.

"Hail the camp!" a sonorous voice called. "May I approach?"

A man stepped out of the darkness. He was tall and wiry with snowy white hair. He wasn't old, but there was nothing youthful about him either. His eyes were dark pools, reflecting the glint of the fire, and he had the angled nose and sharp brow of an eagle. His gaze was keen, as if it held both wildness and intelligence in equal measure.

Kelly knew she should be wary of the stranger, yet he had an air that was at once protective and compelling. She understood instinctively she was safe with this man. She relinquished her branch, adding it to the fire.

"May I join you?" His voice was rolling and deep. Kelly could feel the vibrations of his words as much as hear them.

"Yeah … I guess."

He bowed to her. "Thank you."

She flounced down onto her blanket cross-legged. This handsome stranger had her mind tied in knots. He had the same quality of grace and poise that Brid possessed, and that Kelly lacked. She had no idea what to say.

"I'm known as Cair," he purred.

"I … I'm Kelly." It occurred to her that around her fire, she'd be hostess and this man would be her guest.

"Would you … like something to eat?" She gestured to the plate.

"There's only food for one. I couldn't eat your dinner."

Kelly was suddenly embarrassed by her *frith*. She felt like a child playing Ouija. "I've eaten. That food's … extra."

Cair looked at her, his expression intense but not unkind. "Then I will accept with gratitude." He sat and collected the plate and goblet.

Kelly let him eat for a time in silence. Then she realized he was staring at her bare feet. She tried to tuck them under her.

"My feet … were sore after my hike."

Cair didn't press her with questions, prying into her purpose—he seemed too polite for that. But she felt she should offer some explanation.

"I came out here tonight to think … to try and understand the path I should take …"

Kelly waited, but Cair said nothing. He stared into the fire as if considering her words. After a while, he finally spoke.

"Understanding the future is always a challenge—even for those gifted with the sight. We have only our knowledge of the past, as if we live our lives walking backwards. We choose each step based on what we see behind us. And when that backward vision is obstructed—when the recent past is unsettled—we hardly dare move for fear of a false step."

He paused; the fire's crackles filled the silence.

"Know this, and understand its import: the first steps down any path are the most difficult. If compassion moves you to sacrifice and in doing so you help a person, the next time you see need, your sacrifice will seem less and the decision easier to make." He arched his white eyebrows and looked at Kelly with a fierce gaze. "Just as if greed or jealousy urges you into an action that compromises another, the next time you're tempted, your misgivings will be less. With practice, they'll disappear, shallow justifications filling their place."

Neither spoke for some time. As Kelly reached forward to lay more wood on the fire, Cair removed a velvet-wrapped bundle from his bag.

"Would you mind if I played?"

He pulled back the cloth to reveal a lap harp. The wood was darkened from time and the oils of the harper's hands, but even as antique instruments are measured, this one was immensely old. Every surface was ornamented with carvings, although they were impossible to make out in the firelight. As Cair tuned the pins, each of the silver strings sang out with a clear, ringing voice—the notes lingering in the air, reluctant to fade. Cair played a lilt to test the tuning, but it finished before Kelly wanted it to.

"I've never heard anything like it. What kind of harp is that?"

"It's a *clarsach*." A slight smile played at Cair's lips. "A Gaelic harp. It's an ancient instrument, revered by the Celts. One such as this might have performed for kings or clan chieftains. The music was much sought after."

"I can understand why," Kelly whispered. Her awkwardness forgotten, she wanted only to hear more.

Cair settled with his back against a rock and began to play. The music was magical, with a life of its own. Listening to it was like watching a swallowtail flit in front of your nose. It captured your mind and filled it with wonder, as each note shifted and changed, crowding out all other thoughts. Kelly willingly gave herself up to its enchantment.

The music's beauty was owed in part to the exquisite instrument Cair played, but even more so to his prodigious talent. She couldn't imagine four hands accomplishing what his two produced. Melodies, harmonies, and counter-harmonies spilled from his fingers.

It was hard to say how long Cair played. Kelly drifted, totally under the spell of his harping. She didn't notice whether a tune was mournful, courtly, or spry; she breathed them all in as one, suffused with a restful contentment.

At one point she felt a vague familiarity, but she was too mesmerized to recognize the tune as one of Master David's favorites. Nevertheless, happy memories of time spent with the master played around the edges of her consciousness like snatches of dreams—music lessons, evenings of entertainment, the long talks they shared, the chance meetings in the hallway. Then, as if the images were a runaway train that couldn't stop until it ran its course, the memories turned more troubled—the mountain lion's claws digging into her back, the fearful paws of the white tiger slicing up at her, and finally, the anguishing image of Master David dying in a sea of his own blood ... that scene filled her mind drowning out everything, including the music. The only sounds she could hear were his gasped words: "Kelly ... I'm sorry!"

She didn't know at what point Cair had stopped playing, but when she fought her way back to the present and opened her glistening eyes, he was sitting watching her, his harp at his feet.

"Kelly, what is your real question?"

"I loved him," she blurted, each word stabbing with pain. "How could he have done that?"

Cair waited in the flickering shadows, as if he knew she wasn't finished.

"I thought he was my friend!" A tear escaped and fell down her cheek. "He was always there for me. We would talk, or he'd play a tune, or just sit with me quietly—he always knew just what I needed. He made me feel safe ... and cared for." She looked up from the fire, into Cair's eyes as another tear ran down her cheek. "How could I have been so wrong about him?"

"Were you?" Cair's question was as gentle as a down feather.

"How can you ask that?" Kelly cried. "He tried to kill me. He tried to kill Brid."

"Kelly, sometimes our actions and our thoughts are at odds. You can't always assume one from the other."

"But how could a friend do that?"

Cair stood and fed more branches to the fire. "Did you ask him?"

She nodded mutely.

"What did he answer?"

Kelly thought back to that horrible scene. Master David pierced with arrows, speaking words she could hardly comprehend in her shock. "He ... he said he had to be loyal to his beliefs ... even at the cost of our friendship." She closed her eyes, fighting the memory. "He said he was sorry."

The sound of the fire consuming its fuel was the only sound for long minutes. When Cair finally spoke, the lushness of his voice was soothing.

"We sometimes have to make decisions where no attractive choices exist. It's comforting to believe there will always be a good answer if we look hard enough. But there will be times in your life when there will be no right answers. Don't judge too harshly, Kelly—the world isn't black and white."

"He told me that," she said in a small voice.

Cair arched an eyebrow. "Did he? Then he taught you well—as a dear friend should."

Kelly stared into the fire. "How can I believe anything he said?"

"Was he true to you?"

"What do you mean?" she asked.

"Did David ever ask you to do something against your will? Did he ever try to coerce you to do something, either through intimidation or guilt?"

"No! He was always saying that I should consider other perspectives ... that I shouldn't jump to the obvious conclusion ... and that no one else can choose for me."

"Then he was true to you. He *was* a good friend, and you can trust what he told you."

Kelly sat for a long while digesting such odd advice: that she could trust a man who'd tried to kill her. Yet Cair made it sound so reasonable.

"Was Master David evil?"

Cair retrieved his *clarsach* from the ground and he plucked a single note. The pureness of the sound hovered in the light of the fire, slowly dissolving until its tone was just a memory.

"Have you ever looked through the eyes of a raptor?" he asked.

Kelly nodded.

"And how did you see the world?"

As an owl she had attacked and killed mice, bats, and squirrels—all creatures she herself had been. All creatures with their own unique essence. It seemed brutal, but only if you were the mouse, bat, or squirrel. To an owl it was simply survival.

"It could be harsh," she answered, "but that's how nature is."

He plucked another string. And listened as the note filled the night.

"And evil?" he asked in the ensuing stillness.

"No." She shook her head. "A raptor knows nothing of evil."

He plucked a final string, pausing to absorb the perfect sound before he continued.

"You won't find good and evil in the natural world, because they are not of nature—they are of man. Evil is a consequence of conscience and moral choice—the choice of individuals. I can't tell you what evil is. No one can. We must each find our own answer. And that answer becomes our ethos—our personal value structure."

They talked late into the night. Kelly didn't always understand Cair's words, but she felt comforted by his presence. At times they'd simply sit and watch the fire, each drifting in his or her own thoughts. Then he'd raise his harp and play a tune, occasionally singing along. His voice! If the ocean had a voice, it would sound just like Cair's.

In the early hours of the morning, long after the moon's thin sliver had set, Kelly pointed to the edge of the firelight. Perched on a hawthorn bush was a giant snowy owl.

"Look!" she whispered.

Cair nodded calmly.

"It's so tame to get this close," she marveled.

Cair boomed out a laugh that Kelly feared would scare the owl. "No, he's *not* tame—not that one!"

"Do you know him?" Kelly turned and stared at her guest.

"I do. And now, so do you. What's his name?"

What an odd question. She didn't think he was asking her to name the owl. She looked into its large, golden eyes. She sensed intelligence and purpose.

What is your name?

A voice in her head responded, *I am Riagall. I've waited for you since the days of Parthalon.*

Kelly gasped and turned to Cair. "He spoke to me!"

"That's encouraging—he tends to be taciturn."

Kelly gaped at him and then back at the owl. She suddenly remembered the night of Imbolc. This was the same owl that aided her attack as they tried to distract the tiger away from Brid.

That was you!

Yes, I am your fetch.

"Cair, what's a *fetch*?"

Cair stirred the fire and gave Riagall a wry look. "It's an animal spirit that exists across many worlds. If it chooses a person, as it seems Riagall has chosen you, it will serve as a guide and guardian during that person's life. Don't look for him as you would a pet. He will only take form in this world when *he* chooses—often during pivotal moments. He is the ancient one; he served Parthalon centuries before the *Tuatha de Danann* ever came to the shores of Ireland. He also later served Brid."

"Brid?"

"Yes. For many ages. But he left her a thousand years ago, as the prophecy foretold."

Kelly was bubbling with questions for Riagall, but when she turned back he had vanished. She continued staring at the bush long afterwards.

Riagall, I'm pleased to have made your acquaintance.

Imperceptibly, the sky lightened and slowly the surrounding glade emerged from beyond the light of the fire. Dawn wasn't far off.

Cair arose and swaddled his *clarsach* back into its velvet wrapping. "Kelly, I must take my leave. Thank you for your hospitality and your company. Know that you're always welcome in my home."

"But where do you live?"

"You will find the path to my door when you need it." And with that, her enigmatic guest walked off into the thinning night.

18

PASSAGE

In the stillness of the predawn, Kelly extinguished the remains of the fire, packed her gear, and started back. She felt guilty over how she'd spent her *frith*. It wasn't that she hadn't enjoyed Cair's company—she had. The night had passed pleasantly. But the ritual's intent was quiet introspection, not a companionable evening around the campfire. She felt as though she'd cheated. She doubted Brid would approve. Allisdair certainly wouldn't.

Her long hike back gave her time to consider Cair's words, particularly regarding Master David. Cair said the bard had been true to her. Despite attempted murder. Cair said Master David had been a good friend to her.

Regardless, I know the attacks were wrong.

But if Master David truly believed Bres' cause was just, wouldn't it also have been wrong for him to abandon his pledge?

Kelly had never faced such a lose-lose scenario. She was beginning to appreciate Cair's words. She had once believed Master David to be her friend, and somewhere in her soul she still sensed it. But the shock and hurt of his betrayal wouldn't permit her to return there yet.

I can never forgive what he did—he made an evil choice!

True, but he died for that choice. Isn't that punishment enough?

Perhaps … I can … separate that action from the good memories I know have meaning. Perhaps … I can still love him.

The tears ran freely as she finally allowed herself to mourn her friend's death.

Kenna was waiting for Kelly when she reached the manor grounds. Perched on a low branch of an oak tree, her legs dangling in boredom, Kenna's face brightened when she spied her friend. She scrambled down out of the tree a bit too hurriedly, leaving a trail of bark scrapings running up her sweater.

"There you are! I was afraid you might have taken a different path home and that I'd missed you. I want to hear all about your *frith*. If I get passed to journeyman next year, I'll be holding my own *frith* and I don't know what to expect."

Kenna rushed on to tell Kelly all about the calf she helped deliver the previous day, never returning to the topic of the *frith*, nor pausing long enough for Kelly to comment on anything.

Kelly headed straight to the kitchen when she got back, to find Maggie armed with a basket of warm bannocks, a traditional Scottish oat cake.

"I dunna know how they think starvin' ya young people serves any useful purpose. Now just sit yerself here, lass, an' go ahead an' eat before ya faint on my counter." Maggie poured a steaming cup of cocoa while Kelly bit greedily into a cake.

"I'm so hungry I could eat a sheep—wool and all," Kelly mumbled with her mouth full.

"Ach, now that would be a waste of good wool!" Maggie handed her the mug. "Remember, ya didna sleep last night an' if ya go eatin' yer fill, ya'll be sound asleep by noontime. Ya'll want yer wits sharp about ya for the Questionin'. No more than two cakes!"

Maggie made a good point. Kelly tried to slow her gobbling to a more refined pace.

"I remember yer da sittin' here breakin' his fast followin' his *frith*. Do you know what he says to me? He says, 'Maggie, I'm not worried about the Questionin'. I *know* I'll pass.' An' I says to him, 'Ach, an' how would ya be knowin' that? Are you feelin' you've got some of the second sight in ya?' An' he says, 'No, Maggie, words. It's words. I know what I must do, an' I've found the words to explain it. That's what this test is about. An' I know I'll pass.'

"It just words, Kelly dear, just words. You need to find yer own, an' ya shouldna fear theirs. Now be off and catch what rest ya can."

At noontime Kelly was at the appointed place. She stood outside the closed door, awaiting the summons.

Just words … Sorry Maggie, but there's no "just" about it. Words have power. We're usually too careless to choose them for their strength, but it's there. They can wound, or uplift. They can alter futures. The right words can make me a journeyman … or not.

She knew some of the questions they'd ask, just as she knew the sorts of answers they'd expect. It would be easy enough to tell them what they wanted to hear. And yet …

"How could I not be loyal to my beliefs?"

His dying words gripped her. As if he were teaching her one last lesson ... The door opened and they called her in.

A long table ran down the center of the hall. The masters sat behind it, grim and silent, with Brid in the center and Allisdair to her left. Kelly stood before them, trying to calm the queasiness in her stomach. Her mouth was Sahara dry.

At Brid's nod, Allisdair addressed Kelly.

"Who is it, who comes before this council requestin' passage to journeyman?"

This was a ritual question that expected a prescribed answer. Kelly was supposed to present her ancestral lineage as if she were a prized stud or a champion show dog.

He died for what he believed. How can I do any less?

She took a deep breath and held it for a long moment. The same sort of breath you'd take just before stepping off a cliff.

"I ... am Kelly MacBride." She tried to hold her chin higher and could feel it tremble. "I'm thirteen years old and I've lived here now for six-and-a-half months." Their faces reflected their anticipation; they undoubtedly waited for her to continue. But she didn't.

Allisdair frowned. "Yer to give us an account of yer ancestry that we might better measure who ya are."

It would be tricky to make her point without appearing disrespectful.

"You asked me who I am and that's what I answered." She stared down at a crack in the grout between the great stones laid in the floor. "Whoever my ancestors were, and whatever gifts they may have passed down to me, who I am is defined by what *I've* done with those gifts.

There were murmurs around the table and Allisdair immediately raised his hand for order. His expression altered—his brow was tight and his eyes flashed with either warning or anger, or both.

"Very well ..." he said with slow deliberateness. "Would ya commit yerself to a lifetime of service in the fight against evil?"

Staring back down at the grout, she replied, "I will commit my life, without reservation, to protecting the innocent, to helping those in need, and to nurturing good in all things."

"But whom would you serve?" the Master Smith blurted. "Why wouldn't you fight evil?"

Allisdair indicated Kelly should answer the question.

Kelly pictured Cair leaning back against the rock, half his face lit by the buttery-orange glow of the fire, the other half-hidden in the night shadows.

"I don't think evil exists as an outside force that we can slay like a dragon. I believe that both good and evil are within each of us and they're the two sides of every decision of conscience we make. Any evil that exists in the world comes from our choices."

Kelly looked across at the Master Smith. "I *do* pledge to fight evil ... but I believe it's a different sort of fight than you mean. I can't always see it when considering how to act. I can promise that I'll never consciously support it, but I can't promise I won't make mistakes."

There was silence as the masters considered her answer.

"Oh, this is ridiculous!" Master Roderick snapped. "She wastes our time. This nonsense comes from attempting to educate *girls*. Let's end this farce and get on to serious matters."

"Please, Roderick," Allisdair directed, "save opinions fer our deliberation." He turned to back Kelly. "Why do ya seek to become a journeyman?"

Here it was—the question she had to answer, for which she had no answer. Why was she so sure? She thought of Gordie and his countless hours practicing; of Cameron's long afternoons training with Duffy; of Ina's patient care during Kelly's recovery. Her friends were all dedicated to their crafts; yet, something else drove Kelly.

Time was running out. What happens to journeyman dropouts? Those who fail the Questioning and aren't passed on—or would she be the first? The long silence pressed on Kelly, taunting her. *I know what I must do. And I've found the words to explain it,* her father had told Maggie.

Help me find the words, Dad!

A picture of her father filled her mind. Then her mother was there beside him. More joined the picture: Duncan and Brianna, grandparents she never knew. Fiona, Bearach and others reaching farther back—faces she didn't recognize, but ones she suspected were all her family.

"Kelly, answer the question," Allisdair persisted.

She gazed into Brid's ocean-blue eyes and then turned to Allisdair. "I'm descended from my grandmother, through scores of ancestors who each fought in their own way for our cause."

"But you just claimed that your lineage was irrelevant," Master Roy interrupted.

"I said it didn't define me as a person … but I believe it does define what I must do."

"How so?" the master asked.

An idea was taking hold and it felt very right. "A job was begun thousands of years ago by the original *Tuatha de Danann*—a job that still needs completion. With each generation, my family has carried this work forward, hoping for an eventual conclusion. It's now my turn to take up this charge and to contribute what I can."

Allisdair's chin came up and his eyes were wary. "An' just *what* is this charge yer so eager to take up?"

Kelly looked down at the grout, and then back at Allisdair. Helplessness clouded her face. "I don't know." She gave a deep sigh and then let discretion go. "This is going to sound crazy, but I feel a tugging from the past. In some way I'm bound to it and it has an expectation of me. There's something I must do—I can feel it as surely as I feel the power in these ancient stones … I just don't know what it is. I can't see my path, but I *know* that becoming a journeyman is part of it."

The masters displayed no reaction. Whatever thoughts they had were hidden behind expressionless faces.

After an achingly long silence, Allisdair asked, "An' what makes ya worthy to become a journeyman?"

Worth? What is the value of a thirteen-year-old girl? Greater than a twelve-year-old girl and certainly worth more than most fourteen-year-old boys ... but to this group?

As she looked down the table she saw decades of dedication and service, loyalty and commitment seated before her; she realized that despite her fear of Allisdair, he'd never been unfair or ill-tempered in his treatment of her, and as she looked at Brid she saw the love she shared with her grandmother.

She answered meekly. "As you'd measure it, I'm not worth much ... now. But that's why I need to become a journeyman—so that I can work and learn. I believe I can someday be worthy."

Allisdair looked up and down the table and then, satisfied that there were no further questions, directed Kelly to please step out.

"I agree with the others. It may just be the matter of age, but regardless, I wasn't satisfied with her answers. Nor do I subscribe to her views on evil—you're either against it, or you're not. She prevaricated. I don't think she knows what she wants, and I too felt her deviation from the traditional forms impertinent." There was a murmur of agreement as the Master Smith finished.

Kelly was unsure how long she'd been waiting, but it had been a while. At least the Council's decision hadn't come quickly. That would have signaled certain failure. As long as they continued deliberating, she had a shred of hope. But only a shred. It was ironic that the courage (a quality she never believed she possessed) to speak what she felt would itself deny her this newfound aspiration.

ॐ

Allisdair turned to Brid. "*Bean-rìgh?* Do ya wish to speak?"

"Yes, Allisdair, thank you." Brid rose and paced away from the group, then turned to face them. "After so long, the prophecies are once again in motion. Since Kelly has joined us, there have been signs that those things once foretold are finally drawing towards fulfillment.

"She has a destiny. That feeling has grown so strong within me it's almost corporeal. She maintains she feels it too, and that her passage today is part of this destiny. She has no experience with the sight, to my knowledge, but the power she's already demonstrated might well support her claim of prescience.

"Because I cannot see her path, we must once again rely on faith. I sense tremendous change coming in the next turn of the Great Wheel, and this may in fact be the start."

She turned to Allisdair. "You haven't said much. Would you share your thoughts?"

Allisdair nodded. "I've most feared that without a path, Kelly would be feckless an' wild. If she had come before us today an' claimed to have found her path, I would have dismissed her application for the pretense. Who ever knows his path at twice her age? An' yet, she knows to seek it … an' I admit that surprised me. She spoke with honesty today, an' her truthfulness may indicate some developin' maturity.

"I've long held she's too young an' too immature for passage and trainin'. Now I'm less convinced—she may be ready, or nearly so. I also deem that Brid's words must be given great weight. She's been our guide from the first days." He turned to Brid. "*Bean-rìgh,* if ya believe this will support the fulfillment of the prophecies an' promote our cause, then I nay need proofs."

Allisdair unfolded his hands and laid them on the table in a gesture of finality. "Please consider all that's been said before casting yer vote."

ॐ

Master Roy led Kelly back into the hall. She wasn't nervous now. The decision had been made and there was nothing more to do but accept it. And she would do that with dignity.

When Master Roy had retaken his seat, Allisdair addressed her. "Passage is the movement from one place to another. It's both a transition an' a journey. The Council will only accept candidates when we're satisfied they've already begun this transition fer themselves. Childhood is left behind as responsibility replaces frivolity, knowl-edge replaces ignorance, and duty replaces self-interest.

"In the case of yer petition, the Council has serious concerns about yer age, yer readiness for so serious a charge, an' yer ability to commit a lifetime tenure. Yet, at pivotal times we occasionally need to flex our conven-tions an' consider indefinable measures when choosin' our course. We believe this is one such case, despite the risks.

"After considerable debate, the Council has voted to accept yer application fer passage to journeyman, Kelly MacBride." Allisdair leaned forward, his gaze boring into her. "This path is never an easy one an' will be all the more difficult for yer youth an' newness among us. Yer hon-esty will serve ya best on this journey. There'll be much ya dunna know. When so, ask! Our role as masters is to teach an' to guide. A fool would ignore such a resource. It takes wisdom an' courage to ask for help." As suddenly as that, Allisdair finished and the masters rose from their seats.

"... *Voted to accept your application ...*" Had Kelly heard him correctly, or was she twisting his words into what she wanted to hear? Master Roderick fled the room grumbling, and the other masters filed past her offering polite congratulations.

As the table emptied, Brid leaned to Allisdair. "Would you please ask her to attend me in my solarium when she's finished here?"

"Certainly," Allisdair responded as they both rose. "*Bean-rìgh*, there was somethin' she said ... Does she know of the power within the manor's foundation rock?"

Brid's eyebrows twitched. "*I've* never spoken of it ..."

As the last of the masters left, the room was suddenly empty. Or nearly so. Allisdair was waiting. Her surprise at the Council's decision was still ringing through her and the blunt truth was all she could offer in reaction.

"I didn't think I'd pass."

"Nor did I."

Which way had he voted? His presence made her uneasy, yet he stayed behind for a reason. He had said, "*Our role as masters is to teach and guide.*" Was he offering his help? She took a deep breath, trying to sort her thoughts. "At times I truly feel I can be a good journeyman." She hesitated. "But ... at other times I wonder how I can possibly succeed."

Ugh ... I'm making no sense!

The lines of Allisdair's face were softer than they'd been during the Questioning. "I canna see all of the charges destined for ya. There'll be obstacles—be sure of that—an' you'll likely face perilous tasks before all is done." The tone of his voice was also less severe. "Humility is useful, but too much can cripple ya; if ya lack confidence, you'll undertake nothin' an' ya'll achieve nothin'. Yet, overconfidence is foolhardy an' dangerous. Both humility an' confidence are required, but ya must find yer own balance."

The middle way … he's urging me to find the middle way.

"Kelly, ya have the potential fer greatness. Yet potential means nothing! Hard work an' discipline count more. An' aye, ya'll make mistakes. But if ya let yerself learn from them, they'll teach ya good judgment. This is all I can offer ya—this an' the blessin' that Danu guide yer choices along yer journey.

"Yer grandmother awaits ya in her solarium." He nodded to her and left the hall.

༺

Brid was gazing out the window. Not wanting to interrupt, Kelly stood in the doorway watching her. She had come to rely on Brid as family—someone to provide a home, and a sense of welcome and security. But Kelly began to feel as though she owed Brid something, and something more than just staying out of trouble. It was as if she were seeing her grandmother, not from the perspective of what was important to Kelly, but from the perspective of what was important to Brid.

"… *duty replaces self-interest* …"

Brid turned, and seeing Kelly, she extended her arms. Kelly stepped forward and wordlessly accepted the embrace. It wasn't that of a child clutching for solace;

rather, it was an acknowledgment between comrades with a shared experience, as if to say to the other, "I understand."

They said little while they sipped their tea; there was too much to convey and mere words were inadequate. Brid finally stood and lifted down a small box from one of the shelves above her desk. It may have been brown once, but now the leather was so darkened with age it was impossible to say.

"This was your father's, Kelly. It has been in our family since the beginning, and is presented to the eldest child upon passage to journeyman. It is now yours."

Kelly accepted the box and opened it reverently. Inside was a gold ring with a heavy band supporting a cairngorm the size of her thumbnail. The band was inlaid with precious stones in the shapes of *Ogham* characters. She lifted it from the box. It was unexpectedly heavy for its size.

"I've seen this ring!"

Brid seemed impressed. "Your father's been gone many years. You've an excellent memory from such an early age."

"No ..." Kelly was shaking her head, staring at the ring, trying to remember. "No, it was recently ... it was in a dream I had ... on Saven Eve."

Brid's expression turned hawk-like. "Tell me!"

"There was a woman," Kelly's voice drifted as she thought back. "Asleep on my bed. She was fair, but so pale. She wore the ring. But she wasn't sleeping. A man was with her. He'd been crying. He took it from her hand."

"Was there a book? Do you remember a book?"

"Yes … yes, at the foot of the bed …"

"The lost diary!" Brid whispered.

"… that's why he took her ring."

Brid sat up. "What do you mean?"

"He was going to lock the book and hide it. He said her ring and his pendant would form the key." Kelly added, "I don't see how that would work."

"What makes you say this?"

Kelly shrugged. "Looking at the ring, I just don't see how they'd fit together to form anything."

"Did you see this pendant?"

"Only from a distance. But if it's anything like mine there's no way it'll combine with this ring."

Brid's face paled to the color of chalk. "Show me."

Kelly reached under her shirt and lifted the chain over her head. She handed her mother's pendant to Brid. It was a flat sterling disk, the size of her palm, worked into the shape of a triskelion: three interconnected spirals spinning outward with a diamond sparkling at the tip of each spiral.

Brid stared at it and slowly exhaled. "Cairbre's amulet! Of course—Morgan would have come into this. He was of his line." She looked up at Kelly, her blue eyes incredulous. "Where did you get this?"

"My mother gave it to me. She said it was a family heirloom and I should always keep it safe."

Brid folded her hands around Kelly's pendant and closed her eyes. "Fiona lived a thousand years ago. Descended from me, the old magic ran nearly true in her, as it hadn't for millennia. She was as wise as she was beautiful. And she studied not just the lore of the *Sidhe*, but that of many races. She sought for some ancient power that might help us defeat Bres for all time.

"I never knew the sources of the magic she unearthed. I certainly would have cautioned her against the attempt to wield it. Morgan also was concerned; he had been close to her since her husband Blane's death several years before. But on a Saven Eve, a millennium past, she went off alone and tested her theories, tapping into that primeval magic leftover from the youngest days of the world.

"As great as her power was, it was not sufficient. She didn't survive. Morgan was undone. He had loved her deeply, and I suspect he longed to marry her and to become a second father to Elspeth, Fiona's daughter. He locked himself in her chamber that night battling a profound grief. When he emerged the next day he said little. That was the last we were to see him. He went off that evening, telling no one. Her ring and her diary were missing—we assumed he had taken them.

"We sent scouts to trace his trail, but none succeeded. In one day, we had lost them both—the brightest stars among our people in over fifteen centuries.

"Several years later a strange traveler passed through and delivered the only message we were to ever receive from Morgan. With it came Fiona's ring, which I gave to Elspeth, and an original manuscript: *Morgan's Lament*. Oddly the music was torn, as if verses were missing, but we could never get anything out of the traveler, who himself mysteriously disappeared.

"To this day Morgan remains lost to us. He never returned to the *Sidhe*. Whatever fate befell him, his soul lies trapped and bound somewhere outside of time."

Brid handed the pendant back, a strange gleam in her eyes.

"Your mother was right. It is an heirloom. And you should continue to guard it closely.

"Kelly, we haven't spoken of your *frith*. How was your evening?" Brid leaned forward, as if eager to hear Kelly's response.

"Eh … it was … quiet."

It had been relatively quiet, if you don't count the music.

"Did you see or experience anything … portentous?"

Riagall certainly qualified, but what would Brid say if she knew Kelly had stolen her fetch?

"I saw … an owl just before dawn."

Brid seemed disappointed, but she smile encouragingly. "An owl is a good sign. It symbolizes wisdom and vision. Its nocturnal character represents our ability to sense things we can't see. An owl is a fine portent on a first *frith*."

Brid rose. "Get what rest you can. I'll see you later at the abbey."

Kelly found Gordie waiting for her in the hall outside her residence.

"Congratulations," he offered. "How does it feel?" Gordie seemed unusually subdued.

"Like everything's happening too fast."

He sighed. "Get used to it. After Aidan made journeyman, we hardly saw him at all, they kept him so busy." He dug his hands into his pockets and looked at her with an expression that might have been sadness. "Kelly, you will make time ... I mean, when you can ... for explorations of a scientific nature—won't you?"

He was afraid he was going to lose her!

"Always!" she promised. And then an idea occurred to her. "Gordie, I have to process into the abbey at the start of the ceremony."

He shrugged. "Yeah, been to a few. I know how they work."

"I was wondering if you might lead me in ... piping."

He slowly looked up, his eyes widening as her request registered.

"Really? This would be my first gig. And a passage ceremony!"

"Here's what I'd like you to play ..."

⚛

The masters lined up in two columns. The journeymen were likewise paired off behind them, from the most senior to junior. Each carried a beeswax taper a foot in length. At the signal they silently marched into the abbey, their unlit candles held before them. When the first pair reached the front of the packed church, they halted and

turned to face each other. Allisdair then entered, followed
by Brid, striding through the gauntlet of journeymen and
then masters. They proceeded past the altar and turned
to face the host assembled there.

"Nice outfit." Gordie, dressed in full Highland attire,
colorfully contrasted Kelly's white wool gown and kid
leather slippers. "But don't you think you're rather …
vanilla?"

"Being prone to grass stains, I'm not usually good in
white," she admitted. "But I'm finding there are times
when vanilla is appropriate. I think it's our turn."

Gordie nodded. He filled the bag and struck up the
drones. As their sound stabilized and the chanter blew in,
he squared his shoulders, drew himself tall, and marched
towards the abbey.

As the bagpipe's notes carried into the church, Brid
turned to Allisdair. "Where did Gordie learn this?"

"He told me Kelly wished to be piped in with a specific
tune. Why, *Bean-rìgh*? What is it?"

The disbelief was plain on Brid's face. "Cairbre com-
posed this piece to herald Nuada's return to the throne.
He was the only one ever to play it. This music hasn't
been heard in over three thousand years!" She gazed
towards the door where Gordie and Kelly were about to

enter. "I think my granddaughter had a more interesting *frith* than she let on …"

Gordie began his slow march into the abbey; Kelly followed three paces behind with her unlit taper held like an epée in salute. They processed up the aisle, between the ranks of her soon-to-be-fellow journeymen and then past the masters. When they reached the chancel, Gordie turned off, leaving Kelly with candle in hand to face Allisdair and Brid. The masters then came forward, splitting into rows to either side and slightly behind Kelly, and the journeymen followed suit creating a second row behind the masters.

When Gordie finished, Brid stepped forward to deliver the Invocation:

> "By fire and wind, by sun and moon, by iron and stone,
> By the powers of earth, air, and water,
> You are called to this place and to this time,
> To witness the oath of one who would give over her life
> To the service of the light.
> Let all who answer this summons,
> Observe and stand testament to what is done here."

Brid raised up her unlit candle.

> "I light this candle from the sacred flame.
> May it represent our pledge to serve all things living,

And to honor the memory of all that once lived."

A crackling bolt of lightning split the air above Brid. When it had passed, a brilliant flame danced from her candle. Allisdair lit his taper from Brid's and then moved down the row lighting the masters' candles; they in turn lit those of the journeymen.

Returning to his position, Allisdair took over the ceremony.

"Who comes to this place, seekin' passage an' offerin' service? Name yerself an' be recognized."

Glancing to the back of the chapel, Brid blinked hard in surprise. Standing behind the last pew were the shimmering figures of Hamish and Gwendolyn. Never before had any of the *Sidhe* crossed over to attend a passage ceremony.

"I, Kelly MacBride, seek to be made journeyman."

Allisdair then presented her the oath:

> "An' do you, Kelly MacBride, pledge yerself to the life of a journeyman?
> As a pupil, to ceaselessly study the nature of the world;
> As a shepherd, to guard an' protect those who are weaker;
> As a warrior, to fight those things evil;
> As a teacher, to share yer knowledge an' wisdom with others;
> As a healer, to nurse the ill an' succor the bereft;

An' as a livin' creature, to fill yer place in the circle that is life,
Respectin' and upholdin' the balance of our being?"

"These things, so do I swear," Kelly answered.

Brid's attention flicked to the back of the abbey and she caught her breath. The entire space between the last pews and the entryway was now crowded with the sparkling images of ones not seen in this world for centuries. Duncan and Briana were there; Fiona and Blane; hundreds of others all pressed in. And then she spied Cairbre—even he was present!

Brid focused back on the ceremony as Kelly stepped forward to light her candle from Allisdair's. But movement overhead caused Brid to glance up. Perched on a beam near the ceiling was—*Riagall?* In her astonishment, Brid couldn't help but speak in the great owl's mind.

Brid, he mentally greeted in return. *I serve her.*

Does she know?

Yes.

Kelly set her lit taper on the altar.

Brid recovered sufficiently to resume her role in the service. She announced:

"All here bear witness to this pledge of life service."

Placing her hands around Kelly's as if in prayer, she intoned:

"Kelly MacBride, your oath has been witnessed by all present and we accept your pledge. We welcome your service and give you the blessing of all living things as you embark on your journey. May you find your true path."

As Brid spoke there was shimmering movement in the back of the abbey. Cairbre led it, but as he knelt, the others all followed. As the significance dawned on Brid, she too began to kneel.

Kelly, unaware of the scene behind her, tried to pull her grandmother back to her feet. "No, Brid! Don't kneel—it's not right. You're our leader."

Perhaps, Brid thought. *Perhaps, for a time, yet.*

LEXICAL MATTER

APPENDIX 1
GLOSSARY

Aicme	Family or grouping. Used to describe subsections of the *Ogham* characters.
Bairn	Young child or baby.
Bean-rìgh	Pronounced, "bahn-REE." Scottish Gaelic, meaning "queen."
Ben	Mountain.
Ben Abba	Literally, "mountain of the abbess."
Bodhran	Pronounced, "BOW-ran," rhymes with "COW-ran." An Irish frame drum with a stretched goat-hide skin. The player holds the wooden frame, shaped like a large tambourine, behind the drum head with one hand while striking the head with a double-ended stick, or beater, with the other hand.
Brae	Hill.
Braw	Good or particularly fine.

Bres	Son of a Tuathan mother and a Formorian father, Bres was chosen as king of the *Tuatha de Danann* after King Nuada lost his arm in battle. Bres proved to be an unfit king, exploiting his people for his own benefit. The visiting bard Cairbre cursed him for his poor hospitality, which lead to his overthrow. Bres later sided with Balor and the Formorians in war against the *Tuatha de Danann*, and was defeated in the Second Battle of Moytura. Balor was killed in the battle, but Bres was allowed to live.
Brid	Pronounced, "BREED." Short for Bridghe, one of the first of the *Tuatha de Danann*, and revered as a lord of her people.
Bridies	Traditional Scottish meat pies.
Brogues	Shoes.
Burn	Stream.
Caber	A long wooden pole resembling a telephone pole, tossed in an athletic event of the same name at Highland games.

Cairbre	Pronounced, "CAR-bray." The greatest bard among the *Tuatha de Danann*. When treated with disrespect while the guest of King Bres, Cairbre cursed Bres, which later led to Bres' overthrow as king.
Clarsach	Traditional Celtic harp.
Cycle	A collection of traditional poems or stories that share a common theme or hero.
Fetch	An animal spirit that exists across many worlds, serving as both guide and guardian during a person's lifetime.
Flashes	Elastic with colorful cloth strips attached. Used as garters to hold hose, or socks. Typically worn with a kilt.
Forfeda	Added letters. Used to describe the final aicme of *Ogham* characters, which were added to the alphabet several centuries after the *Ogham* were in use.
Formorians	An ancient race that battled the *Tuatha de Danann* for possession of Ireland. Bres, half Formorian, later became lord of the Formorians.

Frith	The Celtic equivalent of a Native American vision quest. A frith serves to answer some question either through portents and signs, or by providing a glimpse into the future.
Galloglas	Ancient Irish, meaning an elite warrior.
Gealach	Pronounced, "GYEL-ack." The "G" is hard, and the "ack" is soft, barely pronounced. In ancient Gaelic it means, "bright steed of the heavens," and is the name Kelly gives her new horse.
Ghillie	Scottish Gaelic for a Highland lord's chief attendant, often responsible for the running of the estate.
Ghillie brogues	Tongueless shoes typically worn with a kilt, with long laces that wrap up around the ankle. Originally a working shoe, the lack of a tongue allows the shoes to dry more quickly, and by tying the laces up the ankle, the shoe is easier to lift up out of the muck.
Imbolc	One of the four major holidays in the ancient Celtic calendar, Imbolc serves a dual purpose: it celebrates Bridghe, or Brid, lord of the *Tuatha*

	de Danann; and also heralds the coming of spring, as evidenced by the onset of lactation among the expecting sheep and cows. Dairy features prominently in the celebration of Imbolc, observed on February 1.
Ken	To know or understand.
Kith and kin	Family and friends.
Laird	Lord, as in the lord of the manor.
Loch	Lake.
Mhic	Gaelic, meaning "the child of." Surnames beginning with "Mac" or "Mc" are derived from this.
Mods	Competitions of spoken and sung Gaelic.
Muckle	Large.
Ogham[16]	Pronounced, "OH-yum." An ancient Celtic alphabet of runic figures

---

16 The Ogham alphabet is one of several similar, and the author believes related, runic alphabets from early Europe and Asia Minor. While many sources reserve the word "rune" for the early alphabets of Scandinavian and Germanic peoples, specifically the Futhark alphabets, the author believes the Futharks are one of several alphabets derived from an older Celtic proto-alphabet—the source of all runic alphabets—dating possibly as far back as 500 B.C. To learn more about this historic mystery, please visit: www.eyesofaraptor.com.

believed to be over a thousand years old. All of the figures represent letters or phonetic sounds, most also represent trees, and twelve represent months of the year.

Ovate — Librarian; one who maintains the history of the people.

Parthalon — An ancient prince who landed on the shores of Ireland centuries before the coming of the *Tuatha de Danann*.

Passant guardant — A term used in heraldry to describe an animal walking and facing the viewer.

Primus — Latin, meaning "the first."

Quaich — Pronounced, "QUAKE." A flattened bowl, typically of pewter, with two lugs, or handles. It symbolizes sharing and the ancient Celtic law of hospitality. After pouring the drink into the bowl, the host passes it to his guest by one lug. The guest accepts the bowl by grasping the other lug.

Ragna rök — Ancient Norse, meaning "doom of the Gods."

Saven

A Scottish variation of the ancient Celtic holiday Samhain (pronounced "SOW-ween"), celebrated on October 31, marking the end of the harvest year and a time for honoring one's ancestors. It is a day between the end of the passing year and the start of the new year, and thus exists "outside of time." Because of this, the veil between our world and the Otherworld is at its thinnest, and bold souls may pass between on this day. Saven is one of the four major holidays in the ancient Celtic calendar.

Second sight

The ability to see into the future.

Sidhe

Pronounced, "SHEE." When the *Tuatha de Danann* retired from our world, they created three hidden realms beyond the perception of human senses: *Tir na Nog*—the land of youth—a far off isle in the west; *Tir fo Thuinn*—the land under the waves; and the *Sidhe*—the hollow hills. The word "*Sidhe*" refers to the hollow hills and any *Tuatha de Danann* who reside there.

Siren

Monsters from Greek mythology, half bird and half woman, who possessed an irresistible voice. Their song would lure sailors to their island, where the Sirens would devour them.

Skald

Norse equivalent of a bard.

Sporran

The purse or pouch typically hanging over the front of a kilt.

Tanist

Heir to the lord.

The now

Right now; at this time.

Tuatha de Danann

Pronounced, "TOO-ah-ha je DAHN-nun." One of the early races to settle in Ireland, possessing the ability to sense and manipulate natural forces and energies beyond the perception of humans. While the *Tuatha de Danann* can be killed, they do not grow old.

Yggdrasil

The world tree, or tree of life, in Norse myth.

Appendix 2
The Ogham

First Aicme

┠	*Beith*	(BAY)	B	Birch	November
┠	*Luis*	(LWOOSH)	L	Rowan	December
┠	*Fearn*	(FAIR-n)	F	Alder	January
┠	*Saille*	(SAHL-yuh)	S	Willow	February
┠	*Nuin*	(NOO-uhn)	N	Ash	March

Second Aicme

┥	*Huathe*	(WAH-huh)	H	Hawthorn	April
┥	*Duir*	(DOO-r)	D	Oak	May
┥	*Tinne*	(CHIN-yuh)	T	Holly	June
┥	*Coll*	(CULL)	C	Hazel	July
┥	*Quert*	(KWAIRT)	Q	Apple	

Third Aicme

┿	*Muin*	(MUHN)	M	Vine	August
┿	*Gort*	(GORT)	G	Ivy	September
┿	*Ngetal*	(NYEH-dl)	Ng	Reed	October
┿	*Straif*	(STRAFE)	Str	Blackthorn	
┿	*Ruis*	(RWOOSH)	R	Elder	

Fourth Aicme

ᚐ	*Ailim*	(AHL-m)	A	Fir
ᚑ	*Onn*	(UHN)	O	Gorse
ᚒ	*Úr*	(OO-r)	U	Heather
ᚓ	*Eadha*	(EH-yah)	E	Poplar
ᚔ	*Iodho*	(EE-yoh)	I	Yew

Forfeda

ᚕ	*Ebad*	(EH-bud)	Ch	Aspen
ᚖ	*Or*	(ORE)	Th	
ᚘ	*Ifín*	(EEF-in)	Pe	Gooseberry
ᚗ	*Uilleann*	(ILL-ee-in)	Ph	Honeysuckle
ᚙ	*Eamhancholl*	(EH-van-kholl)	Xi	

Appendix 3
Fionn's Shield

978-0-595-42609-6
0-595-42609-3